Moretti: The Making of a Mobster

Britt Richards

and on its cover are trade names, service marks, trademarks and registered trademarks of their respective owners. The publishers and the book are not associated with any product or vendor mentioned in this book. None of the companies referenced within the book have endorsed the book.

The cover art is the original creative work of Aurora Infantino commissioned by Britt Richards. It may not be reproduced in any form or by any means. Aurora can be found on Instagram under the handle @back.stain

To Leslie, my best friend. Thank you for encouraging me to delve into Antonio's story. This book would not exist without you.
And to my students, but especially my 8th grade class of 2022. Thank you for being so encouraging and excited about my writing. You helped make this book happen.

Author's Note

Thank you for picking up Moretti: The Making of Mobster! Before you begin, it is important that you understand the adult and graphic content in this book. The trigger warnings are as follows: death, violence, domestic violence, pregnancy loss, torture, abduction, and a brief description of possible child assault.

Please note, this is a mafia story, and being such, many heavy topics are presented. The actions, thoughts, and words of the characters do not mirror my own.

Each chapter is named for a song from the 70s-90s. I am including a song list at the end of this book so you know who the songs are by, in case you want to give them a listen as or after you read!

Simple Man

March 13, 1970

The quiet spring Los Angeles early morning was suddenly interrupted when Lorenzo Moretti was shaken from his sleep. Opening his eyes, he saw his beautiful, lovely wife gazing at him with pain in her alluring espresso-brown eyes. Sitting bolt upright, he asked, "Carmella, *amore mio, come ti fa tanto male?*"[1]

Taking a deep breath, Carmella lovingly placed a hand on her large belly. Softly, she replied, "*È tempo, amore mio. Il bambino sat arrivando.*"[2]

"The... baby is... *coming!*" Jumping out of bed, Lorenzo started running around like a madman, grabbing their bags for the hospital, and yelling instructions for his guards. In a panic, he nearly collided into his wife who was coming to lay a calming hand on his arm.

"Lorenzo, be still. We don't need to be in such a rush." She nonchalantly scooped up her dark, mocha brown hair into an elegant bun and walked over to their bathroom to grab a few

---

[1] My love, what pains you so?
[2] It's my time, my love. The baby is coming.

extra things.

He watched her walk away, in awe that she was being so calm. His insides felt like they were going to burst, and his heart seemed like it would surely beat out of his chest. Trying to calm himself, he swept his unruly black hair up and tied it back out of his face, rubbing his pale brown eyes and trying to think about what he could possibly do to calm down. A thought came to him, and he quickly ran over and picked up the phone beside his bed.

"Hello?" Came a gruff, sleepy voice.

"Marcus, you're up!"

"*Det är jag nu. Varför ringer du oss klockan tre på morgonen, Lorenzo?*"[3]

Switching to Swedish, Lorenzo rambled, "*Barnet kommer och jag vet inte vad jag ska göra och jag lurar fan. Snälla hjälp mig.*"[4]

On the other end, Marcus laughed and Lorenzo could hear him explain to his wife, Dianne, what was going on.

"Lorenzo! *Lugn ner kära, allt kommer att bli bra. Du arbetar själv över ingenting. Vad gör Carmella? Är hon okej?*"[5] Dianne asked, trying not to giggle at the fact that the fearsome leader of the Black Death Mafia was freaking out about his wife being in labor.

"Um... she's surprisingly calm. Will you meet us at the hospital? I think I will surely pass out if you both are not there to walk me through it." The pair agreed, and arrangements were made.

---

[3] Well I am now. Why are you calling us at three in the morning, Lorenzo?

[4] The baby is coming and I do know what to do and I'm freaking the hell out. Please help me.

[5] Calm down dear, all will be well. You are working yourself up over nothing. What is Carmella doing? Is she alright?

Lorenzo assisted his wife as they walked down the stairs and into the waiting car. They drove to the hospital and he ushered her inside. Marcus and Dianne took turns being in the room with Lorenzo and Carmella as she labored well into the morning, as they had a sweet little two-year-old daughter who would not sit still for long. When it was time for Carmella to push, Marcus excused himself from the room out of respect, and Dianne did her best to comfort both Lorenzo and Carmella, as she held onto them.

At precisely 11:28 A.M., their child was born. Loud, hearty cries filled the room. "You have a son!" The nurse exclaimed, placing the child on Carmella's chest. He weighed 8 lbs and 15 oz and was 20 inches long. "What are you going to name him?"

Lorenzo nodded and smiled lovingly at his wife, trying to put on a brave face for her. Watching his son be brought into the world was both the most amazing and terrifying experience of his entire life, and he was still trying to stay conscious. Knowing Carmella had a name in her heart for their son, he had gladly given her the full rights to his name.

"His name is **Antonio Julius Moretti**," she said proudly, bringing the baby to her breast where he latched on quickly and easily.

Once they had been moved to their next room and were settled, Marcus came in holding Britt in his arms. Dianne was holding their nephew, such a chubby little thing. "Aren't you just the most precious *Patatino*[6] I have ever seen."

Marcus took his turn holding the baby and slapped Lorenzo on the back. "I'm proud of you, welcome to fatherhood."

Lorenzo held his son in his arms, his pride and joy, and sat down on the couch next to the beautiful little blonde-haired,

---

[6] Little potato

blue-eyed child he lovingly called his niece. "Come here Britt, meet baby Antonio."

The toddler crawled over to him and peered down at the child in his arms. "Baby," she stated, before proceeding to smack his soft little head with a resounding "Smack!"

Horrified, Dianne scooped up her child and scolded her in Swedish. Marcus looked like he would surely have a heart attack. Lorenzo looked over at his wife, and almost like they were indeed one person, the pair burst out laughing. Their laughter put their friends at ease. Looking down at his son, Lorenzo remarked, "*Bene, benvenuto nel mondo, figlio mio. Benvenuto al mondo.*"[7]

---

[7] Well, welcome to the world my son. Welcome to the world.

Dream On

The first two years of Antonio's life passed quickly. Lorenzo and Carmella were overjoyed with how sweet and happy he was. He was a chunky little guy, and Dianne, as his honorary aunt, stuck to calling him *Patatino*. Unsurprisingly, the boy reached many of his first milestones quite early in life. At 6 months old, he said his first word. Much to Lorenzo's dismay, Antonio's first word was *"Mamma,"* though it made Carmella so happy. At nine months old he was walking by himself. It did not take long for the family to realize that he would grow up to be very tall, because at only two years of age, he was taller than most four and five-year-old children. He was also well on his way to being trilingual, speaking English and Italian quite fluently, and his family working hard to teach him Swedish as well.

On July 9, 1972, at precisely 8:31 P.M., the Moretti family welcomed a baby girl into the world. Due to complications during the birth, Carmella was unable to have any more children. However, as she and Lorenzo looked into the sweet, little face of their daughter, they knew that their family was complete. She was a mere 6 lbs 2 oz, 16 inches long, and so beautiful. There for the birth once more were Marcus and Dianne Alsup, and as soon as Carmella was situated, they brought in Antonio and Britt, who walked hand in hand.

5

Though their first meeting was somewhat rocky, they had become steadfast little friends, Britt taking the role of a doting older sister.

"Antonio, come here son. It is time to meet your sister," Lorenzo said, scooping up the boy in his arms. He placed him on the bed next to his mother.

"*Ciao mio prezioso ragazzo. Incontra la tua sorellina.*[8] Her name is **Priscilla Angelina Moretti**." Carefully, Carmella placed the baby in her son's outstretched arms. He gazed down upon her face lovingly, and brushed the long black hair, identical to his own, out of her face.

Smiling at her, he whispered, "I love you."

The happy-go-lucky boy bonded instantly with his sister, and as they grew, their bond never wavered. She was his entire world, and he would do anything for her. Once he turned six, Lorenzo and Carmella decided he should be introduced to the Black Death Mafia side of their lives, as he was the primary heir. It became apparent that the boy could handle a gun like a professional, and he became very skilled quite quickly.

Carmella only dabbled in the mafia a little; she preferred to stick to their legal business: Moretti Industries. She was an elegant and sophisticated lady of high stature, and everyone respected her. It was not uncommon for her to have brunch with elite women. Her companions included First Ladies Patricia Nixon, Elizabeth Ford, Rosalynn Carter, and Nancy Reagan. However, when she did assist with the mafia, her role was to convince the mothers, wives, and children of whoever they were after to assist them in any way possible. Her sweet and caring demeanor was something that no one could refuse.

When Priscilla turned six, she insisted that she, too, should

---

[8] Hello my precious boy. Meet your little sister

be trained for the mafia life. Antonio argued her case as well, he could not imagine his sister not being by his side. When they began training her, it became apparent that she was amazingly skilled in finding objects and people. That same year brought sadness to the Moretti family, as the Alsup family had decided to move to Alaska. What a sight it was to see the leader of the Black Death Mafia in tears as he embraced the friends that were family to him as they said goodbye at the airport. Antonio and Priscilla hugged Britt, who they always referred to as their sister.

"Goodbye, *Cerva*," Antonio whispered into her ear. He had lovingly nicknamed her "deer" in Italian, after a day of playing near the lake. She was graceful, agile, and so very sweet.

The next two years passed quickly. When Antonio was 10 years old, on his first day of fifth grade, he was startled when a sweet, feminine voice caught him off guard as he was swinging on the monkey bars. "Hello!" Unable to catch himself in time, he fell and landed awkwardly on his leg, snapping it in half.

He bit the inside of his cheek to keep from crying, rocking back and forth. Curse words that he had heard his dad and some of the other men say were running through his head, threatening to break free.

"Oh my goodness, are you alright?! I didn't mean to startle you!" Antonio looked over as small hands touched his left shoulder. He met the shining, concerned emerald eyes of a girl that he did not know. She had naturally wavy cayenne red hair and a very sweet smile. He recalled his teacher introducing her to the class as a new student, but he had been busy talking to his friend, Edward, so he couldn't remember her name.

"Um… I think it's broken," Antonio managed to gasp through the pain.

Clasping a hand over her mouth in horror, the girl quickly said, "I am so sorry! Let me go get Ms. Troy." She scrambled up off the ground and ran as fast as her little legs would carry her to their teacher.

"Antonio! Dude, are you alright?" A boy asked him. The boy had dark auburn hair, and dark brown eyes laced with red. He was very concerned, noticing that his best friend was still on the ground in obvious pain.

"I'm pretty sure it's broken, Edward. It hurts to move it."

At that moment, Ms. Troy ran up and knelt beside him to check out the extent of his injuries. "Edward, please go to the office and have them call an ambulance and his parents."

Edward nodded and ran as fast as he could, his long legs carrying him quickly from the playground to the doors of the school. Lorenzo and Carmella met the ambulance at the hospital and walked with their son into the emergency room. The X-Ray showed that both bones had been snapped, right above the ankle. They set and cast it, Antonio choosing black for his cast. He was given some pain pills and a set of crutches and sent home. Carmella fussed over her precious boy, who simply laughed at the way she was trying to baby him. He kept a smile on his face for her, even though most of the time he felt like crying.

His parents kept him home the next day, though, unlike most kids, he wished he could have gone to school. He loved learning. Carmella wanted to keep him home the rest of the week, but after promising to take it easy, she allowed him to return to school on Wednesday. Priscilla walked him to his class, carrying his backpack for him. After giving him a quick hug and a peck on the cheek, she skipped off to find Emily, her very best friend, and Edward's sister.

Sitting at his desk, waiting for the bell to ring, Antonio pulled out his book and started reading. A couple of minutes later, he felt a finger poke his shoulder. Looking up, he saw the same girl that had startled him two days before. Her eyes looked so sad, and Antonio saw that she was desperately trying not to cry. "I... I am so sorry. I didn't mean to cause you to fall and break your leg. Please forgive me?" She asked, as a few tears fell down her sweet face.

Antonio was startled, he hated it when girls cried; it made him very sad. Seeing this girl be so upset about a simple accident made his heart hurt. He put on his most charming smile to reassure her that everything was alright. "There is no reason for you to be sorry. It was an accident, it could have happened to anyone. Please don't cry." Reaching into his pocket, he pulled out a handkerchief and handed it to her. If there was one thing that he had learned from both his grandfather and father, it was to always carry a handkerchief, in case a crying lady might need it.

Once the young girl had composed herself, she smiled back at him. "Thank you."

Sticking out his hand, he decided to introduce himself. "I'm Antonio."

Giving him an impressive, firm handshake, she replied, "I'm Cynthia."

That year, Antonio started going on missions with his father, though he was not allowed to carry out any acts of violence. However, he learned a lot from watching the older men, and he was eager to try his hand at doling out punishments. As it turned out, Cynthia's parents were also new hires at Moretti Industries, and the families soon became friends. Antonio, however, had little interest in hanging out with girls, preferring to just stick with Edward.

Priscilla and Emily, however, latched onto Cynthia and the three of them became super close in a short amount of time. When the five did all hang out together, there was lots of laughing and fun to be had. Lorenzo and Martin, Cynthia's father, often would joke about how they would like to see

Antonio and Cynthia marry someday, which earned them eye rolls from their children. Life was going well, and the family was happy and close. They seemed to be living a worry-free life, and no one could have predicted what would come next.

He Stopped Loving Her Today

May 5, 1983

Lorenzo and Carmella were busy packing for a long weekend getaway when Antonio strolled into their room, hands crammed into his pockets. Carmella was slightly taken aback by the sight, as he looked nearly identical to his father. "Good morning, *Mamma*. You look so lovely today." He truly meant it, the sunshine was streaming in through the window on this beautiful spring morning, making Carmella's skin glow.

"Oh *figlio mio*,[9] you flatter me so," she replied as Antonio leaned down to kiss her cheek.

He continued over to his father to hug him. Lorenzo could hardly believe how tall his son was. He, himself, was 6'3, and at only 13 years old, Antonio was barely an inch away from being his height. "You sure you'll be alright for the weekend, *figlio mio*?"

"Of course, *Padre*. You know if anyone had the balls to try anything, that I can shoot better than any of our men." His voice, which had deepened over the winter, was oozing with

---

[9] my son

11

confidence.

Lorenzo belted out a deep, hearty laugh. "You're right, son." Turning serious, he advised his son, "You are so eager to follow in my footsteps and take a life. But Antonio, do not ever make that decision hastily. It changes you, and should not be taken lightly."

"Sí,[10] you're right."

"Of course I am," Lorenzo winked.

"Be sure to take care of your sister, Antonio. And be mindful of Everett and Margaret," Carmella instructed.

Walking them to the porch, Antonio and Priscilla hugged their parents tightly. This family was full of love, and they never missed an opportunity to proclaim it. After saying their goodbyes and I love yous', Lorenzo and Carmella got into their car and began their trip to Oregon, where they would be having a luxurious getaway with Marcus and Dianne at Belknap Hot Springs. The family had moved to Oregon the previous year, and it thrilled the Moretti's to have their chosen family close once more.

Margaret pulled up and as soon as she had parked, Edward and Emily jumped out and ran to join their friends. After a delicious breakfast made by Margaret, the four sat on the floor together, talking about their skills and the progress they had made. Antonio also took this time to tease Emily. He had always seen Edward and Emily as more siblings, and he loved them dearly; he'd do anything for them. Edward had begun training with Antonio, and he was almost as skilled with a gun as he was. Emily, however, wanted no part in the mafia life. She had decided at a very young age that it was not for her, though her justice personality would be a huge asset.

"So, Embug, when are you gonna start training with the

---

[10] Yes

12

rest of us?"

"Antonio, you know that it's not something I want," Emily said, crossing her arms, her blue eyes flashing with annoyance. Even at only 11 years old, she was quite outspoken.

"I know sis, I'm just teasing. I know that whatever you choose to do with your life, you will excel at it, and I'll stand behind you no matter what. Has Jimmy been bothering you again?"

The week prior, a bully in Priscilla and Emily's class had cornered Emily and said some very hateful things to her, and pushed her to the ground, scraping her knees up pretty badly. As a result, Antonio and Edward tracked him down and taught him a lesson. "No, he's left me alone."

"Good. But you better let me know if he ever messes with you again. *La famiglia é tutto, e tu sei una famiglia.*[11] This was one of his family's mottos, one that his father held very dear, and so he, too, strove to live it out in his own life.

After a few more minutes, Antonio and Edward decided to go outside and have a friendly competition to see how many squirrels they could shoot, as the pesky creatures were running rampant on the property and causing an excessive amount of damage. Priscilla and Emily went off to help Margaret with a project she was working on, and the beautiful day seemed like it would only bring joy.

Meanwhile, Lorenzo and Carmella were happily driving through Los Angeles on their way north to Oregon. It was not often that they got to take drives together for fun, and they were quite enjoying themselves. As they paused at a red light in the middle of traffic, a shot rang out and the sound of glass cracking startled Lorenzo. Looking over at his wife, he watched as her eyes rolled into the back of her head, blood

---

[11] Family is everything, and you are family.

dripping down her perfect face from a bullet hole in the middle of her forehead. Before he could fully comprehend what had happened, another shot rang out, and a bullet found its way to the center of his forehead, too. As he took his last breath, his hand clutched his wife's tightly, as they lay there in their car.

Something was thrown onto their car with a loud "thunk!" Within seconds, their escort who had been stuck a few cars back rushed out to help, but it was too late. "Someone call Everett and get him down here now!" Robert, the head guard shouted. Turning to his other men, he shouted orders at them as well. "Canvas the area and bring me those goddamn sons of bitches that did this. And bring them to me alive!" As his men ran off, he moved the car to the side of the road and stood by it, gun in each hand.

Back at the Moretti Mansion, the kids were sitting in the living room. Antonio had been victorious in the squirrel shooting competition, and they were having a good laugh at Edward who was pretending to be distraught. The sound of the front door slamming open startled them, and they looked up as Everett entered the room. His face was pale, he looked like he wanted to kill someone and cry at the same time. "Honey, what's wrong?" Margaret asked, instantly on edge. Her husband was a master at keeping his composure, so she knew something was horribly wrong.

"They... they were..." he paused to collect himself, then knelt beside Antonio and Priscilla on the ground. "I am so sorry... but your parents have been assassinated. We have secured the scene. Antonio... you are the leader now. We need you to come downtown."

Shock. That was all Antonio felt. He went numb. Edward and Emily were pale, and Emily had her hand over her mouth, big blue eyes wide. Priscilla crumpled immediately and sobbed, and Margaret quickly pushed aside her own emotions and gathered her into her arms. Antonio, though numb, wrapped his sister into his arms as well and held her tight for several minutes. "I love you, Priscilla. Be strong for me, I'll be back as soon as I can."

Standing up, he dusted himself off and headed toward the door, following Everett to the waiting car. "Wait up!"

Turning to look behind him, he watched as Edward rushed up. "*La famiglia é tutto, e tu sei una famiglia*. I'm coming with you, brother. We're in this together. I have your back."

Even though the situation was grim, Antonio couldn't help but grin at his friend, the boy who he considered to be his brother. This is why he had chosen Edward as his right hand, his second in command. "Let's go."

Everett drove the boys downtown to the scene of the crime, the three of them remaining silent. He parked right behind Lorenzo's prized Cadillac and took a deep breath. "We left everything as it was, so you could inspect it. The only thing we did was move the car out of the road. Antonio... I am sorry for the circumstances that have caused your ascension over the Black Death Mafia, but son, I need you to focus and use your training."

Antonio nodded, a serious and grim look plastered on his face. Stepping out of the car, he walked over and peered into the driver's side at his father. His heart felt like someone had torn it clean out of his chest. There was a single bullet hole in his father's temple, as well as a single one in his mother's. Her face was serene as ever, but blood had oozed down her face. It brought him a small degree of happiness seeing his parents' hands intertwined tightly. At least they left this world in the manner in which they lived. "I love you, Mom and Dad. I swear on my life that I will find who did this to you, and I won't stop until they have paid for their crimes against our family."

Walking around to the other side of the car, he gently

opened the passenger door. Leaning in, he gently closed his mother's eyes and kissed her soft, lukewarm cheek. Tears wanted to fall, but he held them back. *Now is not the time.* Turning to Robert, who was doing his job well at standing guard and giving instructions, he said, "My sister does not need to see our parents this way. Please have them sent directly to the funeral home and fixed up for burial. Do not allow Priscilla to see them until they have been prepared."

"Of course, boss. I will get my men on it at once. Grant! Come here!"

Once he was satisfied with the orders Robert gave the men, Antonio stepped back and watched as they gently and respectfully removed the bodies of his parents and whisked them away quickly, out of sight from prying eyes. Moving to the front of the car, he stopped dead in his tracks. There, lying on the hood of the car, was a chunk of metal shining in the sun. It was in the shape of a snake... the calling card of the Silver Serpents, the Black Death Mafia's worst enemy in Los Angeles.

"Son of a bitch!!!" Antonio yelled.

"What is it?" Edward asked, coming to stand beside his friend. Seeing the snake on the hood, he let out a hiss.

"Everett!" Antonio called.

Running up to his young boss, Everett had a look of mischief on his face. "Boss, our men caught them. There were two assassins located on the roof of an old warehouse just down the block. The morons didn't think to leave the area. We have them tied up in the warehouse. Follow me."

Antonio gave a curt nod, then walked over and popped the trunk of his father's Cadillac. He unzipped his father's suitcase, shuffling through his belongings for the item he knew his father never left home without. Feeling what he was searching for, Antonio lifted out his father's Plague Doctor Mask, the mask that all the men in the mafia wore when on business pertaining to torture and death. Placing the mask securely on his face, he turned and followed closely behind Everett, with Edward on his heels.

The warehouse was very dimly lit, and an outsider would have been scared out of their minds seeing Antonio take the lead. He was tall and broad, and the Plague Doctor Mask made him look extremely formidable. "Boss." Some of the men acknowledged him with a nod, guns never wavering from the two men's direction.

"Well well well, what do we have here?" The ringleader spat. "A scared little boy hiding behind a mask?"

"How pathetic you coward!" The other put in.

"Is this what the mighty Black Death Mafia has been reduced to? A child?! Too scared to show your face, little boy?!"

Antonio chuckled menacingly as he removed his mask. "No, it was not for me, it was for you. *Hai attraversato la mia famiglia e devi subirne le conseguenze.*[12] From his hip he quickly drew his most prized possession, a custom Colt .45 Revolver, inlaid with ivory and a beautiful pattern on the barrel. It had been a gift to him from his parents on his 12th birthday, just over a year ago. Pointing it at the ringleader, he stared him down.

"You don't have the balls to do it, little boy. You know, the boss ordered us to kill both of your parents, but as I watched your mother through my scope... all I wanted to do was take her and make her mine all night long. With that perfect body and soft skin... then I would have ended her life by slitting her throat and watching her bleed out in my bed. Unfortunately for me, my bullet shot true right into the center of her perfect temple." The man was grinning evilly at

---

[12] You have crossed my family and you must suffer the consequences

Antonio, whose face was full of rage. "Told you that you didn't have the balls to—"

A shot rang out, hitting the man right in the center of his chest, shattering his sternum. Blood sprayed Antonio's face, but he didn't bother to wipe it off. The man coughed and gagged, and screamed in pain. Then the man laughed as he choked on his blood. "You missed, you little bitch. Knew you couldn't shoot properly."

"Oh, on the contrary," Antonio began, grinning sadistically. "I hit right where I was aiming. I wanted to see you squirm. It's more fun to see the light slowly fading from your eyes." He walked over and placed the barrel in the center of the man's forehead, precisely where his parents had been shot. His father's advice, which he had just given him that morning, ran through his head. Taking it into account, Antonio made up his mind. This man's life belonged to him. *"Addio stronzo madre."*[13] He pulled the trigger, leaving quite a mess in his wake.

Next, he moved to the second man that had remained quiet for quite some time. "You must be the man that killed my father. Congratulations, you brought down the nation's most formidable man. But you've also awoken the monster inside of me, I hope you and your boss are ready." Antonio grinned, and the blood spatter on his face made him look demonic.

"Do your worst, Italian bitch."

"As you wish," Antonio winked. Remembering he still had four rounds in the cylinder, he decided to make use of them. Quickly, he fired a round into each hand of the man, who screamed out in pain. Then he fired one into the organ that made him a man. He laughed hysterically as the man screamed and screamed, and the blood oozed out all around him. Placing the barrel on this man's temple as well, he

---

[13] Goodbye mother fucker

18

leaned down to whisper, "In my city, we kill the snakes." Then he fired his last round into the man's forehead.

Taking two Plague Doctor Cards from his pocket, he dropped them on each of the two men, the Black Death Mafia's calling card. Addressing the guards, he said, "Leave them as they are, I want the Serpents to find my message."

Turning to his best friend, he said, "Edward, leave this message on the men: *Non hai posto fine al nostro regno, l'hai rafforzato. Hai chiesto una guerra e ora ce l'hai. Non mi fermerò finché non avrò ucciso ognuno di voi serpenti. È passato molto tempo ... E così inizia.*"[14]

Nodding, Edward grinned as he took out his knife. He had been anxiously awaiting the day when he could let the darkness inside of him out, too. Turning the ringleader over, he ripped his shirt away and began carving the message into his back. Antonio walked out of the warehouse, wiping his face on his sleeve, and got into Everett's car. He placed his father's mask on his lap and stared at it blankly until Everett and Edward joined him.

As soon as they pulled up to the Moretti Mansion, Antonio walked directly inside and took a long, hot shower. When he got out, he went to Priscilla's room, but she wasn't there. He finally found her curled up and sobbing in their parents' bed. Sliding in beside her, he pulled his little sister into his arms and held her tightly, finally allowing the tears to flow from his own eyes. "I love you, *Sorella*.[15] I will take care of you, I promise." The two sobbed together for several hours, before drifting off into a restless sleep. Antonio dreamed of hunting

---

[14] You did not end our reign, you strengthened it. You asked for a war, and now you got it. I will not stop until I have killed every last one of you serpents. It's been a long time coming... **And so it begins.**

[15] Sister

down every single last Silver Serpent and making them pay for their crimes against his family.

Hells Bells

May 6, 1983

The sunlight streaming through the windows woke Antonio up. He sat up, slightly dazed, confused as to where he was. Looking around, he realized he was in his parents' room, sitting in their bed. Priscilla was fast asleep beside him, dried tears on her face. Yesterday's events came flooding back, and he felt as though he had been hit by a truck. He took a deep breath and gently rubbed his sister's back.

"Priscilla, wake up *uno dolce*."[16]

The smaller girl sat up and rubbed her eyes. She looked around the room and tears welled up in her beautiful green orbs. It broke Antonio's heart to see his sister so hurt. Flinging herself in his arms, Priscilla sobbed into his chest for several minutes. "Antonio, what are we going to do?" She asked once her sobs had subsided.

"I am going to take care of you, and I am going to take my place as the leader of the mafia. The Silver Serpents will not get away with this slight against us. I will hunt down every single one and kill them off."

---

[16] sweet one

21

"Let me help you, *Fratello*."[17]

"No, *Sorella*." Before Priscilla could argue, Antonio continued. "I do not want those lovely hands of yours soaked in blood. I... I killed two men yesterday... and already I can feel the hardness in my heart. I don't want that for you. That being said, I do need your help. I cannot run this by myself. *Padre* had *Mamma*, and they made a wonderful team. Will you help me lead?"

With her face full of resolve, Priscilla nodded. "I will. And I will help you find every one of those slimy *bastardi*.[18] They must pay for what they've done."

Antonio hugged his sister tightly and then helped her off of their parent's large four-poster bed. "Why don't you go take a nice long, hot bubble bath? I need to make some phone calls."

Priscilla nodded and walked into her parents' bathroom, closing the door softly behind her. Taking a deep breath and straightening his shoulders, Antonio walked out of his parents' bedroom, down the hall into his room, and quickly changed. Then he made his way downstairs to his father's office. Everett was sitting on one of the dark brown leather couches pouring over some documents. Seeing Antonio, he stood up and walked over to embrace the boy.

"How are you doing, Antonio?"

"Honestly, I'm still in shock. But at the same time, I'm having a really hard time keeping the rage from bursting out."

"Just know that I'm here, we all are. We have your back."

"Thank you, Everett. Would you mind giving me a little privacy? I need to call Marcus and Dianne..."

"Of course. I'll be in the kitchen with my wife."

---

[17] Brother
[18] bastards

Antonio walked around to the back of his father's large, custom, mahogany desk and sat down in his comfortable dark brown leather chair that matched the rest of the furniture. He took a deep breath and picked up the phone, dialing the familiar number.

"Hello?" A woman's voice answered.

"Hello, *Tant.*"[19]

"*Patatino! Hur mår du min pojke? Varför har du inte ringt nyligen? Vi saknar dig så mycket.*"[20]

"*Jag saknar er alla så mycket...*"[21] he paused to take a deep breath. "*Tant,* is *Farbror*[22] and my *Cerva* there? I need to tell you all something..." his voice cracked when he said the last sentence.

Dianne was instantly concerned. She called for Marcus and their daughter, Britt. They gathered around the phone so that they could all hear. "We're here, Antonio," Marcus said into the receiver.

Antonio took another deep breath as tears welled up in his eyes. "My parents were murdered in cold blood yesterday. They're... They're gone."

Silence greeted him on the other end, then the shocked gasps as his words sunk in, followed by sobs. "Who would have done such a thing?" Marcus asked.

"Our enemies, the Silver Serpents."

"Did you catch who did it?" Dianne asked.

"Yes. They've... been dealt with."

They talked a bit longer and then Marcus and Dianne excused themselves. Britt stayed on the line, however, staying

---

[19] Aunt

[20] How are you my boy? Why haven't you called lately? We miss you so much.

[21] I miss you all so much

[22] Uncle

silent until her parents had left the room. *"Björn,*[23] how are you really doing? Don't you dare lie to me either!"

Her quiet, but firm voice left no room for argument. He would have to answer her honestly, and he hoped she would still love him the same after he confessed to her. His bond with Britt, though they lived a couple thousand miles away, had remained strong throughout the years. Whenever he talked about her, he always referred to her as his big sister. He always knew he could be vulnerable with her, and that she would never see him as weak. However, he had never allowed the darkness that he had always felt inside of him to make its presence known, and he wondered how she would react.

"I... I am broken. And I'm scared. I know that I am more mature than most 13-year-old boys due to my training... but how am I supposed to run an entire mafia? I also do not know the first thing about running a business. How am I supposed to keep Moretti Industries afloat? I don't want my parents to have died in vain, but what if I let them down?"

The boy's voice broke and Britt's heart ached for him. She so desperately wished that she could hug the boy that she called her brother, and tell him that everything would be alright, though she wasn't sure if it would be. "Antonio, you can do it. You're a Moretti. And I know you have the best people around you to guide you and teach you. Now don't let this get to your head, but you are the smartest person that I know, you'll pick it up. You are destined for great things, *Björn.* And you know that I will always have your back. *La famiglia é tutto, e tu sei una famiglia.*"

"Thank you, *Cerva,*" Antonio paused, mustering up the courage to continue. "I... I snapped, Britt. There has always been a darkness in me, a hunger for bloodshed. My father

---

[23] Bear

cautioned me about taking a life... but I... I killed the two men that killed my parents. I had no hesitations or second thoughts about it. It was brutal... and it was thrilling. I don't regret it at all. And I vowed to hunt down every last Silver Serpent and make them pay for their crimes against my family. How can you stand behind a monster like me?"

Britt was taken aback. *Why is he calling himself a monster?* She would not have any of that kind of talk. "What do you mean? You are not a monster. The real monsters are those sick, twisted bastards who took the lives of your parents. You are the son of the man that protected my parents when they first came to this country. You are the son of the man who only took a life when absolutely necessary. You did nothing wrong. You know the police will just label your parents' deaths as 'senseless gang violence.' You and I both know that's not what this was. You stand up for them and do not ever back down. Just don't forget who you really are. *Den modiga björnen och den oskyldiga beskyddaren.*"[24]

Tears streamed down Antonio's face as Britt spoke to him. To know that she didn't think poorly of him meant the world to him. There were few people in the world that he was scared to disappoint, and she was one of them. "*Jag älskar dig,*[25] Cerva. Thank you for having my back... and for believing in me."

"*Ti amo anch'io,*[26] Björn."

Antonio hung up the phone feeling relieved but also drained. He grabbed a handkerchief from the top drawer of his father's desk and wiped his face. Noticing a scarf that belonged to his mother sitting in the drawer, he gingerly picked it up, holding it as if it might break. He put the scarf to

---

[24] The brave bear and protector of the innocent.

[25] I love you

[26] I love you too

his face and breathed in deeply, inhaling the scent of his mother's perfume, *Red Door* by Elizabeth Arden. The scent was so familiar and comforting, that it brought some peace to his troubled soul. *I will always keep her bottle of perfume, for as long as I live. I don't want to forget how she smelled.*

Once he had composed himself, Antonio left the study and walked to the kitchen. Margaret set whatever she was cooking down and walked over to embrace the boy that literally overnight had turned into a young man. "Good morning, Antonio, are you hungry?"

"Good morning, Margaret, I am hungry actually."

"Well, young man, you're in luck. I just finished breakfast. If you would go sit down at the table, I will bring it out to you."

Nodding, Antonio went to the dining room and sat down in his father's seat at the head of the table. Priscilla came in, saw where he was sitting, and smiled at him before taking a seat in her mother's chair, directly across from him. Edward sat on Antonio's right and Emily on Priscilla's right. Margaret brought in breakfast and her heart was touched by where the kids were sitting. Their placements were no accident. The five of them dug into their food, chatting here and there until Everett walked in, speaking loudly in Norwegian into the phone. He looked every bit of his Norwegian heritage, as did Emily, though they only tended to speak the language in their own household.

"Flink. Hold dem bundet, ikke la dem slippe unna. Vi vil være der snart for å ta vare på de slimete jævlene."[27] Hanging up, Everett sat down and filled up his plate before turning to Antonio. "One of my contacts working in customs caught two Silver Serpents trying to board a flight to the Bahamas.

------

[27] Good. Keep them tied up, do not let them escape. We will be there soon to take care of those slimy bastards.

He had them detained and taken to our warehouse."

"Excellent. Finish your breakfast and we can head down there. I need a word with them." Antonio stood up to take his dishes to the kitchen, but Margaret shook her head.

"Emily and I will take care of the dishes."

Priscilla stood up as well. "I'm coming too, and you are not going to stop me."

Antonio chuckled but nodded his consent. "Alright, I'm going to change into something more appropriate for the task at hand."

"I'll join as well," Edward stated, standing up and crossing his arms. Emily rolled her eyes, she had a hard time wrapping her head around the excitement they got in hurting people.

The three of them parted ways and changed, meeting on the porch to wait for Everett. They were all wearing black, and they looked formidable. Antonio had his revolver in plain sight on one hip, a fully automatic Glock on the other. Edward had his two Glocks on his hips and was double-checking his case of torture devices to make sure he had everything. Priscilla fastened her knives into the sheaths on her arms and loaded the rest of her tracking equipment into her bag.

When Everett walked out onto the porch, the sight before him warmed his heart, but also made it heavy. *Oh, Lorenzo... you would be so proud of your children right now.* "Let's go you guys."

Once they made it to the warehouse, the trio plastered on a hardened face and walked in. They were greeted warmly by all the men and women they passed, giving them each a nod in acknowledgment. The men standing guard by the door to the holding room opened it, and they walked in. Priscilla gazed upon the two men who smiled up at her, and she felt nothing but hatred toward them. She positioned herself at the table in the corner and got ready to take notes on any information the boys would get out of them.

Antonio and Edward each took a man, taking turns torturing them and forcing information out of their mouths. When Antonio was satisfied that his man had no more information to give, he placed a bullet between his eyes. Edward twisted his knife into the other man's rib cage, drawing out some coordinates for the Silver Serpents' headquarters, then shot a bullet into his heart.

"Clean this up," Antonio instructed a couple of the guards who immediately got to work. "You get anything, *Sorella*?"

Priscilla looked up and grinned at her brother. "I have the headquarters location here on my map. We need to storm it. Even if they have evacuated, hopefully, they were dumb enough to leave personal information behind. I can track them down wherever they may run."

"Edward, call your father and have him assemble his team of snipers at the locations Priscilla gives you. I'm going to gather up a team to storm the place."

Two hours later, snipers were ready on the rooftops of all the buildings surrounding the Silver Serpents' headquarters. Margaret and Everett, the best of them, were placed directly in sight of the entrance to cover Antonio, Edward, and the rest of the team, which included about 20 people. Priscilla was poised behind her brother and Edward, ready to comb the building for anyone hiding and for their files. On Antonio's command, they broke the door down and marched stealthily inside. Although mostly empty, some people tried to escape from the back and side entrances, and were immediately taken out by the snipers.

The next ten minutes were full of bloodshed. Anyone they found were killed immediately. Antonio himself took out 10 of the enemy's men. No one was spared. Priscilla found a few people that were hiding, with Edward following to ensure her safety, as she was as much his sister as Emily. He quickly took out the seven that she found. Using her knowledge, Priscilla was able to locate the records room and laughed maniacally when she pulled out all of the files. Not only did they have a file for each member, but the files included their addresses, family addresses, and their likes and interests.

After doing a final sweep and finding no more people, the team raided the building, taking all arms and money, and information that they found. Any equipment of use to the Black Death Mafia was also taken, then the building was set on fire, with a lot of accelerants; it was burned to the ground in a matter of minutes before the fire department arrived.

The rest of the weekend was spent at the Black Death Mafia headquarters. Priscilla poured over the files and made notes on maps that she hung up in her new office. She hardly came out of the room and slept there for two nights. Antonio soaked up as much information as he could regarding the running of the mafia and Moretti Industries. The week at school the siblings tried as best they could to act normal, shying away from the sympathies expressed by everyone they came into contact with. Even though they did not want to be at school, education was important, their parents had made that very clear.

Their nights were spent coming up with a plan of attack. Antonio made it known that he would not stop until every last member of the Silver Serpents was dead. He was overjoyed to learn of their strict policy that no female members were allowed, as he did not want to have to kill any women and leave orphans in his wake, even though that very thing had been done to him. When the weekend rolled around, he gathered his team once more, geared up, and headed out to take out three of the prominent members who were having dinner at the big house. Placing his father's Plague Doctor mask over his face, he gave the signal for entry. *"La morte sta arrivando,"*[28] and with that, he led the charge into the bloody night.

---

[28] Death is coming.

Let it Be

Standing in front of his mirror, Antonio adjusted his black tie and stood back to look at his reflection. He had donned an all-black suit; black was most certainly his color. Margaret had cut his hair for him the previous evening, so he was looking very well put together. Digging around in a small drawer in his dresser, he pulled out a black silk handkerchief that he folded neatly and tucked into his pocket. *Priscilla might need this today.*

A soft knock on his door interrupted his thoughts and he turned around to see the beautiful young lady whom he referred to as his older sister, Britt. She smiled softly at him, her blue eyes watery, but she was doing the best she could to maintain her composure. "Good morning, *mio Cerva,*" Antonio greeted her, pulling her into a hug. He had to stifle a laugh because although the Alsup family had arrived a few days ago, it was comical to him that he had grown to be so much taller than the girl who was two years older than he was.

"Good morning, *Björn,*" Britt mumbled into his chest.

Pulling away, Britt rolled her eyes and mumbled something in Swedish, something along the lines of how

31

Antonio did not know how to put on a tie. As Antonio went to adjust his tie, Britt swatted his hand and undid the whole thing, putting it back on him correctly. "Much better."

"Thank you."

"Are you ready, Antonio?"

"Almost. I'm going to go check on Priscilla. I'll meet you all in the car, alright?"

Britt nodded and quietly left the room. Antonio took a deep breath and walked back over to his dresser. Sitting on top was his mother's bottle of perfume. He took off the cap and held the bottle to his nose, taking a deep breath. Tears began to well in his eyes, so blinking quickly, he returned the bottle to its place and turned on his heel, and walked out the door.

When he got to his sister's bedroom, he knocked twice and then walked in. Priscilla was sitting on her bed staring out the window. Her long black dress nearly touched her toes, and she had tamed her curly black hair by putting half of it in a ponytail. "You look beautiful, *Sorella*."

"Thank you," she whispered.

Antonio walked over to where she was sitting and held out his hand to help her up. Pulling her into his arms, he murmured into her ear, "You are the spitting image of *Mamma*, just as beautiful too. Your black hair that we got from *Padre* makes you even more beautiful."

"You really think so?" Priscilla asked.

"I do."

Stepping back, Priscilla flashed Antonio a small smile. Taking her arm in his, he led her down the stairs to where the Alsup family was waiting for them in the car that was to take them to the church for their parents' funerals. Everett was waiting for them outside the church when they pulled up.

"The building is secure, we have men and women placed all over the perimeter to make sure nothing happens."

"Thank you, Everett."

The entire church was full, and it was a very large building. So many people showed up, that many had to stand. The audience included members and former members of the Black Death Mafia and their families, people from the community whom the Moretti's had helped in some way, the mayor, the governor, and their families were also in attendance. It warmed Antonio's heart because although the Black Death Mafia was mostly known for their destruction, they also positively touched the lives of so many people.

They had decided to have an open casket service, and once the preacher had finished his message, he and Priscilla went to say their final goodbyes. Priscilla leaned down and kissed both of their parents and whispered some words to them before bursting into tears once more and walking away to take her place in the line where people could greet her. By this time, she had already soaked Antonio's handkerchief. Antonio placed his forehead against his father's for a few seconds, trying his best to maintain his composure.

"Padre, farò del mio meglio per renderti orgoglioso e portare avanti la tua eredità. Ti amo tanto."[29]

He walked over to his mother and kissed both of her cheeks softly, taking in her beauty once more. It was all he could do not to break down, and he longed for her to just sit up and hold him. Placing his forehead against hers, he whispered, *"Mamma, devi essere l'angelo più bello del Paradiso. Ti amo moltissimo, ma so che ci stai guardando. Cercherò Priscilla fino alla mia morte, lo giuro.*[30]*"*

---

[29] Father, I will do my best to make you proud and carry on your legacy. I love you so much.

[30] Mama, you must be Heaven's most beautiful angel. I love you very much, but I know you are watching over us. I will look out for Priscilla until my death, I vow it.

Taking his place beside Priscilla, they waited for their Moretti family to say their goodbyes and take their places. Then the Alsup family took their turn and went to stand behind them for support. Antonio and Priscilla must have shaken a couple of thousand hands and heard just as many condolences by the time the last person filed through. They rode silently to the cemetery and placed flowers on their parents as they were lowered into their graves, side by side, forever.

Antonio took the time to reflect on his parents' marriage, and it brought a smile to his face. They were so desperately in love with each other, and never missed an opportunity to let the other know. Whenever Lorenzo would come home from a mission, Carmella would run into his arms, he would pick her up and twirl her around kissing her passionately. Antonio remembered late nights where his parents would dance in the living room together without a care in the world, teaching their children how to dance as well. He could not recall one single moment where his parents were angry at each other, and he was glad that they would be spending eternity just as they had spent their life: together.

Back at the Moretti Mansion, Antonio and Priscilla changed out of their formal attire and into something more casual, both choosing to stay in black for their mourning. Dianne Alsup bustled around the kitchen to prepare a giant dinner. It helped keep her mind off the heartache that she felt. Smiling to herself, she pulled out the ingredients for Antonio's favorite goodies, *Lussekatter* and *Polkagriskola*, dishes she only typically made at Christmas time. Margaret Sommerset joined her, and the two women chatted while they cooked a meal for the nine of them.

Everett Sommerset and Marcus Alsup busied themselves in Lorenzo's study. The Moretti's lawyer had called and asked for some specific documents. Antonio was relieved that the two men had offered to find the documents, as he felt drained of all his energy. Edward and Emily walked in carrying some packages and sat down in the living room where Antonio, Priscilla, and Britt were relaxing.

"Here, Priscilla," Emily said, handing a package to her dearest friend.

Priscilla opened the package to find handwritten cards and handmade gifts from her classmates. She found a small box and opened it up to find a necklace that had a beautiful mint-colored gemstone, which was her favorite color.

"That one is from me!" Emily exclaimed. "I used my special savings to buy it, and look! I got one for myself too." She pointed to her neck where a matching necklace had been placed, except it had a pink-colored gemstone.

"Thank you, Emily, I love it! I will keep it forever," she smiled.

Edward handed the other package to Antonio. It, too, had handwritten cards from his classmates. "Think fast!" Edward said and Antonio whipped his head up and quickly snatched the knife that was thrown at him out of the air. The two boys grinned while Britt rolled her eyes. She was certain those two boys would eventually end up hurting themselves if they weren't careful. Antonio studied the knife, it was an exceptional piece of art, with the Moretti crest engraved onto it.

"Thank you."

"No problem."

Something slipped out of the box onto the ground, and when Antonio reached down to pick it up, he noticed his name written in perfect cursive writing. He opened the card to find a sweet note from Cynthia Springer, who signed her name with hearts over the I's. It wasn't a particularly special note, but something made him want to keep it. After checking to make sure no one was looking at him, he slipped the note into his pocket. With nothing else to do before dinner, they turned on the T.V. and put in the brand new *Star Wars: Return of the Jedi* VHS tape that Antonio had gotten for his birthday back in March but had not had the opportunity to watch it yet.

Dinner was excellent, and as Antonio sat at the head of the table, his heart couldn't help but feel full. Even though the pain of the absence of his parents ate at him constantly, he looked around at the loving faces of the Alsups and Sommersets and he knew there was no one else he would rather be with at this very moment. These people were his family, and he knew that no matter what was going to happen in the future, they would always have his back and be there for him and Priscilla. Since the Alsups were visiting, Margaret and Everett had decided to give them some space and took Edward and Emily back to their own house. Dianne and Marcus wanted to spend as much time as they could for the short time they were visiting doting on Antonio and Priscilla, and showing them how much they were loved.

"Tomorrow is a big day for the both of you," Dianne started. "Why don't you head on up to bed? It's been a really long day, and you both seem exhausted."

It was true, Priscilla could hardly keep her eyes open and Antonio couldn't go five minutes without yawning. "Come on Priscilla, I'll braid your hair for you," Britt said softly, taking the younger girl by the hand and walking toward the stairs.

"*Tant*, let me help you clean up." Antonio stood up to clear what was left on the table but Dianne swatted his hand.

"You will do no such thing. Go on now."

"*Jag älskar dig,*" Antonio murmured into her ear in Swedish as he leaned in to kiss her cheek.

36

"*Jag älskar dig också,*"[31] she replied, hugging him tightly before shooing him toward the stairs.

Marcus chuckled and hugged the boy as well, before assisting his wife with the cleanup. Antonio trudged up the stairs and decided he would stop and tell Priscilla good night. Peeking into her room, he saw Britt sitting on the edge of Priscilla's bed, calmly stroking her head. His sister was sound asleep. Walking in quietly, he leaned down and kissed her forehead gently. "*Buonanotte dolce Sorella, ti amo,*"[32] he whispered.

"Thank you," Antonio said quietly to Britt before turning and walking to his room. He quickly changed into some shorts and slid into his bed. A few minutes later, Dianne and Marcus came in to tuck him in. Though he was 13 years old, he did not mind the treatment. They prayed over him, and Dianne kissed his forehead before they took their leave. Shortly after, Britt walked in to check on him.

"Are you still awake, *Björn?*"

"*Sí*, my mind will not turn off, *mio Cerva.*"

Antonio patted the spot beside him on his bed, indicating that Britt should sit beside him. He pulled the blanket up for her and covered her up once she had laid down beside him. "What is on your mind?" She asked.

"I miss them... so much..."

"I know you do, we all do."

"It was so hard for me today. I wanted to just break down and cry, but I couldn't. As the leader of the Black Death Mafia, I cannot show any weakness. But it was almost too much today."

"I did notice that you didn't cry. *Björn*, it's ok to cry, you need to let it out. It's just you and me now," Britt encouraged.

---

[31] I love you too
[32] Good night sweet sister, I love you.

With hardly a second thought, Antonio moved closer to Britt and laid his head on her much smaller shoulder. The tears came flowing, as though a great dam had suddenly burst. There was no stopping the torrent. He sobbed as silently as he could, and Britt wrapped her arms around him as best she could to comfort him. Her heart broke once more for the younger boy weeping in her arms. He had always been a feeler, always letting his emotions shine through, no matter what they were. Though, she had always known him to be so happy and could hardly even remember ever seeing him without a smile. It pained her knowing that he felt he had to hide his true self for the sake of his image as the new leader of the mafia. He had so much pressure and responsibility thrust upon him too soon, and too young.

He mourned for the loss of both his parents. He mourned for the loss of his childhood and his innocence. He mourned for the loss of such a great love as he had never seen, and the feeling that he would never know that kind of love again overcame his senses. He mourned for his sister, and how she had even less time with them than he'd had. There was rage building inside of him, but the tears overpowered even that. Antonio knew there would be a time for the rage to have its turn, but now was not that time. He never said a word to Britt, just cried and cried. She didn't say anything either, she knew that her being there was enough.

Britt stroked Antonio's head and rubbed his back soothingly. He wept for at least an hour. When she finally heard his breathing even out, she reached over and grabbed the handkerchief that was on his nightstand and gently wiped the tears off of his face. Though he was sleeping, his face still held so much grief. She attempted to shift him over to his pillow, but he was too heavy for her to move very well, and she did not want to wake him.

The door slowly opened, and Dianne and Marcus peeked

their heads in. They had finished up downstairs and had gone to check on Britt, but she had not been in her bed. Britt looked up and put her finger to her lips to indicate that Antonio was sleeping. She made a motion to show that she couldn't move him either. Marcus looked at his wife, and the both of them shrugged. Britt blew her parents a kiss as they shut the door softly. In any other circumstance, they would not have allowed their teenage daughter to sleep in the same bed as a teenage boy. However, they knew without a shadow of a doubt that the two saw each other as siblings, and they knew that Antonio needed the comfort of someone being there.

Pulling up the large black comforter, Britt tucked it snuggly around Antonio and herself and relaxed comfortably onto the pillow. *"Jag älskar dig lillebror, vila väl."*[33] With sorrow in her own heart, Britt fell asleep praying that Antonio and Priscilla would never feel such heartache again.

The next morning, Antonio woke up to find a pile of blonde hair covering his face; there was even some in his mouth, and he had to restrain himself from gagging so as not to wake up the young lady sleeping soundly beside him. Slowly, he got out of bed and tucked Britt in. It was only 6:30, and though he still felt a bit drained, he also knew that he had gotten as much rest as he could. He grabbed some clothes and headed to his bathroom where he took a quick shower.

Marcus and Everett were chatting in the kitchen when Antonio walked in, and Dianne handed him a steaming hot cup of coffee. He greeted them and then took a sip; it had the perfect amount of cream and sugar in it, exactly how he liked it. It was exactly how his dad took his coffee.

"Thank you, *Tant*."

---

[33] I love you little brother, rest well.

"Antonio, the lawyer will be here at 7:30 to go over your parents' will. Do you want all of us to be there with you and Priscilla?" Everett asked.

"Where are Edward and Emily?" Antonio asked, noticing Margaret cooking with Dianne.

"Emily woke up last night with a fever. Edward offered to stay home and take care of her today."

Nodding, Antonio walked back upstairs to wake up his sister. When the lawyer arrived, they all gathered in the study, with Antonio sitting in the big leather chair behind the mahogany desk. "Well, Mr. Williams, what do you have for us?"

The older man smiled warmly down at his late employer's protege. He had been the Moretti lawyer from the very beginning when Lorenzo's parents started the business and the mafia. His silver hair was still speckled with black here and there, and he had smile lines around his eyes. There was not a kinder-looking man that Antonio or Priscilla had ever seen. "Where would you like me to start, Mr. Moretti?"

"Please, Mr. Williams, you've known me since I was born. Call me Antonio."

"Very well, Antonio. I can start at the beginning if you would like?"

Antonio looked at his sister who smiled encouragingly at him, so he nodded his consent for Mr. Williams to begin.

Taking a deep breath, Mr. Williams began reading the will that Lorenzo and Carmella had updated just months before.

We, Lorenzo and Carmella Moretti, leave our children in the care of Everett and Margaret Sommerset should our lives be taken before they turn 18 years of age. For Margaret and Everett, we bequeath upon their family a bank account, account number XXXXXXXXXXXX. A fund has been set to deposit monthly into the account for the care of our and their children. Our son, Antonio

Julius Moretti will act as the executor and is the primary heir to Moretti Industries and the Black Death Mafia. We bequeath upon him all the accounts and property held in those trusts, and he shall be given the utmost respect and the training required to carry out his tasks. Our daughter, Priscilla Angelina Moretti, we bequeath upon her one-third of the rights to and accounts of Moretti Industries and the Black Death Mafia, that one-third shall be decided by her brother.

The mansion shall be placed into Antonio's name upon our deaths. Antonio and Priscilla shall be granted access to the bank accounts created in their names following the reading of this will. To our beloved family, Marcus and Dianne Alsup, we bequeath the following account, number XXXXXXXXXXXX, which will have a monthly deposit from Moretti Industries for as long as they live. Following their deaths, their account will be inherited by their daughter, Brittney Elise Alsup. Immediately following the reading of this will, funds will be released to pay off the mortgage of their business and home in Oregon. To our niece, Brittney Elise Alsup, we bequeath the following account, number XXXXXXXXXXXX. It, too, will receive a monthly deposit from Moretti Industries. She will be able to access the funds after her 18th birthday. The same respect and care that is shown to the Moretti family shall always and forever be shown to the Alsup family and their descendants. They have the right to use all facilities and properties owned by the Moretti family, including but not limited to the private jet, private homes, and security details. Everything stated herein is true and shall not be infringed upon.

Lorenzo Hadrian Moretti and Carmella Elaine Moretti.

Mr. Williams' closing words left the room in a state of silent dismay. Antonio and Priscilla had always known that they would inherit their family's empire, but they realized that they truly had no idea how vast it was. Margaret and Everett had always known that Antonio and Priscilla would be left in their charge, but had not expected their dear friends to provide for them so heavily. They were grateful but wished that they could have their friends back instead of their money. Probably the most shocked of all were Marcus and Dianne. Since they were teenagers, Lorenzo had always looked out for them and never allowed them to go through any financially hard times. The fact that he had put into his will that they and their daughter should always be provided for took the breath straight out of their lungs. In a way, they were grateful that Britt was still sleeping, for they did not know how they would be able to ease her shock while they were currently in tears.

"Mr. and Mrs. Moretti also provided instructions for disbursements to be made to all members of the Black Death Mafia as a 'thank you' for their service to the family. Now, if you all do not have any questions, I must go down to the bank and have all of the funds released." Mr. Williams scanned the room and finding no questions, turned to leave.

Antonio walked him to the door and shook his hand before turning back to talk with his family. Britt walked downstairs and found all of them to be quite silent. "What did I miss?" She asked.

"Well, *Cerva*, my parents left you a little something..." Antonio explained.

A couple of days later, Marcus, Dianne, Britt, Antonio, and Priscilla clung to each other at the airport in the private hangar that belonged to the Moretti's. The jet's engine was going, awaiting its passengers, but the five did not want to let go of each other. They did not know when they would see each other next, though they promised it would be a lot sooner than the previous time. With tears and heartfelt goodbyes, the Alsups boarded the jet and took off down the runway toward Oregon.

Once they got home, Antonio began packing a bag and

some supplies for a trip he was going to be making down to San Diego to pay a visit to the home of the Silver Serpents' leader. He was not going to be leaving there until the man was bleeding out on his own floor. Priscilla came in to tell him that lunch was ready but stopped in her tracks.

"*Fratello*, what are you doing?"

"I'm getting ready to go to San Diego, *Sorella*. I have a group of men ready to accompany me and I will be leaving after lunch."

"But what about school? We can't keep missing school, Antonio."

Sighing, Antonio stopped what he was doing and walked over to sit on his bed. He patted the space next to him, indicating that Priscilla should sit. Once she was beside him, he took her hands in his and looked into her eyes. "*Carissima sorellina*,[34] you will be staying here. Do not protest, *per favore*.[35] With the information that you have found, I have come up with a plan. I... I do not want you to be exposed to all of the bloodshed. And about school... I am dropping out."

"*Scusa! Chi diavolo credi di essere? I nostri genitori si aspettavano che finissimo la scuola. Non puoi abbandonare!*"[36] Priscilla yelled, face turning red.

"*Calmati dolcemente.*[37] I will still finish school. There is an accelerated homeschool program that I have found that I can complete while I travel. I will still graduate and everything."

"Then let me do it too! I need to be with you!"

"You know that I love you, Priscilla, but I need you here. I need you to run things while I am away, and I know how

---

[34] Dearest little sister

[35] please

[36] Excuse you! Who the hell do you think you are? Our parents expected us to finish school. You cannot drop out!

[37] Calm down sweet one.

much you like being at school."

Sighing with defeat, Priscilla nodded her consent and then flung her arms around her brother. "You better come back to me, I can't bear to lose you, too."

"*Tornerò sempre da te, lo prometto.*"[38]

After lunch, Antonio, Everett, and Edward loaded up into the armored car and headed toward San Diego with their entourage. The closer they got, the more excited Antonio became at the upcoming bloodshed that was about to occur. He would be sending a message to anyone that dared think of crossing his family again, that only a gruesome death would follow. As they arrived at the house under the cover of darkness, Antonio kicked in the door and grinned at all of the men that had just sat down for dinner and to discuss plans.

"*La morte è qui per te, il mostro è fuori,*"[39] he grinned before launching himself at the nearest person.

---

[38] I will always return to you, I promise.
[39] Death is here for you, the monster is out.

War Machine

Antonio wiped the sweat and blood off his face with his sleeve. He looked around him at the massacre he had just finished and grinned wickedly. Three of the top-ranking members of the Silver Serpents lay in a pool of their own blood, along with six other members. Having only expected the top three to be here, it was a pleasant surprise to find the others; it meant less work for him in the future. After documenting who it was that he had killed and having his men raid the large house for anything of use to them, Antonio and his crew left a calling card on each body before walking out the front door into the black night. His only disappointment about the evening was that Casimir Szymanski, the leader of the Silver Serpents, had gone escaped.

Arriving at the hotel where they would be staying, he was handed his key at the entrance in stride as he walked through the door. He immediately went straight to his room, shed his clothes, and stepped into the bathroom for a steaming hot shower. The water ran red for several seconds as he scrubbed the blood off of his face, out of his hair, and from his hands. Leaning back into the steady stream, Antonio closed his eyes, hearing his father's words ringing in his ears. *Dad, I know you warned me about this... But I had no choice. I hope that you're proud of me.*

Satisfied that no traces of what had occurred that evening remained, Antonio stepped out of the shower and quickly got dressed. Relaxing comfortably onto the soft hotel bed, he grabbed the phone to call Priscilla. If he didn't, he knew she would be very angry with him. After his phone call to his sister, Antonio thumbed through the hotel menu and ordered some room service. Turning on the news, he smiled to himself as he watched the footage of the police taping off the house that he had just destroyed. He soaked it up while he could because once word got back to the authorities that his Plague Doctor cards had been found, the story would be wrapped up and discarded.

That night he dreamed of a simpler time when his parents would dance the night away in their parlor while he and Priscilla would snuggle on the couch drinking hot cocoa and watching their parents with delight. A single tear fell from his eye as he slept, wishing he did not have to wake up to reality. With the monster inside of him tucked safely away, he still very much felt like a vulnerable, lonely, little boy.

July 1983

Two months after Lorenzo and Carmella's deaths, Antonio was sitting at his desk in what was now his personal study in their home. He could still smell traces of his father's cologne, and he breathed in deeply as he poured over some papers from Moretti Industries. The shrill ringing of the phone on his desk made him jump. Rolling his eyes at his own reaction, he picked up the phone to answer it.

"This is Antonio," he said gruffly.

The person on the other end giggled half-heartedly at his greeting, but Antonio could hear a heavy-hearted sigh. He knew that the person on the other end had been crying, and he recognized exactly who it was by the giggles that he loved.

"*Cerva*, is that you? Have you been crying?"

"Hi, *Björn*... Yes, I..." Britt started before sobbing into the phone.

"*Cerva*! You tell me who the *bastardo* is that made you cry and I will be there in a couple of hours to make them pay! No one gets away with causing you pain."

In any other circumstance, the fire in Antonio's voice would have made Britt burst into laughter and all would have been well knowing that he had her back through anything. However, today her heart was too heavy, and there was too much weighing on her mind.

"*Björn*, as much as I appreciate the thought... you may want to reconsider. Your parents, God rest their souls, would never forgive you."

"Ah... *Sí*, I could never hurt your family. They are the cause, correct?"

"Yes... I messed up... big time. There's no going back. My life is over!"

"Britt, I'm sure you haven't made a mistake as great as you think. Whatever it is, we can fix it. What happened?"

"Well... if I tell you, you'll hate me too. I have never felt so alone."

Antonio sighed. "There are only a few things I can promise you, *mio Cerva*, and one of those is that I could never hate you, no matter what. I love you too much."

"I'm pregnant and have to get married. They are giving me until the end of the year at least before the wedding. I have to do this. They left me no other choice."

Feeling the brevity in Britt's voice, Antonio paused for a few moments before responding

"*Sorella*, I love you. While this is... unexpected, I know that your baby is a blessing. You will be a great mother, I know it. They will be born into such a loving and caring family. I already love them, and I'm going to be the best *Zio!*[40] As for you having to get married, that seems harsh. I'll talk with *Tant* and you can come live with me. I'll make sure you have everything you need and the best doctors! They cannot refuse my request."

Breathing a moment, Britt had to do the one thing hardest for her: deny Antonio. "They could never deny you, *Björn*, but I have to. It wouldn't be fair to Cade or his family."

"*Quindi questo è il nome del bastardo che ha osato metterti le mani addosso. È meglio che sia pronto perché quando arrivo lì imparerà cosa è cosa, e se mai ti farà male, lo farò a pezzi...*[41] But you are right, I would never wish for anyone, especially your precious baby, to have to grow up without their parents."

"Just so you know, *Patatino*, I am just as guilty as Cade. It does take two to make a baby. After the devastating news of your parents, I was in such a dark place. I didn't know how to take it and Cade was just there. He really is a good boy, and I think if it weren't for this...news... you guys would get along."

"I shall try to get along with him, for you, but only after I do my brotherly duties and *spaventare la merda da lui.*"[42]

"Why don't you and Priscilla come visit around Christmas time?"

"I think we can arrange that, and we will be bringing you lots of gifts. You send me a list of what you need for wherever you will live and we shall go shopping together."

"Perfect! And Mom will bake your favorite sweeties."

"My mouth is watering already! How are you feeling? I

---

[40] Uncle

[41] So that's the name of the bastard that dared to lay his hands on you. He best be ready because when I get there he's going to learn what's what, and if he ever hurts you I will tear him apart...

[42] scare the shit out of him

hear that pregnant people are often sick."

"Umm... The way I 'announced' to Cade and his whole family *and* dad was... well..."

"You're killing me, *Cerva*! Out with it."

"Must I relive the most embarrassing moment of my life?"

"*Sí*, you must."

"*Fine*! I may or may not have puked all over the dinner table... and everyone there."

Unable to contain his laughter, Antonio roared into the phone, doubled over with tears coming out of his eyes. He imagined Dianne and Marcus' faces when this happened, and could imagine the horror on Britt's face as well. Hardly able to breathe, he tried desperately to regain his composure but ended up going into another fit of laughter. He was still a typical 13-year-old boy, after all.

"Sure... laugh at my misery, why don't you!"

"I... I'm s-sorry..." Antonio giggled, once more sounding like the little boy that she knew.

"Can I ask you something?"

Hearing the seriousness in her voice, Antonio's laughter quickly subsided. "You can ask me anything."

"So... if the baby is a boy, I have always loved the name Logan and will give him Cade's middle name. However, if the baby is a girl, would it be okay... if I named her after your mom?"

Antonio was taken aback by her question, and he tried as hard as he could, to not choke up. "The name Logan is wonderful... and both Priscilla and I would be so honored if you had a girl and named her after *Mamma*. I know that she would be honored, too."

"Thank you, *Björn*! I'm going to have to let you go because... oh god!"

All Antonio could hear on the other end was the loud, disgusting sounds of someone throwing up. There wasn't much that made him queasy, but this sound was definitely it. "Uh... I love you *Cerva* bye!" He said quickly, hanging up the phone.

Shaking himself, Antonio decided that he should go tell Priscilla the news and headed out of his office to find her. She loved babies, and said her goal in life was to be a mom, though she did not get to spend much time around them. As he walked through the house, Antonio was already thinking about how he could spoil Britt's baby and what he could do to be the best *Zio* ever. The thoughts of a teenage boy that has a great love for his family can shock just about anyone.

Antonio spent the next year of his life traveling all over the United States and even to Spain, Italy, France, and Mexico, chasing the members of the Silver Serpents that were running and hiding in fear for their lives. Edward often joined him on his missions as his loyal second-hand. However, when it came down to the actual killing, Antonio only rarely relinquished his right to take their lives. There was so much bloodshed in his wake, and he soaked up the publicity and thrived off of the fear. He made sure he was gaining a reputation. If he were to be respected and feared as the leader of the Black Death Mafia, at such a young age, he had to go to extreme measures.

When the bodies of those he had slain were being cleaned up, the authorities were stunned at the ruthlessness and the degree of violence that had befallen them upon their deaths. It did not take long before seemingly every household in the United States, especially in California, knew the name of Antonio Moretti. His favorite weapon by far was the revolver that his father had given to him, though he became quite adept at murdering his enemies with various firearms, knives, and brass knuckles. He had a custom set of brass knuckles, each knuckle engraved with a plague doctor. During this time, Edward became very skilled at the art of torture and relished the opportunities that Antonio gave him. He, too, became adept at dispatching their enemies.

Meanwhile, Priscilla was thriving in school. She and Emily were tied at the top of their class. Priscilla honed in her skills as well, directing Antonio on where to go and where to look. No one could hide from her forever. Emily did her best to avoid anything relating to the mafia but was always there to support her best friend. Although they had promised to see the Alsup family more regularly, they were so caught up in tracking down every last Silver Serpent that they only managed to spend a few days in December during their first winter break without their parents in Oregon with them. However, Antonio and Priscilla both made sure to call them as often as they could. If they did not call in over a week, Dianne would ring them until they answered to chastise them and then give them all her love. Although he missed the birth of Britt's child, Antonio was overjoyed when he got the call that she had delivered a very healthy baby boy whom she had named Logan Asher Warren. Britt sent him pictures and in return, Antonio sent several gifts for his beloved *nipote*[43] whom he was so in love with even though they had never met.

When Antonio wasn't off hunting down his enemies, he was spending the majority of his time at Moretti Industries. All of his employees were very loyal and determined to teach him all that they could. They wanted to see him thrive, and if he was successful, they would be also. Some former employees who had originally worked for his grandparents and had retired came back to personally train him. He made sure that all who helped him received extra pay as well. It wasn't long before his name was also well-known in business circles.

---

[43] nephew

There were many times that Antonio became so stressed with his responsibilities that he did not think he could do what he was supposed to. However, Priscilla was his biggest supporter and the way she looked up to him helped him to carry on. He always made sure to put his duties aside to spend time with Priscilla, and they grew closer than ever. Margaret and Everett did their best to raise them how Lorenzo and Carmella would have wanted, and they always told Antonio and Priscilla how much they loved them. The Moretti children loved the Sommerset family immensely and were grateful to have them in their family.

Another year passed, and after two years of hunting, Antonio had finally killed off the last of his enemies from the Silver Serpents. Well, almost. Casimir Szymański had managed to evade Antonio's wrath, and Priscilla had to beg him to give up the madness and stay home with her. With the rage still burning inside of him, but no one left to take it out on, Antonio busied himself in Moretti Industries even more. He made sure that all of the accounts were in order and that the business was running smoothly. The Black Death Mafia was also running smoothly. No one wanted to cross them in fear of Antonio's wrath, and their business dealings were successful as well. By the time Antonio turned 16, he was every bit of the adult that everyone expected him to be. The Sommerset family moved back into their own home, though they came by often to make sure all was well.

Edward started taking an interest in girls, and convinced Antonio to come on a double date with him, stating that he was 16, things were in order, and he needed to still be a teenager. Figuring he might as well, Antonio went and was plunged into the world of women and hormones. He quickly discovered that he was quite charming, and could make any woman he wanted fall for his charms. The rage inside of him still burned brightly, but he found that it could be tamed through sex, and he felt no regret for using the women he slept with to tame the monster inside of him. It was a cycle that he kept himself in often, though he never brought anyone to their home, as he did not need his sister to know what he was doing.

In the background of it all, however, a little redheaded girl was growing up into a beautiful young woman. She stood in the shadows, preferring to blend in during her middle school years. However, in high school, she started to stand out. Her grades were excellent, she treated everyone kindly, and she was very involved in the community. She watched with sad eyes and a torn heart as the boy she had once been close to virtually cut her out and forgot about her as he plunged himself into his world of darkness, and she wondered if she would ever get to know the real him again.

Hello Darlin'

"Antonio Julius Moretti!" A voice bellowed as Antonio's office door burst open. Priscilla's face was red; she was fuming.

"Yes, *uno dolce*?" He asked nonchalantly.

"Oh no you don't! Do not '*uno dolce*' me you *stronzo madre*," she hissed.

"Now hold on just a minute. I better not hear that kind of language come out of your mouth again, Priscilla," Antonio replied, eyes narrowed as he stood up and glared at his 15-year-old sister. She rolled her eyes at him and glared back at him even more angrily. Taking a deep breath to calm himself, he asked, "What seems to be troubling you this afternoon?"

"Don't act like you don't know, *stronzo*.[44] How *dare* you tell Gabriel that I'm not allowed to go to homecoming with him?! You made the poor guy nearly piss himself and now he won't even look at me!!!" Her face was getting redder by the second as her voice grew louder.

Antonio gulped, as he had not intended for his sister to

---

[44] asshole

find out what he had done. When he overheard Priscilla talking to Emily two days ago about being asked to homecoming, he decided to do some digging on the guy. Turns out, the guy was a senior while Priscilla was a sophomore. He seemed to enjoy the company of several girls in the high school and there was no way that Antonio was going to let that guy put a finger on his sister. He'd tracked him down after football practice and put the fear of God into him. "*Sorella*, don't be mad. He is a manwhore and I'm not about to let him use you. Guys like him are no good."

"And who the hell do you think you are to judge him like that? You're out doing the exact same things that you're calling him out for. You're such a hypocrite!" Priscilla whirled around to storm out but Antonio caught her by the arm and pulled her in for a hug. She fought him for a moment before sighing and collapsing into his arms and sobbing.

"I really did not mean to upset you, *uno dolce*. And I know I'm a hypocrite... I just... I have to control the monster inside of me somehow. Please don't cry."

"It's not that... no one else has been brave enough to ask me to homecoming. Everyone is afraid of you. I don't want to go alone."

Stepping back, Antonio gently wiped her tears away with his handkerchief. "I'll take you! It's been a while since I've stepped foot in a school anyway."

Putting her hands up, Priscilla shook her head rapidly. "Absolutely not! Are you trying to embarrass me further? You don't go to homecoming with your sibling! *Signore, abbi pietà.*"[45]

Antonio chuckled and shook his head. He knew she was right though, and he truly did not want to embarrass her. "You know, if you want to come to the school, I'd appreciate

---

[45] Lord have mercy

it if you actually came to one of my games this season," Priscilla started. "You didn't come to any of my games last year, and I am the only sophomore on the varsity volleyball team. And your best friend is the star tight end on the football team, you should really watch his games. Edward has been with you through thick and thin, it's the least you could do."

Rubbing his stubbled chin, Antonio thought for a moment. "You're right. I've been a *merda*[46] friend and brother when it comes to those things. You have a game tonight, *sí*? I'll be there."

Clapping her hands in delight, Priscilla kissed his cheek and ran out of the room to get ready for her volleyball game, nearly running right into Edward on her way out. "What about me? Will you come to my game tomorrow?" Edward asked with puppy dog eyes.

Rolling his own eyes, Antonio chuckled, "Of course."

"I have an idea. Hear me out..."

Later that evening, Antonio and Edward walked into the gym together and found a seat on the bleachers behind their team's seats. For the occasion, Antonio had foregone his usual suit in favor of some jeans and a Knights t-shirt, the school's mascot. His hair was tousled and for the first time in years, he truly looked like a high school boy. During the warm-ups, Priscilla caught sight of him and grinned, waving briefly before going into her steps and slamming the ball with a powerful hit onto the other side of the net.

Antonio was in complete shock. He knew that his sister was talented, otherwise, she would not have been a starter on the varsity team her freshman year, but he never expected her to be this good, and it was just warm-ups. Her 5'6 frame was muscular, and her vertical was amazing. The game was bound to be good. Edward grinned as he watched his friend's

------

[46] shit

face, and Emily teased him about his lack of knowledge about the sport.

The game went well, and Antonio found himself on his feet cheering and clapping more than he had anticipated. Priscilla was an amazing outside hitter, the position that Emily had explained to him. She'd had 15 kills during the three matches that they won in a row, and also 5 aces when she served. The power behind her hits was extremely impressive, and Antonio made a mental note to stay off of her bad side at all costs.

During the game, he had turned to Emily and asked why there was a player that was wearing a different colored jersey. She explained to him that she was the libero, who was a special and talented player who only played the back row. The girl that played the position seemed very familiar. Her bright cayenne-red hair was braided elegantly down her back, and she flew all over the court, diving constantly for the ball. Her digs went precisely where she sent them and she had a ton of amazing plays. Antonio was impressed.

Following the game, the four went out for dinner at their favorite restaurant and celebrated the big win. The team that they had beaten was the state champions last year, and Priscilla's team was well on their way to winning this season. They made plans to attend Edward's game the following evening, then went their separate ways. Football was a sport that Antonio knew well. When he had still gone to school, he had played wide receiver for the team. He missed it, but he knew his position as head of Moretti Industries and the Black Death Mafia was more important. The Friday night game was a blowout. Edward was also impressive to watch and Antonio got loud cheering for his best friend as he scored two touchdowns and made some impressive catches.

October 10, 1987

The weeks had flown by, and as each day passed, Priscilla was becoming more and more discouraged at the fact that she had yet to be asked to homecoming. With the dance now less than a week away, she was losing hope and had decided that she would just go by herself. The good news, however, was that they had one more playoff game before heading to the state tournament. Her team had gone undefeated the entire season, and everyone was pumped. The football team had their playoff game the following Friday that would determine if they were heading to state, and it was also the homecoming game.

Sighing, Priscilla rolled out of bed and headed to take a shower. When she walked back into her bedroom, she found a note on her pillow. *Meet me outside when you're ready. E.* Slightly confused, but curious, Priscilla quickly donned her favorite pair of black leather pants, a mint long-sleeved shirt, and a pair of black heeled boots. Her long, curly hair was a bit unruly, so she quickly brushed it and put half of it up in a high ponytail. She had already done her makeup in the bathroom, and satisfied with her look, grabbed her purse and sprinted downstairs.

Outside, she found Edward leaning against the hood of his brand new black 1987 *Buick GNX*, awkwardly holding a bouquet of the most beautiful mint green roses she had ever seen. "Um, good morning, Priscilla," he greeted her with a nervous smile.

"Good morning, Edward," she smiled back, restraining herself from laughing at how nervous and awkward he looked.

Edward coughed as he handed her the flowers which smelled heavenly. "Alright, I'm going to get right to the point. I know you probably would prefer someone else... but... Priscilla Angelina Moretti, will you do me the honor of being my homecoming date?"

"Um, what?" She nearly choked, unable to believe what she was hearing.

Running a hand through his messy hair and straightening his Letterman's jacket, Edward continued, "You know, you are as close to me as my own sister, and I love you as such. To be honest with you, going to homecoming is not exactly my thing, but it kills me to know that the most beautiful girl in school is going alone. There is no one else I'd rather take than you, and I hope that you will come with me."

Tears formed in Priscilla's eyes at his words. While only having ever seen Edward as an older brother, there was no denying that he was extremely attractive with his messy mahogany hair and reddish brown eyes. He could take any girl he wanted to homecoming, in fact, he could probably take multiple. The fact that he had chosen to ask her, and called her beautiful while he was at it, meant more to Priscilla than he would ever know. "I would love to go to homecoming with you, Edward!" She threw her arms around him, careful not to destroy the flowers, and hugged him tightly.

He chuckled as he squeezed her tight. "Well, at least you won't have to worry about your date trying anything inappropriate," he winked at her as she stepped away, causing her to giggle. "So, I assume you are going to be wearing a beautiful mint dress?" When she nodded he continued, "If you will excuse me, I need to go find something suitable to wear and order a corsage. See you Monday."

Priscilla waved as she watched him drive off then went inside to put her flowers in a vase and let her brother know the news. Antonio loved his best friend even more for asking him if he could ask Priscilla to homecoming and told his sister that he hoped she had the most magical night next week. When homecoming finally came, Edward placed a beautiful white rose corsage on her wrist and danced every dance with her, making her feel super special. Several people gave them jealous looks, but they did not let anyone ruin their fun. For Priscilla, it was a night she would never forget.

December 24, 1987

After celebrating two state championships and heading into basketball season, which his sister and best friend were also quite talented at playing, Antonio found himself slammed with planning Moretti Industries' annual Christmas banquet and ball. All employees of Moretti Industries, as well as members of the Black Death Mafia and their families, were invited to attend. He thanked God every day for Margaret Sommerset who took the lead on the decor, catering, and invitations. All he had to do was sign checks and make sure that everything was in order.

At last, it was Christmas Eve, and Antonio was relieved that all of this party planning was about to be over for another year. After taking a long hard look in the mirror one day, especially after Priscilla's comment about him being with several women, he had decided to stop sleeping around. The monster inside of him raged on, and he desperately had been searching for a new hobby. Britt called to check in on him and had suggested he try his hand at gardening. He'd rolled his eyes but bought some rose bushes for their greenhouse, as well as several other plants.

Surprisingly, he loved it. The time he spent there was peaceful, and it put his mind at ease. He couldn't wait for spring to come so he could plant them in the gardens around the mansion. Shaking himself from his thoughts, Antonio gazed at his reflection in the mirror and began styling his hair. Running his hands over his face, he decided not to shave because he liked the facial hair; it made him look like a man. Discarding his towel, he dug through his closet for a suitable outfit for the event.

He chose a pair of slim black dress pants and a black dress shirt that he found to be tighter than he remembered. His arms had beefed up quite a bit since he had last worn it and it hugged his muscles tightly. The black suit jacket was also tight around his bulging muscles. He grabbed his black diagonally striped tie and set about tying it around his neck, but he had never quite mastered the art. *"Mi stai prendendo per il culo, cazzo!"*[47] He yelled, throwing the tie on the bed after several failed attempts.

"What are you yelling about now?" Priscilla asked as she waltzed in the door wearing a beautiful floor-length mint dress. She had tamed her curls and they fell beautifully down her back. She'd added some bobby pins adorned with pearls throughout her hair and topped the look off with a pearl necklace and pearl earrings. She looked absolutely stunning. Noticing the tie on the bed, Priscilla laughed as she walked over and picked it up.

"Fratello, non c'è bisogno di urlare. Chiedi aiuto.[48] You look quite handsome by the way." The tie was quickly and beautifully fashioned around his neck before he could say a word in protest.

"Grazie Sorella. Sembri semplicemente affascinante.[49] And if any man looks at you the wrong way, I will kill him with my bare hands."

"No, you won't," Priscilla rolled her eyes as she headed out of the room.

Quickly, Antonio pulled on some black socks and his black

---

[47] You have got to be fucking kidding me!

[48] Brother, there is no need to yell. Just ask for help.

[49] Thank you sister. You look simply ravishing.

dress shoes. He finished off the look with his large black metal studs, black hoops through the top of his ears, his black hoop through his nose, and his silver lip piercing that was somewhere between a spider bite and a vertical labret; he simply called it: *the Moretti*. He'd gotten all of his piercings within the past year, and he liked how it made him look even more like a bad boy. Priscilla was already in the car when he climbed in, and the two sped off into the city listening to *Never Gonna Give You Up* by Rick Astley.

The siblings arrived shortly after the event began, not caring that they were fashionably late. Priscilla caught sight of Emily and left her brother behind. Antonio and Edward discussed some things before Edward headed off to find his parents. In the lobby, Antonio grabbed a cherry martini from one of the waiters and pulled a cigar out of his pocket. He'd picked up smoking cigars and drinking in the past year as well, though he refrained from it as much as possible. His father had a box of Cuban cigars in the office and Antonio occasionally helped himself to one. Seeing how it was going to be a long night, he decided to relax by smoking one of them.

"Good evening, Mr. Moretti," a man's voice broke him out of his thoughts.

"Good evening, Mr. and Mrs. Springer. It's great to see you both. You look quite elegant this evening, Mrs. Springer," Antonio greeted the couple. They had been loyal employees since he had been a child and had been supportive and patient in his endeavors to learn how to run the business. The three shook hands before the Springers made their way into the dining hall, muttering something about their daughter taking her own sweet time.

Seeing that most of the guests seemed to have arrived, Antonio leaned back against the wall to relax a moment before he went in to give his speech. He looked around and admired the beautiful decorations that Margaret had chosen for the event. "These damn heels," He heard someone mutter as the sound of footsteps coming up the stairs reached his ears. A beautiful young woman made her way to the top of the staircase and began walking toward him. She lifted her gaze, and spotting him, stopped dead in her tracks. "Antonio? Is that really you?" She asked, eyes wide and a hint of a smile playing on her lips.

"Cynthia?" Antonio barely managed to choke out. He was simply stunned by the sight in front of him. The little girl that he had once called his friend so many years ago had grown into a beautiful young woman. Her bright, cayenne-red hair was curled elegantly and framed her face perfectly. The lights in the room made it shine. She was wearing a dark green, sparkly dress that complimented her figure quite nicely. There was a beautiful silver choker around her neck and a silver bracelet on her wrist. What captivated him the most, though, were her bright emerald-green eyes that seemed to stare right into his very soul. *Damn, she is the most stunning woman I have ever seen. How I would love to pull her into my office upstairs and make her scream my name. She's changed so much, how have I not noticed her before?*

While Antonio was busy ogling her, Cynthia took a moment to look him up and down as well. After the death of his parents, Cynthia had only seen Antonio a handful of times, and only from a distance. She had hoped they would remain friends, but he had distanced himself from everyone his age except for the Sommerset siblings. When she had seen him at the volleyball game in August, she was stunned and could not quite believe that he was there. She figured he didn't recognize her though. As the libero, she was not exactly her usual self. *It's so weird seeing him up close. That suit is quite tight... I'd love to feel those muscles of his. Get it together, Cynthia! You should not be having these kinds of thoughts...* She found his facial hair and piercings to be quite attractive, too, and had to shake herself from her thoughts before she could act on any of them.

"It's nice to see you, Antonio. Maybe we'll run into each other again soon," she smiled at him as she started to walk by. Turning to look back at him, she said, "Smoking is a disgusting habit you know."

For some reason, which he could not explain, her comment got to him and he immediately put his cigar out and threw it in the closest trash can. Antonio watched her walk away, appreciating her body from behind. *Oh don't you worry, Bel Fiore,*[50] *we shall run into each other quite soon.* Setting his unfinished drink on a tray, Antonio made his way into the dining hall. He found his sister, then took his spot at the head of the table. Immediately, the room went quiet as everyone turned to look at their young boss. Antonio spotted Cynthia and locked eyes with her as he began his speech.

"Welcome, everyone. I'm glad you all could make it to our annual Christmas banquet and ball tonight. I would just like to give my gratitude for all of you. Because of everything you do, Moretti Industries has had its most successful year to date. We could not have had this level of success without the sacrifices and time that each and every one of you put into the company. You have given up countless hours of family time and some of your own sanity to make this company run and to help me learn how to manage it. As a thank you, I have a few people walking around the room handing out envelopes. Inside you will find your Christmas bonus, and I hope that it is sufficient. Moretti Industries will also be closed until after New Year's Day, but you all will still receive your pay. Take the time to go on vacation, relax, and just enjoy yourselves. Merry Christmas, everyone!"

---

[50] Beautiful Flower

Everyone in the room stood up and clapped. Some people whistled, and others cheered. Antonio's face lit up in a huge smile, and Cynthia couldn't help but smile back as his eyes bore into hers. Everett stood up once everyone had been seated and said Grace, dismissing everyone to eat. Priscilla, never missing anything, leaned in close to her brother. "So, wanna tell me why you were staring at Cynthia the whole time? And don't tell me that you weren't, I saw it."

"Well... She's just so... beautiful," he replied, feeling his face flush slightly.

Priscilla rolled her eyes. "You're just now noticing? If you would have been paying attention you would have noticed how beautiful she's gotten a lot sooner. But no, you dropped everyone. You know, she told me that she misses your friendship."

"There is no possible way I can be friends with her."

"And why the hell not?" Priscilla asked, glaring at him.

"Just look at her... She is far too beautiful for that. I think I want to be more than friends with her."

"I know that look. Don't you dare try to use her! She's different from the other girls you've been with. Cynthia deserves someone who only has eyes for her, not a manwhore looking to get laid."

Antonio rolled his eyes and took a deep breath. "*Sorella*, I don't know how to be a boyfriend. But... I think I wanna see if I have a chance with her. Where do I even start?"

"You could start by being her friend again and getting to know her."

Taking his sister's words to heart, Antonio ate his meal and pondered how on earth he was going to get a girl like Cynthia to give a guy like himself a chance. *I'll have to ask Britt tomorrow when I call to say Merry Christmas.* As people finished their food, they began heading towards the ballroom where a live band was playing. Antonio strolled in and looked around. *Ah, there is the bel fiore.* She was standing behind a group of people, her back against the wall watching her parents and the other couples who were on the dance floor as they danced.

He quickly made his way over to where she was standing. "Cynthia?"

She jumped slightly but smiled when she saw who it was that had snuck up on her. "You startled me."

"I'm sorry, I didn't mean to," Antonio said, rubbing his neck sheepishly. He coughed a little before bowing, "May I have this dance?"

Cynthia giggled as she took his outstretched hand and curtsied. "You may."

Antonio led her out onto the dance floor right as the band began playing a song that was perfect to Waltz to. The pair danced gracefully around the room, each having learned the dance from their parents. As they danced, they took the opportunity to catch up on each other's lives, Antonio being nearly unable to look away from her eyes the entire time. They captivated him, as did she. For nearly an hour they danced, no matter if it was a slow or fast dance. The two laughed and had more fun than they'd had in years. Cynthia marveled at how this young man, who was by all accounts a ruthless, cold-blooded, hardened killer, could still laugh his boyish laugh that she had grown to love so many years ago as children; albeit his voice was much deeper now.

At the toll of the midnight bell, everyone proceeded to yell Merry Christmas before parting ways. Cynthia's parents were waving to her, letting her know that it was time to leave. "Thank you for tonight, Antonio. I had a lot of fun."

"As did I," he replied, sad that the night was ending.

"Good night, Antonio. Don't be a stranger."

"Good night, *Bel Fiore*," Antonio smiled down at her.

"Beautiful flower, huh?" She asked, slightly puzzled.

"Wait, you know Italian?"

"Well, when your family works for an Italian family, it helps to pick up the language," she winked playfully. "Why the nickname?"

"Maybe I'll tell you someday, on one condition," he leaned in and whispered playfully into her ear.

"And what might that be?"

"Come on a date with me."

"A date? Are you serious?"

"Yeah? Or do you not want to be associated with me?"

"That is not at all what I was implying," she said quickly. "I just meant that... it's hard for me to understand why you would want to take a girl like me on a date."

"A girl like you? I don't understand."

"I'm neither blind nor deaf, Antonio. I know the types of women that you've been with. I'm nothing like them, nor am I beautiful like they are."

Antonio was flabbergasted. *How does she not see her own beauty? I haven't even been able to acknowledge another woman's presence in this room.* "Cynthia, trust me when I say that you are more beautiful than anyone I have ever seen." She rolled her eyes but blushed at his compliment. "So, will you go on a date with me?" He asked once more, hope in his eyes.

Chuckling softly, Cynthia reached into her purse and pulled out a small piece of paper, and quickly wrote something on it before handing it to Antonio. "Here is my number. Call me and let me know when and where." With that, she turned on her heel and walked over to her parents who waved at Antonio.

Non so cosa ti riguardi, ma non vedo l'ora di farti sentire la donna più speciale del mondo, Bel Fiore.[51]

---

[51] I don't know what it is about you, but I cannot wait to make you feel like the most special woman in the world, Beautiful Flower.

Mama He's Crazy

December 25, 1987

Christmas morning, Priscilla came bounding into Antonio's bedroom at 9:00 A.M. and snuggled up next to him on his bed. "Wake up, *Fratello carissimo!*"[52]

Antonio groaned, he wasn't ready to get up yet, but knew that Priscilla would not leave him alone until he got up. Faster than should be humanly possible, Antonio turned over and pinned his sister with one arm and tickled her with his free hand. "*Tocco, tocco!*"[53] She squealed with laughter.

"That's what you get for waking me up before I'm ready," he winked, releasing her. "*Buon Natale,*[54] Priscilla."

"Merry Christmas, Antonio! Now come on, you have to see what I got you!"

Chuckling, Antonio swung his legs out of bed and slipped a t-shirt on before following his sister downstairs where she was waiting impatiently in front of the Christmas Tree. The two exchanged gifts and savored the remaining pieces of

---

[52] brother dearest
[53] I tap, I tap!
[54] Merry Christmas

their *Tant's* Christmas goodies for breakfast. Antonio had gifted Priscilla a custom set of mafia gear that was black and mint, and she was excited to try it on. She rushed to shower and get ready for the day, leaving Antonio to clean up all of the wrapping paper.

I guess this would be a good time to call Britt. He headed into his office and sat down in the large, leather chair behind his desk. Picking up the phone, he dialed the number that he had memorized several years ago. "Hello?" A soft voice answered after a few rings.

"*Buon Natale, Cerva!*"

"Merry Christmas to you too, *Björn!*" Britt laughed into the phone.

"Did you get your gifts?"

"I did! Thank you so much for the necklace, I love it so much!"

Antonio had given her a custom-made gold necklace with a raw amethyst inset into it. It was both her and Logan's birthstone. "I'm glad. Britt... I need some advice."

Hearing the seriousness in his voice, and the fact that Antonio had called her "Britt" instead of "*Cerva*", concerned her. "*Va tutto bene?*"[55]

"*Sí*, nothing serious. I just... Do you remember when I told you about the girl that caused me to break my leg?"

"How could I forget? I was so worried about you and upset that we lived so far away from each other. What about her?"

"Well... I may have cut her out of my life when my parents were killed. Being around people my age was too distracting, and frankly, it made me sad because at the time most of the kids still had their parents and were living quite happily." Antonio paused to take a deep breath, just thinking about all

---

[55] Is everything alright?

that he had missed out on due to his parents' deaths, and the sorrow that filled his heart because he missed them terribly, made him emotional. Britt's heart ached for the brother of her heart, and she wished she could hug him through the phone. "Anyway," Antonio continued, "Her name is Cynthia. I saw her last night at the banquet... and *Cerva*, she is the most beautiful woman I have ever seen and I want nothing more than to have her as my own."

"*Kvinnor är inte föremål du äger,*"[56] Britt chastised, switching to Swedish as she became frustrated. "*Du kan kalla henne en följeslagare, men inte din egendom.*"[57]

"*Jag menade inte det så! Jag är ledsen att det kom ut så. Gud, jag vet inte vad som är fel med mig.*"[58]

Laughing, Britt sarcastically retorted, "*Låt mig notera att den stora, dåliga björnen för första gången i historien är mållös!*"[59]

"Ha. Ha. Very funny." Britt could practically hear Antonio roll his eyes. "We reconnected yesterday, and there is no way I can just be friends with her. But I don't know how to be a boyfriend. I'm ashamed to admit it, but I don't really know how to treat a woman that I'm not just trying to get into my bed."

Britt thought for a moment, before she lovingly responded, "Well, start with just being honest and being the kind boy your family knows and loves. Show her the heart behind the '*fä*'."[60]

---

[56] Women aren't objects that you own
[57] You can call her a companion, but not your property.
[58] I did not mean it like that! I'm sorry that it came out that way. God, I don't know what's wrong with me.
[59] Let me make note, that for the first time in history, the big bad bear is speechless!
[60] beast

"I think I can do that... I just have no idea what women like. I asked her to go on a date with me but I have no idea what to do. Girls like flowers, right?"

"Why don't you have Priscilla and Emily play a little recon and you can find out exactly what she likes? I love lilies, but not all girls do."

"Can I tell you something without you teasing me?"

Laughing Britt jested, "Maybeeee....of course, you *dum björn*."[61]

"I'm glad that I am safely in Los Angeles because if you saw the amount of times I've rolled my eyes you'd hurt me," he replied sarcastically. "So, I definitely already gave her a nickname... *Bel Fiore*. Her hair reminds me of the *gigli di tigre*[62] growing in my greenhouse. I think I might cut some and give them to her."

Britt instantly became as giddy as a schoolgirl, "Oh my gosh *Björn*, that is literally the most precious thing ever." Preening triumphantly, Britt continued, "See, this is what I am talking about. *This* is who you are. Also, gardening huh? You're welcome, by the way."

"Again, I am rolling my eyes. But yes, thank you. It's very... peaceful. Thank you, *Cerva*, for the advice. Now, is *mio nipote* around?"

Britt chuckled once more, "Of course he is! You know, this little one never leaves my side. I can't believe my baby will be four soon." Holding back a few motherly tears, Britt softly spoke, "Logan, tell *Zio* 'hi'."

"*Zio*! I wubs you!"

"*Ciao*[63], Logan! I love you too buddy. Merry Christmas! Did you get lots of cool presents?" Antonio's heart melted to

---

[61] silly bear
[62] tiger lilies
[63] Hi

72

the floor hearing the little boy speak to him, he loved him dearly.

"*Jultomten*[64] dibs me teddy beaw. *Io chiamo*[65] *Zio Björn* tus mommy call you *Björn!*"

Antonio wiped away a couple of tears, this boy was truly so special. "*Skit,*[66] Logan that is so sweet! Thank you, buddy."

"Mommy, you dunna panks *Zio*? Him say potty wowds." Logan asked, worried for his loving uncle. Britt spoke through the phone with a chuckle, "The next time I see him baby mine, yes I will. Tell *Zio* what Daddy and I got you for Christmas."

"Oh yeah! Dems dibs me Misser Potato Head!"

"We'll have to play with him when I come to visit!"

"Otay *Zio*! Me go play wiff toys! Wubs you!"

"Love you too, Logan! Uh... sorry *Cerva*, I try and have a filter but sometimes it just sneaks out. Please don't kill me when I come to see you. And when are you gonna have another baby for me to spoil?"

Britt laughed, a bit too hysterically, "Cade and I can barely keep up with Logan as it is. He's pretty wild. I don't know if I could handle another one of him running around. Also, I'm just 19, almost 20. I'm enough of a stereotype as it is. I really don't want to be another one."

Antonio sighed, sometimes he wished that Britt would not care about what other people thought of her. To him, she was absolutely spectacular, and an amazing role model, no matter what had happened during her teenage years. "Well, I think you are doing amazing with him. What do you think about a visit after New Year's?"

"That would be amazing, but be polite to Cade, please. He

---

[64] Santa Claus
[65] I call him
[66] Shit

is working super hard and I couldn't ask for a better husband."

"I suppose I could try," Antonio groaned. "Anyway, I'll let you go, I'm sure you have a lot going on today with it being Christmas. Tell *Tant* and *Farbror* I'll give them a call later. I've got a date to figure out..."

With a joking wink, Britt, after she knew Logan wasn't within earshot, said, "Make sure you wrap it before you tap it, buddy!" After her laughter died down, she said, "I will and I love you *Björn*! Merry Christmas."

"*Che cazzo*,[67] Britt!" Antonio groaned, slightly embarrassed. "I love you too... Merry Christmas. Now if you'll excuse me, I'm going to go die of embarrassment." He hung up and rubbed his face, noticing that it was very red.

The rest of Christmas day was spent with the Sommerset's who had made a delicious supper. Priscilla and Emily were very gracious in the information they provided to Antonio on what Cynthia liked. "She likes simple things, like lunch in a diner. Nothing fancy, especially for a first date," Priscilla instructed.

"And this," Emily gestured at his outfit, "Needs to change."

"What's wrong with my clothes?" He asked, slightly offended.

"Too much black. Wear a little color for goodness' sake."

Antonio rolled his eyes but took a mental note to wear a shirt that wasn't black.

December 26, 1987

The following morning, he worked up the courage to call Cynthia. He dialed the number on the piece of paper and

---

[67] What the fuck

waited for her to answer. "Hello?" A soft, feminine voice answered.

"Hey, it's Antonio."

"Oh! Hi, Antonio," she replied.

"So I was thinking... if you're not busy tonight, would you like to get some dinner with me? There's this new diner that opened up downtown that I've been wanting to try." His hands were shaking as he spoke.

"Maggie's Diner?! I've heard amazing things about it. I would love to go!" "Great! I'll pick you up at six. Uh, is your dad there by chance?"

"He is, let me grab him."

"Good morning, Antonio," Came a man's voice.

"Morning, Mr. Springer. I realize I probably should have spoken to you first, but I have just asked Cynthia to go to dinner with me tonight. Is that alright with you?"

Mr. Springer chuckled at the fact that his boss was asking permission to take his daughter to dinner. "That is fine by me, just have her home by 11. And I know you're my boss, but don't try anything with her, got it?"

Swallowing a nervous lump, Antonio nodded his head. "Absolutely! I will treat her with the utmost respect, Sir."

He could not quite understand why he was so nervous, but he wiped a little sweat off his brow. Suddenly, he felt a little panicked. "Priscilla!" He yelled as he ran upstairs and burst into his room.

"*Sí, Fratello?*" She asked, looking up from the book that she was reading.

"*Mi devi aiutare! Non so cosa indossare!*"[68]

Bursting into laughter, Priscilla grabbed his arm and dragged him into his bedroom. "Sit," she commanded, pointing to his bed. He immediately sat and watched as she

---

[68] You have got to help me! I don't know what to wear!

dug through his dresser. After several minutes, Priscilla was finally satisfied with her choice of outfit for her brother. "Put these on, then come see me when you're ready. My book is calling me."

After she left the room, Antonio shrugged and walked into his bathroom to take a quick shower. He looked at the clothes briefly before deciding he might as well give them a try. Looking at his reflection in the mirror, he was amazed at how normal he looked. Priscilla had chosen a pair of dark wash jeans, a burgundy long-sleeved shirt, and a pair of casual brown boots. *Not bad at all... though I would still prefer my black clothes.* Making his way back to Priscilla's room, he stood at the foot of her bed until she realized he was there.

"Antonio! You look fantastic, if I do say so myself!" She grinned at him.

"Thank you, *Sorella*. How should I wear my hair?"

"Go with the messy look. No need to make it so neat and tidy. Now go away, I'm reading," she dismissed him with a wave of her hand.

Antonio spent the next several hours trying and failing to make the nervousness he was feeling go away. Edward and Emily came over to keep Priscilla company, and they teased him as he paced in the living room. At 5:00 P.M., Antonio grabbed his brown leather jacket and his keys and walked outside toward the back of the house where his greenhouse stood. Inside, he made his way to the thriving bunch of tiger lilies and cut seven of them, wrapping the stalks in a wet paper towel and a piece of parchment paper that he tied with a piece of twine.

He was glad he left so early, as it took longer than he anticipated to get to the Springer family's house. Pulling up in his loud, black, 1974 *Chevy Impala*, he parked and grabbed the bouquet out of the passenger seat. Walking up to the door, he took a deep breath and knocked. Within seconds, the door opened and Martin Springer was grinning at him. "Nice to see you, Antonio," he greeted him as he stuck out his hand.

"Nice to see you too, Mr. Springer," Antonio said as he shook the older man's hand.

"Daddy, I hope you're not giving him a hard time," Cynthia said as she rounded the corner and came to stand next to her father at the door. "Now go away."

"Have fun you two," Mr. Springer chuckled as he walked back into the house.

"Hi, Antonio," Cynthia smiled at him.

"Hi, Cynthia. You look really nice," he replied shyly. She was wearing a light pink jean skirt, a white long-sleeved blouse that was tucked in, and white sneakers. There were large silver hoop earrings in her ears and she wore a beautiful nude shade of lipstick that topped off the look quite well. "Oh, um, these are for you," Antonio mumbled nearly dropping the bouquet as he shoved them into her hands.

"Thank you, they're beautiful," she said, bringing them up to her nose to smell them. "Hang on just a minute, I'm going to go put them in a vase!" When she returned she shut the door behind them and started walking toward the car.

"*Bel Fiore*, it's December! Why don't you have a coat?" Antonio gasped.

Cynthia shrugged, just realizing that she was, in fact, coatless. "Here, take this," Antonio chuckled, taking off his jacket and putting it around her shoulders.

"Thank you. So, where did you get those amazing flowers this time of year? What kind of lily are they?" She asked as they got in the car.

Antonio backed out of the driveway and headed toward downtown. "Well... do you promise not to laugh if I tell you?"

"Cross my heart," she smiled, making an X over her heart with her finger. "I still am curious about the nickname too, don't think I forgot. And why seven?"

Chuckling, Antonio took a deep breath. "They're *gigli di tigre*, tiger lilies... that I grew in my greenhouse. I chose seven because we met seven years ago..."

Cynthia blushed, finding the sentiment to be extremely sweet. "You garden?" She asked, somewhat shocked.

"Yeah... as you are well aware, my hobbies included killing my enemies and sleeping with women. I, uh... decided that I needed a new hobby. Surprisingly, I love gardening, and I'm pretty good at it. I know it's not a manly hobby, but it's peaceful."

"I think that's wonderful," Cynthia said, placing her tiny hand on his broad shoulder. "So, why tiger lilies?"

"Well, they are my favorite flower, and I've been growing quite a bunch. And... well... your hair reminds me of them. That's why I gave you the nickname."

His admission took her breath away. If she couldn't hear the sincerity in his voice, she wouldn't believe the words he was saying. *Maybe the boy I once knew really is still in there.* "I like it," she whispered.

Antonio heard her, though, and winked. "Hey, can I find some music?" Cynthia asked.

"Sure," Antonio shrugged as they drove through the city.

Giddily, Cynthia turned the radio to the country station. "What the hell is this?" Antonio asked, repulsed.

"It's country music, duh. Now no complaining, I love this song!" She exclaimed as she turned the volume up to George Strait's song *Ocean Front Property*. He rolled his eyes, but couldn't help but smile as she sang along beautifully.

Finally pulling up to Maggie's, Antonio hopped out of the car and quickly rushed over to open the passenger door for Cynthia. They walked in together and were greeted by a woman in her early thirties. "Goodness me. Is that really you, Antonio Moretti?!"

The woman pulled Antonio into a hug as he chuckled. "It is, Mrs. Whitacker."

"I'm so glad you came! And how many times do I have to tell you to call me Maggie?"

"I told you I'd come, didn't I? How are Roger and Amelia?"

"You did indeed. They are doing well. Amelia just turned four!"

"Four already? That doesn't seem possible."

"I know! And, we are expecting another," Maggie exclaimed, pointing to her rounded stomach.

"Congratulations, Maggie! Oh, this is... Cynthia," he said, gesturing to her, not knowing how to introduce her.

"Well, aren't you just a pretty little thing? I'm Maggie, and this is my restaurant. This young man helped my husband and me start it up. Here, let me show you to a booth."

"It's nice to meet you, Maggie," Cynthia said as they followed the busy woman.

Once they were seated, Cynthia took a deep breath before initiating a conversation that might be hard to hear, but there were things that she needed to know. "So, I am a very curious person... and I have a lot of questions for you..." she began, shyly.

Antonio took a deep breath, knowing full well the kinds of questions she was going to ask him. "Ask away. For you, I'm an open book."

"You said your hobbies included killing your enemies... Did you kill as many people as the rumors say?"

Sighing, Antonio ran a hand through his hair and looked out the window for a moment before meeting her captivating emerald eyes once more. "To be perfectly honest with you... any rumor that you have heard about me is probably true. If you must know, I've taken over 500 lives." He was scared to look at her, so he turned to look back out the window. There was a lump in his throat that he struggled to swallow, and for some reason, he did not want this woman to see him as the monster that he was.

Two small, warm, soft hands enveloped one of his large ones. "Antonio, look at me." He turned his head reluctantly and met her gaze once more. Instead of disgust and hate, he found compassion in her eyes. "While I don't exactly condone what you've done... I understand why you did it; why you had to do it."

"You... you don't see me as a monster?" He asked, voice barely above a whisper.

"Not at all. You're not a monster, no matter the darkness that lives inside of you." Seeing that Antonio was having a hard time responding, Cynthia moved on. "Your next hobby was women... how many have you been with?"

"Do you need to know that?" He groaned. Seeing her unwavering stare, he sighed, "I'm not sure... around 20 I think."

Cynthia's face went pale, briefly. There was one more thing that she needed to know, so she worked up the courage to ask. "What exactly are your intentions with me? Why did you want to take me out tonight?"

"If you think that I'm doing this to get you in my bed, you don't have to worry about that," Antonio started, blushing as he ran his hand through his hair once more. "I gave up sex a couple of months ago, and I truly want to avoid it until I'm with the person I can see myself marrying. To be honest with you, you have completely captivated me. I'm not quite sure what it is, but I desperately want to get to know you. You're absolutely beautiful, and the way you carry yourself so elegantly impresses me. I... I've never actually been on a date, nor have I considered the idea of actually having a girlfriend, but I would like to learn how to do it. And hopefully, *un angelo come te potrebbe considerare di dare una possibilità a un mostro come me."*[69]

Satisfied with his answer, and doing her best to keep her emotions in check, Cynthia squeezed his hand. *"Voglio darti una possibilità."*[70] She withdrew her hands as Antonio snapped his head up to meet her eyes, and she admired the warmness of his brown eyes. "To be honest with you... I've had a crush on you since we were 10 years old. But I never figured I would be your type."

"Well, that makes me very relieved. I've never had a type... but if I were to have one, you would be it."

Before they could continue talking, Maggie set their food down in front of them, winked, and headed back to the kitchen. The two dug into their burgers and fries and had fun sharing a large chocolate malt. It was the perfect first date, and they both couldn't wait to see where this would lead. When dinner was over, Antonio drove Cynthia home, keeping the country music station turned up loud for her to sing along with, even though it was definitely not his type of music.

He parked in the driveway and took Cynthia's hand before she could get out of his car. "Hey, so... Priscilla and I are having Edward and Emily over on New Year's Eve for some games and movies. Would you like to join us? We have a spare bedroom you can use."

"I'd love to. I'm sure my parents won't mind. Maybe... I could come over tomorrow? It's been a while since I've been to the Moretti Mansion, and I did tell Priscilla I would help her with some math homework."

"Cynthia, you are welcome at our home anytime."

He walked her to the door and took a deep breath. "Thank

---

[69] an angel like you might consider giving a monster like me a chance.

[70] I do want to give you a chance.

you for dinner, Antonio," she said softly, turning to open the door.

"Thank you for coming with me. Good night, Cynthia." He gently brushed her hair behind her ear and leaned in, kissing her softly on the cheek.

"Good night, Antonio," she whispered, blushing. Quickly, she went inside but watched from the window as he drove away. *I can't believe Antonio Moretti just kissed me on the cheek... Oh Antonio, how happy I am to see that the real you is still there.*

December 31, 1987

Cynthia spent three of the next five days at the Moretti Mansion, spending time with both Priscilla and Antonio. She even got to see the beautiful flowers that Antonio was growing in his greenhouse. New Year's Eve finally came, and Antonio was anxiously pacing in the living room waiting for Cynthia's arrival.

"Dude, chill. She'll be here soon I'm sure," Edward said, trying to help ease his best friend's mind. He'd never seen his best friend like this, and he was having a hard time restraining the laughter that desperately wanted to escape his chest.

Five minutes later, a car pulled up and Cynthia got out and waved goodbye to whoever had dropped her off. Before she could even make it to the porch, Antonio was bounding down the steps. "Hey," he said sheepishly. "Let me take that for you."

"Hi. Thanks," she replied, handing him her bag.

The evening passed quickly, the five of them playing several different games, eating take out and watching movies. They were having so much fun, that they didn't even realize that it was almost midnight. "Oh my gosh, you guys! There's only three minutes left. Come on Emily, let's go set up the fireworks!" Priscilla exclaimed, grabbing Emily's hand and pulling her outside, the two of them laughing hysterically.

"Wait for me!" Edward yelled, chasing after them. He did not trust them with explosives and figured he should do his brotherly duty and help them out.

Antonio laughed heartily but stopped when he noticed Cynthia grinning at him. "What?"

"I just, really love your laugh," she said sheepishly. "There's only a couple of minutes till midnight..."

"Yeah?"

"Well, most people tend to, um, ring in the New Year with a, um..." Cynthia trailed off as Antonio moved her way, stopping directly in front of her.

"With a kiss," he finished, voice husky.

"3... 2... 1..." Yelled the three from outside. The clock struck midnight, and fireworks were immediately shot up into the sky from the front yard.

Cynthia swallowed nervously as Antonio slowly leaned in towards her. Unable to contain herself any longer, she reached up and pulled his head down, their lips meeting in a passionate kiss. Antonio wrapped his arms around her waist and pulled her tiny frame up against his large one, leaving no space between them.

Antonio pulled back, and stared at her, his eyes darker and full of desire. "Happy New Year, Cynthia Elizabeth Springer," he whispered, voice even huskier.

"Happy New Year, Antonio Julius Moretti," Cynthia replied, trying to catch her breath.

He smiled down at her, then dropped his arms and turned to sit back down. "Oh no you don't, Moretti," she said, grabbing his arm and pulling his face back down to meet hers. Antonio didn't hesitate, holding her tightly once more as they gave in to the passion for a few more moments.

Girls Got Rhythm

February 14, 1988

Antonio spent the next month and a half taking Cynthia on dates, spending every second he could with her. They spent a lot of time smiling and laughing, and even more time making out. Kissing her was something he could never get enough of. Sitting up in his bed and stretching, Antonio grinned to himself. Today was a very special day. Not only did he have his first-ever Valentine's date, but it was Logan's fourth birthday. Seeing that it was only 8 A.M., Antonio decided to get ready for the day before giving his favorite nephew a call.

After getting himself dressed up in appropriate date attire, Antonio made his way downstairs to his office. The black dress pants and peach-colored long-sleeve button-up looked good on him. He'd chosen a peach shirt because it was Cynthia's favorite color, though he still much preferred black. Sitting comfortably in his leather chair, he dialed the number and waited until he heard the sweet voice of his nephew on the other end.

"Hewo?"

"*Buon compleanno, nipote!*"[71]

---

[71] Happy birthday, nephew!

"*Zio!* I is four today!"

"Four? No way! You must only be two, you're not big enough to be four."

"I am *Zio!*"

"I hope it is the best birthday ever, buddy. I sent your birthday presents in the mail. You will have to call me tomorrow and tell me if you like them."

"I will *Zio.* Momma says I haf to eat my bweakfast fwirst before I opens pwesents."

"That's right, Logie, you better listen to your mom. I love you, Logan Asher, happy birthday!"

"I wubs you too *Zio,* bye bye!"

After having a brief conversation with Britt, Antonio hung up and went to make himself a cup of coffee. Priscilla was bustling around the kitchen humming a tune. "Antonio Julius, did you call Logan without me?" She asked sternly with her hands on her hips.

"Um... good morning *uno dolce,* did you sleep well?" He sputtered nervously.

Signore, dammi la pace,[72] she thought, rolling her eyes. "I did, thank you. You know I miss our nephew just as much as you. You could have told me when you were making the call. I'll go call him myself."

"I'm sorry, *Sorella.* I should have told you. But before you go, do I look alright?"

Priscilla looked at her brother and tried not to laugh at how nervous he was. Though he and Cynthia had been seeing each other for almost two months, he still got anxious before each date. "You look as handsome as ever, *Fratello.* I like that color on you. Are you finally going to make things official with Cynthia?"

"*Sí,* I figure it's time."

---

[72] Lord give me peace

86

Squealing with excitement, Priscilla hugged her brother and wished him luck before skipping off to call Logan. Chuckling to himself, Antonio poured himself a cup of coffee, ate some breakfast, and did a few chores around the house. After making sure everything was in order, he walked to the greenhouse and cut a few peach-colored calla lilies. Placing the flowers in a vase, he secured it in his car and headed downtown to Moretti Industries. Even though it was a Sunday, he wanted to get a head start on the week.

At 5:00 P.M., Antonio got into his car and made the drive to Cynthia's house. He grabbed the flowers and walked up to her door and knocked. When the door opened, he was stunned. Cynthia stood there looking absolutely stunning. Her cayenne red hair was curled elegantly with a braid crown and she was wearing a short, peach lace dress. *I'm fucked...* Antonio thought to himself as he swallowed hard. "Happy Valentine's Day, *Bel Fiore*," Antonio blushed as he handed the flowers to her.

"Happy Valentine's Day, Antonio! Oh my goodness, we are matching!" She squealed. Quickly, she ran inside and put the flowers on the table before rushing back outside and throwing her arms around the young man that had stolen her heart. After placing a passionate kiss on his lips, she grabbed his hand and pulled him to his car. "Thank you for the flowers."

"Aren't you worried about your parents seeing us kissing?" He asked, still slightly dazed.

"No, they're already out on their date," Cynthia grinned.

"Well in that case," Antonio smirked, leaning her against his car and smashing his lips to hers once more. Cynthia responded by grabbing onto his shirt and pulling him closer. *She drives me absolutely insane. I've never felt like this before. Fuck —We've got to stop before I lose control.* "Alright babe, I think it's time to go. Don't worry, we can resume later."

Cynthia giggled but allowed him to step away so he could open the door for her. It made her heart happy hearing the country music playing from his radio as he started the car, even though it wasn't his kind of music. Antonio made her feel so many emotions, and she realized just how quickly she was falling for him. Even though she knew he was a cold-blooded killer, he was sweet, playful, and gentle with her. When they were together, he wasn't Antonio Moretti, mafia leader, business leader, stone cold; no, he was simply Antonio.

Arriving at one of the most prestigious restaurants in Los Angeles, the pair walked hand in hand. They were immediately seated at the VIP table, and Cynthia was taken aback by how gorgeous the interior was. The restaurant also had the most amazing view of the city. Dinner was phenomenal, and the two enjoyed each other's company, talking and laughing throughout the evening.

After sufficiently gorging themselves, Antonio stood up and offered Cynthia his hand. Making their way to the balcony, Antonio closed the door behind them and stood beside her as they looked out over the city. "What's on your mind, Moretti?" Cynthia asked after several minutes of silence had passed.

Antonio was shaking, and he took several deep breaths to compose himself. *Enough with this shit. You kill grown men for a living. There is no reason for you to be so nervous with a woman. No matter how amazing and beautiful she is. Snap out of it Antonio before she thinks you're even creepier than you are.* "Cynthia—" he croaked, then cleared his throat to start over. "Cynthia, I'm not very good at this. I've never done this before... But you are absolutely amazing, and I feel like the luckiest guy in the world that such a perfect woman like you would give a monster like me a chance. What I'm trying to say is that I really like you and I was wondering if you would like to officially be my girlfriend?"

Unable to help herself, Cynthia giggled at the way he was struggling. She blushed as she stepped closer to him and touched his face softly with one of her hands. "Antonio, you really need to stop saying that. You are no monster. I'd love to be your girlfriend."

Before he could react, Cynthia stood on her tiptoes and planted a soft kiss right on his lips. "Now come on, boyfriend. You said something about a movie night?" She smirked as she walked away from him.

Damn. I can't believe this woman is mine... "Wait for me, *Bel Fiore!*"

Once they were back at the Moretti Mansion, the two cuddled up under a blanket on the couch and turned on *Rambo III*. It had been a long time since Antonio had felt so relaxed and at ease. About a third of the way through the movie, the phone in the living room began ringing. Rolling his eyes, Antonio made his way over to the phone to answer it. "This better be a fucking emergency because I specifically said I was not to be called this evening," Antonio growled into the phone.

"Antonio, you know I wouldn't call unless it was important," the ever calm voice of Everett Sommerset replied.

"Sorry, Everett. What happened?"

"Sampson Hayes sent some of his men to mess with our weapons shipment. They stole a third of our supply."

"Are you shitting me right now? Who the fuck does Hayes think he is? He's nothing more than a petty criminal."

"I know. He's messing with the wrong people, that's for sure. We did manage to track them down, and we've got them surrounded. Boss, we need you to come finish this."

"I'm on my way. Don't do anything else until I get there."

Hanging up the phone, Antonio started heading upstairs, unbuttoning his shirt as he made his way up. "Wait!" Cynthia called, following him. "What's going on?"

"I'm sorry, babe… but we've had some issues at the warehouse that I have to take care of," Antonio explained, shrugging off his shirt and letting it fall to the ground. "I have to go down there and take care of it but I'll be back as soon as I can."

He dropped his pants and stepped out of them, turning to see that Cynthia was standing there gawking at him, her face extremely red. "Um… I should, uh, probably turn around…" she gasped.

Antonio laughed heartily and winked at her. "I'm not shy, babe. And now that I'm your boyfriend, you can look at me all you want. I don't mind," he flexed playfully, but his bulging muscles made Cynthia feel even more aroused.

Shaking his head and chuckling, Antonio dug around in his closet for his Black Death Mafia gear. Finding it, he quickly got dressed, much to Cynthia's dismay. "Will you still be here when I get back, *Bel Fiore*?" He asked, standing in front of her and looking at her with concern.

Swallowing hard, Cynthia nodded with a mischievous glint in her eyes. "I will. I told my parents I wouldn't be coming home tonight. Which is a good thing because I sure as hell do not want to hear what they'll be doing."

Laughing once more, Antonio hugged Cynthia tightly and placed a quick, but passionate kiss on her lips. "I'll see you soon, *Bel Fiore*."

She watched as he grabbed his Plague Doctor mask and made his way downstairs. *You better come home to me Antonio Moretti…* Sighing, she decided to finish the movie while she waited for his return. Priscilla was spending the night with Emily, so she was all alone in the house by herself.

When Antonio arrived at the warehouse, he found several of Sampson Hayes' men surrounded in what he liked to refer to as "The Execution Room." With his mask on, he was an extremely formidable sight; he stood at 6'4 and was 200 lbs of pure muscle. His broad shoulders made him look even larger as he crossed his arms and stared down at the men. "So," he chuckled evilly. "You think you can steal from a Moretti and get away with it? Wrong move. Edward, it's torture time."

The grisly scene before him made the darkness inside of him giddy with excitement. When the last man finally gave up the remaining pieces of information that Antonio was looking for, he silenced him forever with his revolver. The blood and gore covering the floor was a beautiful sight. "Clean this shit up, and make sure Hayes gets our message," he instructed before walking out of the warehouse and hopping into his car.

Back at home, Antonio walked inside quietly and noticed that Cynthia was not in the living room. Feeling relieved, he headed into one of the guest bathrooms to shower. He did not want her to see him like this. After a quick shower, he put his clothes in the washer and found a pair of shorts to wear. Wondering where Cynthia could be, he made his way to his bedroom and paused at the door. Cynthia was sound asleep on top of the duvet on his bed, and she was wearing nothing but one of his t-shirts, though he could see the pink lace of her underwear peeking out. The sight drove him crazy, and she had never looked so sexy. *No. Do not think about that right now...*

As carefully as he could, he climbed in next to her. Stirring, she opened her eyes and smiled sleepily up at him. "You're back," she murmured.

"Of course I am. I'm so sorry that it took longer than expected," Antonio said softly, covering both of them with the duvet.

"It's alright, I'm just glad you're safe. I hope it's ok that I'm wearing your shirt."

"It definitely looks better on you... though I think it would look even better on the floor."

"Antonio Julius Moretti! Get your mind out of the gutter," Cynthia said with mock sternness, slapping his shoulder playfully.

"My apologies, *il mio bellissimo fiore.*[73] Now come here, let's sleep," he said, pulling her close.

Laying her head on his chest, she looked up at him and kissed him softly. "Goodnight, boyfriend."

"*Dormi bene, amore.*"[74]

---

[73] my beautiful flower.
[74] Sleep well, love.

Growing Up

March 13, 1988

It was a peaceful Sunday morning, and Antonio was taking the opportunity to sleep in so he would feel well-rested for the day. With his eyes closed, he stretched and attempted to shift to a more comfortable position. However, he realized his bed felt extra heavy and the hushed giggling confirmed that there was indeed an extra person in his bed that had not been there previously. *What the fuck?*

Cautiously, he opened his eyes to find Priscilla's smiling brown eyes directly in front of him. She had an extremely mischievous grin on her face, and as a Moretti, that could not be a good sign. However, he realized that she was not the only one in his bed. Turning, he nearly smacked his head on Edward's face, and Edward belted out laughing and cuddled closer to him. Sitting on the end of the bed were Cynthia and Emily who simply could not contain their laughter anymore and erupted into a fit of giggles.

"Can someone please tell me what the fuck is going on and why you all are in my bed?" Antonio groaned, slightly irritated that his precious beauty sleep had been interrupted.

"HAPPY BIRTHDAY!!!" The four of them yelled, making Antonio jump.

"What?" He asked, puzzled.

"Did you seriously forget your birthday, *Fratello*?" Priscilla asked, giving him a weird look.

"Shit, is it really?"

"Yes!"

"Now get up, we have a fun outing planned," Cynthia commanded sweetly.

"And please wear something other than black," Emily rolled her eyes.

"Only because you said please, EmBug," Antonio winked.

"Don't you think I'm a little old for you to be calling me EmBug?"

"Never!"

"Dress nicely please," Priscilla added.

Cynthia came over and kissed him good morning before taking off with Priscilla and Emily to get ready for the day. Antonio swung his legs over the bed and rubbed his eyes. "Aw, you don't wanna snuggle with me anymore?" Edward whined.

"Quit your whining, you've gotten enough snuggles for one day," Antonio rolled his eyes.

"You're no fun," Edward laughed, rolling out of the bed and grabbing his backpack.

"So where are we going?" Antonio asked, yawning.

"Bowling!"

"And you had to wake me up at 8:00 a.m. on a Sunday to get me ready for bowling?"

"Yes. We're not just going bowling... we're going bowling in Las Vegas," Edward smirked.

"Fuck yes!" Antonio shouted, shoving his fist in the air. He ran into his bathroom and took a quick shower, running out with his black towel just barely staying on his hips.

Rummaging around in his dresser, he pulled out a pair of ripped black jeans and quickly put them on. He grabbed a black t-shirt and pulled it over his head and looked in the mirror. While this was his go-to look, he frowned at his reflection. *Dammit, I told EmBug I wouldn't wear black.* Edward sat on the bed and held back a laugh as he watched his best friend try to figure out what to wear.

Antonio tried on a button-up navy blue shirt, but it was too formal so he threw that on the floor. Next, he tried a long-sleeved maroon shirt, but that was much too heavy and warm; it, too, went on the floor. It was followed by a random Hawaiian shirt, a yellow t-shirt, a black long-sleeve shirt, and a red hoodie. Half an hour later, a loud roar could be heard throughout the whole wing of the mansion. The girls rushed into Antonio's bedroom to see him standing on a pile of shirts with a murderous glare on his face as Edward rolled around on his bed laughing so hard he was crying.

"What is going on in here?" Priscilla asked.

"Y-your... b-brother..." Edward gasped between fits of laughter. "Can't f-find a... s-shirt to wear!"

"*Mi stai prendendo in giro, Antonio?*"[75] Priscilla groaned, hands on her hips, glaring at him with a look that matched his.

"*Cosa ti ho detto di quel tipo di linguaggio?*"[76]

"You're a damn hypocrite. Just put on a damn shirt!"

Cynthia couldn't help but laugh at the frantic look on her boyfriend's face as he searched and searched for a suitable shirt to wear. "You guys aren't fucking helping! I need to look damn good. We are going to Vegas, damn it!"

Emily rolled her eyes and marched over to his closet where she pulled out a baby blue short-sleeve button-up shirt and a pair of black combat boots. "God, Antonio, I swear you act like a child sometimes. Put these on and let's go," she

---

[75] Are you fucking kidding me, Antonio?

[76] What did I tell you about that kind of language?

commanded, tossing the clothing to him.

Antonio mumbled something incoherent but put the shirt on anyway. Looking at his reflection in the mirror, he ran a hand through his hair and was satisfied. Turning to grab the boots, a repulsed look crossed his face. "I'm not wearing these. They don't go with the outfit!" Everyone groaned but watched with interest as he rummaged through his closet and pulled out a pair of brand-new *Maison Margiela* low-top, mirror-leather sneakers. "Now, I'm ready."

"You look good babe," Cynthia complimented him.

He turned to face the group and pulled on a pair of Ray Bans sunglasses and smirked. "Nah, I look like *the shit!*"

The nearly four-hour drive to Las Vegas was filled with laughter and loud singing to the rock songs that were blaring out of the brand new jet black 1988 *Land Rover Range Rover* that Antonio had purchased specifically for outings that involved the five of them. He was having a grand time speeding down I-15 belting out Bon Jovi, Poison, and whoever else came on the radio. Cynthia was sitting shotgun, where he felt she always belonged, and their hands were intertwined. It was a great feeling, and in this moment, he didn't have a care in the world.

Las Vegas was already bustling when they made it to the city. Edward was giving directions from the backseat where he was holding a map. Priscilla rolled her eyes and snatched it out of his hands, turning it the right way up and correcting the directions he had given. When they finally arrived, the five of them dashed inside the bowling alley as quickly as they could in search of the bathrooms.

Edward walked up to the counter where a girl that had to be their age was working. He laid on the charm and had her batting her eyelashes and flirting with him the entire time he was paying for their game. Antonio watched his friend and laughed, knowing that he would probably disappear for a while with that girl before they left. He watched as the girls grabbed their bowling shoes and began lacing them up, and as he watched Cynthia smile and laugh, it dawned on him that he truly did not miss sleeping around and flirting with any attractive girl that would look his way.

Once their lane had been paid for, they typed in their names and chose their bowling balls. They decided that whoever lost the game had to slide like a penguin down the lane as fast as they could. As Antonio went to pick up a ball, Priscilla's small hand gently pushed his arm down. He looked down at her smiling face, and for a second wondered where the sweet, innocent little girl had gone. *She's really just about all grown up... how did I miss it? My baby sister... so beautiful.*

"*Fratello*, we all pitched in to buy you an extra special birthday present for the occasion," Priscilla said sweetly, hiding something behind her back.

Before Antonio could ask what it was, she handed him his very own bowling ball. It was painted to look just like a potato. A goofy grin spread across his face as he looked at it, and it didn't take long for him to belt out laughing. The other four laughed too, but it was clear that Antonio appreciated the gift and truly loved it. "Did *Tant* and *Cerva* have something to do with this?"

Priscilla just winked as she placed the ball in his arms and ushered him to the lane. Since it was his birthday, he got to go first. The game was fun and it was head-to-head between Cynthia and Emily. During the last round, Emily pulled ahead and won the game. Unfortunately for Edward, he was the loser and he groaned as he took off his hoodie. Backing up a bit, he took off running and dove on the floor, sliding on his belly clear down the lane where he smacked the bowling pins. Rubbing his head, he carefully walked back to where the group was laying on the floor howling with laughter.

"Here, let me get some ice for your head. I can help you feel better," The girl from the counter cooed as she walked up and grabbed Edward's hand, pulling him to the back room.

"God, I swear my brother is worse than you ever were, Antonio," Emily groaned. "Please, for the love of everything holy, do *not* take him to a strip club next week on his birthday."

"Aw, why not Embug? It would be so fun—" Antonio started, but the glares from both Emily and Priscilla cut him off. The hurt look in Cynthia's eyes instantly made him regret the joke. "I'm just kidding, I swear! You guys know I do not go near those places anymore."

After about fifteen minutes, Edward came strolling out of the back with a huge grin on his face. His hair was tousled and his clothes a little rumpled. "Hey, Edward?" Antonio smirked at his best friend.

"Yeah?"

"Your fly's undone."

"Oh shit!" He exclaimed while quickly zipping up.

Laughing, they strolled out of the bowling alley and climbed into the *Land Rover*. The rest of the afternoon was spent eating lunch at one of the most highly rated restaurants in Vegas and strolling the strip. Antonio was given several gifts and was just grateful to be able to spend the day with the people he cared for most. It was nice to forget about who he was to the world and what he did for a living for a while, and just to enjoy being a "normal" 18-year-old boy hanging out with his friends. The girls did some shopping and played "tourist." They had brought several disposable cameras and by the time evening rolled around, they had filled them all up.

"You know, if you guys weren't so goody goody about school, we could stay at the *Stardust* tonight," Antonio grinned, knowing his charm could probably sway the group.

"You know, your charm would have swayed us, *Fratello*, but you're forgetting one thing," Priscilla smirked at him.

"What's that?"

"It's Spring Break. If you had stayed in school with the rest of us, you'd have known that!" The look of victory on his sister's face made him proud. *That's my girl. A true Moretti, through and through.* "Lucky for you, we packed you a bag."

"And, we already have a suite booked at the *Stardust*. You aren't the only resourceful one here, Moretti," Cynthia winked.

Giddy as a child, Antonio threw the car in drive and rushed down the busy street. Pulling up to the magnificent hotel and casino, he allowed the valet to take his car and they made their way into the building. Their suite had three separate bedrooms, a living room, and a kitchen. Edward groaned about how he was the only one with a room to himself, then realized he could bring a guest back with him if he wanted. They even had a private pool and hot tub, which they took advantage of. The week they spent there flew by, and Antonio was grateful for Everett who had called and assured him that he had everything under control.

July 8, 1988

The next few months sped by. Antonio kept his promise and did not take Edward to a strip club for his birthday. Instead, the five of them had gone to San Diego to go mini golfing and exploring. Today, however, Antonio had some big plans, for the following day was a big day. Tomorrow was Priscilla's 16th birthday, and while he had already bought her the most amazing present, he wanted to surprise her with a cake. However, it couldn't just be any cake, no, Antonio wanted to make it himself, with their mother's recipe. But as Antonio stood in the large kitchen looking at his mother's beautiful handwriting on the recipe card, he realized he knew nothing about baking and panic began setting in.

What am I going to do? What the fuck is a cake pan? What does sifting mean? I need to get some help. He was grateful that Priscilla was out of the house today; Emily had insisted on a spa day and a sleepover at the Sommerset household. *Edward is probably even more useless than I am when it comes to baking... I hope Cynthia is available. I could call Britt, but she'd just make fun of me and I am **not** in the mood for her teasing.*

After the trip to Las Vegas for his birthday, he and Cynthia hadn't seen each other a whole lot. She had explained that since it was her last quarter of her senior year, she desperately wanted to keep her 4.5 grade point average. It was expected of her, as the Valedictorian. While Antonio missed seeing her during the week, it made the weekends even sweeter when he had her full attention. However, as summer began, he found that work, both sides of it, began pulling him away as well. Moretti Industries scored three new contracts with other companies in June alone, and while it was barely the second week of July, he had already closed a deal on two more contracts and there were at least five more he would get to before the month was out. And then there was the mess with Sampson Hayes, who seemed to think that he was some sort of big shot that could keep messing with their supply lines.

Taking a deep breath, Antonio set down the recipe card and picked up the phone. It had been over two weeks since he'd seen Cynthia, and he didn't want to seem like he was smothering her. She had gone on vacation with her family for two weeks and he had called her every night. Not wanting to be seen as clingy, he had decided that he would wait for her to call from now on, at least for a while. They had gotten back the previous day but she had been exhausted from the flight, and after a quick call, had gone to bed. *Just call her, you need the help.*

Dialing the familiar number, Antonio waited as it rang. After the sixth ring, he was about to hang up when he heard an out of breath voice answer, "Hello?"

"Hello, *Bel Fiore*, is everything alright?"

He heard giggling on the other end and grinned; he'd missed hearing her laugh. "I'm so glad I got to the phone in time. I was in the shower when I heard it ring and I was hoping it was you. So yes, everything is alright. Please tell me you're inviting me over?"

"*Sí*, I am in desperate need of some help. It's an emergency!"

"Are you ok?!" The concern in her voice made him chuckle.

"Everything is alright, I'm probably just overthinking..."

"No, you're probably being a diva. I'll have my dad drop me off, see you soon babe!"

Half an hour later, the front door flew open and slammed closed as Cynthia rushed into the kitchen. The sight of her left Antonio speechless, and he could feel his face go red. In that moment, she had never looked so beautiful. She was wearing a pair of light-wash jean shorts and a floral tank top. Her face was free of makeup, and her cheeks had a rosy hue. She had let her hair air dry, and it fell in beautiful red waves. The natural her was his favorite, and when he finally shook himself from his stupor, he strode over to her in three long strides.

"So, what's the emergen—" Cynthia was cut off when his lips slammed against hers. She didn't mind though.

"I take it you missed me?" She giggled when he finally released her.

"You bet I did."

"Alright, Moretti, what's the emergency?"

"Um... I want to bake Priscilla a cake, but I don't know the first thing about baking."

"So, you're saying that just because I'm a woman I must know how to bake?" She raised an eyebrow at him, crossing her arms.

"What? N-no. I just… I figured that if I'm gonna attempt to do this thing and fail miserably at it, I would rather have my girlfriend with me so we can fail together but still have some fun. I swear I'm not a chauvinist!" Antonio was shocked that Cynthia would think that, and he was desperately trying to put her mind at ease.

When she winked at him, he hung his head and rubbed his face. It was still weird for him to be on the receiving end of some teasing. "I'm just messing with you, Antonio. I know you're not. Luckily for you, I love baking and happen to be very good at it."

"And you're just sharing this bit of information with me now? All this time you could have been making me delicious goodies?"

"Can't give up all my secrets at once, now can I?" She winked once more, walking to the counter to pick up the recipe card.

"It's… my mom's recipe. She always made everything homemade, and I figured it was time to pull out her recipe box. I haven't opened it since…" Antonio couldn't finish the sentence. So many emotions were fighting to come to the surface. He was angry. Angry that his parents hadn't been able to be there for his milestones, but even more angry that they couldn't be there for Priscilla's. Then there was the immense sadness he felt, and the huge hole in his heart that he didn't think could ever be filled.

Tears clouded his eyes, but he felt two arms wrap around his waist and pull him close. "I understand… We will follow her instructions and do our best to make it just like she did. She would be so proud of you, Antonio. They both would."

"Thank you…"

"Come on, let's preheat the oven and get started."

"Preheat…?"

"You have a lot to learn. Don't you know how to cook?"

"Yeah? But I've never preheated anything. You're supposed to do that?"

Cynthia laughed and rubbed her face with her hand. After explaining what everything on the recipe card meant that Antonio didn't know, the two got to work mixing. Cynthia put Antonio in charge of the dry ingredients while she combined the wet ones.

"This sifting shit is too time-consuming!" Antonio exclaimed, slamming the sifter down on the counter, showering Cynthia with flour in the process. "Uh… oops."

"Really Antonio?" She rolled her eyes and attempted to dust off. She grabbed the bowl from him and finished the sifting, and then combined the wet ingredients expertly into the bowl. Smirking, she grabbed the spatula and flung what was left onto Antonio's face.

Laughing, she finished mixing the batter and gently poured it into a cake pan. Once it was safely in the oven, she turned and gave instructions on how to start the icing. As Antonio poured the powdered sugar into the mixer, he accidentally bumped the switch and turned it on, sending a layer of white powder all over both of them. "Just let me do it," Cynthia giggled. When the icing was finished, Antonio stuck his finger in the bowl and scooped some out.

"This is delicious!"

"Antonio! Stop eating the icing! It's for the cake."

"But it's so good," he said, sticking his finger back in the bowl.

He's lucky the timer just went off or I'd give him a piece of my mind, Cynthia thought as she pulled the cake out of the oven and set it on a tray to cool. As she turned around, she bumped into Antonio who had come up behind her, and instantly saw his eyes go wide as she felt something stick in her hair. Nervously, he pulled a spoon covered in icing out of her hair and gave her an awkward grin.

"Oh, that's it!" She exclaimed, scooping up a bit of icing in her hand and smearing it all over his face.

He looked at her in shock before wiping some of the icing off his face and smearing it on her nose. For the next few minutes, they took turns flinging sugar and flour at each other before Cynthia put her hands up in surrender, the two of them laughing hysterically. She leaned forward against the counter across from him, eyes closed and laughing. Antonio stared at her, icing on her face and in her hair, her body covered head to toe in white powder, and he was in absolute awe of her and how perfect she was.

"God, I love you," he breathed. For a split second, he was shocked that he had spoken his thoughts out loud. *Oh, what the fuck. I love this woman and she sure as hell deserves to hear it.*

"What did you just say?" Cynthia whispered, eyes wide as she snapped her head up to look at him.

Antonio walked around to the other side of the counter and placed one hand on her waist and pulled her close. He put his other hand on her cheek and his warm brown eyes bored into her emerald green ones. "I said, god, I love you."

"Y-you love me?" She whispered once more, still in shock.

"With everything I have," he said softly. "I love you too, Antonio."

As soon as the words left her mouth, Antonio's mouth crashed onto hers once more. This kiss was different though. It wasn't hard and demanding. The passion was still there, but it was soft, gentle, and loving.

"Come on, let's go get cleaned up," he murmured against her lips, then picked her up and slung her over his shoulder.

Taking the stairs two at a time, Antonio rushed into his bathroom and set her down, then turned to turn the water on. "Um, Antonio?"

The nervousness in her eyes was always unsettling for Antonio. He never wanted her to feel nervous or uncomfortable with him. "Just stripping to my boxers babe, we don't need to be completely naked to have a shower. Unless you want to," he finished with a wink.

Feeling a little bit better, Cynthia watched her boyfriend as he took off his dirty clothing and tossed them into a laundry hamper. Nervously, she began tugging at her tank top, but her fingers were shaking. Antonio had seen her in a swimsuit before, but this would be more than he had seen of her and her stomach was flip-flopping. Her heart rate sped up and breathing was becoming harder. *What if he doesn't like what he sees? What if I end up not being enough to satisfy him? What if...* She was shaken from her thoughts when she felt his large, warm hands cover hers.

"Cynthia? You don't need to be nervous or afraid. You're beautiful. Please... let me help you?"

Nodding, she took a deep breath and forced herself to relax a bit as Antonio gently lifted the tank top over her head. He focused on her eyes but carefully unzipped her shorts and pushed them off of her hips to the ground. Without letting his eyes stray from her face, he turned his back to her and stepped into the shower, turning to offer his hand to her. She took it and stepped in beside him, grateful that he was respecting the fact that she was uncomfortable. However, as she studied his well-sculpted body, she couldn't help but want him to do the same.

"Antonio..."

"Yes, *Bel Fiore*?"

"You... you can look at me," she said, mustering up as much courage as she could, and blushed furiously when she saw his eyes darken as they met hers.

Antonio let his eyes wander her body from head to toe. She

was wearing a simple black bra and panty set, but she was the single most sexiest and beautiful thing he had ever seen. Her curves seemed to be calling to him, begging him to touch her, and she definitely filled out the bra she was wearing. Unable to keep his hands off of her, he gently grabbed her waist and pushed her against the shower wall.

"*Dio sai quanto sei bella, bel fiore?*"[77] He breathed against her neck as he kissed her soft skin. "*Sei così perfetto, amore mio.*"[78]

Cynthia sighed with pleasure and contentment. One thing that she had learned was that when Antonio was feeling extremely passionate, he reverted to Italian and the way he was speaking to her sent shivers through her whole body. *He called me "my love."*

Claiming her lips once more, he let his hands wander a little, reveling in the feeling of her skin. The hot water raining down on them did nothing to calm his feelings. "A-Antonio... stop..." Cynthia squeaked awkwardly.

Confused as to what had happened, Antonio dropped his hands and took a step back. "Did I do something wrong?" He asked nervously.

"N-no... It's just... I hope you don't think that just because you said you love me that I will have sex with you because I'm not. I'm... I'm saving myself for marriage," the last part she said timidly, unable to meet his eyes.

"What? Cynthia, *amore mio*,[79] look at me." He lifted her chin so he could see her face. "I'm not trying to have sex with you. I respect you way too much to do that, I know you're not ready. The fact that you want to wait doesn't bother me, and I promise you that I won't leave you because of it. It'll make our wedding night that much sweeter."

---

[77] God do you know how beautiful you are, beautiful flower?
[78] You are so perfect, my love.
[79] my love

"Our wedding night? You want to marry me?"

"Did you think I'm just dating you to pass the time?"

"I... I hoped you weren't."

"Cynthia, you're it for me. I love you. I know that we are not anywhere near being ready to take it to that next step yet, but I have no intention of ever letting you go."

His confession made her speechless, and instead of replying, she pulled his head down to kiss him once more. The rest of the shower was spent getting cleaned up, with an added soap fight. They finished decorating the cake and fell asleep content to be in each other's arms after being separated for a couple of weeks.

July 9, 1988

"Can I open them yet?"

"No, *uno dolce*, not yet," Antonio chuckled at his sister's impatience as he led her, blindfolded, onto the driveway.

As soon as she had gotten home that afternoon, they had done presents and had eaten an early dinner. Priscilla loved the cake; she said that it tasted just like their mother had made it. Cynthia and Antonio high-fived at their success, and the joy on Priscilla's face made his heart swell. However, he had saved the biggest and best present for last.

"Antonio Julius! I simply cannot take this suspense any longer!"

"Well, then it's a good thing it's time to take the blindfold off."

Priscilla ripped the blindfold from her face and stood in shock as she looked at the object in front of her. Several weeks prior, she had seen the most amazing car and had mentioned it in a passing comment to her brother. She couldn't believe that he had remembered, but she shook her head in amazement and knew she shouldn't have underestimated

Antonio. There, in front of her, was a red *Mustang* with white stripes. It was beautiful, and she blinked several times, making sure it was really there.

"Catch!" Antonio yelled.

Without looking, Priscilla stuck her hand in the air and caught the keys that had been thrown to her. "Is... is this really mine?"

"She sure is. Wanna take her for a spin?"

"Fuck yes!" She yelled, opening up the driver's side door and sliding in.

"What did I tell you about that kind of language?" Antonio scolded as he slid into the passenger seat.

Priscilla rolled her eyes but the look of pure joy and amazement on her face as she delicately touched the interior, the stereo, and the steering wheel was enough for the sternness to dissipate quickly. "It's my birthday, Antonio, and you've just given me the most amazing gift ever."

"I'm glad you love it. What are you waiting for? Start this baby up!"

Giggling, Priscilla started the engine and squealed as she roared to life. Putting the car in drive, she took off down the street, loving the way the car shifted. She felt as though she were on top of the world. Antonio smiled at her proudly, glad that he could fill the empty space in her heart, even if it was only for a little while.

We Are Family

December 3, 1988

Antonio stood in the back of his office, staring out the large window, watching as the snow came falling gently from the sky. It didn't snow often during the winter in Los Angeles, but whenever it did, he made sure to treasure the moment. The snowflakes were large and fluffy, and he took in their beauty. Closing his eyes, he recalled a memory of his mother from when he had been a small child. Carmella had bundled him up and ran out into the snow holding his hand all the way. He remembered how she had fallen backward into the snow and proceeded to make a snow angel. Looking down at her as she lay in the snow with her eyes closed, a smile on her lovely face, and her hair spread beautifully upon the white ground, he had been convinced that his mother was truly a real life angel.

A single tear rolled down his face as he squeezed his eyes tighter, trying to make the picture of his mother last longer in his mind. Though he never really talked about it, he missed his mother most of all. He'd been close with both of his parents, but he was unashamedly a mama's boy. Even now, over five years later, he craved her presence like he craved air to breathe. Taking a deep breath, the image of his mother faded into the back of his mind as he opened his eyes to watch the snow fall once more.

A soft knock came at his door, and without turning, he mumbled, "Come in."

"So, this is what your office looks like," Cynthia's sweet voice mused.

The sound of her voice was music to Antonio's ears, and it calmed his soul in a way that nothing else could. Turning to face her, he smiled as he watched her emerald green eyes study every bit of his office. "You haven't seen it?" He asked, slightly puzzled.

"Not really. You'd think after nearly a year of dating that I would have spent a copious amount of time in here. But all I've gotten were little glimpses," she chuckled.

"My apologies, *amore mio*. Have a look around," se said softly as he walked up and placed a loving kiss on her cheek.

Moving back to the window, he leaned against the wall where he had a perfect view of both the snow and the beautiful woman that had stolen his heart. He loved the way she inspected the bookshelves and the picture frames and the way her delicate fingers ran along the various weapons on display. She finally made her way beside him, where she intently studied a photo for the longest time.

"I've never seen this one before. You were so young! Who is that precious baby sleeping on you?" Cynthia asked softly.

Antonio grinned proudly as he positioned himself behind her and wrapped his arms around her slim waist as they gazed at the photo. "That, *amore mio*, is my *nipote*, Logan. It was taken the day after his first birthday. There were a lot of circumstances that prevented me from meeting him before then, and I just did not want to part with him for a moment. I never knew that you could love someone so much, but I found out the moment I met him. It's a strange thing for a nearly 14-year-old boy to discover."

Cynthia's heart nearly burst with love and pride at this side of her boyfriend. She had heard a lot about Logan and Antonio's chosen family, though she had never met any of them. It was obvious that he loved them dearly, and she hoped that he would introduce them someday. "I can see how much you love him in this picture. Although, it's a little misleading."

"What do you mean by that?"

"You look so innocent. And we all know you were far from innocent," Cynthia smirked.

"Oh yeah? I can certainly show you how impure I am," Antonio growled in her ear as he lifted her up and set her on his desk, spreading her legs and wrapping them around his waist as he leaned in and gazed into her eyes. "I've always wanted to do this," he smirked before claiming her lips passionately.

Cynthia was startled by his abruptness, and he had never been even remotely rough with her, but the feeling passed briefly as she eagerly kissed him back. She didn't even mind as Antonio laid her back against the desk, nearly laying on top of her as he deepened the kiss, his hands exploring her body. This would have normally made her freak out, but she trusted her boyfriend to respect her boundaries. Sure enough, within a minute or two, Antonio released his claim on her lips and rested his forehead against hers, desperately trying to control his breathing. *Dammit, you almost lost control, you can't do that*, he chastised himself.

"Sorry, *amore mio*," he breathed as he straightened himself and adjusted his pants before helping her off of his desk. Antonio turned from his girlfriend and stared back out the window, his cheeks flushing red as he tried to make the burning desire he felt for her go away.

"*Fottimi,*"[80] he groaned.

"Are you ok?" Cynthia asked, wrapping her arms around him from behind.

"*Sí.* I... I'm really sorry that I pushed it, *Bel Fiore*. It won't happen again," Antonio murmured, his voice tinged with sadness.

"Hey, look at me," she commanded softly. Sighing, Antonio did as she asked and tried to make the tears in his eyes go away. He never, ever, wanted her to feel like he was pushy. He'd sworn to respect her and her boundaries, and he was ashamed that he had let himself act like that with her. "I'm not mad at you, Antonio. If I was upset by your actions, I would have pushed you away, not pulled you closer."

"But I pushed your boundaries," he whispered.

"Antonio, you may have gone close but I knew you wouldn't cross the line. I trust you, and I love you," She said, putting her hands on either side of his face and kissing him softly.

"I love you too. Damn, I don't know what I ever did to manage to have such an angel in my life, but I am grateful."

Smiling, Cynthia hopped back up on the desk and watched as Antonio turned back to gaze outside. Smirking to herself, she decided she wanted to tease him before asking him a most pressing question. "You know, *amore mio*, I am quite looking forward to when you will truly take me on your desk."

Antonio whirled around, eyes wide and jaw dropped. He couldn't believe she had actually said it, and while he knew she was probably teasing, he was completely stunned by the absolute honesty in her eyes. "*Fanculo amore mio, stai cercando di farmi avere bisogno di fare un bagno di ghiaccio?*"[81]

---

[80] Fuck me

[81] Fuck my love, are you trying to make me need to take an ice bath?

"*Voglio solo che tu sappia che non sei l'unico ad avere tali pensieri. Li nascondo solo meglio,*"[82] she winked.

Antonio grinned at her. Her confession made him feel relieved, and he loved the way she sounded when she spoke Italian. Every little thing she did made him fall more and more in love with her, and he wanted nothing more than to make her his wife. He considered asking her when she pictured herself getting married, but he always got too nervous.

"So, I have a question," Cynthia started, breaking him from his thoughts. "Why does your family call you *Patatino*, and will I get to meet them?"

Antonio's laugh boomed out from his chest as a huge smile spread across his face. "Well, I know it's hard to believe seeing as how I have a body like this," He started, flexing and playfully smirking at her. "But when I was born I was quite round and was a bit of a chunk the first few years of my life. *Tant* gave me the nickname and it stuck. But *only* my family gets to call me that. And actually, I was going to ask you if you wanted to come with Priscilla and me to Oregon to celebrate New Year's with my family."

"You actually want me to come with you?" Cynthia gasped, eyes wide.

"Of course! Why wouldn't I? Besides, it's time you met them. And I think if I don't introduce you guys soon, Britt will stomp all the way down here and cut my balls off."

Cynthia giggled, especially seeing the serious look on Antonio's face. They spent the rest of the afternoon discussing their plans, and it was decided that Cynthia would be joining them on their trip to Oregon at the end of the month. In the meantime, Antonio managed to find some time

---

[82] I just want you to know that you aren't the only one that has such thoughts. I just hide them better.

alone with Mr. and Mrs. Springer. He had never felt so nervous in his life than the day he asked them for Cynthia's hand in marriage. After a long and stressful conversation, the couple hugged him and gave him their blessing. They knew that Antonio would treat their daughter right, and protect her with his life.

December 30, 1988

The alarm blared in Antonio's ear, and he audibly groaned as he rolled over and slammed his fist on the button. *"Figlio di puttana,"*[83] he muttered into his hands, eyes still closed. Rolling over, he reached his arm out to the sleeping form of his girlfriend and pulled her against his chest.

"Antonio, shouldn't we be getting up?" Cynthia asked sleepily.

"Five more minutes, *Bel Fiore, per favore?*"[84] He mumbled against her neck.

Stifling a laugh, Cynthia rolled over to face him and gingerly reached her arm over to set a timer for five more minutes. She nuzzled against him, his heavy breathing comforting her as she allowed herself to wake up fully. When the timer rang, Antonio bolted upright and smacked the button once more, rubbing his eyes in complaint.

"Come on, *amore mio*, it's time for you to wake up," Cynthia giggled as she untangled herself from his arms and slipped out of bed. She walked a few feet and stooped down to grab some clothes from her bag. When she stood up she turned back to see Antonio sitting on the bed, feet on the floor, staring at her with a goofy expression. "What?" She asked, quizzically.

---

[83] Son of a bitch
[84] please

Smirking, Antonio made his way over to her and put his arms around her waist, pulling her closer until she was firmly pressed against him. He gazed down at her, brushing some hair out of her eyes. "You don't know how attractive you look first thing in the morning, wearing my shirt, and hardly anything underneath. It's amazing that I've been able to control myself. It should be a crime for you to look this good before we are married."

Cynthia smirked back up at him, fighting back a blush at the thought of marrying him, though he had not indicated if he would even ask her. "Well you know, this family is notorious for crime," She winked and sashayed off to the bathroom for a shower.

Questa donna sarà la mia morte,[85] Antonio sighed as he grabbed his towel and trudged to one of the nearby guest showers. While he and Cynthia had showered together numerous times, neither of them had ever been completely naked and he wasn't sure that he could control himself this morning. However, as the hot water rained down on him, Antonio's thoughts quickly moved to the trip they would be taking today. He was extremely excited to see his family again; he missed them and it had been far too long since he had gotten to hug them. Besides that, he could hardly contain his excitement at the fact that he would finally be introducing Cynthia to them. He hadn't told Britt that she was coming; he knew that she wouldn't mind the surprise.

Walking back into his room, Antonio ran a hand through his hair, tousling it as he dug through his dresser. Deciding on something comfortable, he took out a pair of ripped black jeans, a soft black t-shirt, and a red flannel. Dropping his towel, he heard a squeal and whirled around to see Cynthia covering her eyes with both hands. Chuckling, he quickly put

---

[85] This woman is going to be the death of me

a pair of boxers on and walked over to his girlfriend.

"I've told you before, I don't mind if you see me naked," he chuckled.

"I... I know. I just wasn't expecting that. I'm sorry, I didn't even think about the fact that you'd be getting dressed in here. I didn't see anything!" She rambled.

"I wouldn't mind if you did," Antonio winked, kissing her forehead before turning back to his dresser so he could finish getting dressed.

"Look at you," Cynthia mused. "You look like a normal young man in those clothes."

Antonio belted out a laugh as he ran his fingers through his hair once more. "I figure I don't need my suits for this trip, though it feels weird to be wearing normal clothes."

"Come on you two! If you're not outside in five minutes, I'm leaving your asses here and going to see our family by myself!" Priscilla called out as she walked past his bedroom.

"Oh no you don't!" Antonio yelled as he grabbed his bag and dashed out after her.

The flight to Oregon went by quickly, though it felt like an eternity to Antonio. He had a whole load of Christmas presents with them, though the majority of them were for Logan. That little boy was his whole world and he missed him greatly. The plane had barely come to a stop when Antonio flew down the stairs and across the tarmac to where his Oregon car was parked. It took him a minute to realize that Priscilla and Cynthia were still carefully making their way off the plane.

If Antonio could have driven faster, he would have, but the traffic out of Portland made it a bit difficult. When they finally pulled up to Britt and Cade Warren's house, he took a deep breath and helped both his girlfriend and his sister out of the car.

"Do you think they'll like me?" Antonio heard Cynthia

whisper to Priscilla.

"Of course, they will! We love you, and so will they," Priscilla reassured her.

Grinning, Antonio led the two up the porch and placed himself in front of them. He pounded on the door a couple of times, then rang the doorbell for good measure, knowing it would make his dear *Cerva* grumble. Standing back, he crossed his arms and smirked as he waited for the door to open.

"Whoever is pounding on my door is going to get their asses handed to them, if they wake Logan up from his nap," a frustrated and beleaguered Britt called out, before opening the door to find Antonio, Priscilla, and a lovely red-headed young woman she had yet to meet.

"*Björn*, you're lucky I love you! Now move out the way so I can meet who I presume is Cynthia."

Antonio stuck out his lip in an exaggerated pout as Britt went to move past him. "Hello to you too, *Cerva*. Don't mind your favorite brother who traveled all this way to see you. I guess I'm just chopped liver now."

"As long as you don't wake Logan up, you'll be my favorite. That boy is wild, I swear," Britt sighed before giving Antonio a big hug.

"It's ok, *Sorella*," Priscilla laughed as Britt untangled herself from Antonio's arms. "Unlike this *perdente*,[86] I can wait my turn."

Laughing, Britt gave Priscilla a big hug as she whispered into her ear, "This is why you're actually my favorite!"

Priscilla kissed her cheek and gave her a knowing look. Cynthia stood behind them, watching with wonder at the reunion. She wasn't sure what she should be doing, so she just stood silently. Having been an only child, it was

---

[86] loser

118

interesting to her to see that the Moretti siblings had chosen to have another in their lives as a sibling.

Noticing Cynthia's quiet nature, Britt walked over to her and embraced her in a warm hug. "You must be Cynthia! It is amazing to finally meet you. I'm Britt by the way. Also, please tell me you are keeping *Patatino* in line! He can be a bit of a handful, especially with the sweets Mom makes."

"I'm so happy to finally meet you too! Antonio speaks so highly of you and I've wanted to meet you for so long. I do my best to keep him in check, but I definitely witnessed how out of hand he can get with the sweets!" Cynthia exclaimed.

"I... didn't tell her about that," Antonio coughed, looking like he wanted the ground to swallow him up whole as he recalled the events of the past week.

"Oh, good Lord, *Björn*, what the hell did you do," Britt asked as she drug her palm across her face; knowing all too well how "testy" Antonio could be.

Antonio sighed as he slumped his shoulders and did his best to avoid eye contact. "I just got here and already the love of my life has sold me out to my big sister," he grumbled. "Um, let's just say that someone decided they were going to steal my sweeties and now we will be getting a new mailman."

Walking over to Priscilla, Britt asked for a lift up onto her shoulders and to be carried over to Antonio. Once they were beside him, Britt reached out and smacked Antonio as hard as she could and shouted in her 'Mom voice,' "Antonio Julius Moretti! What the hell were you thinking?! Well, obviously you weren't. I mean seriously, killing a man over a box of damn sweets. I swear, Logan is more mature than you sometimes and the boy isn't even five yet. I oughta beat the shit out of you for not just calling mom and asking for a new box!"

Bowing his head in defeat, Antonio mumbled something

incoherent before straightening up and making his way into the house. "I'm gonna go find Cade... maybe he'll treat me better," he pouted.

Cynthia doubled over laughing, clutching her sides. When she had caught her breath, she followed Britt and Priscilla inside. However, she caught Britt's arm gently and pulled her aside. "I don't normally condone what he does... but he did explain why he did it. He said it wasn't really about the sweets, but the fact that they came from the only mother he'll ever have. That man loves you guys so much, and it's one of the things I admire most about him," she said softly.

Feeling slightly guilty for chastising Antonio so severely, Britt said, "I know he does. I just know that Mom would much rather have let that man have the box and make one with double of everything for him, instead of him having to kill the man... but as for me, yeah, I say he deserved it," with a wink Britt continued, "Just don't tell *Björn* that though. Gotta big sister rep to maintain after all."

Cynthia giggled once more. Though she had just met Britt, she instantly knew that they would become fast friends. "My lips are sealed. And I must say, that boy could use a slap or two every now and then. *Ha bisogno di un assaggio della sua stessa medicina.*"[87]

Hearing Cynthia speak in Italian caused Britt's eyes to light up. "Antonio has been teaching you? I am so excited!"

"He has definitely been helping me become more fluent, but my parents had me start learning when they were originally hired by Lorenzo and Carmella, God bless their souls..."

"I have been teaching Logan Italian and Swedish and it is the cutest thing hearing him blend all three languages together," Britt laughed with tears coming from her eyes.

---

[87] He needs a taste of his own medicine.

"Maybe Antonio could teach you some Swedish, too."

"I'm so looking forward to meeting Logan! I saw the cutest picture of him and Antonio in his office. I didn't even know Antonio knew Swedish! He will definitely have to teach me someday!" Cynthia exclaimed.

Recalling the memory of Antonio and Logan asleep on her couch, Britt couldn't help but smile; it wasn't often that Antonio had the chance to just be a regular teenager and that moment was forever etched in her heart.

Hearing childish laughter, Britt smiled warmly and said, "Well, Cynthia, it looks like you won't have to wait too long to meet Logan. I am 99.999 percent positive Antonio woke him up."

As the pair walked into the living room, they both couldn't help but smile at the sight of Antonio on the floor hugging the sweet little red-headed boy tightly to his chest and talking in a childish manner to him. Antonio was excitedly giving Logan the Christmas presents he had brought for him, and the smiles on both of their faces lit up the whole room.

After dinner that evening, Logan excitedly asked his *Zietta*[88] and Cynthia to play with the new toys he had gotten. The two young women could never deny the sweet boy anything and happily let him lead them by the hand to his bedroom. Antonio watched with a grin on his face as they walked out of sight. His heart felt so full in that moment.

Turning, Antonio followed the sound of Britt's voice and found her and Cade chatting in the sunroom. Knocking softly on the door frame, Antonio alerted them of his presence. "Hey... do you have a minute, *Cerva*?"

Turning her attention from her husband, Britt remarked, "For you, dear *Patatino*, I have all the minutes in the world. Why don't you join us?"

---

[88] Auntie

Nodding, Antonio plopped down on the couch next to Cade and squeezed his shoulders in a side hug. While he hadn't been too sure of the man when he first heard about Britt's pregnancy, he had grown to become friends with him and enjoyed his company greatly. Taking a deep breath and running his hand through his hair nervously, Antonio looked toward the entryway once more to make sure they were alone. "I'm... um..." he began nervously.

Seeing how nervous Antonio was, Cade excused himself briefly before returning with two cans of beer. "Here you go man," Cade said, "A little liquid courage never hurt anyone."

"Thanks, brother," Antonio said as he raised the can, opening it and taking a rather large drink. "Alright, let me try this again," he chuckled. "I'm desperately in love with Cynthia and I'm gonna ask her to marry me."

Britt squealed in delight, "Oh my God! This is so exciting. I was about to question your sanity for not already locking her in."

Cade chuckled as he kissed his wife's cheek, "She's a great girl, brother. Her eyes light up every time your name is even mentioned."

The nervousness began to fade from Antonio as he took another drink of his beer and smiled sheepishly at the couple. "I needed to get your approval first. It's important to me that you love her, too. But I will say, I was scared shitless when I went to talk to her parents! I kid you not, I felt like I was going to piss myself the entire time!"

Cade couldn't help but laugh as he finished a swig of beer, "Man, you're lucky though. At least y'all weren't 15 and knocked up. I wouldn't change it for the world though," he remarked, looking lustfully at the beautiful blonde beside him.

"No kidding. Her parents are kind-hearted, but I'd hate to think about what they'd do to me if we were in that situation.

And Lord knows I'd let them... But um, we haven't done... that..." Antonio mumbled, blushing, and feeling like a little kid that was afraid to say the word 'sex'.

Britt smiled lovingly at Antonio, "It takes a strong man to not act on fleshly desires. Cade's sister, Kayla, and her husband, Daniel, waited until they got married and they say it was the most amazing experience ever. Although, I think they were a little wary of sex since it literally took once and the proof is the world's most adorable red-headed little boy."

"I love that little red-headed boy more than life itself. I'm not really worried about anything, you've pounded the 'wrap it before you tap it' into my head for so long," Antonio rolled his eyes and grimaced. "Plus, when the time comes, I know how to take care of her. She wanted to wait, and I'd do absolutely anything for that woman. Respecting her boundaries was the least I could do to show her how serious I am about her."

Feigning tears, Britt playfully remarked, "My little baby is growin' up." Noticing Antonio rolled his eyes, Britt chuckled, "Fine, fine. I am proud of you though and I know *Zio* and *Zia* would be too."

Antonio swallowed the lump in his throat, washing it down with another swig of beer. "Thank you, *Cerva*. So, what do you think of my *Bel Fiore*?"

"She's going to be my new best friend, right after Priscilla," Britt blurted out.

Smiling proudly, Antonio dug around in his pocket and pulled something out. He gazed at the object for a moment before handing a large, shiny, diamond ring in an emerald cut, to the sister of his heart. "Well, what do you think? Is it too small? Should I get a bigger one? Do you think she'll like it?" He rambled nervously.

Looking at the ring, Britt couldn't help but tear up, "It looks... it looks so much like your mom's." Taking a minute to regain her composure, Britt put her game face back on and retorted, "Dear Lord, how much does this thing weigh? I definitely think it's large enough. I will tell you though, that a girl like Cynthia won't care about size, shape, cost, whatever. What she'll care about is that it's from you, and most importantly, from your heart."

"I... I had it designed after Mom's. I did consider giving it to her, but then I also thought it might be a little weird since... well... since I took the ring off of my mother's dead hand myself," He sighed, shaking the image from his mind. That had been one of the hardest things he had ever done. "I've decided that I'm going to give Mom's ring to Priscilla. I think it would mean a lot to her to have it."

Handing the ring back to Antonio, Britt stated, "I think that's an amazing idea to pass it on to Priscilla. I don't think Cynthia would have minded the ring, but by the expression your face just held, it would have been too hard for you. So, why not start a new life with new memories?"

Grateful that Britt understood and that he didn't have to explain it further, he quickly slipped the ring back into his pocket. "As much as I want to march right up to her and ask her this very second, I'm going to wait until March. There is this beautiful garden that starts blooming in downtown L.A. in March that I think would be a romantic place to take her. Is that too cheesy?"

Shaking her head in laughter, Britt replied, "Honestly, I would expect nothing less from you, *Björn*. I mean, you have always had a flair for the extravagant."

"Shit! I only have a couple months to find the perfect outfit to wear too! Fuck, I'm gonna need to start shopping when I get home."

Shaking her head once more, Britt turned to Cade and exclaimed, "See what I'm talking about? People say women are bad... nope! No woman has anything on Antonio Julius

Moretti and his shopping addiction!"

That night, Antonio held Cynthia in his arms as she slept, and he knew without a shadow of a doubt that she was the one for him. The next few days flew by, and Cynthia was lovingly welcomed by Dianne and Marcus. As they rang in a second New Year together, Antonio leaned in and promised her that it would be the greatest year of their lives. After a blissful few days in Oregon, the trio arrived home, and Antonio immediately set to work preparing everything for March.

Welcome to the Jungle

March 18, 1989

Antonio woke up to the sunlight shining in through his bedroom window, warming his face. Whenever the sun hit his face like this, he felt as though his parents were smiling down upon him. Closing his eyes, he savored the moment before the realization of what today was, dawned on him. Sitting bolt upright in bed, he double-checked the calendar near his nightstand to confirm that it was indeed Saturday, March 18th.

Shit! I need to hurry up and get ready! Antonio thought in a panic as he noticed that it was already 9:00 A.M. He was supposed to pick Cynthia up at noon for their special date, and he only had three hours to get ready. *I should have set an earlier alarm! Three hours is not nearly enough time to get ready for this special day!* Quickly, he shed his clothes as he strode into his bathroom and hopped in the shower. Taking a deep breath, he tried to quell the nerves that were already starting to turn his stomach inside out. Stepping out of the shower, he gazed at his reflection in the mirror and decided he should shave. He'd let his facial hair grow out for nearly three weeks to help him look older for the various meetings he'd had.

Once he was clean-shaven, Antonio made his way back

into his bedroom to get dressed. True to his word, the day they got back to Los Angeles after their trip to Oregon, he had immediately begun shopping for the perfect outfit to wear for the occasion. After searching for two weeks, he finally found the perfect suit and gotten it tailored to fit him exquisitely. Grinning, Antonio reached into his closet and pulled the suit out. Getting dressed quickly, he took a look at his reflection before picking up his tie.

Sighing, he turned to yell for his sister. "*Uno dolce!* I need your help!"

"What do you need, *Fratello*?" Priscilla asked as she walked in a few moments later, but paused and looked her brother up and down. She'd only gotten glimpses of the suit as he'd kept it hidden, but he looked so handsome in it. In fact, he looked just like their father. The gray suit had a minute houndstooth pattern with a blush-colored shirt and a navy tie adorned with pink roses in bloom. It was far from his usual style of various gray, black, and navy suits, but he looked amazing. It made him look normal, too. "You look so handsome, *Fratello*... just like *Padre*."

"Thank you, Priscilla. Are you alright?" He asked, furrowing his brows in concern as a couple of tears escaped her beautiful brown eyes. Striding over, he gently brushed the tears away and pulled her in for a hug. "What's wrong, *uno dolce*?"

"I just miss them so much, Antonio. Sometimes, I can barely remember what they look and sound like. But you just look so much like our dad right now... it's just a little overwhelming."

"I miss them too...and I often have the same troubles. You look a lot like our *mamma*, and I often shed a few tears myself. Now, would you mind helping me with my tie?"

Laughing, Priscilla grabbed the tie out of his hands and expertly tied it around his neck. It amazed her that at 19 years old, her brother still could not properly fashion a tie by himself. His birthday the previous week had been comical, with him spending two hours trying to do it by himself before they went to dinner. It ended with him screaming in rage and her coming to the rescue once more. "There you go. Man, Cynthia is going to swoon seeing you in this suit. How are you feeling?"

"I hope she likes it, it feels a little weird wearing it, but it's kinda nice to wear something different. Honestly, I am so nervous. What if she says no?"

"Antonio Julius Moretti, that woman loves you with her whole heart. She is *not* going to say no. Plus, no one can resist the Moretti charm! Now, grow a pair and calm the fuck down and go get yourself a *fiance*!" Priscilla exclaimed, flashing her most charming grin at him.

Normally he would correct his sister on her use of language, just to irritate her, but today, her reprimand was fitting. He was Antonio Julius Moretti, and he needed to stop being a pussy. Walking back over to his dresser, he grabbed his cologne and sprayed a pleasant amount on himself before opening the top drawer. Reaching inside, he took out the ring he'd had custom made for his beloved and slipped the small box into the inside pocket of his jacket. Taking out another object, he turned toward his sister once more.

"*Sorella*, come here."

Raising an eyebrow, Priscilla inched closer and crossed her arms. "Yes?" She asked quizzically.

"I've been holding onto this, but I think it's about time that I give it to you. *Mamma* and *Padre* would want you to have it, and it belongs to you. Here, open your hand."

Doing as she was told, she gasped when Antonio gently placed a ring on the palm of her outstretched hand. "It's *Mamma's*," she whispered as tears welled up in her eyes. "Thank you."

"I love you, Priscilla," Antonio murmured into her curly black hair as he embraced her.

"I love you too, Antonio. Ugh, you've gotta stop making me cry. Now go on, get out of here! Cynthia will be waiting for you."

With a chuckle and a shake of his head, Antonio released his hold on his sister and grabbed his shoes. He put them on quickly then headed down the stairs and out the front door. Before climbing into his *Impala*, Antonio walked over to the greenhouse and cut a bouquet of the most beautiful dark pink roses that he had been growing. They went well with the tie he was wearing, and he knew that Cynthia would love them. Wrapping them in a wet paper towel and some burlap tied with twine, he climbed in his car and took off toward the Springer's house.

He got there quickly, as he had been in a hurry, and before he could knock on the door, it swung open. Mr. and Mrs. Springer greeted him with smiling faces and a warm hug; they knew what was going to happen today, and they were filled with excitement that they could hardly repress. "Cynthia! Antonio is here!" Alexandra Springer called out once she and her husband had released the young man from their embrace.

"I'm coming!" She replied as she started descending the stairs. The look on Antonio's face when he saw her made her stomach burst into butterflies, and she felt her face heat up as she took him in as well. He had told her to get really dressed up for a spring date, and so she had chosen a floor-length, ballet slipper pink strapless a-line gown. It had an organza overlay with hand-embroidered roses blooming throughout, giving her an ethereal glow. She'd pinned her beautiful cayenne hair into an elegant updo, which showed off her rosy, bare shoulders.

Antonio's eyes felt like they would bulge clear out of his

head as he took in the sight of the woman he loved. His heart began beating erratically just looking at her, and in that moment, all he wanted was to take her in his arms and ask her to marry him right then and there. Swallowing hard, he took a deep breath as Cynthia walked up to him. Taking her hand in his, he leaned down and kissed it gently, right where he was going to be placing his ring. "I can barely manage to form a coherent thought right now, but you look truly divine, *amore mio*," he breathed into her ear as she put her arms around his neck and hugged him.

"You are looking very sharp yourself, Antonio. You have yet to tell me where we are going, and I am quite curious given the fact that we are even more dressed up than we were for our first anniversary," she responded, looping her arm with his as they walked outside to his waiting car.

"It's a surprise, *Bel Fiore*, but I am sure that you will love it. Here, these are for you," He said with a sheepish grin, handing her the bouquet of roses.

She brought them to her nose and inhaled deeply. "I love them, thank you."

"And I love you," Antonio smirked as he sat down in the driver's seat.

"I love you, too," Cynthia smiled back.

They hadn't gotten to see each other that week, save for Antonio's birthday, as Cynthia had been swamped with homework. This was her second semester of college, and she had decided to take an extra class. He loved hearing her talk about what her college experience was like, and it made him smile when she got excited about one of her classes. While he would have liked to attend college as well, it just wasn't the right time for him. Moretti Industries was booming and it took all of his time during the week. On top of that, his weeknights and weekends tended to be consumed with Black Death Mafia business. If it weren't for Priscilla and Cynthia making him rest and take the time to be a normal human being, he wouldn't do anything else.

The pair chatted as Antonio drove through downtown L.A., weaving in and out of traffic as he made his way to their destination. However, the closer they got, the more nervous Antonio was becoming, and he was doing his best not to start sweating. Finally, he pulled up to the beautiful park and helped Cynthia out of his car. It was sunny and warm, with a light breeze carrying the wonderful scent of the many flowers blooming all around. "Wow, look at all the flowers! It's so beautiful, but what are we doing here?"

"This is where we are having our date. I hope that's alright with you," Antonio blushed.

"I love it! It's such a beautiful day, though I don't think I've dressed very appropriately for a park date."

"Trust me, you are dressed perfectly. Come on, *amore mio*," he grinned, taking her hand in his. "There's something I want to show you."

With a soft giggle, Cynthia let Antonio lead her down the well-worn path in the park. They soon came to a small creek with a gorgeous bridge spanning it. He led her to the middle of it before stopping. Noticing that there was a breathtaking view of the whole park, Cynthia placed her hands on the rail and leaned forward, taking it all in. Antonio's heart was pounding in his ears, and he was desperately trying to control his breathing. However, Cynthia's back turned to him provided the perfect opportunity for him to surprise her. He looked over to where he knew that Edward was hidden. His best friend had taken an interest in photography during the first semester of college when he had chosen to take it as an elective, and he was very skilled. When Antonio told Edward he was going to propose, he immediately offered to capture the moment on film.

Taking a deep breath, Antonio reached into his jacket

pocket and grabbed the ring box before kneeling behind the woman he loved more than anything in the world. "Antonio, this view is breathtaking. Thank you for bringing me here!"

"It is indeed, but not as breathtaking as the woman I'm looking at right now," he replied, doing his best to control his nerves. This was it; she was going to turn around at any moment.

"Why aren't you admiring the view, silly? It's such a beau—" Cynthia started as she turned around. She gasped as her eyes met Antonio's brown orbs that seemed to be glowing as he gazed at her with love and desire. As her gaze lowered to the large diamond ring in his hand, it dawned on her what was happening and she struggled to keep the tears at bay as she started to shake with emotion.

"Cynthia Elizabeth, *mio Bel Fiore*, how do I even begin to describe how much you mean to me? The very first day we met, it became apparent that you had the power to break my leg, even though you didn't mean to. How was I supposed to know that a mere eight years later, you'd also have the power to break my heart should you ever choose to release it from your grasp? Love has always been something that I wanted, especially after watching the passionate love my parents shared, even if only for a short time... but it was never something I had any interest in looking for. That was until you waltzed back into my life that Christmas Eve. I had never seen a more beautiful woman in all of my life. The way you looked in that sparkly, dark green dress and the way it made your eyes shine nearly brought me to my knees. Over the past year, I've fallen so deeply in love with you, that the thought of not having you by my side and as the keeper of my heart terrifies me. Your beauty, grace, kindness, and compassion have no rival, and you leave me in awe every single day. You are my soulmate and the love of my life. Everything about you is perfect, except for one tiny thing:

you don't have my last name. Cynthia Elizabeth Springer, would you make me the happiest man alive by becoming Cynthia Moretti? Will you marry me?"

Tears began to flow freely from her eyes as Cynthia looked down at the man who could take her very breath away with his smile, and the way he had bared his heart to her was nearly more than she could handle. She never thought she could love someone so deeply, but she fell even harder as Antonio took her left hand in his and rubbed her ring finger with his thumb. "I love you more than words can say, Antonio. And it would be an absolute honor to bear your name. Of course, I'll marry you!"

With a smile that made her nearly melt, Antonio took the ring out of the box and gently slipped it onto her finger; it was a perfect fit. Before she could get a good look at her ring, Antonio stood up and put his arms around her, lifting her up as he claimed her lips passionately. They stood there on the bridge, kissing for several moments before loud whistling and clapping came from a few feet away. Antonio laughed heartily as Edward walked up and gave him a congratulatory slap on the back, camera hanging from his neck. Cynthia looked at the two men quizzically, unsure of what had just occurred.

Edward grinned and held up his camera. "I captured the proposal on film so you'll have pictures," he shrugged. "Welcome to the family, Cynthia!"

"Oh! Thank you, Edward!" She laughed as he hugged her. Antonio pulled her close and kissed her once more as soon as Edward let go of her.

"Aaaannnnndddd this is where I take my leave," Edward laughed. Winking at the couple, he turned and walked away up the trail toward the parking lot, whistling happily.

"So, now what?" Cynthia asked breathlessly once Antonio stepped away. His kisses always made her feel a little lightheaded.

"And now, you and I are going to have a picnic lunch over there," He grinned, pointing to where Edward had laid out a blanket and a picnic basket.

"Oh my gosh! Antonio!" Cynthia exclaimed, running over to the blanket and plopping down. "I've got the most romantic man ever."

"Damn straight," he preened.

Antonio sat down and opened the basket and began pulling things out. He'd packed mostly finger foods: cucumber sandwiches, some fruit, and a charcuterie board. Smirking, he pulled out two wine glasses and a bottle of champagne. He filled them both about halfway and handed one to his fiance who seemed to have gotten even more beautiful now that they were officially engaged.

"My my my, spoiling me with expensive champagne, are we?" Cynthia giggled, clinking her glass with his and sipping it. For the first couple of months that they had been together, the underage drinking thing had bothered her, but he rarely ever drank, and when he did, it was mostly only one drink at a time. Realizing that he wasn't the kind to just get drunk all the time, she had shaken her feelings away and occasionally enjoyed a glass of wine when they spent time together in the evenings at his house.

"Only the best for my *fiance*."

"I love the way that sounds: *fiance*. Gives me butterflies," she said playfully, batting her eyes.

"I do, too. But you know what I'm gonna love even more? When I get to call you my *wife*."

Blushing, Cynthia picked up some food and began eating. People were starting to make their way through the park and they kept staring. Antonio didn't seem to mind, but she was getting anxious to be out of the public eye and alone with her man once more. Sensing her growing discomfort, Antonio ate quickly, packing up the remainder of their meal to take home with them. Cynthia breathed a sigh of relief when they got to the car and drove toward the Moretti Mansion.

"So... I tend to be very good with my words, but when it comes to you, it's hard for me to focus. But, I found the perfect song," Antonio explained, smiling as he put a cassette in.

As soon as the song came on, Cynthia's heart swelled with happiness and love for the man sitting beside her. She recognized it instantly: *Soul Song*, by Joe Stampley. It meant even more to her that he had chosen a country song since he was not fond of the genre at all. "You're my soul song," he said softly.

Arriving at the mansion, they walked inside where Priscilla greeted her future sister-in-law with a big hug. Antonio excused himself; he needed to get some things in order in his office real quick, but he told Cynthia she could change into some of his clothes while she waited so she would be comfortable. She watched him walk away with pure happiness on her face. "I'm so excited for you guys!" Priscilla exclaimed. "You gonna torture him a little bit?"

"I'm considering it. I do love to see how riled up he gets when I wear his t-shirts," Cynthia laughed. "Well, as much as I love this dress, I do want something more comfortable. See you in a bit?"

"I'm actually staying with Emily tonight, but I'll see you tomorrow," Priscilla winked.

The girls hugged once more, and then Cynthia hurried upstairs to Antonio's bedroom. She felt extremely giddy at the prospect of this becoming her bedroom, too. Opening his shirt drawer, she dug around in it until she found an old, faded black t-shirt that had definitely seen better days. Reaching behind her, she unzipped her dress and let it fall to the ground. She'd gone braless but had packed one in her purse, which she pulled out and quickly put on, followed by the shirt. She breathed in Antonio's scent as she sat on the bed and admired her ring once more. The diamond was enormous, cut exquisitely into an emerald cut and inset with many small diamonds in the band. She had never been one for excessive, expensive jewelry, but she loved the ring because she knew Antonio had designed it himself.

A few moments later, the door opened and closed gently as Antonio walked in, loosening the tie from around his neck. He discarded it on the floor, followed by his jacket and belt as he untucked his shirt. "Sorry that took so long, *amore mio*. But now you have my sole attention for the rest of the night." Antonio ran a hand through his hair, mussing it up. The action made him look even more attractive, and Cynthia found herself biting her lip as she stared at him. "Do you know you look extremely seductive when you bite your lip like that?"

"Oh? Do I?" She asked, smirking as she stood up and walked over to where he was standing. It was then that he realized she was wearing one of his old shirts, and it was a little short for her, and the sight of her lacy pink underwear peeking out nearly made him lose his cool. Blushing at the way he sucked in a breath as she put her hands on his chest, Cynthia slowly unbuttoned his shirt and pushed it off of his shoulders before running her hands on his bare chest. It was something she had done numerous times before, but it all felt different this time. As her hands moved lower, she got a burst of bravery and confidence and unzipped his pants, pushing them to the floor.

In response, Antonio pulled Cynthia up tight against him and claimed her lips roughly. She hopped up and wrapped her legs around his waist, deepening the kiss. Letting out a groan, Antonio moved towards the bed and laid her down gently. Straightening up, he gazed down at his beloved, and the desire for her rose up nearly uncontrollably. Reaching down, he grabbed the collar of the shirt and ripped it right down the middle, baring her chest to him, save for the bra she was wearing.

Cynthia reached up and pulled her beloved down on top of her and kissed him once more, letting out soft sounds as Antonio explored with his warm hands. *"Fanculo! Prendimi adesso, amore mio,"*[89] she groaned against his lips.

Antonio let out what sounded like a growl, kissing her passionately once more before rolling off of her and sitting on the edge of the bed with his head in his hands as he tried to catch his breath. *"Fanculo!"*[90] He yelled, standing up abruptly and slamming his fist into the wall.

"What's wrong?" Cynthia asked, doing her best not to cry as she sat up and brought her knees to her chest. "Did I do something wrong? Do you... not want me?"

"What? *Perché si potrebbe pensare che?"*[91] Antonio asked as he turned around and stared at the woman he loved with wide eyes. It broke his heart seeing the look on her face and the tears in her eyes. Moving quicker than any normal human being should, Antonio scooped Cynthia up and sat her down on his lap, pressing her hard against him as he wiped the tears from her eyes with one hand. "Cynthia... you feel that? I want you more than anything and it took my every last ounce of self-control to stop."

"But why did you stop?" She whispered.

"Because I love you. Even though you basically gave your consent, I'm going to respect your wishes about wanting to wait until we're married. We are both feeling a lot of emotions about being engaged, and I'm sure you would have

---

[89] Fuck it! Take me now, my love
[90] Fuck
[91] Why would you think that?

been upset in the morning if we had slept together. It's all I can do not to change my mind and let the heat of the moment take over. I love you, Cynthia, and I want to do this right."

"I love you, too," Cynthia sobbed, wrapping her arms around his neck. The fact that he had stopped even after she told him to do it made her love him even more than she already did. "I'm sorry that I put you in that situation."

"Don't be sorry, *amore mio*. Now, why don't you grab a new shirt while I go take a long, cold shower," he chuckled as he stood up, clearly very uncomfortable.

"A cold—oh," she giggled. Right before he disappeared into the bathroom, she added, "You tearing off my shirt like that...was really hot."

Turning around with a boisterous laugh, Antonio winked and flashed her his most charming grin. "Don't you worry, *Bel Fiore*, that won't be the last time."

Fifteen minutes later, Antonio strutted out of the bathroom with his towel hanging dangerously low on his hips. Looking up from the book she was reading, Cynthia blushed and made a little squealing sound as he smirked at her and dropped his towel. "Antonio!" She yelled, squeezing her eyes shut tightly. The urge to roll her eyes was overwhelming as he laughed loudly.

He couldn't help it; he loved to tease her. Quickly putting some clothes on, he opted to wear a t-shirt instead of remaining bare-chested since his shower had nearly chilled him to the bone. Walking over to the bed, he tapped her shoulder gently until she opened her eyes. She smiled when she saw that he was fully clothed, but frowned as she took his hand. "Why is your hand so cold?"

"I told you I was taking a cold shower."

"I didn't think you were actually serious."

"Very serious. I needed it. Anyway, I have one more surprise for you. Come with me," he grinned, leading her out of the room and down the hall.

Raising an eyebrow, Cynthia followed him down the dark hallway to the door at the very end of the hall. She had only ever set foot in the room that lay beyond the door less than a handful of times, and she wondered why Antonio was bringing her here. Sensing her discomfort, Antonio squeezed her hand and smiled at her before putting his hand on the knob and pushing the door open. He flipped the light switch on and waited for her to take in the view of the room. The sight in front of her made her gasp, and she stood in the doorway unsure of what to make of it.

The once full and untouched bedroom of Lorenzo and Carmella Moretti was now almost completely empty. All that remained was the large armoire and the king-sized four poster bed. The bed was stripped down to the bare mattress, and even the pictures and art pieces that had once hung on the walls were gone. "Antonio?" Cynthia whispered.

Taking her by the hand once more, Antonio led her to the bed and lifted her onto it. Jumping up beside her, he took a deep breath as he gazed around the room. "As you are well aware, this used to be my parents' room. I have so many happy memories in here... and on the worst day of my life, this was where I retreated to. Priscilla and I left it as our parents had left it all these years, only coming in to keep the room from getting dusty and to take in the scent of our parents from their clothes and try to feel close to them once more."

He paused for a moment as the memory of his mother telling him that one day this room would be his, flooded his mind, and it nearly took his breath away being able to see the smiling image of his mother so clearly for the first time in a long time. "When I was young, my mother often told me that someday, this bedroom would be mine. I was never ready to take it over, the thought brought me a lot of pain, and so I just left it as it was."

Turning to look at his *fiance*, he smiled down at her and put an arm around her, pulling her close. "I'm ready now. With us now officially engaged to be married, I wanted to make this *our* bedroom. Instead of you moving into mine, I figured we could move in here together. It's also the biggest bedroom in the place, and better suited for two people. What do you think?"

"I think it's a very good idea, Antonio. Are you sure you're alright with it?"

"I am. Priscilla and I went through the bedroom together last weekend. It was really hard, but also really therapeutic. We cried together, laughed together, and shared a lot of memories as we packed their things. This room was once filled with the purest, most amazing love, and it's time for it to be filled with love once more. However, it's been several years since this room was last decorated, and it requires some updating. As an engagement gift to you, I am giving you complete freedom to decorate this room as you see fit. Any color, theme, decoration, etc., you may choose. I want this space to reflect you because you bring out the best in me. And cost is no issue, so you don't need to worry about a budget, either. How does that sound?"

"Are you serious? You want me to design our bedroom?" Cynthia gasped, eyes wide, a smile spreading from ear to ear.

"Absolutely! And no, I do not care if you decorate the entire room in peach or pink," he winked.

"This is the most wonderful gift. Thank you, Antonio."

"You don't need to thank me, *Bel Fiore*. I love you. I'd give you all the stars in the sky if I could."

"I love you, too, you charmer," she giggled. "Now come on, *fiance*, let's go get snuggled up in your bed so we can start discussing dates."

Chuckling, Antonio stood up and followed Cynthia to the

door. Pausing in the doorway once more, he took one last look at his parents' former bedroom before turning off the light and shutting the door behind him.

Head Games

May 6, 1989

Cynthia finished pinning up her hair into an elegant chignon and gave herself a once over in the mirror before applying a final coat of mascara. She smoothed out her tea-length peach gown and then slid on her favorite pair of Mary Jane's. It was a simple dress, made of tulle with a delicate a-line cut and spaghetti straps, but it was perfect for date night. Her semester had ended a couple of days prior, and Antonio had insisted they celebrate.

He had made a reservation for them at *Pacific Dining Car*, and after dinner, they were going to go dancing. She'd been looking forward to the evening all week, especially since Antonio had gotten fairly busy in the weeks following their engagement. However, he always managed to make time for her. A sharp whistle sounded from behind her and she turned around quickly to see Antonio eyeing her appreciatively.

"Tell me, *amore mio*, how do you get more and more beautiful each time I see you?" He smirked.

Chuckling softly, Cynthia made her way over to her fiance and wrapped her arms around his neck, meeting his warm brown eyes with her emerald ones. "You flatter me. I love you," she murmured before kissing him softly. "Now come on, we have a reservation to make."

The couple descended the stairs hand in hand, and once they reached the bottom, Cynthia headed to the living room where she had left her purse. Antonio leaned against the banister as he waited for her, looking forward to their evening. His thoughts were interrupted when the front door burst open, and Everett and Edward ran inside. The first things that Antonio noticed were the look of panic on his best friend's face, and the bloody wrap around Everett's arm.

"What the fuck happened?" Antonio exclaimed.

"We were at the hangar, unloading some cargo when someone started firing. I was only grazed, but we've lost a couple of men. We're under a standoff, and we came to get you," Everett exclaimed, panting.

"It's Hayes' men," Edward added, narrowing his eyes.

"Oh, fuck no!" Priscilla yelled, startling the three men as they hadn't noticed her come into the room.

"What's going on?" Cynthia asked, stopping suddenly in the entryway to take in the scene. "Is everything alright?"

Sighing, Antonio turned to the woman he loved as he loosened his tie to take it off of his neck. "I'm sorry, *Bel Fiore*, I've got to go. There's a situation that I have to take care of. I'll make it up to you, I promise."

"Are you fucking kidding me?" Cynthia exploded as she followed Antonio upstairs. He was shedding clothes as he made his way to his bedroom to change into his gear. "Are you seriously going to just leave?"

"Yes. My men are being shot and killed as we speak. I can't just leave them."

"But you'll leave me," she spat back, crossing her arms and glaring at him.

"I don't know what you want me to say, Cynthia."

"I want you to stay! You promised me."

"I have an obligation to my men. I'm their leader. I have to take care of this shit."

"For once, why can't you just leave it to someone else? Why does it always have to be you?"

"You knew who I was when you started dating me, and when you said yes to marrying me. This is who I am, Cynthia. If you can't accept every side of me, then what the fuck are we doing?" Antonio yelled, doing his best not to let his voice break. It was all he could do not to break down and cry as he saw tears start to stream down her face.

"I don't know! I just don't know..." she yelled back, sobbing. "I thought you might put me first."

"Right now, I can't." he replied coolly, letting ice fill his voice. It was the only thing he could think to do at that moment, lest he cave. "Maybe you should think about what you want. I'm the leader of the Black Death Mafia. I protect my men and kill anyone who threatens them. And right now, they need me. I don't have time to squabble with a silly woman who can't understand the weight of responsibility I carry." With that, he stalked down the stairs and slammed the front door behind him.

Following slowly, Cynthia found Everett, Edward, and Priscilla staring at each other with eyes wide and mouths agape. "Erm, we should go..." Edward coughed, heading out the door with his dad following closely.

Turning to the sister of her heart, Priscilla wrapped Cynthia in her arms and hugged her tightly. "I know you're angry... But please... Please don't leave him. You're his very reason for living." Kissing her cheek softly, Priscilla turned and ran out to join her brother.

When the door closed for the last time, Cynthia crumpled to the floor and sobbed her heart out. The realization that she sent the love of her life out into a shootout following a fight, without telling him she loved him, ate at her. She felt an overwhelming amount of guilt. Taking a deep breath, she shakily made her way upstairs to change out of her dress and into an old pair of jeans and one of Antonio's worn-out t-shirts as she pondered how they were going to get past this.

Meanwhile, as soon as Antonio got himself seated in the back of the car, he immediately burst into tears. *"Fanculo!"* He yelled, slamming his hands onto the seat.

Everett slid into the driver's seat, and Edward and Priscilla each hopped into the back, one on either side of Antonio. *"Fratello…"* Priscilla started, but Antonio cut her off.

"What have I done? How could I have spoken to her like that?" He cried.

"You guys were feeling intense emotions. It's alright," Edward said, trying to comfort his brother.

"It's not alright! Fuck! I yelled at her! I've never yelled at her. And I… I didn't tell her I love her. I didn't tell her that she's the reason I wake up in the morning, the very reason I breathe. She doesn't know that I'd give up everything for her. That she's my whole world. And now I'm going to a gunfight, and she doesn't know…" Unable to contain himself, he sobbed once more.

Priscilla took his hand in hers and squeezed it tightly. "She knows, Antonio. She knows," She said softly.

Nodding his head, Antonio took a few deep breaths and readied himself for the fight that they were quickly approaching. He forced all thoughts out of his mind, except for the rage that always smoldered deep down in his chest. As they approached the hangar, seeing the bodies of the men and women he considered family lying dead on the ground, he saw red, and the monster within woke up with a vengeance. Everett slammed the car into park, and the four of them drew their guns and ran into the chaos.

Cynthia had never felt this much anxiety in her life. It had been nearly three hours since Antonio had left, and she felt as though she might have a panic attack with each minute that passed. She'd deep cleaned much of the house to keep her imagination at bay, but most of the house was already clean, as the housekeeper had been in only yesterday. Not knowing what else to do, she decided to make dinner. She knew they would all need to eat something when they returned. *If they return,* she thought, tears welling up in her eyes for what seemed like the millionth time.

Turning off the stove once the soup she'd made was done, Cynthia turned to begin washing the dishes when the front door finally burst open. She started to exhale in relief until she heard Priscilla's voice.

"Cynthia!" Priscilla screamed in a full-blown panic.

Knowing that something was terribly wrong, Cynthia dropped the bowl she was holding and sprinted into the entryway, not caring that it shattered as it hit the ground. All color left her face and all she could hear was the pounding of her heart in her ears as she came to a screeching halt and took in a sight she hoped she would never have to see. Edward and Everett were struggling to carry Antonio, who was unconscious and covered in blood. So much blood. It was seemingly pouring out of him, but from where, Cynthia couldn't quite tell.

Hearing Priscilla call out to her once more snapped Cynthia into a calm, steady mode that she didn't realize existed. "What happened?"

"He was shot!" Priscilla exclaimed, tears and snot streaming down her face.

"Come on, let's get him to the infirmary room. Quickly!" Cynthia instructed.

With a grunt, Edward and Everett followed her down the hall, thankful the room was on the first floor. Cynthia opened the door for them and they quickly, but gently, laid Antonio on the bed. "W-w-we can't get a hold of Dr. Raymond," Edward panted, trying to catch his breath.

Taking a deep breath, Cynthia turned away from her love lying motionless on the bed and stared evenly at the trio. "Well, it's a good thing I've been taking night classes to become a certified RN."

All three of their jaws dropped. Cynthia rolled her eyes and pointed to Antonio. "Look who I'm marrying. I figured I should know how to remove bullets and stitch up wounds. According to the doctors and nurses I've been training with, I'm the best student they've seen perform sutures. And it's a good thing I've familiarized myself with this room."

Turning to the sink, Cynthia turned on the hot water and scrubbed her hands and arms as she gave directions. "Everett, grab a bag of A- out of that cooler over there. Edward, open the top drawer over there and grab the suture kit. Priscilla, grab me some gauze and antiseptic."

She smiled to herself as they all sprung into action. Once her hands and arms were sufficiently cleaned and dried, Cynthia pulled on some latex gloves and grabbed an I.V. bag and some morphine. Walking quickly back over to the bed, she grabbed the scissors from the suture kit and expertly cut Antonio's shirt from his body. Once his shirt was removed, she could see an entrance wound in his abdomen.

"Could you guys please gently roll him so I can see if there's an exit wound?"

Without hesitation, Everett and Edward did what she asked. Cynthia breathed a sigh of relief seeing that there was no exit wound, and moved into high gear once Antonio had been rolled back onto his back. Finding a decent vein, Cynthia put an I.V. into his arm and hung the bag, then injected morphine into the second port to keep him out and relieve any pain he felt. Then she quickly got to work to stop the bleeding as best she could.

Satisfied that Antonio's wound was bleeding less, Cynthia grabbed the tweezers and inserted them into the bullet wound, relief washing over her when she found the bullet and easily pulled it out. There seemed to be no damage to any internal organs. After thoroughly cleaning the wound, she quickly sutured the wound closed, then began a blood transfusion, since he had lost so much.

When it was all said and done, Cynthia felt more weary than she'd ever felt in her life, but she couldn't help but smile as she noticed the color slowly returning to his face. Turning to Everett, she motioned for him to come closer. "Let me see your arm."

Grinning sheepishly, Everett carefully unwound the bloody bandage from his arm and turned so she could get a good look at it.

"Oh, this isn't too terrible, but it does need to be cleaned and it looks like you'll need at least two stitches. Sit down in that chair for a moment."

He did what he was told and within a couple of minutes, his wound had been cleaned and stitched. "Thank you, Cynthia. Not just for my arm, but for what you just did for Antonio. We are all in complete awe of you."

"You don't have to thank me. I love all of you. Now, I made some soup. Go eat it and rest. I'm going to sit here with him."

With a nod, Everett and Edward quietly left the room, but Priscilla hung back. "Cynthia... are you ok?"

At that moment, it was all Cynthia could do to keep herself standing upright. She started shaking as tears streamed down her face once more. "I'm so scared, Priscilla."

"Hey, it'll be alright," Priscilla reassured her as she pulled her into her arms.

"I hope so. I did the best I could. But shit! He almost died... and I didn't tell him I loved him. I never got to tell him how I feel about him. That he's the best thing that's ever happened to me!" She sobbed.

"Shhhh, it's ok. You will get to tell him, I promise. Have some faith. And Cynthia, he knows you love him."

Cynthia nodded and did her best to calm herself down. She grabbed a chair and pulled it over beside the bed. "Uh, what are you doing?" Priscilla asked, raising her eyebrows.

"I'm going to sit beside him until he wakes up."

Priscilla laughed and shook her head. "He may have just been shot, but he's not that fragile. I can tell how badly you want to be up there beside him. Get up there, girl! He'll be fine, and I know he would much rather come to with you laying beside him than with you sitting in a chair." With that, she left the room and closed the door softly behind her.

Pondering that bit of information for a moment, Cynthia decided that her sister was correct. As carefully as she could, she slid into the infirmary bed beside the love of her life and snuggled up against his non-injured side. She gently laid her head against his chest, and upon hearing his steady heartbeat, allowed herself to break down once more. The whole experience had been extremely traumatic, not just because he had been shot, but because they had screamed at each other just hours before. She quietly sobbed against his chest until exhaustion overtook her and she fell asleep.

In the early hours of the morning, Antonio finally stirred and winced at the sharp pain in his side. Remembering the shootout, his eyes flew open and he took in his surroundings, relief settling over him as he recognized the infirmary room in his house. Feeling a soft, warm weight on his chest, he looked down and saw the woman he loved sleeping, though not peacefully. Her forehead was creased with worry, and he could see her face was covered in dry tears. "Cynthia..." he murmured softly.

Sitting bolt upright, Cynthia stared at him with her eyes wide. "Antonio?" She whispered, tears welling up in her eyes.

"*Sí*, it's me."

Taking a deep breath, Cynthia looked him over. "Are you in any pain?"

"A little. Where's Dr. Raymond?"

Jumping out of bed, Cynthia made her way over to the cabinet and grabbed a syringe of morphine. "He never answered his phone."

"Then who did this?" Antonio asked, gesturing to the bandage covering his abdomen.

"I did," she said softly as she turned around and made her way back to his side to administer the morphine.

"You did?" He gaped up at her, eyes wide.

Cynthia couldn't help but giggle at the look on his face. After setting the syringe down, she carefully got back into the bed beside him. Antonio immediately sat up, much to her horror. "Antonio! What are you doing? You need to lay back down!"

"I'm fine, see? I'm not even bleeding anymore. But tell me, how did you do this?"

"I've been secretly taking night classes to become a registered nurse."

"You have?" He gasped. "Why?"

Taking his hand in hers, her voice quivered as she spoke. "Because I'm marrying the leader of the Black Death Mafia, injuries come with the territory. I mean, that is, if you still want to marry me..."

"What?" Antonio gasped once more. "*Bel Fiore*, come here." Cynthia shook her head, unable to meet his eyes as tears streamed down her face. His heart shattered seeing her in so much pain.

Before Cynthia knew what had happened, Antonio had lifted her up and placed her on his lap so she was basically straddling him. "Antonio! What are you doing? You're going to rip your sutures!"

150

"I asked you to come here," he shrugged as he lifted her chin so he could look into her eyes. "And ripping my sutures would be worth it if it meant having you close to me. Why wouldn't I want to marry you?"

"Because of our fight!" She sobbed, all of her emotions and fears swarming in her eyes. "We've never fought before. And then you left, and I... I didn't get to tell you how much you mean to me, how I feel about you. Then when they brought you in, I was so scared that I'd never be able to!"

"You could tell me now..." he breathed, his heart catching in his throat.

Taking a deep breath, Cynthia gently placed her hands on his face and stared deeply into his eyes. She wanted him to see how much he meant to her. "Before we were together, I never knew how lonely I was. I didn't know what real love looked or felt like. You are the best thing that has ever happened to me. When we're apart, it feels like I can't breathe. My world doesn't feel right until we are together again. It doesn't matter what's happened during my day, your voice, your touch, your scent... is all I need to be ok again. I need you like I need air. You're the love of my life. Antonio, a life without you, simply wouldn't be a life worth living... I love you. Every side of you. Your fun, playful side, your loving side, the darkest part of your soul. Everything. All of it. I just love you."

Antonio felt as though he could hardly breathe as she spoke. The intensity of her gaze and each word she spoke made his heart swell. As soon as she finished, he slammed his lips on hers, drinking her in. She stiffened at first but soon melted into his embrace. "I love you so fucking much, Cynthia Springer." He murmured against her lips.

"Oh? Do you, now?" She grinned.

Leaning his forehead against hers, he teared up as he whispered, "I was so scared I wouldn't be able to tell you how I felt, either. And I am so sorry for the way I spoke to you. Forgive me?"

Brushing the tears from his eyes with her thumbs, she kissed his forehead softly and murmured, "Of course I forgive you. Do you forgive me?"

"There is nothing to forgive, but if you think I need to, then yes, I do." Taking a deep breath, he pulled her close once more. "You're the reason I wake up every morning. The very reason I even breathe. Cynthia, you are my whole world. Before you, I was hardly even existing. But now, I'm alive. If you asked me to give everything up for you, I couldn't tell you no. I'd walk away from everything if it meant getting to love you each and every day. Without you, life is meaningless. I'd be an empty, hollow shell of a man with a monster I could never contain. You're the air to my lungs, the light in my days, my everything... I love you more than life itself."

This time, Cynthia kissed him first, as if her life depended on it. "I could and would *never* ask you to walk away from who you are. I love you for you, and I always will."

"Marry me?" Antonio breathed, his voice hoarse and full of emotion.

"Anytime and any place," she whispered against his lips as she kissed him once more.

Both of them felt as if a huge weight had been lifted off of their shoulders, and Antonio wearily brushed a strand of hair behind her ear. It was then that Cynthia noticed how exhausted he was. She quickly removed herself from his lap and gently pushed on his chest until he laid back down. "You need to rest, *amore mio*."

He nodded, but reached out and grabbed her arm as she turned to get off the bed. "Not without you. Please don't go."

She turned and smiled softly at him. "I'm going to turn off the light. I know it's dim, but we both rest better when it's dark." Walking over to the light switch, she shut it off and hurried back to the bed. Sliding back in, she placed her head against his chest once more, Antonio's arm wrapped firmly around her. Within minutes, they were both sleeping soundly, with everything right in their world once more.

Night Moves

July 20, 1989

Edward stretched out on his bed as he thumbed through his syllabi for the upcoming semester. Even though it was summer break, Edward liked to be prepared. His apartment was situated close to campus, and he liked the solitude. That is, when he didn't have any female guests over. He paused to take a drink of his water, thankful that Antonio hadn't needed him to go to Italy with him for the week. A knock on the door interrupted his thoughts, and with a sigh, Edward begrudgingly got out of his bed and made his way to the front door.

He opened the door to find Priscilla standing outside, wearing a black trench coat and her favorite mint green high heels. "Priscilla? What are you doing here?"

"Can I come in?" She asked, raising an eyebrow as she moved some of her curly black hair out of her face.

"Sure," he replied, opening the door wider and allowing her to step in before closing it behind her. "So, what's up?"

With a smirk, Priscilla locked his front door and let her jacket fall to the ground, causing Edward's eyes to go wide as he tried to look anywhere but at her naked body. "What the fuck, Pris! Put that back on, what are you doing?"

With a giggle, Priscilla made her way over to Edward and lifted his chin to make him meet her eyes. "Edward... I'm sick and tired of the fact that no one wants to touch me. Everyone is afraid of Antonio, and I'm done with this shit! Please, Edward, please spend a night with me. Men aren't the only ones with needs, you know."

Edward gulped and did his best to keep his eyes on her face. "Priscilla, you've always been a sister to me, I can't do this. And you know Antonio will kill me when he finds out"

"He won't find out. We never have to speak of it. And I'm not asking you to date me or have romantic feelings for me. I'm asking you to have a night of meaningless sex so that I can experience what it's like. I'm getting to the point where I don't think anyone will ever touch me in fear of my brother. Please, Edward, don't make me get on my knees and beg."

"Why me?" He whispered.

"Because you are the only man I trust, aside from my brother. And it helps that you're experienced," she blushed.

"I can't believe I'm doing this," Edward started, taking a breath. "Just one night? And we never speak of this again?"

"Exactly," she grinned.

Edward sucked in a breath as she pulled his t-shirt off and ran her hands over his muscular chest. He found it hard to breathe as he let his eyes wander over her body, and knew it would be hard to ever look at this beautiful woman as the little sister he had always seen her as. She had blossomed into womanhood, and she was by far the most gorgeous woman he had ever laid eyes on. As he placed his hands on her waist to pull her close against him, he marveled at how soft her skin was.

"Edward... Kiss me," Priscilla rasped.

Without hesitation, Edward closed what space remained and claimed her lips, groaning at the feeling of them on his. "God, what are you doing to me?"

"You're making my wish come true. Now shut up and take me to bed."

Early the following morning, after three hot and heavy rounds, Priscilla untangled herself from Edward's arms and quietly slipped out of bed. The experience was everything she had dreamt it would be and more. While she in no way held romantic feelings for him, she was grateful that he had fulfilled her request. As quickly and as quietly as she could, Priscilla put her jacket and shoes on, then made her way back to the bed.

She gently swept some hair out of Edward's face and leaned down to kiss his forehead. "Thank you," she whispered. Turning away, she silently let herself out of his apartment and drove home.

Edward rolled over just in time to watch her leave, and as the door shut behind her, he breathed, "You're welcome, *uno dolce*."

With a groan, he got out of bed and headed straight to his shower, where he let the hot water pelt down against him. *What have I done... God, I hope Antonio never finds out.*

True to her word, Priscilla never breathed a word about their night together, and acted completely normal, as if nothing had happened. Edward found it a little harder to do so, but he managed alright. He was relieved when his college courses started because he spent less time around the Moretti siblings, even though he always enjoyed hanging out and working with his best friend.

Priscilla started her senior year of high school with more confidence than ever. Her volleyball team was on track for a third championship in three years, and she knew the college scouts would be eyeing her and her teammates. Emily remained her biggest fan, and even though she was knee-deep in dual credit courses, she always made sure she was at every single game. As September rolled around, Antonio and

Cynthia finalized wedding plans and made sure to make time for each other even though they both had a busy workload. However, September would bring about something that would forever impact Priscilla's life.

September 27, 1989

The Lady Knights had beaten their biggest rival in three games, and Priscilla had been a huge contributor to that fact; she'd had eight blocks and 20 kills, and her serves had been spectacular. Her team was going wild, and she grinned from ear to ear as they celebrated out on the court following the game. Reaching down, she slid her knee pads down to her shins as her coach made her way over to where she was standing.

"Ah, there you are, Priscilla," Jean Hartford began. "There's someone I'd like you to meet."

Straightening up, Priscilla faced her coach and smiled. "Here I am, Coach Hartford."

"Priscilla, I'd like you to meet Jack Taylors. Mr. Taylors is a scout from Stanford," Jean all but squealed as she introduced the pair.

"It's nice to meet you, Priscilla," a voice came from behind her.

Whirling around in surprise, Priscilla's eyes widened as she took in the man that was there to meet her. "Erm, uh, it's nice to m-meet you too, Mr. Taylors."

The man, who appeared to be in his late 20s, chuckled and grinned at her, "Please, call me Jack."

Swallowing hard, Priscilla grasped his hand and shook it firmly, shaking herself from her stupor. Jack was a handsome man, about 6'1" with pale skin, dirty blonde hair, and brown eyes a shade darker than her own. His eyes sparkled with mischief, and she couldn't help but want to partake in whatever it was that he had in mind.

"Well you two, I'll leave you to talk. Mr. Taylors, please meet me in my office when you are finished so we can finish talking," Jean said as she walked away.

"So, um, how can I help you?" Priscilla asked, trying to ease her nerves.

"Actually, what I'm here for is to see what I can do for you," Jack smirked as he led Priscilla to the bleachers and sat down. "As your coach pointed out, I'm the recruiter for Stanford. We've been keeping an eye on your stats since your freshman year, and we are very impressed. Stanford would like to sign you on to play volleyball for them next year."

"Are you fucking serious? Uh, I mean, really?" She exclaimed, blushing at her outburst.

Jack threw his head back and laughed heartily. "No need to watch your language, I don't mind at all. I'd rather see the real you. The very gorgeous, you," he winked.

"Oh, um… Well, I would love to play for Stanford. What do I need to do?" Priscilla asked, flustered by the compliment.

"Well, right now, they are having me scout for a couple of people, but you are at the top of the list. I will personally be attending the majority of your games, but my money is that you will make the final cut. Toward mid-season, I will have the papers from Stanford that you will need to sign, with your parents present, of course," Jack explained.

"Alright. Well, my legal guardian is my brother, as my parents died several years ago… but that sounds good."

"Oh! My apologies, Priscilla. Here is my home phone number. Feel free to call me any time. And I mean any time. Say, I'm pretty hungry, would you like to join me and get a bite to eat?"

"Sure! Um, just let me get showered and changed first! Where would you like to go?"

"How about the diner down the road?" He asked with a grin.

"Sounds good to me. I'll meet you there since I drove here. See you in a bit, Jack," Priscilla grinned before jogging toward the locker room.

I look forward to it, Jack thought as he shoved his hands in his pockets and whistled as he walked out of the gymnasium. Twenty minutes later, Priscilla found herself sitting across from Jack in a booth at the local diner. They had each ordered a chocolate malt and were happily drinking them as they waited for their food to arrive. "So, are you 18 yet?" Jack asked.

"Not yet. I turned 17 in July. How old are you?" Priscilla responded.

"I'm 27. Are you seeing anyone?"

"Like dating? Hell no! Everyone is too scared of my brother. Why?"

"I apologize, but I am a very forward man, and you are the most gorgeous young woman I have ever laid eyes on. I would like to know if I stand a chance. Besides, I'm not scared of anyone's older siblings."

Priscilla was a bit taken aback by his forwardness, but she quickly recovered. Leaning forward on her elbows, she batted her eyelashes at him. "I don't see why there'd be any reason you wouldn't have a chance. But aren't you concerned that I'm a minor?"

"Psh. You're a senior, on your way to 18. I'm not concerned at all. So, can I take you on a date next weekend?"

"I'd like that."

The two spent the rest of their time getting to know each other over dinner. Jack was quite charming, and Priscilla could see herself dating him for a long time. However, they both agreed that they should keep the fact that they were seeing each other on the down low, due to their age difference. She didn't mind the 10-year age gap and knew that if they proceeded with the relationship, the difference could be very beneficial when it came to other matters. In the back of her mind, though, she knew she was going to have to be very careful not to let Antonio catch on to the fact that she was seeing an older man, not only for her sake but more importantly, for Jack's.

Waiting for a Girl Like You

November 18, 1989

Antonio did his best to calm his nerves as he stood in front of the floor-length mirror and picked up his tie. Knowing that he would not be able to tie it properly, and not wanting to get angry on his wedding day, he decided he would ask his best friend for help. "Edward!"

"Yeah?" Edward asked, stepping into view as he buttoned up his suit coat.

"I need help," Antonio grumbled as he rolled his eyes.

Edward barked out a laugh and shook his head as he took the tie from his best friend and proceeded to place it around Antonio's neck. "There you go. You know, it means the world to me that you chose me as your best man... but I fucking hate suits."

"What's wrong with a suit? They look sophisticated and like you mean business. Trust me, my friend, someday you'll feel the same way I do."

"Doubt it. Anyway, are you ready?"

"I've been ready from the moment I laid eyes on her at that Christmas party. God, I love her so much. Can you believe that angel of a woman even wants to marry me?"

"It truly is hard to believe, you're ugly as sin," Edward

winked, ducking out of the way to avoid Antonio's fist.

"You're just jealous that I'm hot as fuck," Antonio preened, smoothing out his hair and giving himself another once over in the mirror. "Hey, Cade! Has my precious *nipote* woken up from his nap yet?"

"Britt just dropped him off with me," Cade grinned as he walked into the room holding Logan by the hand.

"*Zio!*" Logan exclaimed. "Look at my suit!"

"You look very handsome, *nipote!* I think you look even more handsome than me in those colors!"

Logan puffed out his chest and grinned. While their beige suits and peach ties were typically colors reserved for spring, Cynthia had wanted that palette for their wedding; and Antonio would always give her whatever she wanted. Edward and Cade grinned as they watched Antonio interact with his five-year-old nephew. It was hard to fathom that he was also a big bad mafia man. Satisfied that Logan would not be getting into any trouble, Cade went over and finished getting ready himself, grateful that he and his family were being included in Antonio and Cynthia's special day.

Sitting down and placing Logan on his knee, Antonio did his best to quell the rising grief he had felt for days now. Today, it was stronger, and he felt a tear roll down his face. He missed his parents and wished that they could be there to see their little boy, who was now a man, marry the woman of his dreams. At that moment, the sun beamed through the window, landing on his face. Turning his face into the sun, Antonio knew that his parents would be proud of him, and swallowing the lump in his throat, he was determined to keep the sadness at bay for the rest of the day.

On the other side of the venue, Cynthia sat at the lit vanity as her hairstylist curled her hair. Her dress hung from a hook on the wall beside her, and she gazed at it lovingly. She hoped that Antonio would love it, but knowing him, he would always find her ravishing no matter what. Hearing laughing from another part of the room, Cynthia adjusted her view to watch the sisters of her heart as they chatted and got ready.

"Cynthia, you know I love you with all my heart, but peach is so not my color," Priscilla teasingly grumbled as she tied the halter top of her dress on. "You know I'm a mint kind of girl, and dark colors, too."

"I like it!" Emily exclaimed, twirling in front of the mirror. "I'm not really into dresses, but I adore this."

Britt laughed as she walked up to Cynthia and gave her a loving kiss on the cheek. "The colors you chose are beautiful, and I love the style you chose."

"Of course you and Emily like the color, it compliments your skin tone!" Priscilla called out.

Everyone laughed at the playful banter, but the three bridesmaids truly did look beautiful in the peach floor-length gown with a sweetheart neckline and halter top. The hairstylist quickly sprayed a layer of hairspray over Cynthia's curls, then stood back to admire her work. "All done! You look beautiful! I'll see when you walk down the aisle."

"Thank you, Joanne!" Cynthia exclaimed as she stood up and hugged her friend.

Once Joanne had exited the room, Priscilla turned to her sister-in-law with a mischievous gleam in her eye. "So, sister, what are you planning on wearing tonight?"

Cynthia turned a deep shade of crimson as she thought about what on earth she would say in response. "Um…"

"Don't be shy! Tell us!" Emily added.

Britt rolled her eyes at the girls but patted Cynthia's arm encouragingly. "You don't have to tell us, and I'm sure whatever you wear, *Patatino* will think you look absolutely gorgeous, even if it's a burlap sack."

Cynthia giggled, knowing full well that what Britt said was true. Walking over to her bag, Cynthia rummaged around until she found what she was looking for. Holding up a skimpy, black lace piece of lingerie, she smirked at her best friends. "I figured I'd wear his color tonight."

"Hot damn! My brother is gonna tear that to shreds!" Priscilla grinned, fanning herself.

Hearing the doorknob turn, Cynthia quickly hid the lingerie back in her bag right as her mother walked into the room. The four women gave each other knowing looks while Alexandra Springer set the bouquet down on the end table. "Well my darling, shall we get you into your gown?"

"Oh yes!" Cynthia exclaimed. "I am so ready to walk down that aisle."

With a cheerful laugh, Alexandra gently unzipped and took Cynthia's wedding gown off of the hanger. She held it down to where her daughter could easily step in and then zipped up the back. "Oh, my darling, you look breathtaking," Alexandra sniffed as she dabbed at her tears with a handkerchief.

"Thank you, Momma," Cynthia beamed.

Her gown was absolutely stunning. While Cynthia was typically all for traditions, she had left traditions by the wayside when it came to her dress. Instead of going with the traditional white, Cynthia had chosen a satin, ivory, floor-length gown with a ballgown silhouette and a basque waistline. It had an off-the-shoulder, ruffled bodice with small flower details along the neckline. The train was chapel length with bustling in the back. She had a crown of peach roses around her head and topped the look off with a hip-length veil.

A knock at the door interrupted the moment, and as the maid of honor, Priscilla took it upon herself to see who was bothering them. Opening the door, Priscilla was surprised to find Edward standing there, a small, white, elegantly wrapped package in his hands. Sucking in a breath, Edward

164

coughed quickly and held the package out to her. "Uhm, this is a wedding gift from Antonio to Cynthia. Would you please give it to her?"

"Of course," she replied, taking the package from him. As she turned to go back into the bridal suite, Edward gently grasped her arm.

"You look beautiful, Pris."

"Thank you, Edward. You look very handsome yourself," Priscilla said as she flashed him her most charming Moretti smile. With a wink, Edward jammed his hands in his pockets and walked away while Priscilla went back inside. "This is a wedding gift from my brother," she explained as she handed the package to Priscilla.

"Oh! That devil! I told him not to get me anything," Cynthia rolled her eyes, but she smiled as she slowly untied the ribbon.

"He never listens to anyone," Britt laughed.

Without tearing the white wrapping paper, Cynthia opened her gift and found a box with a dual-stranded pearl necklace inside. "This is so beautiful! Pearls are my favorite."

Britt gently took the necklace out of Cynthia's hands and walked behind her. After sweeping her beautiful ginger hair out of the way, Britt carefully clasped the necklace around her neck. "Beautiful."

"Well, that takes care of something new," Cynthia giggled.

"I have your something blue!" Emily exclaimed. She grabbed her purse and pulled out a diamond bracelet with a round sapphire pendant. Taking Cynthia's arm, Emily fastened the bracelet around her wrist.

"Emily! This is beautiful! Thank you!" Cynthia cried.

"You're welcome. This is my family's gift to you."

Another knock came at the door, but this time, Britt went and opened it. Her mom, Dianne, came in and paused as she took in the bride. "You are such a lovely bride, Cynthia,"

Dianne said softly, dabbing at her eyes. "Lorenzo and Carmella would have loved you so much, and they would be so happy that you're marrying our *Patatino*. I've held onto something that I know Carmella would have wanted you to have. May I?" She asked, gesturing to her.

With tears in her eyes, Cynthia nodded and stepped over to where Dianne was standing. From her purse, Dianne pulled out an ivory silk ribbon, which she cradled in her hands for a moment. After taking a deep breath, Dianne explained, "I was Carmella's maid of honor when she married Lorenzo. She wore this ribbon in her hair on her wedding day, which was a gift from me for her birthday. When I saw her put it in her hair when she was getting ready, I was shocked. She didn't wear a veil or anything, only the ribbon. It meant the world to me."

Dianne had to pause once more as the loss she felt bubbled up inside of her; she missed her friends greatly. "When they were killed, our dear friends generously made sure we would always be financially stable. However, Carmella had also asked that I hold onto her wedding items for either Antonio's bride or Priscilla's wedding; whoever got married first. This ribbon, though a simple gift, meant the world to her, for some reason. Here, this is for you."

Cynthia gingerly accepted the ribbon, then pulled Dianne in for a hug. "Thank you, *Tant*," she whispered in the older woman's ear.

"You're welcome, sweetheart."

"I have a perfect idea!" Britt exclaimed, grabbing Cynthia's bouquet and marching to where she and her mother stood. "The ribbon is your something old, and I brought you my grandmother's cameo to wear as your something borrowed. What if we loop the ribbon through the cameo and wrap it around your bouquet?"

"I love that idea!" Cynthia beamed.

Britt quickly got to work, and within a matter of seconds, her task was completed. "Here you are, sister."

Taking the bouquet in her hands, Cynthia breathed in the scent of the peach pink and yellow roses. The baby's breath complemented the colors wonderfully, and the silk was smooth and soft against her fingers. A couple of soft taps came at the door, followed by Martin Springer poking his head in. Seeing that everyone was ready, he stepped inside the room and took in his daughter, beaming as he looked at her.

"You are the second most beautiful bride I have ever laid eyes on," he said softly, pulling Cynthia in for a hug. "Your mother is first, sorry sweet pea."

With a giggle, Cynthia squeezed his neck. "I'm not offended, Momma is gorgeous."

"You ready to get married?"

"I am. Are you ready to give me away?"

"As ready as I'll ever be, I guess."

With that, the group made their way to the doors of the church sanctuary, and with a kiss on Cynthia's cheek, Alexandra walked in and took her seat in the front row, followed by Dianne and Marcus, who had come out to accompany her after giving Antonio some last minute advice. Since they did not have a flower girl, Antonio had covered the aisle with rose petals personally when they got to the church that morning.

Edward walked up, and Emily and Priscilla each took an arm before making their way down the aisle. Cade took Britt's arm, giving her a quick kiss before taking their spot. "You ready, Baby Blue?" He asked.

"I am. Lead the way," Britt replied as the doors were opened once more to allow their entry. Turning back real quick, she made sure her son was fully ready, and satisfied, allowing her husband to lead her down the aisle. Seeing

Antonio all dressed up and patiently awaiting his bride caused Britt's heart to swell with pride.

After taking their places, Britt leaned over and whispered, "You look very handsome, *Björn*. I'm so proud of you."

"Thank you, *Cerva*," Antonio murmured as he watched Logan carefully pick his way through the petals, bearing the pillow where the wedding rings lay.

Taking a deep breath, Cynthia squeezed her father's arm as the doors were opened a final time, and as the wedding procession began to play, the pair began their descent down the aisle. Cynthia blushed as she saw and felt Antonio's eyes rake over her body before finally meeting her eyes. The smile on his face made her feel as if she were floating on air, and she felt tears in her eyes when she noticed that he was letting tears freely run down his face.

"Who gives this woman to this man?" The pastor asked.

"Her mother and I," Martin smiled. Kissing his daughter's cheek, he handed her over to Antonio and sat down by his wife.

Antonio leaned in and whispered in her ear, "I do not view you as a possession. And if anything, I belong to you."

The pastor began the wedding spiel, though Antonio and Cynthia hardly listened; they were too busy getting lost in each other's eyes. When it was time for the vows, Antonio took a deep breath and lovingly smiled at his bride. "Cynthia. Several years ago, I met a cute little girl at school, who startled me so much that I fell off the monkey bars and broke my leg."

Several people in the audience chuckled. "Even though you were a girl, you became one of my friends, and I always enjoyed it when you came over to hang out with me, Edward, and the girls. When I lost my parents... I lost a big part of myself. I pushed everyone who wasn't in what I considered my immediate family away. And I'm sorry and ashamed to admit that one of those people was you. A couple of years ago, at our annual Christmas party, I saw you for the first time in years, and your beauty, grace, and personality blew me away. Every day I became more and more in awe of you. You managed to wrestle the monster inside of me into submission, and there is nothing in this world I wouldn't do for you. I love you with all that I am, and all that I will be. I vow to be your lover, your friend, and your biggest supporter. I vow to always put you first, and listen to you whenever you need my ear. Thank you for taking a chance on me, and for loving me as much as I love you, Cynthia Elizabeth."

Cynthia knew without a shadow of a doubt that Antonio meant every single word he said, and she graciously took the handkerchief that Britt held out to her and dabbed her eyes. Emily handed her the folded piece of paper that she'd written her vows on, and with shaky hands, she began with a smile, "Antonio Julius, where do I even begin?"

This also caused some chuckling in the audience, which helped with her nerves. "I'm not sure I could ever explain the degree of pain I felt being the cause of your broken leg, but I promised myself that I would spend as long as necessary to make up for it. I know people don't think it's possible, but I fell for you as a child. You captivated me, and I always wanted to know you better. When you distanced yourself, it hurt me, but I did not take it personally. I knew I could never feel the level of grief that you felt, though I wished you would have allowed me to grieve with you. When we reconnected, it made me happier than you even realize. No matter what reputation you'd garnered, I knew the real man deep down beneath the surface. I fall harder and harder for you each day, and I'm so blessed that you chose me. Antonio, I vow to love you more every day, and no matter what challenges we face in life, I promise to always stand by your side. I vow to create a loving home filled with warmth so that you never know loneliness again, and I vow to do whatever I can to grow with you. I love you, Antonio, forever and always."

Antonio was grateful for the advice his father had given him many years ago as he pulled his handkerchief from his pocket and wiped his eyes and nose. After repeating after the pastor, the couple exchanged rings and said "I Do." Grinning, the pastor proclaimed, "It is my absolute pleasure to pronounce you husband and wife. You may kiss your bride!"

With a smirk, Antonio pulled Cynthia into his arms, dipped her, and claimed her lips with unrestrained passion. Everyone in the audience stood and applauded as their kiss stretched on longer than was normal. Edward hooped and hollered while Priscilla and Emily whistled. Finally releasing her, Antonio brushed his lips against her ear as he murmured, "I cannot wait to ravish you tonight, my beautiful wife."

Giving him a smirk of her own, Cynthia whispered back, "Not if I ravish you first."

Coughing and doing his best to not get utterly turned on, Antonio straightened up and took his wife by the arm as they walked down the aisle and out of the sanctuary doors. They had hired a photographer to photograph the wedding party and met everyone outside to do so. Once their pictures had been taken, everyone went inside the reception hall for food and dancing. However, Antonio desperately wished that he didn't have this obligation so that he could take his bride home and love the shit out of her.

Even though he wanted to take Cynthia home, he enjoyed their first dance together. Cynthia had given him free rein over the first dance song, and while he had wanted to choose a country song to please her, he decided to choose *Waiting for a Girl Like You* by Foreigner. When she heard the song, Cynthia giggled but softly sang along as Antonio expertly led her around the dance floor. Not wanting to disappoint her, the next song that followed was *Deeper Than the Holler* by Randy Travis, and many guests crowded the dance floor to dance to it.

When it was finally time to leave, Antonio and Cynthia ran out the front doors hand in hand, while also trying to block rice from hitting their faces. Finally reaching the *Impala*, Antonio opened the passenger door for her and shut it quickly as soon as she was in. Cynthia laughed watching him scramble around to the driver's side, and he grinned at her as he slammed the door shut, started the engine, and sped off down the road. The cans that had been tied to the rear bumper clanked noisily, but they didn't care. Reaching the Moretti Mansion, the newlyweds breathed a sigh of relief, happy to finally be alone.

As they made their way into the house and upstairs, Antonio felt himself becoming increasingly nervous the closer they got to their bedroom. Cynthia giggled when he picked her up and crossed the threshold, but scrunched her eyes when she noticed he was visibly nervous. "What's wrong, my love?"

"Nothing, *Bel Fiore*," he mumbled.

"Antonio Julius Moretti, don't you lie to me. Tell me what's on your mind."

"You know me too well, *amore mio*. I guess I'm just nervous about disappointing you tonight. We've done everything right, yet, now that the time is here, I just want it to be perfect for you."

Standing on her toes, Cynthia snaked her arms around her husband's neck and stared directly into his eyes. "There is no way you could disappoint me. While I'm nervous to have sex for the first time, I know that it will be perfect, because I will be wholly giving myself to you, my husband. Don't overthink it."

Without allowing him to respond, she softly kissed his lips and smiled when she felt him relax. "Now, if you could please unzip my dress for me, that would be great."

Nodding, Antonio slowly, almost painstakingly unzipped her wedding gown. But before it could fall off of her, Cynthia put her hand up and held the dress at her bosom. "I'll be right back," She smirked over her shoulder as she made her way to the bathroom, only pausing to grab her bag.

Shrugging, Antonio removed his shoes, then carefully hung his jacket in his closet so that it wouldn't get ruined. As he went to loosen his tie, Cynthia called out, "Don't you dare remove your tie, husband of mine."

Antonio chuckled, and not knowing what else to do, sat down on the large four poster bed as he waited patiently for his bride. A few minutes later, the bathroom door opened and Cynthia slowly walked into the bedroom. Antonio was on his feet before she fully made her way into the room, his eyes wide as he took her in. While he had expected her to wear a lacy little number for their first night together as a married couple, he'd thought she would have worn a soft color like peach or pink. However, she hadn't chosen a soft color at all. Instead, she was wearing black, and it was enough to nearly bring him to his knees as she made her way over to him.

"You're wearing black," he rasped, unable to form any other words.

"I am. I wanted to wear your color," she grinned.

"You look hot as fuck in my color," he smirked, his senses coming back to him. Taking her by the hand, he gently commanded, "Turn around for me."

Cynthia obliged, allowing him to fully view her body as she slowly turned around. She could feel her body heat up under his gaze. As she came around to face him once more, she dropped his hand. Before he could reach for her once more, she grabbed his tie and pulled him against her, their bodies and lips crashing into each other passionately. Her nimble fingers soon had Antonio's clothes on the floor, and for the first time, Cynthia allowed herself to take in all of her husband's body. Blushing deeply, she refused to take her eyes off of him. Slowly, she backed up and leaned against their bed.

Antonio loved the fact that she was unashamedly staring at him. It lit something up inside of him, and releasing a small growl at the way she was leaning against the bed, quickly closed the distance. He quickly, but gently tore her lingerie off of her body, throwing it behind him and letting his hands freely explore her soft skin. "Don't worry, *Bel Fiore*, I'll buy you a new one."

She giggled in response, her hands roaming his body as well. Unable to take the space between them any longer, Antonio picked up his bride and tossed her on the bed with a smirk, coming to rest on top of her, his elbow keeping his full weight from crushing her. "Tonight, I'm going to take you to places you never thought you could go. I'm going to show you how much I love you, over and over."

Grinning herself, Cynthia sat up, and before Antonio could comprehend what had happened, found himself lying on the bed with his wife sitting on top of him. Seeing her body from this angle nearly made him lose all control. "And I, *amore mio*, am going to show you how much I love you. And you can bet that I won't be holding anything back."

Their lips met in a fiery passion, and neither one of them held back.

The following morning, after several rounds of lovemaking, and sleeping in as long as they wanted, the newlyweds loaded their suitcases into Antonio's *Impala* and took off to the airport. They were taking the private jet to Venice, Italy, where they would be spending their three-week honeymoon. Although this was neither of their first time in

Venice, they both were in awe of the breathtaking views as they exited the plane.

Later that night, after a fancy, romantic dinner, the couple made their way back to their waterside flat. Antonio ran a hot bubble bath, and slowly undressed his wife, placing her in the tub before joining her in the water. Pouring two glasses of champagne, Antonio handed one to Cynthia and they clinked their glasses together before taking a sip. Setting her glass down, Cynthia cleared her throat, grabbing her husband's attention.

"Antonio, there is something I would like to discuss, now that we're officially married."

"Oh, of course. What's on your mind, Cynthia?"

"I wanted to discuss the topic of having children," she stated.

Antonio choked on his champagne and coughed for several seconds, trying to breathe. "My apologies, you just caught me off guard. Um, what about having children?"

Cynthia giggled and slid over onto his lap. "I want to know what your thoughts are on when you would like to start a family."

Thinking for a moment, Antonio squeezed her thigh. "I do want to have kids with you. I've always wanted to be a dad. I at least would like to wait a year. Even though we've been together for nearly two years, I know that there will still be plenty of adjustments as we figure out what it's like to not only be married but living together. Plus, I'm selfish and want you all to myself. After a year, though, I wouldn't mind trying."

Cynthia mulled over his words before responding. "I agree with wanting to wait until we have adjusted to married life. However, I think I may want to wait longer than a year. I'd like to graduate from college first before we grow our family. Is that ok?"

Antonio felt a small pang of disappointment, but it quickly dissipated as Cynthia adjusted herself on his lap, straddling him and pressing her body firmly against his own. "Whatever you want, you shall have, *Bel Fiore*. We can wait as long as you like, gives me more time to savor your body without having to share you with anyone else."

Relieved at his response, Cynthia kissed her husband softly, slowly, loving the way his breath hitched. She loved how he reacted to her touch and knew without a doubt that making love to Antonio Julius Moretti was her new favorite activity. "I love you, Antonio," she murmured against his lips.

"I love you, too, Cynthia," he replied, breaking their kiss and staring deeply into her eyes. The emotions she saw there left her speechless, and as he pulled her closer once more, all other thoughts quickly left their minds replaced with bliss.

Bad Reputation

The sun shone brightly as Antonio walked up to his parent's car, stepping lightly over the shattered glass. Peering inside, he saw his parents' lifeless bodies, the bullet holes in their foreheads the only thing marring their serene faces. Suddenly, Lorenzo opened his eyes and turned his head. "Antonio?" He asked.

Shocked, Antonio backed away from the car quickly. However, Carmella's voice soon called out to him, too. "*Figlio mio*, please, come back."

Unable to stop his feet from moving, Antonio soon found himself back at the driver's side door. His mother was smiling at him, her eyes beaming with pride. Lorenzo smiled kindly while gazing at his son, before stating with his signature grin, "I am so proud of the man you've become."

"You've grown so much! And gotten so handsome. We are so glad you married Cynthia. She's perfect for you," Carmella added.

"We've been waiting for you, Antonio," Lorenzo's voice took on a more serious tone. "What took you so long?"

"What do you mean, *Padre*?" Antonio asked, confused.

"You may have succeeded in avenging our deaths, *figlio mio*, but there are things you have yet to uncover," Carmella said softly.

"What did I miss?"

"Think, Antonio, think! Your mother and I were on our way to Portland. No one knew when we were leaving or what route we were taking, except for a select few of the mafia. How did the Silver Serpents know where we would be?" Lorenzo pressed.

Realization dawned on Antonio, and he felt chilled to his very core. "We have a rat," he whispered.

"Find them, Antonio. They must pay for what they've done," his father nodded. "I love you. This will be hard, but you can do it, my son."

"I love you, my sweet boy. Remember, you can only trust so many people. Be careful," his mother added.

With those final words, Lorenzo and Carmella once more locked hands and turned their heads. Then they became still. "*Mamma*? *Padre*?" Antonio cried but did not receive any sort of response.

No no no! I can't lose them again! Reaching into the car, he shook his parents, but they were ice cold. Unable to stay on his feet any longer, Antonio collapsed to the ground and screamed.

"Antonio! Antonio, wake up!" A frantic, feminine voice called out through the darkness.

Opening his eyes, Antonio found himself sitting bolt upright in bed, cold sweat running down his body, and Cynthia hugging him from the side as best as she could. He drew in several ragged breaths as his body shook, and as his heart rate calmed down, several sobs left his mouth. Even though he now realized it had all been a dream, the pain of losing his parents once more was still very, utterly real.

"My love, what happened?" Cynthia asked, voice full of concern as she removed her arms and moved around on the bed until she was sitting and facing him.

"I dreamt of my parents," Antonio croaked before

explaining every single detail and word of his dream turned nightmare. "I think they're right, though. It never occurred to me that there was no way those bastards should have known where my parents were heading and where they would be. Cynthia, the Black Death Mafia has a rat. A rat that has been under my nose for six years!"

Gasping, but trying to keep her emotions in check so she could comfort her grief and rage-filled husband, Cynthia gently placed her hands on his chest and pushed him slowly back into a lying position. Climbing on top of him and straddling his hips, she bent down towards him until their faces were inches from each other, and she was staring directly into the warm brown eyes she loved so much. "Then what are we going to do about it?"

"I don't know. First I need to—" he started, but was cut off when Cynthia placed a finger on his mouth, shushing him.

"I didn't ask what are *you* going to do. I asked what are *we* going to do," she emphasized.

Cocking his head slightly, Antonio gazed deeply into the green orbs that always captivated him. "I thought you didn't want anything to do with that part of my life, *Bel Fiore.*"

Cynthia sat up a little and took a deep breath. "I know what I said... but Antonio, you're my husband. I'm going to stand by your side and do whatever I can to help you. For most things, I won't get involved, but this is serious. I want to be involved. I need to be involved. Those bastards took away my mother and father-in-law, and even though we were young, I loved your parents. They were so kind to me."

Antonio didn't think it was possible to fall harder for the woman who was now his wife, but in that moment, he did. Tearing up, he rasped, "I don't think you realize how much that means to me. I love you so much."

"I love you, too. Now, how about we get the crew together in the morning? And for tonight, let me help you forget about everything," Cynthia murmured, running her hands along his chest as she bent back down and placed a heated kiss on his lips.

With a throaty growl, Antonio pulled her down against him and flipped them over. He loved the fact that her body instantly reacted to his, her fingers lacing his hair. Even though he'd just come to a major realization, all thoughts left his mind as she moaned against his lips. *Yes, everything can wait until morning.*

The following morning, Cynthia locked the door behind her as everyone shuffled into Antonio's office. Antonio sat at his desk while Margaret, Everett, Edward, and Priscilla took a seat on the couches. Cynthia sat on the edge of her husband's desk and smiled softly at everyone. As Antonio took a deep breath to explain the situation, a soft knock came at the office door. Scrunching her brow, Cynthia walked back over and opened it to find Emily standing nervously outside.

Stepping into the room, Emily put her hand up and said, "I know I've said I want nothing to do with the Black Death Mafia, but I could tell by Antonio's voice that something is dreadfully wrong. So, if you'll let me, I'd like to be here."

"Embug, you're welcome anytime, you know that. Thank you, I appreciate you coming," Antonio grinned. Once more taking a deep breath, Antonio decided to just drop the bomb on them. "We have a rat."

A gasp went through the group as they stared at him. "Come again?" Everett asked, hoping that he'd heard wrong.

"The Black Death Mafia has a rat," Antonio repeated.

"How did you come about that?" Margaret asked, with concern all over her face.

Even though he felt slightly silly, Antonio explained most of his dream from the night before to everyone, and how the more that he thought about it, the more the conclusion that they had a rat rang true. "Everett, as my father's right-hand man, you would know more about who would have known about my parent's travel plans. Would you please comb through our people and bring me the names of everyone in charge of their guard detail?"

"Of course. I'll bring the files over this evening from my house," Everett nodded, determination in his eyes as he set his mouth in a hard line. It had also never occurred to him that a rat in their organization could have been the cause of his best friend's death.

"Margaret, once I have the names, please discreetly interview the wives. See if they suddenly came into more money or something after my parents' deaths."

"You got it."

"Priscilla, once we get the files, I need you to find everything about these people. Who are their family members, where have they traveled to, and what houses have they lived in? Shit, even who their dentists are."

"No stone will be left unturned, *Fratello*."

"Edward, I need you to keep your ear to the ground with the members. I assume they talk more when I'm not around. Also, discreetly ask questions."

With a sly grin on his face, Edward replied, "Those fuckers won't be able to hide for long."

"Emily, since you have agreed to help us, I need you to use your unique skills. Any and all records of the members your father gives us, and the known leaders of the Serpents, I need. Criminal records, bank statements, transcripts, everything."

"I'll get everything you need," Emily stated, her eyes twinkling.

"And do I just sit here and look pretty?" Cynthia asked, knitting her brows together as she crossed her arms.

"Of course not, *amore mio*. I need your help digging through all of the paperwork. Since you are going to school for business management, you are trained to look for certain details. I need your eyes to help me find pieces of information that I am likely to miss myself."

Seeing that Cynthia was satisfied with his answer, he concluded their meeting. "This investigation needs to remain completely confidential. Nothing we have spoken about leaves this room, not that you guys need to be told that."

When everyone left, Antonio sat back down at his desk and started going through some things. Still seated on the desk, Cynthia swung around to face her husband. "You know, I seem to recall you told me you'd take me on this desk someday. We've been married for two months and it hasn't happened yet," she mused.

Startled, Antonio immediately looked up and swallowed hard when he saw the heated look in her eyes. "You know I'm not one to make a promise I don't keep. Are you saying you want to do that now?"

"Yes. Yes, I am. I don't see any reason not to. Besides, there's nothing else you can do about our situation until Everett brings the files over. So, how about it?"

"Who knew you had this side to you," he chuckled as he stood up and made his way to the door to lock it once more.

"I did," she smirked. "I just did my best to keep it hidden. Though, having you as my boyfriend made it extremely difficult to remain chaste. Oh and by the way, do you want to hear a secret?"

"Of course," Antonio said as he cocked his head and paused unbuttoning his shirt.

"I'm not wearing any underwear," Cynthia whispered slyly.

Antonio's eyes nearly fell out of his head as his jaw dropped to the floor. It only took a couple of seconds for the rest of his clothing, followed by hers, to end up on the ground. "I love you, *Bel Fiore*," he murmured against her lips as he gently laid her back on his desk.

"I love you, too," she replied breathlessly as she lost herself in her husband once more.

Later that evening, the crew met up once more, but this time at the Sommerset household where Margaret had prepared a large meal; she believed that the best work was done on a full stomach. Since her husband was the son of Norwegian immigrants, she had perfected several Norwegian dishes. For this evening's meal, she had chosen to make her husband's favorite dish, *Fårikål*, a hearty stew packed with sliced lamb, cabbage, and peppercorn. On the side, she served boiled potatoes topped with parsley. When everyone had arrived, she had stated that no work matters were to be discussed until everyone had eaten their fill, which no one complained about.

"Would anyone like any more *Fårikål*?" Margaret asked.

Everyone shook their head, except for Everett, who loaded his bowl up with his third portion of stew. "Don't mind me, we can start discussions now. Emily, will you please pass these files to Antonio?"

Nodding, Emily took the stack of files her father handed her and passed them to Antonio who took them and began thumbing through them. "So it looks like the men on my parents' guard detail were Robert, Trent, Tahir, Jeremiah, Roy, Grant, Zachary, and Michael. One of these eight men betrayed *la famiglia* and we are going to find out who. We will start by looking into Zachary since at the time, he was the newest member of the detail. Thank you for getting these together for me, Everett."

Priscilla and Emily were both writing down the names of each man, and Cynthia took her turn thumbing through the files, confirming their last names and date of birth for them. "Tahir and Zachary aren't married, so that whittles my interviews down to six," Margaret mused as Cynthia handed her the files. "However, I'll see about talking to their mothers, who seem to still be living."

"My dad and I will be keeping our ears to the ground, and will report anything suspicious we pick up on," Edward added.

"Great. Thank you all for your help. I don't think I could get through this without all of you. I say we meet in a week here to discuss our findings, if that's alright with you, Margaret, and Everett?" Antonio asked. "It will seem less suspicious to meet here than at my place if any of the members take notice."

"That is perfectly fine with us, sweetheart," Margaret smiled. "Now, don't any of you move. I made some fresh *krumkake*[92] and *fattigman*[93] for dessert."

"Oh my!" Cynthia exclaimed as Margaret and Emily returned to the table with the traditional Norwegian desserts. "I think I'm in heaven."

"I second that!" Priscilla agreed as she licked the powdered sugar off of her fingers before grabbing a second *fattigman* cookie.

Everyone laughed and dug into their dessert before discussing some different strategies. Even though the topic of discussion was both serious and treasonous, Antonio was glad he had all of these people on his team that he could count on. *Don't worry, Mom and Dad, I'll catch the fuckers who took you from us.*

When Antonio, Cynthia, and Priscilla arrived back home, Priscilla excused herself and went upstairs to get ready for bed. Turning to his wife, Antonio softly kissed her forehead. "If you don't mind, Cynthia, I'd like to have a few moments to call Britt. I could use her advice as well. I'll meet you in bed before too long, *sì*?"

---

[92] Pronounced CRUM-cock-uh
[93] Pronounced FOUGHT-ee-mahn

With a smile, Cynthia hugged her husband and kissed him softly. "Take all the time you need. And give our sister my love." With that, she, too, headed upstairs for the night.

Feeling the weight of the world crash down upon his shoulders, Antonio trudged to his office and shut the door. Sitting down in his leather chair, he grabbed his phone and swiveled around to face the window. Dialing the familiar number, he placed the phone to his ear and waited for Britt to answer. He hoped she could help calm the storm brewing inside him in a way only a big sister could.

"Hello?" Came Britt's voice as she picked up the phone.

"*Ciao, Cerva!*" Antonio grinned, forcing as much cheer into his voice as he could muster.

"Hey, *Björn*," Britt greeted, "Why do you sound off? You're newly married, so don't tell me you already fought with Cynthia. If I need to get on a plane to set your ass straight, I will!"

Antonio chuckled then sighed heavily. "No, Cynthia and I are fine. But I appreciate the vote of confidence," he rolled his eyes.

"You know I have to give you a hard time. After all, that's how this sibling bond works, right?" Britt lovingly teased, before turning serious. "If you two are fine, then what's really going on?"

"I expect nothing less, sister. I had a bit of a dream last night which opened my eyes to a blaring problem that I've missed all of these years. Britt... we have a rat. We've had a fucking rat living under our noses for nearly seven years and it never occurred to me! I'm about to lose my goddamn mind!"

"*Jävel!*"[94] Britt cursed. "Who in their right minds would have thought to betray your parents?"

---

[94] Son of a bitch!

"I don't know. I'm so lost, *Cerva*. It never occurred to me that no one should have known where my parents were going or when. But the Silver Serpents did. The only people that knew were their guard detail. It's one of them. One of the eight men my father trusted with his life and saw as his brothers. I don't know what I'm gonna do."

Taking a moment to compose herself as warm, bitter tears fell down her cheeks, Britt finally asked, "How's the gardening going?"

Shaking his head, he chuckled. "It's going well, helping to keep the monster at bay. Though, since the discovery this morning, I haven't been out there. It's taking a lot to keep my composure and not destroy things."

Normally a lady of even composure, Britt briefly entertained the darkness hidden deep within her heart. "That's good to hear, *Björn*. However, it sounds like you really could use better *fertilizer*. And while I don't wish to witness the mulching process, I do hope you will let me know once the new blooms begin to grow with the new brand of fertilizer." Clenching her fists, she continued, "In fact, I think that special blend would be perfect to grow flowers to put on your parents' graves. Then show the loved ones of the *förrädare*."[95]

Antonio paused for several moments, crinkling his eyebrows at her words. "Alright, one, are you talking in code because *mio nipote* is around? And two, how have I known you for this long and you haven't revealed this darkness to me, *Cerva*? You want to come help me out yourself?"

Britt laughed as she smiled down at her son while speaking into the receiver. "Glad to see you catch on quickly, *Björn*. Logie bear is taking a nap across my lap. And as for the truth behind the words, I guess I've just had it locked away

---

[95] betrayers

deep inside. Your parents were so precious to me, and… to think someone would betray the kindest, most selfless people in the world? My brain literally can't comprehend it. I won't be helping you in the garden, since it sounds like a messy task, but know that I love you and support you fully."

"What did I do to deserve a big sister like you? Thank you, Britt. I don't know if you realize how much that means to me. Can I admit something?"

"Of course!"

"I'm scared. Scared shitless. I look at each of these men as an extension of my family. I know what I have to do, but how am I supposed to look into the eyes of someone I'm so close to and know that they betrayed me, and take their life? I'm not sure if I'm strong enough…" "Björn, do you remember why I decided to call you by this nickname?"

"I like to think it's because I'm really just a big teddy bear and I give the best hugs," he chuckled.

Laughing warmly, Britt continued, "While that is very true, the real reason I gave that name to you is because of your unwavering strength. Bears are great protectors, and my dear brother, true strength and bravery never come when it is easy. Instead, it comes in the moments that truly measure a man's worth. When they made their choices, they removed themselves as family. Remember the mailman after all."

Antonio coughed, trying to make the tears in his eyes go away. "*Grazie.*[96] You always know just what to say to help calm my soul. I love you, *Sorella maggiore.*[97] Give Cade and Logan my love."

Britt promised she would before asking him to return the affections to Cynthia and Priscilla as she ended the call.

After hanging up, Antonio sat at his desk for several

---

[96] Thank you
[97] big sister

minutes staring at the pictures of the eight men that he had trusted for so many years, wondering which smiling face had stabbed him in the back, and made the monster inside of him come alive. Robert had been with the mafia the longest, so he very much doubted that he was the rat, though he couldn't imagine any of these men being the rat. Trent was someone that he'd always been able to count on, and he was rather quiet, always watching.

Tahir, a self-proclaimed heartless son of a bitch from Egypt, had been his father's go-to man for torturing enemies for information. However, when it came to his mother, there was nothing the man wouldn't do. Antonio knew that getting information out of his mother would be the best option. He also knew that they would need to tread carefully with Tahir because although he was loyal to the Black Death Mafia, he had ties to other criminals and the money to make them do his bidding should he feel slighted.

Jeremiah was a bit of a loose cannon, but fiercely loyal. He grew up in the projects on the bad side of Los Angeles, and his first taste of death came when the local gang murdered his pitbull, EJ, whom he had raised since he was a puppy that had been rejected by his mother. He'd only been 10 years old at the time but was hellbent on revenge. Lorenzo had caught Jeremiah snooping around the warehouse, trying to learn how to shoot, and had taken him under his wing. Together, they figured out where the people responsible for the death of his dog lived, and they taught the gang a lesson or two. Since then, Jeremiah had completely given himself over to the Black Death Mafia and was living the high life.

Roy was a former MMA fighter who'd joined the Black Death Mafia after discovering that one of his fights had been staged by a rival mafia and he had no choice but to lose. When Antonio was a small child, Roy had always taken the time to teach him how to fight. It was because of Roy that

Antonio was a good fighter and knew when he needed to control the urge to knock someone out. He had taken a lesser role about a year after Lorenzo and Carmella had been killed to focus on raising his own children, which Antonio could not fault him for.

Grant had become a member at the same time Robert had, but had spent several weeks here and there laid up in the hospital as a consequence for protecting Lorenzo. However, he had a rare condition in which he didn't feel pain, which was not always a good thing. Lorenzo had always made sure that whatever injuries he sustained while on the job were treated thoroughly, and that he had more than enough time to heal.

Michael, one of the Black Death Mafia's elite assassins, was a bit of a paradox. When he wasn't working, he was extremely loud and rambunctious, always calling attention to himself. However, when he was on the job, he was quiet and stealthy, his target never realizing he was there until it was far too late. He hailed from Cleveland, but the LA life called to him, so he traveled to the big city when he was 19. One cloudy night, Lorenzo was chasing a rival mob leader through some back alleys when a shot rang out, dropping the man in his tracks. Michael stepped out of the shadows, pistol still smoking, and asked to join. He'd been a part of the mafia ever since.

Last but not least, was Zachary. He was their undercover spy in the drug scene, making sure that no members were using, and that their territory wasn't being overtaken by rivals. Originally from Detroit, Zach made the move to LA after his girlfriend left him and took the kids, claiming he was too weak to care for them. After stealing a car, he traveled cross country to Los Angeles, where he made the mistake of attempting to break into Lorenzo's car while it was parked outside of Moretti Industries. He'd been caught and thrown into the warehouse, and when Lorenzo came to deal with him, he saw something in Zach that made him hesitate. Offering him a second chance, Zach wholeheartedly threw himself into mafia life, quickly becoming one of the most dependable men around Lorenzo. Within two years, Lorenzo had also helped him get custody of his kids, who were loving their new life in California.

Groaning, Antonio ran a hand through his hair in frustration and defeat. He hoped they would be able to solve the mystery of who the rat was quickly, as he didn't know how long he could take the feeling of dread and rage that had rooted itself in the pit of his stomach, and the back of his mind. After staring at the files for far too long, Antonio finally stood up and drug himself upstairs where he found Cynthia sound asleep in their bed. Slipping in beside her, he pulled her against his chest and succumbed to the darkness of sleep.

Working for the Weekend

February 14, 1990

Antonio, Cynthia, and Priscilla quietly snuck into the Warren household early in the morning to surprise Logan for his sixth birthday. Even though it was a Wednesday, Cade and Britt had decided to keep their son home from school so he could make the most of his time with his *zio* and *zias*. Knowing the special tradition that Dianne had started with Britt, which was making her own mother's homemade Swedish pancakes, Cynthia and Priscilla made their way to the kitchen to get started. While Britt would normally make the pancakes for Logan's birthday, the two Moretti women wanted to do it so she could sleep in a little longer.

Britt had left the recipe out on the counter for the trio, though Antonio wasn't sure he would be of much help. However, once he glanced at the recipe, he realized there was something that he could do. While Cynthia and Priscilla got to work on the batter, Antonio started making the lingonberry syrup. Whenever he spent time with his Oregon family, he always looked forward to the syrup that Dianne made from scratch, and he would eat it with anything. Dianne would always laugh at him because he would put it on pancakes, toast, crackers, cookies, pretty much anything.

Before long, breakfast was ready, and Britt and Cade sleepily made their way into the kitchen. They were both ambushed with hugs, which caused them to laugh merrily. A few minutes later, Logan woke up, and still half asleep, followed his nose to where everyone was waiting for him in the dining room. "Happy Birthday Logan!" Everyone yelled, startling the boy so much that he dropped his favorite stuffed teddy bear and well-worn, small blue quilt that he carried around with him in the mornings.

"*Zio! Zietta* Priscilla! *Zia* Cynthia!" Logan squealed happily, eyes wide as he caught sight of his loved ones, completely surprised that they were in his home.

"*Buon compleanno, nipote!*" Antonio exclaimed, scooping Logan up into his arms and hugging him tight. "Are you surprised?"

"Yes!" The boy exclaimed, his messy red hair falling into his deep blue eyes as his uncle twirled him around.

"Alright, alright. *Patatino*, give me my son please," Britt giggled, taking her son into her arms and showering him with kisses.

"Oh my goodness, Logie Bear! You grew so much already! You're going to be as tall as me soon!" Priscilla exclaimed.

"How much has he grown since November?" Cynthia asked as the group sat down at the table to eat breakfast.

"Five full inches!" Cade grinned, ruffling Logan's hair.

Antonio whistled sharply before grinning at Logan, "I think you're going to be taller than me someday, Logan!"

Logan puffed out his chest and flexed his arm, "I'm gonna be taller and stronger, *Zio!*"

Throwing his head back, Antonio barked out a laugh and everyone at the table joined in. "You very well might be."

The rest of the day was filled with love and full of fun. Logan got several presents, and the Moretti clan soaked up every second they spent with their Alsup/Warren family.

Cynthia loved watching her husband with his family. While he was always himself with her, she noticed that when he was around his Oregon family, he was much more carefree. It was like the mafia side of him ceased to exist, and the worries he carried on his shoulders were left back at the border of California and Oregon. For a split second, Cynthia wished that things could be like this all of the time. But no sooner had the thought crossed her mind than she dismissed it. She loved every part of her husband, even the darkest parts of his soul. For now, though, she reveled in the carefree moments.

The following afternoon, once Logan had returned home from school, Antonio, Cynthia, and Priscilla bid their farewells to Britt, Cade, and Logan, then headed to the airport for their flight home. As they touched down in Los Angeles, Antonio sighed as he felt the weight of the burden he was carrying settle back on his shoulders. While it had only been a few days since he realized they had a rat, it felt like it had been an eternity and that they would never figure out who it was. Shaking the notion from his head, he set his jaw and resolved to spend every free moment he had trying to figure out who had betrayed his family.

So far, Everett and Edward had nothing to report, but that was to be expected, as it was unlikely that anyone would freely speak about treason. Priscilla was still working on finding out everything about the eight suspected men, and Emily hadn't managed to gather all of their records yet. Margaret had invited the wives and mothers of the men to a brunch, but she had nothing suspicious to report. However, Cynthia had yet to go over all of the files with him, as she was trying to get ahead in her classes so she could devote her attention to the task at hand.

Seeing that something was bothering her husband, Cynthia pulled Antonio into his office when they got home to talk to him. "Antonio, what's on your mind? Your whole mood shifted the moment we touched down."

Sinking onto the leather couch with a sigh, Antonio rubbed his face tiredly. "I know it's only been a couple of days, but I feel like we should have caught the rat by now. It's completely irrational to feel that way because I know whoever betrayed us must have thoroughly covered their tracks, but I feel like I've failed my parents. I feel so guilty because it never occurred to me that we had a traitor. I just… I just want to solve it and get it over with."

"These things take time, and we have no experience dealing with this kind of problem. But we will figure it out, Antonio. We'll figure it out together. There is no reason to feel guilty. You were only 13 for fucks sake. You're not failing your parents, you're making them proud. Would you like to go through the files right now? It's still early and I don't have any homework to do right now."

He nodded, and with a smile, Cynthia walked over to his desk, picked up the files, then plopped down beside him on the couch. Licking her thumb, she began going over each piece of paper in each file, her eyes scanning the documents with a keen focus. "Hmmm," she mused. "Babe, look at this."

"What are you referring to?"

"Your father kept meticulous records for each day his men worked or took days off for both Moretti Industries and the Black Death Mafia. Everett included their work records from the year your parents were killed and the previous four years. Most of the men took a day or two off here and there, but look at Robert's records. It looks like starting about a year and a half before your parents were killed, he took every Tuesday off. The notes for those days off simply say 'appointment.' Do we know where he was going?"

Taking the document from his wife's outstretched hand, Antonio leaned forward and scrutinized the record. "Very strange. I don't recall Robert ever having any medical issues.

He always passes his physicals. Unless he's seeing a therapist, I don't know what kind of appointment he'd be having. We need to look into this more."

"What are you feeling right now?" Cynthia asked pointedly.

"Confused, worried, angry. I've got a mixture of emotions running through me. After Everett, Robert was the man my dad trusted most. He's been with us the longest, save for Everett who grew up with my dad. If he betrayed us... I don't know what I'm going to do. I've trusted him my whole life. If it's him, why would he do it? What did he gain?"

"Well, that's what we're going to find out. Why don't you go spend some time and tend to your garden, my love? I'll start on dinner, and I'll come grab you when it's ready. Okay?"

Setting the documents down, Antonio pulled Cynthia onto his lap and kissed her passionately. "I don't know what I'd do without you, *amore mio*. Thank you."

"You don't need to thank me. We're a team. Now go on!" She giggled, kissing him once more before hopping off of his lap and sashaying to the kitchen.

Unable to help himself, Antonio whistled as he stared at her backside as she walked away, and he grinned when she laughed down the hall. Shrugging on a jacket, he went out the back door and made his way to the greenhouse. Once inside, he felt a sense of peace settle over him as he hung his jacket on the coat tree and rolled up his sleeves. While most people tended to wear gloves when gardening, Antonio loved the feeling of the warm soil in his bare hands. His tiger lilies and rose bushes were thriving, which made him smile proudly. He trimmed some dead stems and flowers off, then removed the few weeds that somehow made their way into the greenhouse.

There was one large planter that was empty, as the vegetables he'd grown during the summer had all been harvested and either eaten, canned, or frozen. Rummaging around in the seed drawer, Antonio pulled out a bag of Stargazer Lily bulbs. With a happy grin on his face, he cleared the planter out and dumped a new bag of soil inside, mixing in some fertilizer as well. Then he carefully planted eight Stargazer bulbs. They would bloom just in time for Mother's Day, and he would personally deliver a bouquet of them to Britt, as they were her favorite flower.

Moving over to another planter, Antonio stared off into space as he thought about what he should plant, and completely lost track of time. A half-hour later, Cynthia opened the door to the greenhouse to find her husband gripping the side of the planter, leaning forward, completely lost in his thoughts. "Whatcha thinking about?" She asked.

Startled, Antonio jumped and whirled around, his response causing Cynthia to laugh. "You scared me. Um, I was thinking about what I wanted to plant and then got lost down memory lane."

"Well, dinner is ready. Were they good memories?" Cynthia queried as she took her husband's hand and headed back towards the house.

"They were," he nodded.

"Do you want to tell me about them?"

Antonio smiled as he once more got a far-off look in his eyes. "I was five. *Padre* stayed home with Priscilla, and *Mamma* took me to the botanical gardens. She loved things like that. I remember running all through the place, pulling her along by the hand. There were so many different kinds of butterflies, of all different colors, and I remember being so in awe of them. I can still see her smile and hear her laugh as I took in everything. I loved both of my parents so much, but I loved those moments when I got *Mamma* all to myself. Shit, I miss her so much."

"I know, my love. I'm glad that you have those happy

memories, though. Maybe we could take Priscilla to the botanical gardens sometime. I've only ever been once, and I'd love to go again."

"Let's do it! Tomorrow. You, me, and Priscilla!" Antonio exclaimed, feeling giddy.

"Priscilla has school tomorrow. Why don't we go on Saturday," Cynthia giggled.

"Fine," he said, rolling his eyes. "I love you, *Bel Fiore*."

"I love you too. I hope you're hungry!"

"I know I am!" Priscilla yelled from across the room, a mischievous grin on her face. "If you two don't hurry up, I'm gonna eat all the food without you."

"Oh no you don't!" Antonio called back, running over and picking up his sister and mussing up her hair.

Saturday morning, the trio piled into Antonio's *Impala* and made their way to the Los Angeles botanical gardens. As they entered the building, they all stopped to look around in awe. Even though it was February and chilly outside, it was hot and humid inside and all of the plants were green and vibrant. Tropical plants and flowers grew everywhere, and the sounds of gently flowing water, birds, and other small animals met their ears. Butterflies of all colors and sizes flitted through the air, some small, some as big as Antonio's hand.

Several butterflies landed on Antonio, and Priscilla pulled out her camera to take a picture. A curious lizard poked its head out of some bushes and stared up at them. Cynthia turned fully in a circle, and as she took everything in, all her cares and worries vanished. Loving the joyful look on his wife's face, Antonio took her hand and together they slowly made their way through the gardens. Priscilla, however, waited back a while to give them some space, but also for her own privacy. When her brother and sister-in-law were out of sight, two arms wrapped around her waist and turned her around.

"Jack!" Priscilla giggled as her boyfriend captured her lips and kissed her deeply.

"Hello to you too," Jack winked before kissing her once more.

The two had officially begun dating in November but were keeping it on the down low. Every spare moment they could find, they secretly saw each other, and Priscilla found herself falling head over heels in love with the older man. He seemed to feel the exact same way. "So, have you told your brother yet?"

"I was going to tell him tonight! He's going to be so proud of the fact that Stanford wants to sign me for both volleyball and basketball! Though, he'll be sad that I'll be moving to Stanford and won't be in L.A.," she replied with a grin.

"But that will make things easier for us until your birthday. I can't wait until you turn 18 so we don't have to hide anymore."

"I can't wait either. Come on, we better start making our way through the garden before Antonio comes looking for me."

The couple managed to avoid detection for the remainder of the time they were there, and before they got to the exit, Jack kissed her passionately before hiding in the shadows. Stepping outside, Priscilla found Cynthia and Antonio wrapped up in each other's arms, kissing almost hungrily. She fought the urge to roll her eyes and make gagging noises, but as she passed them, she teased, "Can y'all stop eating each other's faces so we can get some actual food?"

"I suppose," Antonio chuckled. "But I want to stop somewhere on the way first."

Driving into an upscale portion of downtown lined with five-star restaurants, Antonio pulled up in front of one of the restaurants and parked. Two men were standing on the balcony overlooking the street, a painter's sheet covering the sign above them. Cynthia and Priscilla climbed out of the car and followed Antonio to where he was standing, nearly below the balcony. Looking in through the windows, the women could tell the space had been recently renovated and it was very modern and fancy inside. All that it was missing were staff and customers.

"Hey, Boss!" One of the men called down with a grin.

"Hey, DeMarcus!" Antonio called back, with a grin equally as big.

"You ready for us to pull this?" Tyrone asked.

When Antonio nodded, the two men pulled the sheet down to reveal the restaurant sign. In an elegant peach font, with fluorescent light bulbs around the entire outline, read *Bel Fiore*. Cynthia gasped as she stared up wide-eyed at the sign, tears in her eyes. Priscilla was also speechless, and in unison, the two women turned to stare at Antonio who had the proudest smile on his face.

"Antonio, what is this?" Cynthia whispered.

"It's a bit late, but this is my wedding gift to you, *amore mio*. I know that you've dreamed of running and managing your own restaurant, which is why you are going to school for business management and hospitality. This restaurant is yours, to do with as you will," he replied lovingly.

"I don't know what to say! Thank you, my love! I love it so much!" She exclaimed, throwing herself into his arms and kissing him passionately while happy tears streamed down her face.

"You're welcome. Now, come. Inside are two Michelin five-star rated chefs that are waiting to blow our minds and hopefully get hired. Shall we?"

Antonio strode to the door and held it open wide for his two favorite women to walk through. Once inside, Cynthia gasped as she took in the interior of what was now her restaurant. The atmosphere had an air of modern Italian opulence blended with neoclassical designs found in angles and columns. Antonio had chosen the perfect color scheme that fit her tastes: stone white and rose gold. The flooring was an Axminster broadloom carpet in stone white, and an ornate, real crystal chandelier hung from the ceiling.

Cynthia was delighted to see that Antonio had chosen round, cafe-style tables with a polished peach wooden top and a white marble base. The contemporary-styled cushioned chairs were also stone white. As she looked up, she noticed intricate detailing on the ceiling in rose gold; rosy, calming light reflected off of it.

"Well, what do you think of *Bel Fiore, mio Bel Fiore*?" Antonio grinned down lovingly at his wife.

"I am beyond speechless. It's so beautiful, Antonio!"

"I'm glad you like it."

"I love it! But, may I ask why you chose white for the color scheme? White is kind of a hard color to keep clean."

Antonio shrugged, a smirk on his face. "You know I'm bougie as fuck."

Priscilla, who had just taken a drink of water out of her water bottle, spewed water all over her brother's back as she laughed. The action made Cynthia snort loudly, and she covered her face in embarrassment, though she couldn't stop giggling. Antonio, on the other hand, was using every last ounce of self control he had to keep from freaking out and losing his shit. He could tell his back was entirely soaked and his perfectly styled hair was no longer in place.

Taking a deep breath, he slowly turned around and walked toward the exit. "I'm getting a new shirt," He muttered through clenched teeth as he walked out the door.

"Whoops," Priscilla shrugged before taking Cynthia's arm.

Laughing, the pair made their way into the kitchen where the two chefs were waiting. Antonio joined them a few minutes later, a fresh, dry shirt on. Once he'd been seated,

Antonio introduced the chefs, Gregory and Judith Ricci, a husband and wife team. They were a sweet middle-aged couple who worked perfectly together. Gregory's specialty was all things sweet while Judith's was all things savory.

For their testing, the trio was served a refreshing Caprese salad. The couple had grown the tomatoes and basil in their personal garden and had acquired the fresh mozzarella from a local artisan. To top it off, the balsamic glaze was Gregory's own recipe. The pair also laid out a delicious charcuterie board, filled with cheeses, meats, and olives that were locally sourced; the crackers were made by the Riccis. For the main course, Judith served *Saltimbocca Alla Romana Con Torta Di Risotto*, which was scallopine of veal tenderloin, prosciutto, sage, sautéed spinach, a *vermentino* reduction, and an herb risotto cake. She poured a small taste of wine that paired perfectly with the dish.

To finish the meal, Gregory brought out his pride and joy, a slice of tiramisu, crafted from his family's generations-old, secret recipe. Cynthia let out a soft moan as she let the small bite she took melt in her mouth. "This is the most heavenly thing that has ever been in my mouth."

"Psh, I see how it is," Antonio muttered with a wink.

Priscilla choked on her bite, as she sent her brother a glare. "Could you please keep such comments to yourself! *Brutto figlio di puttana.*"[98]

"Language!" He replied, returning her glare. With a sigh, Antonio turned back to his wife and asked, "Well, what do you think?"

With a grin, Cynthia turned to the Riccis and exclaimed, "You're hired!"

---

[98] You gross motherfucker

Moretti The Making of a Mobster

Carry on Wayward Son

A knock at his office door broke Antonio from his thoughts as he was looking over reports from Moretti Industries. "Come in," he called out, without looking up. Someone slipped in and closed the door behind them, and came to stand in front of his desk. After a few moments of silence, Antonio finally looked up from his paperwork to find Emily fidgeting nervously with a manila folder.

"Hey, Embug, what's up?" He asked, noticing that her fair skin was much paler than usual. Her big blue eyes seemed to be brimming with tears that she was desperately trying to hold back.

Taking a deep breath to calm herself down, Emily straightened up and handed the folder to Antonio. "I found him. It's all here in his records," she said evenly, though her chin quivered.

Realizing what Emily meant, Antonio felt his stomach drop, and he swallowed hard. He carefully opened the folder and saw the name of the man who had betrayed his family at the top of the page: Robert Santoro. It felt like time stopped at that moment. Robert had been a part of the family for years. He had become Lorenzo's third, his left hand, when he had taken over as the leader. How could this man, who had been like an uncle to not just Antonio, but Priscilla, Edward, and Emily, betray them in the worst fathomable way?

He felt numb as he began going over all of the records that Emily had found on Robert. There was nothing to be said about his criminal history that Antonio didn't already know, nor were there any medical records that weren't available through Dr. Raymond, which they already had in their possession. On the days he was absent from work, labeled "appointment", there were no records of any appointments. However, the most damning thing that Emily found were bank statements. Not just any bank statements, but statements from an offshore account. It was not the account in which Robert was paid for his work at Moretti Industries, or for his role in the Black Death Mafia.

Each deposit lined up with each day Robert had an "appointment," for two whole years. They were $5,000 each, a substantial amount of money. Except for the last one. The last deposit Robert received was on May 5, 1983. Antonio swallowed hard once more, rage, confusion, and sadness welling up inside of him. It was the very day his parents had been murdered. That day, Robert received 2 million dollars, which set him up for life, yet, he hadn't even touched a penny.

And while all of that was damning in and of itself, it was the name of the person depositing the funds that was the icing on the cake: Casimir Szymański, the leader of the Silver Serpents. The one man who had managed to evade Antonio's wrath for the last nearly seven years. "What do we do now, Antonio?" Emily whispered, pulling Antonio out of his own head.

He gave her a small smile as he stood up, walked around his desk, and wrapped her in a hug. "Your work here is done, Embug. I will never be able to repay you for discovering who the rat is, but I am forever in your debt. I will take it from here. The next steps... are ones that you need not be involved in. Thank you, Emily."

"You owe me nothing, Antonio. I loved them too," she said softly, tears rolling down her cheeks. "I'll call my parents and let them know they're needed here, *sì*?"

Antonio nodded and followed Emily out of his office. She paused in the family room to use the phone while he made his way upstairs to find his sister. Knocking on her door, he waited until she called him in before entering. Priscilla was sitting at her desk working on her homework intently, chewing on the end of her pencil as she thought over her next answer. Looking up and seeing her brother's pained, pale face, she gently laid her pencil down and swiveled in her chair to face him better.

"What happened?"

"Emily found the rat."

"Who?" She gasped in a whisper.

"It's Robert..."

"No," Priscilla whispered, standing up, tears filling her eyes as she shook her head back and forth rapidly.

"I don't want to believe it either, but it's all there. He was meeting with Casimir for two years before our parents were killed, and getting paid each time. Obviously, whatever he was telling them, was worth a lot of money."

"How much were our parents' lives worth?" She snapped angrily.

"He received 2 million dollars the day they were killed."

"What the fuck!" Priscilla yelled as she stormed over to her closet and yanked the doors open. Clothing went flying as she mumbled angrily to herself. "*Farò a pezzi quel figlio di puttana, arto per arto, a mani nude.*"[99]

Her long, curly hair whipped around her face as she tore her hoodie off and pulled on her mafia gear over her tank top and shorts, strapping her favorite knives into their various sheaths along her body. Antonio watched her patiently, knowing she needed to get it out in order to carry out the task at hand with a clear mind. As clear a mind as she could have given the situation, anyway. With her gear all ready, she hastily put her hair up in a tight bun and whirled around to face her brother.

"I'm ready. Let's go feed this rat to the rats!"

"Slow down, *Sorella*. We need to have a clear head before we grab him. The Sommersets aren't here yet, and I can't do this without Cynthia's blessing. She should be home from school soon."

With a huff, Priscilla nodded in acquiescence and trudged downstairs to the living room where Emily was waiting. Taking a deep breath, Antonio decided to give the girls a few minutes to process together while he, too, donned his mafia garb. Before he headed downstairs to join the girls, Antonio carefully attached his holster to his belt and slid his beloved revolver inside. It took the lives of hundreds of Silver Serpent members, and today, it would take the life of the Black Death Mafia's betrayer.

Hearing the front door open, Antonio headed downstairs to find that Everett, Margaret, and Edward had arrived. He filled them in on what Emily had discovered, and they went over the plan of capturing Robert unaware and taking him to the torture room of the warehouse. Everett and Edward would be in charge of grabbing and delivering Robert, while Priscilla and Margaret gathered the rest of the bodyguard

---

[99] I'm going to tear that motherfucker apart, limb by limb, with my bare hands

entourage. They deserved to be involved in the Black Death Mafia's version of justice, too. Antonio would be waiting for everyone at the warehouse, ready to make the rat answer for his crimes against his family.

Once the plans were made, everyone split to go about their respective duties while Antonio waited for Cynthia to get home. She arrived about five minutes after everyone had left, the smile on her face vanishing in a second when she saw the look plaguing her husband. "You know who the rat is, don't you?" She asked.

"That obvious?" He replied, forcing a smile on his face, though it came out more like a grimace.

"I'm your wife. I know you. What's the plan?"

Antonio quickly filled her in, and took her hands in his, taking a deep breath. "This is something I need to do. But *amore mio*, I need your blessing first."

Standing on her tiptoes, Cynthia placed a gentle, loving kiss on his lips as she whispered, "You have it."

"I love you," he murmured as she embraced her tightly for a moment.

"I love you, too. While you guys do what you need to do, I think I should call the rest of the mafia in for a meeting. They deserve to know what's happened. I'll have everyone meet in the ballroom at Moretti Industries, and you guys meet us there when it's over. Alright?"

"Maybe you should be the boss instead of me," Antonio smirked before grabbing his mask and heading out the door to drive to the warehouse.

One moment Robert Santoro was sitting at his table eating dinner with his family, the next a sack was over his head before he was unconscious. The next thing he knew he was sitting in a chair, hands and feet bound, and the sack was being jerked roughly from his head. Squinting to get his bearings with a bright light aimed directly at him, it took him a moment to recognize his surroundings, and the tall, broad figure standing in front of him. The fear he'd felt quickly turned into relief as he playfully chuckled, "What the fuck, Antonio?"

No sooner had the words left his mouth than Antonio's fist slammed into his face. Shock blocked out the pain as Robert spit out a mouthful of blood and a tooth. "You don't get to call me by my name," Antonio growled. "It's Mr. Moretti or 'Sir.' Do. You. Understand?"

Eyes wide, the fear hastily returned to Robert. There was only one reason, and one reason only, why he would be in this position. They'd finally caught him. He swallowed hard, knowing that today was going to be his last day on earth. It was then that he noticed the four other figures surrounding Antonio. Shit, this is not good.

"Antonio, I didn't–" he was cut off as a knife slung through the air and took off the corner of his right ear. "He told you to call him Mr. Moretti or Sir! And you will keep silent until spoken to, motherfucker," Priscilla seethed through clenched teeth. He nodded quickly to indicate that he understood as blood poured from his ear down his neck.

"I am going to ask you some questions, and if you lie or answer incorrectly, Edward and Priscilla will take turns removing pieces of your body. Have I made myself clear?" Antonio stated evenly, with no hint of his fun, silly side in his voice. The monster had awoken, and awoken with a vengeance. His tone made Robert shiver, the hair on his body stand on end. Once again he nodded.

"Did you receive payments in an offshore account from Casimir Szymański for two years?" Antonio started.

"Yes," Robert whispered.

A knife flicked out from Edward's wrist and removed the

corner of Robert's left ear. "So we can hear you, *cagna*,"[100] Edward grinned.

"Yes," Robert repeated, louder.

"Were you paid on the day my parents were killed?"

"Yes, Sir."

"How much?"

"$100,000."

"Wrong answer," Antonio spat as his fist slammed into Robert's face once more. "I'm going to ask you again, and you best answer correctly. How much were you paid on the day my parents were killed?"

"$1 million," Robert choked, once more spitting out blood.

"Priscilla, pick a body part."

"With pleasure." Walking up to Robert, who tried in vain to shift himself away from her, she pulled out a scalpel and quickly removed his left ring finger, ring and all.

Robert's screams of pain echoed around the soundproof walls, but there was no pity to be found in this room. Margaret and Everett watched from behind the younger adults, they knew it was not their justice to take. But they would show no mercy to the one that had betrayed them all.

"How. Much. Were. You. Paid."

"$2 million!" Robert finally squeaked.

"Ah, so the rat can tell the truth. Did you give Casimir my parents' route to Oregon?"

"I did."

"How long were you under Casimir's employ?"

"One year."

"Edward, pick a body part."

With a wicked grin on his face, Edward stalked up to the bound man and kicked his right knee so hard, it shattered from the force of the impact. Once more, the room echoed

---

[100] bitch

with screams. "You should know by now that I always wear steel-toed boots at work," Edward said evenly when Robert's screams died down.

"I'm going to ask you again, and this time, you better answer honestly. My patience is wearing thin, and the monster inside of me thirsts for blood. Your blood. How long did you work for the Silver Serpents?"

"Two years! That's the truth!" Robert cried out in utter agony.

"What information were you feeding them?"

"Shipping schedules, supply lines, routes, anything they asked for, Sir."

"Why, Robert? Why did you cross us?"

"Casimir caught me one night and threatened to make my daughter the Silver Serpent's whore. They were going to keep her chained up in a room for their men to take their pleasure with whenever they wanted, day or night. I couldn't let that happen! She was only six years old, An–Mr. Moretti! I had to protect my baby," Robert sobbed.

For a brief moment, a small wave of sympathy washed over the group, but it dissipated quickly. Taking a step closer to Robert, Antonio stared down at him evenly. "You didn't have to. You know you could have gone to my father and he would have taken care of the issue. Why didn't you?"

"They were watching me. Someone was always following me!"

"I know for a fact that you, Everett, and my father had a code. You only had to say the code and he would have known something was wrong. But you chose not to. Why?"

He knew it was a mistake, but Robert laughed anyway. His laughter earned him another strike to the face, and his left eye immediately began to swell because of it. "I may have been third in command, but Lorenzo would never have paid me like Casimir did. It was financially beneficial to me. My family will never want for anything."

"That's where you're wrong, Robert," Antonio chuckled, a wicked grin gracing his face. As we speak, Emily is transferring the funds from your offshore account into a new account under a name they do not know. All they will have is whatever you have saved from working for us. After that, they're on their own."

"You monster! You'd have my daughter go without?!" Robert yelled.

"You had Priscilla and I orphaned. We've grown up without our parents. I'm not completely heartless. I'll make sure your daughter is never homeless or hungry, but they will not be getting that blood money. That belongs to Priscilla and me."

The pain from his wounds was becoming unbearable at that point, and Robert knew it was only a matter of time before he succumbed to the darkness of unconsciousness. He willed it to come faster, so he no longer had to deal with the pain and torture that he knew had yet to be inflicted.

Ice-cold water hit him and broke him out of the trance he was slipping into. "Ah ah ah, no you don't. We aren't done with you yet," Priscilla purred.

Robert's eyes widened in surprise as Trent, Tahir, Jeremiah, Roy, Grant, Michael, and Zachary filed into the room. Each of them held a close-up photograph of Lorenzo and Carmella from various stages of their autopsies. He closed his eyes tightly; he didn't want to see the dead faces of the man and woman that had treated him like family, whom he had sold to the enemy to be killed. He was a coward, after all.

"Look at them!" Antonio's voice boomed. Edward came around and jerked Robert's head up, hot gluing his eyelids open.

Robert screamed once more, but there was nothing he could do. The blank eyes of Lorenzo and Carmella stared back at him. Their flesh flayed open as the medical examiner did his work. A close up of the bullet wounds in their heads. "You did this, Robert. You caused this. And for that, you will pay with your life."

Each man in the guard gently set their pictures down and took turns yelling at Robert and hitting or stabbing him, making sure none of their aims were fatal. By the time Antonio cleared his throat to indicate they should stop, Robert was unrecognizable. Both of his eyes were swollen shut, blood pouring out of too many wounds to count. After managing to quell his screaming and spitting out yet another mouthful of blood, Robert muttered, "Carmella was a whore anyway."

With a roar that surprised everyone in the room, Priscilla grabbed a rusted stake off of a table, marched up to Robert, and shoved it up into his rib cage diagonally, piercing one of his lungs and who knew what else. Leaning in close, she growled, "You keep my mother's perfect name out of your fucking mouth!" With that, she twisted the stake. Robert couldn't shoot back a retort, for his breathing was shallow and difficult.

Backing away, Priscilla nodded at her brother, who in turn lifted his beloved pistol out of its holster and aimed it toward the center of Robert's forehead. "*Addio topo.*"[101] With those words, he pulled the trigger once, the bullet piercing the very center of Robert's forehead, blood, and brain matter flying as he was instantly killed. Turning around to face his loyal companions, Antonio mused, "You know, Santoro means 'feast of all the saints.' Turn him into a feast for his patron saint: the rat."

With that, everyone in the room raised their gun and unloaded on the battered corpse until they had no

---

[101] Goodbye rat

ammunition left. What remained could not be identified as being formerly human. The cleaning crew would dispose of the remains somewhere they knew he would never be found, and would, in fact, be devoured by hordes of rats.

Half an hour later, Antonio strolled into the ballroom at Moretti Industries headquarters, followed by his 11 companions. Every member of the Black Death Mafia that was in Los Angeles was gathered inside, and the room fell silent as they made their way to the stage. Cynthia bowed her head toward her husband as he walked up, then moved to the back. All eyes were on him as he cleared his throat. He knew they were all a sight, not having bothered to clean up following the execution, but he didn't care.

"Thank you all for meeting me here on such short notice. I know I've interrupted your evenings, and for that, I apologize. However, I would not be a very good leader if I did not share with you the events of the past few weeks that culminated in the execution of one of our own this very evening."

Several gasps could be heard, and everyone seemed to lean in closer, wondering who could have been killed and for what reason. They only had to wait a moment longer to find out. Antonio took a deep breath and began once more.

"It occurred to me, a few weeks back, that we had a rat in our midst. I came to this conclusion because no one, especially the Silver Serpents, would have known the route my parents were taking to Oregon to visit *la nostra famiglia*.[102] The only people that knew, aside from my parents, were their guard detail. As you can see behind me, all of them are here but one. Everett, Margaret, Edward, Emily, Priscilla, Cynthia, and I have spent the past few weeks discreetly investigating the guard detail."

---

[102] our family

212

He had to pause to take another deep breath, his body shaking from the adrenaline and all of the overwhelming feelings inside of him. Cynthia walked up beside him and gently placed her hand on his arm, hoping the small gesture would calm him enough to get through what he had left to say. She was right.

"The investigation, which brought us no pleasure, was a necessary evil that made me quite ill. After compiling indisputable evidence, we revealed that the traitor to our organization, and my family, was Robert Santoro. This evening, we brought him to the warehouse, interrogated him, and executed him. I know that this is a shock to all of you, as it was to me. What is done is done. My hope now is that all of us can heal and move on from this betrayal. You all are being given a week off to be able to process this news in whatever ways you need to. I will be unavailable tomorrow, but you all are welcome to stop by our home to talk with me if you feel the need. Now if you'll excuse me, I need to wash the remains of the rat off of me. But before I go, just remember: *la famiglia è tutto e tu sei la famiglia.*"

With those final words, Antonio stalked off the stage, unable to hear anything going on around him, though there was not much to hear as everyone was dead silent. He felt numb and stumbled a bit as he walked outside. Cynthia ran after him and guided him to her car, where she helped him into the passenger seat before hopping in and driving them home as quickly as she could. Priscilla had whispered to her during Antonio's speech that she was going to stay with Emily, to give them some time alone. When they pulled into the driveway, Cynthia led Antonio upstairs, through their bedroom, and into their bathroom. He hadn't said a word the whole drive home. Letting go of her hand, he blindly pulled off his shirt and pants, turned the water on in the shower, and stepped in where he immediately sank to the ground, knees to his chest, and began to sob.

Not knowing what else to do to help her husband, Cynthia stepped in and sank down beside him, clothes and all. She wrapped her arms around the much larger man as best she could and held him as he wept all of his feelings out. They stayed that way for hours, long after the water had run cold.

Before the Next Teardrop Falls

June 1990

The next couple of months went by quickly. While Antonio and Priscilla struggled to come to terms with the brutal betrayal and subsequent execution of Robert, there were also exciting times coming. It was June, and Priscilla was finally graduating high school. She was looking forward to finally being done and moving on to the next season of her life. In August, she would begin her college career at Stanford, where she had received a full-ride scholarship to play both volleyball and basketball for the Cardinals. However, one thing that she was not looking forward to doing was telling her brother that she was planning on stepping away from the Black Death Mafia unless her skills and expertise were absolutely necessary.

It wasn't that she hated her role or her life as one of the leaders of the BDM, she just wanted to focus on college, and her relationship with Jack Taylors. The two of them had been going strong for months now, and she was planning on moving in with him while she was attending Stanford. The thought made her blush, as did most thoughts pertaining to the man she had fallen in love with. They had many clandestine meetups, and she was surprised that her brother hadn't found out yet. She knew that if he had known, he would definitely have brought it up.

Stepping out of her bathroom and into her bedroom, Priscilla made her way over to her closet where the dress she had chosen to wear for graduation hung, ready to be worn, along with her cap and gown. For graduation, she had picked a gorgeous, black, fitted, off-the-shoulder silk evening gown. The asymmetrical hemline rested about two inches above her knees, and the color complimented her glowing, tanned complexion well. Deciding against wearing tights, she stepped into a pair of black heels.

She then quickly tamed her curly hair, which Jack lovingly referred to as her mane, then applied her makeup. Finally, she donned her silver graduation gown, which had a navy blue border, and her navy blue graduation cap with a silver tassel. A soft knock at her door broke her from her thoughts. "Come in!" She called.

"I can't believe you're graduating!" Cynthia exclaimed as she walked in and paused to take her sister in. "You look beautiful, *Sorella*."

"Thank you, Cynthia. I can hardly believe it myself!"

"Your brother and I got you something to wear this afternoon," Cynthia smiled as she handed Priscilla a small, wrapped box. "He's going to meet us there because something came up, but he wanted to make sure you got this before you left."

Loving that her brother was always so thoughtful, she quickly removed the wrapping paper and opened up the box. Inside, she found a beautiful pair of mint green diamond studs, set in silver, and bordered with small white diamonds. They were absolutely stunning. "Thank you," She whispered, throwing her arms around her sister-in-law, as tears welled up in her eyes.

"You're welcome. I'll leave you to finish getting ready, and

I'll see you when you walk across that stage," Cynthia replied as she made her way out of the room.

Priscilla donned the earrings and admired them in the mirror for a few moments before grabbing the last two pieces of jewelry she was going to wear to complete her look. The first piece was her mother's wedding ring, which now fit her right ring finger perfectly. Whenever she wore it, she always felt closer to her mother, and she had to brush a few stray tears away before they ruined her makeup. Finally, she placed the simple necklace with a mint green crystal around her neck that Emily had given her all those years ago after her parents had been killed. She wore it as a staple nearly every single day.

A few hours later, Priscilla walked across the stage and received her diploma. She had graduated with honors, and had declined to share the Valedictorian or Salutatorian spot, as she didn't want to give a speech, but had earned that right. Antonio surprised her with a huge bouquet of gardenias and honeysuckles from his garden when the ceremony was over, and she had to use his handkerchief to wipe the proud tears from his eyes. She spent the remainder of the evening traveling to various graduation parties with Emily, who had also worn her matching crystal necklace. The two girls shared their graduation party, which only lasted about an hour, as there were many parties to attend.

When she had finished party hopping, Priscilla met Antonio and Cynthia at *Bel Fiore*, where she was treated to a fancy, mouthwatering meal. Her brother produced a bottle of the most expensive champagne the restaurant carried and permitted her to have a couple of glasses with them in celebration. She felt extremely loved and almost forgot about her parents' absence on this important milestone.

July 9, 1990

It was finally Priscilla's 18th birthday. And while she was excited to finally be an "adult," she was also extremely nervous because she would finally be introducing Jack to her family. She was worried about how they would take the news, especially because of the age gap, but she hoped they would see how much they loved each other. Priscilla also prayed that her brother wouldn't take Jack's head off, because it wasn't out of the question.

To add even more to her nerves, it wasn't just Antonio, Cynthia, Edward, and Emily that she was introducing her boyfriend to. Her Oregon family had arrived the previous night to celebrate with her. They hadn't been able to make it for her graduation, so it was going to be a double celebration. She was beyond happy that they were all here, as any time spent with them was always so memorable and full of love; but she was worried about how they, too, would react.

Quietly, Priscilla made her way downstairs so that she could go pick up Jack from the airport. Part of the benefits of his job as a recruiter was that he racked up airline miles. It also helped that his brother worked for the airlines, so he could fly for nearly pennies. And for the past few months, he had been taking frequent flights to Los Angeles from Stanford. Priscilla paused outside of the sitting room where she could hear Antonio, Cynthia, Britt, and Cade visiting quietly. With a smile on her face, she grabbed her keys from the table in the entryway and made her way to the airport.

In the sitting room, the two couples lounged on the couches sipping their hot cups of coffee, as they basked in the stillness of the house and each others' company. Britt and Cade especially appreciated this time to spend with Antonio and Cynthia, because they could get in some adult talk before Logan woke up for the day. Though, Antonio had to basically be restrained from waking his nephew up.

"Quit pouting, *Björn*. We're going to be here for a few days, you can go without seeing Logan for another hour," Britt giggled, rolling her eyes at the childish display of annoyance on her brother's face.

In response, Antonio stomped his foot and stuck out his lip before giving his sister a wink. "I've gotta soak up all the time I can with him. Even though I'm not a parent yet, I know how valuable quiet time is. I'll restrain myself... For now."

Cynthia smiled as she watched their interaction, loving the way they teased each other. They may not have been related by blood, but their bond was stronger than any Cynthia had ever seen. She stifled a yawn as she brought her mug to her lips to sip more of her coffee. Since it was Priscilla's birthday, she and Antonio had woken up extra early to prepare her favorite, traditional Italian breakfast: *Maritozzi*. The dish consisted of a sweet bun split in half and filled with homemade, fresh whipped cream.

While Antonio was admittedly worthless when it came to baking, he made the most delicious whipped cream. It had just enough sweetness to satisfy a sweet craving but wasn't overly sweet where it would overpower whatever it was paired with. Cynthia, though, had mastered the sweet buns. The bread was light and fluffy, and most of them didn't make it till the end to be filled with whipped cream, as whoever was in the house while she made them would devour the buns by themselves.

Cade stretched his arms as he yawned before putting one of them around Britt and gently pulling her closer to his side. "I'm curious to see who this mystery person is that Cil is going to introduce us to."

Leaning lovingly into her husband, Britt mused, "Ya know, I'm curious too. For as long as I've known her, Priscilla hasn't shown any interest in dating anyone... Well, now that I give it another thought, it could be because *Björn* is only *slightly* overprotective."

Antonio opened his mouth to argue but a stern look from his wife made him close it just as quickly. "You most certainly are. Don't give me that look. Priscilla told me all about how you threatened a boy her sophomore year."

Smiling nervously, Antonio scratched his head as he recalled his sister's reaction to that incident. "Yeah... she almost cut my balls off for that. I'm not quite sure how I'd take her dating someone. She's my little sister."

"If it turns out she is dating someone, you will smile and welcome him warmly. Is that clear, my love?" Cynthia grinned coyly.

"Crystal," he gulped.

Trying not to laugh at Antonio's pained face, Cade remarked, "I just hope Logan behaves himself. Apparently, he's been getting into fights at school. He's only six, and when Blue and I asked him why he was fighting, he said it's because he doesn't like people who are mean."

Providing further explanation to a very confused looking Cynthia, and proud looking Antonio, Britt stated, "One of the new boys in his Kindergarten class last year moved from Cuba, and some of the other boys were making fun of him for only being able to speak broken English. Although his mom is American, they only ever spoke Spanish at home."

"Those little *stronzi*[103] are lucky they're just little kids, though I have half a mind to teach their parents a thing or two," Antonio stated through gritted teeth.

As if he knew he was being talked about, Logan strode quietly into the sitting room, dragging his well-worn blue blanket behind him. Instead of greeting his mother with a good morning snuggle like he usually did, he climbed up into his *Zio's* lap and got comfortable. Antonio placed a small kiss

---

[103] fuckers

on Logan's soft rose-red covered head before sticking his tongue out at Britt.

Before Britt had a chance to say a word in retort to the brother of her heart, the front door opened and Priscilla's sweet voice called down the hallway, "I'm home!"

Marcus and Dianne had filed in behind Logan and had barely taken their seats before Priscilla danced into the room, followed by a man that no one recognized. A much older man, everyone in the room noted. "Oh good, everyone's here!" Priscilla exclaimed with a broad smile on her face. "I'd like you all to meet my boyfriend, Jack Taylors."

Your what now?" Antonio asked, picking his jaw off the floor.

Priscilla glared at her brother, and Cynthia quickly resumed the conversation. "It's very nice to meet you, Jack. I'm Cynthia, Priscilla's sister-in-law. How long have you two been together?"

"Pleasure to finally meet my girl's family. We've been dating since September," Jack replied casually.

"Oh my, that's quite some time," Cynthia said, not really knowing what else to say.

"I kept it a secret because, well, Antonio," Priscilla rolled her eyes. "And because we have a slight age gap..."

"And what, pray tell, might that age gap be?" Antonio muttered, doing his best to control the rage building inside of him.

"Erm, 10 years."

"10 *YEARS*–" Antonio roared, standing up abruptly. However, a scathing look from both his wife and Britt cut him off and he swallowed hard, willing himself to calm down. Clearing his throat, he stuck out his hand to shake Jack's. "Excuse me, I'm Antonio. Priscilla's brother."

Picking himself up off the floor where he'd fallen in Antonio's haste to get off the couch, Logan gave the strange new man a brief once over before quietly walking up to him. While he tried to be on his best behavior, just like his parents had told him, Logan couldn't help but feel sick in his tummy just looking at the man standing by his precious *Zietta*. Now standing directly in front of this stranger, Logan really tried to be good, however, something inside overtook him, as he punched the man straight in the groin, and screamed, "Go away, you bad, bad man," before quickly scampering back between his father and *Zio*.

Unable to help herself, Priscilla started laughing hysterically, especially when she saw the look on Britt's face. Jack had doubled over, trying to catch his breath. He hadn't thought a child as young as that one could be so strong. Antonio grinned down at his *nipote*, his chest about ready to burst with pride. He almost said as much but thought better of it.

Doing his best to stifle his own laughter, Cade quickly ushered both Britt and Logan to the other room, in hopes of properly disciplining his son, but also encouraging him to trust his gut instincts.

Britt, on the other hand, was completely mortified. "Logan Asher Warren! I know I have raised you better than this. We do not treat someone's guest so rudely!"

Looking up at his mother with watery, deep blue eyes, Logan refuted, "He's bad momma! And scary!"

Bending down to comfort her son, Britt took a deep breath before she continued. "Baby mine, I want you to look at me, okay?" Having her son's attention once more, she continued. "Now, if you have a bad feeling about someone, you need to talk to daddy, or me, or some other adult you trust. You can't just go around assaulting people for the heck of it. People might let that behavior slide because you are the cutest little boy in the world, but you're gonna grow up. And as grown-ups, we have to face big, big consequences."

"Like time out?" Logan asked with as much seriousness as his little heart could muster.

"Like the worst time out ever," Britt concluded.

"Okay, momma. I'll be good. Do I have to say sorry though?"

"Are you sorry, son?" Cade asked.

"No!" Logan vehemently protested.

"Well, are you sorry you embarrassed Cil?" Cade proceeded to ask.

Thinking for a moment, Logan sighed heavily. "Yes. I hope I didn't make *Zietta* sad. Can I only apologize to her and not the bad man? You and momma said lying is bad. And if I say sorry when I'm not, isn't that a lie?"

Once again amazed at her son's intelligence and maturity, Britt admitted that he was right and he only needed to apologize to Priscilla.

When the trio returned to the sitting room, they found that Priscilla and Jack were nowhere to be seen. Seeing the confused look on their faces, Cynthia said softly, "Jack wanted to take Priscilla out for breakfast since it's her birthday today. So, it looks like we'll be eating the *Maritozzi* without them."

Britt took Logan into the other room and put some cartoons on the T.V. for him while he ate his breakfast and returned to the sitting room to see Antonio about to lose his mind. She'd never seen his face that red before. "*Quella madre fottuto figlio di puttana!*"[104] He roared, unable to contain himself any longer. He hated for his *Tant* and *Fabror* to see him like this, but he couldn't help it. "That man is way too old for her! I should break his fucking neck for ever touching my sister!"

"*Amore mio*, calm down," Cynthia tried to soothe him by

---

[104] That mother fucking son of a bitch

putting a hand on his arm but he shook it off.

"What the hell is she thinking?! He's a fucking pedophile in my book, and pedophiles are only good for one thing: rat food."

Clearing his throat softly, Marcus gently spoke up. "*Patatino*, I understand that you are scared and angry by this whole situation, mainly because it is beyond your control. When my *Älskling*[105] daughter first announced she had a boyfriend, it also came with that of a pregnancy."

Pausing briefly to look at his daughter and son-in-law, Marcus continued. "As you know, I am not an angry man, in fact, your father used to laugh all the time, saying I was blessed with the patience of all the saints. However, on that day, I actually wanted to... I wanted to kill Cade. In my eyes, as Britt's father, he stole something precious from her."

Taking another deep breath, Marcus paused while reaching for his wife's hand. "But my heart, she gave me the best advice possible. If I were to be too strict and harsh, it would only make things worse. I think we can all guess that I didn't listen, because I have often regretted forcing Britt and Cade to get married. They could have had a good life either way, but I often feel I forced my daughter to give up too much. So please, Antonio, be patient with your sister."

Antonio's body slowly relaxed and stopped shaking as he, too, took a deep breath. His eyes welled up with tears as he looked at his beloved aunt and uncle. "*Fabror, Tant*, I beg your forgiveness for my outburst. I will be as patient as I can be, I promise. I just love her so much, and anything with the potential to hurt her... needs to be destroyed, in my mind. I will heed your advice. I love you both so much."

In response, everyone in the room gathered around Antonio and hugged him tightly. He unashamedly let his

---

[105] Darling

tears flow because with them, went the last of his anger. It had been a long time since he had felt such a tangible love, and the group hug made everything seem less meek. After a solid two or three minutes, everyone headed into the dining room to enjoy their breakfast and a much-needed second cup of coffee as they awaited Priscilla and Jack's return.

When Jack and Priscilla came back to the house, with Emily and Edward in tow, everyone took the time to get to know Jack better. The one thing that eased Antonio's mind was that he had a good, solid job, with tenure, as the top recruiter for Stanford. Priscilla was in such a happy mood, and Logan's heartfelt apology for embarrassing her earlier made her giggle as she hugged him tightly and kissed his cheeks. She was beyond happy that everyone she loved was there for her birthday. Margaret and Everett also came by later that evening for dinner, gifting Priscilla a beautiful mint, black, and white patterned dishware set since she would be moving off on her own for college.

The rest of her birthday was filled with love and laughter, and she was glad to not be carrying the burden of a secret relationship anymore. Antonio was understanding of her wanting to step away from the mafia to focus on college, and encouraged her in living life the way she wanted. It made her heart both happy and sad at the same time. She knew that Antonio had never even explored what he might have liked to do with his life, and probably never even let himself think about it. He had just jumped into leading the mafia at the tender age of 13 because that was expected and needed of him. And the fact that he lovingly and happily encouraged her to focus on her own life, just proved how much he loved her. She couldn't wait to both start her classes and begin playing both of the sports she loved.

October 28, 1990

Priscilla swallowed hard as she stared down in disbelief at the two pink lines on the home pregnancy test she had taken minutes before. She had known that getting pregnant was a possibility, as she and Jack were never very careful, but she just never thought it would happen so unexpectedly. Especially with how much time and energy she was putting into volleyball. Practices were often over three hours long, and she had proved herself worthy of being a starter, so she played during most of every game. And before too long, she would be doubling up as basketball would start in November. A baby just didn't fit in her plans right now, even though she wanted nothing more than to be a mom.

But plans can change, right? Priscilla thought as she shakily placed her right hand on her flat stomach, a smile gracing her face as she thought about the baby growing inside of her. *Sports aren't everything. But this baby... they are everything.* Feeling herself calm down, she resolved to tell Jack the news as soon as he got home, and that she was going to step away from her obligations as part of the volleyball and basketball teams. Besides, it's not like she needed the full-ride scholarship she had received; she had more than enough money to cover any and every degree she ever wanted to get.

Hearing the front door open, Priscilla excitedly flew down the hallway to greet her boyfriend, a huge smile on her face. Her smile faltered, however, when she caught both sight and smell of him. He had very obviously spent his day drinking. Cautiously, as Jack didn't like to be startled when he was drunk, Priscilla made her way up to him. "Hey, baby. How was your day?" She asked, placing a soft kiss on his lips.

"It was fine," He retorted, kissing her back and then heading to the kitchen where he proceeded to open the refrigerator and pull out a can of beer. "Spent the day with my buddies, it's been a while since we just had a free day.

How was yours?"

"Oh it was good. I wasn't feeling well this morning, but I feel great now. Um, I have some news to share with you."

"Yeah?" He asked, his attention piqued.

Taking a deep breath, Priscilla smiled as she said, "I'm pregnant."

The mouthful of beer that Jack had just drank spewed out of his mouth in surprise at her statement. "What did you say?"

"I said I'm pregnant. We're having a baby!" She exclaimed.

In that moment, Jack's entire countenance changed. His eyes narrowed and darkened, his whole face contorting in an almost unnatural rage. He was seething. "Jack? What's wrong?" Priscilla asked, feeling a sense of fear come over her.

With only two quick strides, Jack was in front of her, and his fist flew out and landed squarely in her stomach. Priscilla doubled over in pain, shocked that he had just hit her. "What the fuck, Jack!" She yelled, only to receive a punch to the face.

"You stupid whore!" Jack roared. "Who the fuck said I wanted to have a kid?! We aren't having a baby!" He seemed to lose control of himself, becoming more of a monster than a human being. All Priscilla could do was try to shield herself from the barrage of blows she was taking all over her body, but mostly her abdomen. Jack picked her up and threw her to the ground as hard as he could, only to pick her up and throw her through the large window in the living room.

Priscilla screamed as the glass sliced her body, landing hard on the ground outside. Her body was in so much pain. Doing her best to get up, she tried to crawl towards her car, but Jack came outside and caught her by the leg, dragging her back. He began stomping on her abdomen, and Priscilla could do nothing but scream as she felt her ribs crack and darkness begin to seep in as she slowly began to lose consciousness.

She vaguely heard some yelling, then a car starting and peeling off. Soft, warm hands cradled her head as a woman's voice yelled to someone. As her world went dark, she heard sirens in the distance. And then everything went black.

When she woke up, she found herself in a hospital bed, all sorts of things hooked up to her. And she was utterly alone. Everything that had happened came crashing back and she started sobbing. A nurse rushed in, checking all of her vitals before gingerly taking her hand. "Priscilla? I'm Robin. Do you remember what happened or how you got here?"

Through her sobs, Priscilla nodded and replied that she did not remember coming to the hospital. Robin explained that a neighbor had called an ambulance and had brought her unconscious to the hospital. "Let me grab the doctor so he can explain the extent of your injuries. Is there anyone I can call for you? Family maybe?"

"No!" Priscilla yelled, then took a breath. "Please don't call my family. Um, call my friend Edward. His number is XXX-XXX-XXXX. Just tell him I need him."

Robin nodded and quickly left the room. A moment later, a kindly older man came in and offered her a comforting smile. "Hello Priscilla, it's so nice to finally make your acquaintance and see those beautiful brown eyes of yours. I'm Dr. Richardson. Let's get down to what happened this evening, yes?" He asked calmly.

Seeing the young woman nod, Dr. Richardson took a deep breath before diving into the extent of the injuries that tore his heart to shreds. "You came in with multiple lacerations all over your body, deep bruising to your tissue, and several broken bones, including five of your ribs. We had to operate on you to repair one of your lungs which collapsed. I am sorry to tell you this, you came in about four weeks pregnant, but due to the blunt force trauma your body received, the fetus did not survive. You are undergoing a miscarriage right now."

She didn't hear much else as numbness took over. Jack had done this to her. He had killed their baby. Her baby. She felt Dr. Richardson squeeze her hand encouragingly before he left the room. Then she just sat there in her bed in silence and disbelief.

In Los Angeles, Edward was panicking. He had received a call from a nurse from a hospital in Stanford and all she would tell him is that Priscilla had been in an accident and she needed him. He hated that Stanford was so far away, but was grateful he had a private jet at his disposal. Without thinking, he jumped in his car and sped towards the airstrip, not worried about the fact that he had nothing with him but the clothes he was wearing. The flight was the longest 50 minutes of his life. A car was waiting for him when they landed, as the pilot had radioed ahead. One of the things Edward appreciated about his best friend was that Antonio was always prepared. When Priscilla moved to Stanford over the summer, he'd had a car sent to the Stanford airport for their use when they visited.

He sped the entire way to the hospital, slammed the car in park, and sprinted inside. Running to the nurses' station, he asked, "Where can I find Priscilla Moretti?"

Another nurse walked up to him before the woman at the desk could respond. "You must be Edward. I was just coming to let the front desk know to be on the lookout for you. Follow me. I'm Robin, we spoke on the phone."

"Hi, Robin. What happened to Priscilla?" Edward asked, worry evident in his voice.

"I think you need to ask her," she replied, turning to smile sadly at him.

The pit in his stomach sank lower, and he just wanted to get to her room. When they finally got there, Robin held his arm for a moment and looked at him with every ounce of seriousness she could muster. "She's going to need you. Be there for her as best you can." With that, she left him to go in by himself.

As soon as he saw her, his heart shattered. She was black and blue all over, and he had never seen such a look of defeat in her warm brown eyes. "*Uno dolce...*" he whispered, hardly able to get the words out.

She looked up, somehow hearing his whisper, and when their eyes met, she burst into tears. He rushed to her side and managed to join her on the small hospital bed, pulling her into his arms as gently as he could. "Priscilla... what happened?"

Through her sobs she told Edward everything, from her finding out she was pregnant that afternoon to everything Jack had done to her, and that she had lost her baby. He did his best to listen to and comfort her, but all he could see was red. "When Antonio hears about this–"

"No!" She exclaimed. "Please Edward, please don't tell him. Antonio will kill Jack!"

"That *madre di puttana*[106] doesn't deserve to breathe for another second after what he did to you!"

"Please... please don't... for me... I know what he did is inexcusable, but I love him, Edward. I wouldn't be able to live with myself if you guys killed him. Just please. Edward, I just need you to promise me you won't tell anyone. Just be here for me," her voice broke as she began sobbing again.

As much as Edward wanted nothing more than to slowly squeeze the life out of the man that dared to lay a hand on this precious young woman whom he loved as much as he loved Emily, he could refuse her nothing. It had always been that way, and he knew that it always would be. Sighing in defeat, he took her hand and rubbed his thumb along the

---

[106] mother fucker

back of it, doing his best to comfort both her and himself.

"You know I can't refuse you... I won't say anything to your brother, and I won't kill Jack. But if he ever puts his hands on you again, I can't promise anything."

"Thank you, Edward... And thank you for coming to be with me. There's no one else I felt like I could trust. Emily wouldn't have been able to handle it. I know that I can trust you. Will you stay here with me, for a while?"

"I'm not going anywhere. Rest now, *uno dolce*. You're safe now."

With that, Priscilla laid her head against Edward's shoulder, and feeling safe in his embrace, let herself close her eyes and sleep. When she had finally settled into a deep sleep, Edward, at last, allowed himself to cry and to grieve all that she had been through.

Shameless

May 8, 1993

Antonio swallowed hard as he gripped the large bouquet of tiger and calla lilies with white knuckles. He was stalling in front of his bedroom door, scared to open it and let down his wife with what he needed to tell her. After taking several deep breaths and wiping the sweat from his brow, he opened the door and stepped inside. Cynthia was sitting at her vanity finishing up her makeup. She looked stunning in the outfit she had chosen for the evening.

Her beautiful red hair was elegantly braided into pigtails, each one resting on a shoulder. Seeing her husband in the mirror behind her, she smiled as she applied a layer of lipstick before standing up and turning to him. The smile on her face vanished when she saw the nervous look on Antonio's face, however, and she raised her brow in question.

Seeing her in her peach and pink flannel shirt tucked into a short jean miniskirt and gorgeous heeled cowboy boots made him nearly come undone. He tried desperately to think of anything besides her bare legs as he eyed his wife. "Well, spit it out, Antonio," Cynthia sighed as she crossed her arms over her chest.

"That obvious?" He asked.

"Mhmmm. What is it?"

"I, um… I can't come with you to the concert tonight. Alejandro Torres called and said he's in town this evening only before he heads to Chicago. It's the only time we can meet. I'm sorry, *amore mio*."

Cynthia sighed heavily and turned away from her husband, not because she was angry, but so he wouldn't see the tears in her eyes. It had been a few weeks since they'd been on a date, and she had been looking forward to going to this concert with him since their anniversary in November. "It's fine," she mumbled as she reached for her tan, faux leather earrings in the shape of a leaf.

As she put in her earrings, Antonio gently set the bouquet down and wrapped his arms around his wife, knowing she was trying not to cry. "I'm so, so sorry. I know how much you've been looking forward to this. I will make it up to you, I promise, *Bel Fiore*. I love you so much."

"I love you too," she breathed before turning around to kiss him. "And you sure as hell better make it up to me." Before Antonio could respond, Cynthia stepped away and called out the door to Priscilla, who was there for the week to visit. "Priscilla! You wanna go see Garth with me?!"

"Fuck yeah! Give me five minutes to get ready!" She yelled from down the hall.

Turning around, she grinned at her husband. "Got a replacement. Give Alejandro my regards, and tell him he needs to bring María and little Mateo for a visit next time." Grabbing her off-white cowboy hat and placing it on her head, she sashayed out the door and down the stairs, leaving Antonio alone in their room, groaning and rethinking his decision.

An hour later, Cynthia and Priscilla were standing front and center in front of the stage, waiting for Garth Brooks to step out. While she was sad Antonio hadn't been able to come, she was very happy to be spending the evening with the sister of her heart. They didn't see each other very often anymore, since Priscilla was still living in Stanford with Jack, and had just finished her junior year of college. The women had a drink in each hand, and they toasted each other as they visited. Before long, they were screaming with the rest of the crowd as the country music superstar graced the stage.

About halfway through his set, Garth slowed it down as he took the mic in his hands. "Alright! Before I start this next song, can Cynthia Moretti raise her hand? I know you're in the front row."

With her eyes wide in shock, she slowly put her hand up in the air. Garth Brooks caught her eye and grinned at her. "There you are, young lady! Your husband wants you to know that he loves you more than anything. And you make him shameless!" With that, the band started into the rhythm of *Shameless*, and Garth winked at her as he started to sing.

Cynthia was speechless. Even though he hadn't been able to come, Antonio had still made her feel overwhelmingly loved, and it took her breath completely away. He never missed an opportunity to tell her how much he loved her, and her heart swelled as she sang along. Priscilla waggled her eyebrows at her sister as the song ended, and the two women burst into laughter. With her sadness completely melted away, she fully immersed herself in the experience for the rest of the night.

Meanwhile, at Moretti Industries, Antonio sat in his office waiting for his guest to arrive. Without warning, the door burst open and Alejandro Torres glided inside singing "*Hola mi amigo!*"[107]

Grinning, Antonio stood and embraced his friend. While it was common for various mafias to be rivals and enemies, it

---

[107] Hello my friend!

was not the case for the Black Death Mafia and *El Matadors*. Antonio and Alejandro had met by chance in Chicago when Antonio had been on his rampage to strike down every Silver Serpent member. He had just struck a man down in an alleyway when Alejandro happened upon him in a moment of exhaustion and vulnerability. From that moment, Alejandro, who was seven years older than Antonio, had taken the young man under his wing as an older brother figure.

El Matadors was a mafia based in Spain, with a sector in Chicago. The two mafias allied, each agreeing not to encroach on the other's territory while monitoring those who would slight them. "*Alé!* My friend, it's been far too long," Antonio laughed.

"Indeed it has," Alejandro replied, running a hand through his thick, jet-black hair. His dark brown eyes tinged with burnt orange shined with mischief.

"I know that look. You wanna kidnap me and take me to Chicago with you," Antonio chuckled.

Alejandro shrugged. "What can I say, I miss you, *hermano*.[108] Mateo and María want to see you as well."

"How old is Mateo now?"

"He's seven!" Alejandro beamed.

"Seven already! Man, how time flies."

"It sure does. Say, when are you and Cynthia going to bless us with a little terror?"

"I honestly don't know. Cynthia asked to wait until she finished college, which I didn't mind at all. But that was a year ago... I don't want to pressure her, but I really want to start a family with her, you know?" Antonio sighed.

"I get it, man. María and I got pregnant unexpectedly, and she told me that she wanted to wait for quite some time

---

[108] brother

before we tried for another. Women know when they're ready and when they aren't. And just a few months ago she told me she was ready, and damn, these months have been the best sex we've ever had," he winked. "She'll let you know, and you best be prepared for her appetite."

It wasn't often that Antonio blushed, but he did at his friend's words, causing Alejandro to chuckle. Coughing, Antonio decided to steer the conversation to the matter at hand. "So, what's this about inventory being swiped from your shipments and mine?"

When Cynthia finally arrived back home, she felt like she was floating on air. The concert had been a dream come true, and she was looking forward to thanking her husband properly for what he had done for her. She'd dropped Priscilla off at Emily's place, which she shared with her *fiance*, John. They were an adorable couple, and so clearly in love. As she opened the front door, she found the house to be dark and quiet. However, she knew she wasn't alone because her husband's shoes were in the entryway.

Taking the stairs two at a time, she burst into their bedroom to find lit candles everywhere. Their king-sized bed was covered in peach rose petals, and Cynthia's heart exploded with the effort her husband was putting into his apology. Hearing his wife, Antonio emerged from the bathroom where he had another surprise waiting for her. He'd come home and traded his suit for a pair of basketball shorts, not bothering to add a shirt. Cynthia bit her lip at the sight of her husband's bare chest glowing in the candlelight.

"Welcome home, *Bel Fiore*," he grinned.

"What's all this?" She asked.

"I promised you I'd make it up to you for not being able to go with you tonight. And I always keep my promises. Come," Antonio held out his hand, which she gladly took and allowed him to lead her into the bathroom.

The large jacuzzi tub was filled with water and Cynthia's favorite bubble bath. Antonio had lit candles all around the bathroom, giving the room a romantic glow. A bottle of champagne sat in a bucket of ice on the floor, two glasses by its side. "Oh, Antonio," she breathed, turning around and kissing her husband. "Thank you."

"My pleasure. Now, why don't you relax in the tub? I'll pour us some champagne and give you a shoulder massage while you soak."

Cynthia threw her head back and laughed, looking at him with a playful look in her eyes. "No. You, sir, will be joining me."

He swallowed hard, but this time it wasn't from nerves, it was the burning desire in her eyes. Even though he'd let her down, she still wanted him badly. His body shuddered as she ran her hands lovingly over his chest, then she backed away and removed her clothes, slowly sinking into the tub. She loved the way he watched her, knowing that his full focus and attention was on her and her alone. Antonio wasted no time in joining her, pulling her against him and kissing her passionately.

She giggled against his lips and then pulled away, resting her back against the tub. "You said you were going to pour us some champagne?"

Taking a deep breath to calm his pounding heart, Antonio nodded and uncorked the bottle. As they sipped their champagne, Cynthia gushed about the concert, thanking him repeatedly for having *Shameless* dedicated to her. "You know I'm not a big country fan, but I've never heard a song that describes how I feel about you so accurately. I'm completely shameless when it comes to you."

Unable to control herself anymore, Cynthia downed what remained in her glass before sliding over to her husband and straddling him. Antonio set his glass down and gently held her as she kissed him softly, slowly. She slowly kissed her way to his ear where she whispered, "I'm done waiting, my love. Let's start a family."

Antonio gasped, holding her out at arm's length to search her eyes. She smiled and nodded at him, letting him know that she was serious. Without skipping a beat, Antonio pulled her back to him, standing up quickly, her legs wrapped firmly around his waist. He didn't even pause to dry off, just headed straight for their bed. They lost themselves in nearly tangible passion, holding nothing back.

June 19, 1993

"Hello?" Antonio answered his phone sleepily at midnight only to find Emily's panicked, rambling voice on the other end. "Whoa, Embug, slow down. What's going on?" He asked, as he, too, tried not to panic. If one of the people from his closest circle was upset, so was he.

"Something's happened to John, I just know it!" Emily cried, wiping the tears from her face.

"What do you mean? What would have happened to John?" Antonio queried. He'd met Emily's *fiance* a handful of times, and he was a genuinely nice guy. He was five years older than Emily but treated her with the utmost respect and love. They'd met during Emily's freshman year, when John, who had just graduated with his law degree, was a student teacher for one of Emily's law classes.

Taking a deep breath, Emily shakily explained, "He's been receiving threatening letters and phone calls for several weeks, and he is pretty sure they're coming from a man he helped prosecute and put in prison for three years. I told him he needed to be careful and not be alone outside when it was dark, but he hasn't come home yet. I went to his office and his car is still there but he's not. I... I found blood on the ground by his car. Antonio… I'm so scared!"

"Holy shit. Why didn't you tell me sooner that he was receiving threatening letters and calls?"

"You know I don't get involved with the mafia… but I'm desperate, Antonio. It's hard for me to ask for help, but please help me. Help him. I love him so much. I can't live without him," she sobbed.

"Hey, shhh. Lock your doors, just in case. I will find him, Emily. I promise I'll bring him home to you," he assured her before hanging up the phone.

Cynthia had woken when the phone rang as well and had heard the entire conversation. As Antonio was talking, she had gotten out of bed and grabbed her husband's mafia gear out of the closet. She shoved the gear into his hands and urged him to hurry. "I love you. You best keep your promise to Emily. Go!"

Kissing his wife quickly, he pulled his clothes on, told Cynthia he loved her, then ran down the stairs and out of the house. He sped quickly to John's office to see the scene for himself. There was definitely some blood, but not a lot. He could see droplets leading away from the car and noticed a security camera in the parking lot. Pulling out his brand new, massive cell phone, he called a contact in traffic enforcement who was able to tell him that John was put into a gray Silverado at gunpoint.

Cameras caught the truck as it sped through main streets and ended up at an abandoned warehouse. Receiving the coordinates, Antonio hopped back into his car and made his way across town to the building. Making sure his gun was loaded, he crept silently towards the building, a large knife in his mouth in case he needed it.

Looking through the window, he could see John sitting at a table, sweat dripping off his brow, as he ran his hands over a keyboard. His right eye was swollen shut and a dark purple color and it was obvious his nose was broken. Standing behind him was a single man, resting the barrel of his gun against John's head. Slowly and silently, Antonio made his way to the back of the warehouse and found a broken window, which he pulled himself through. Without a sound, Antonio crept up behind the kidnapper and slit his throat.

John jumped in his seat, but due to the restraints tying him to the chair, could only turn his head. Never in his life had he been so relieved to see someone that belonged to the mafia, specifically the leader. "Antonio?"

"Hey, John. Emily called me. What the fuck happened?" Antonio grinned as he cut the restraints off of him.

Groaning as he stood and stretched, John replied, "Thank you, really. That guy you just... erm, killed, is Paul Hansom. I was on the prosecution team that put him in prison for three years for sexual assault of a minor. He should have gone away for life, but the justice system failed that little girl. She was five... Anyway, he was required to register as a sex offender, and I oversaw that he did so. It appears that he believed that I was the one that made the law and that I could somehow hack into the system and remove him from the registry. He blamed me for getting beaten and almost killed while he was in prison."

"Well, too bad they didn't succeed. You alright, John? How long have you been here?"

"Roughly five hours. I can't believe I'm saying this, but thank you for taking him out. If you hadn't... he was getting more and more angry that I couldn't get into the system... I think he was about to kill me."

"You don't have to thank me. I'm glad I could help. Come on, I'll drive you home. Emily is losing her mind."

They walked side by side to Antonio's car and started toward John and Emily's house. After driving in silence for a few minutes, John glanced at Antonio and asked, "Why, knowing that I don't approve or condone what the mafia does, why would you come to save me?"

Antonio smiled at him before putting his eyes on the road once more. "Emily may not be my blood, but she is my family. I would refuse her nothing, nor would I allow her to be crushed by losing the love of her life. We have a motto in my family, John. Since you don't speak Italian, I'll just say it in English. 'Family is everything, and you are family.' You're engaged to one of the sisters of my heart, you're family now."

John was silent for a few moments before replying, "I owe you my life, Antonio. How can I ever repay you?"

"As I said, you're family. The best way you can repay me is to love Emily with everything you have."

At that, a huge smile spread across John's face. "I love that woman more than anything in this world. She's everything to me. Thank you."

As they pulled into the driveway, the front door opened and Emily rushed down the front steps and flew into John's arms as soon as he stepped out of the car. She kissed him through her sobs and tears, holding him close as they took in the moment of safety and love. Antonio had gotten out to make sure they didn't need anything else, but seeing that the couple were happily kissing, he turned to walk back to the driver's side.

"Antonio! Wait!" Emily called, running towards him and throwing her arms around him. "Thank you, thank you for saving my love," she smiled up at him, tears streaming down her face.

Brushing a few tears away, Antonio smiled down at her. "La famiglia è tutto e tu sei una famiglia. You don't need to thank me, I love you, Embug."

"I love you too, *Patatino*."

"Now go to your man, he's going to need tending to."

Driving home, Antonio knew that his actions that night had

earned him a new friend, and he was glad he had made it in time. As he parked his car, his heart soared when the front door opened and Cynthia rushed out to greet him, thankful he had returned unharmed once more. Kissing her husband passionately, she pulled him inside and ushered him back upstairs to bed.

"I've gotta say I love being greeted like that. But why are you still up, *Bel Fiore*?"

Closing the bedroom door behind them, she turned to face her husband, a smile playing on her lips. "I had to make sure our baby's daddy returned home in one piece."

Antonio's jaw hit the floor. "Our what?"

"Our baby. I was going to wait to tell you until tomorrow, but I couldn't bear the thought that you might not come home in one piece and I hadn't told you. I'm pregnant!"

"P-pregnant?" His eyes widened as he eyed his wife up and down, not quite believing it. But seeing her nod in confirmation, excitement flooded his entire being. "Fuck yes!"

He lifted Cynthia in his arms and smashed his lips on hers as he twirled her around a few times before laying her on the bed. "You've just made my dreams come true, *Bel Fiore*. Now tell me, how can I take care of you tonight?"

"Love me sweet and tender," she murmured. "And also grab the garbage can and bring it beside the bed, just in case."

Antonio did as he was asked, not wasting a single second. He marveled at the fact that her body was carrying their baby and loved her more for it. His dreams of having a family were finally coming true, and he couldn't wait to embark on the journey of parenthood with his beloved.

July 9, 1993

Priscilla woke up on her 21st birthday with an overwhelming feeling of excitement. She couldn't pinpoint where it was coming from, but she smiled broadly as she stretched and got out of bed. Jack was already up and downstairs chatting with Antonio; she could hear them laughing about something as she got dressed. While she and Jack had long since reconciled what had happened between them and were living happily in Stanford, she missed being home with her brother and sister-in-law.

The plan for the day was to have breakfast together, attend a comedy show, dine at Bel Fiore, then bar hop. Feeling ready, Priscilla floated downstairs where she was immediately greeted by Cynthia who was coming out of one of the downstairs bathrooms. Seeing tears in her sister's eyes startled Priscilla. "Cynthia! What's wrong?"

Cynthia laughed and shook her head. "Nothing at all, Priscilla. I wasn't feeling well is all, but I'm better now. Happy birthday, sweet one!"

"If you're sure. Thank you!"

Hearing that the women had come downstairs, Antonio and Jack met them in the entryway. "Happy birthday, babe!" Jack grinned, pulling Priscilla into his arms and kissing her.

When Jack released her, Antonio embraced her as well. "*Buon compleanno dolcezza!*"[109]

Priscilla laughed, shaking her wild curly hair free from his arms. "Thank you. Shall we head to Margaret's to have breakfast?" Margaret and Everett had offered to make breakfast for her birthday, and she had readily accepted.

"Soon. But if you guys wouldn't mind, could we head to my office first? Cynthia and I have a gift we'd like to give you before we go."

As they filed in, Priscilla and Jack sat on the brown leather couch while Cynthia and Antonio sat on top of the large mahogany desk. With a grin, Antonio grabbed the phone and

---

[109] Happy birthday sweet one

dialed Britt's number. "Hello?"

"*Ciao, Cerva!*" Antonio smiled as he spoke into the receiver.

"Hi, *Björn!* I assume I'm on speaker. Happy Birthday, Priscilla!" Britt replied joyfully.

"Thanks!" Priscilla called out.

"*Cerva,* are Cade and Logan around?"

They are," Britt replied before calling for them to come and stand by the phone. She let Antonio know when they were all there.

Turning back to face his sister, and grabbing Cynthia's hand, Antonio took a deep breath and grinned broadly. "So, we don't have your physical present quite yet. It won't be here until the first week of February."

Seeing the puzzled look on Priscilla and Jack's faces, and hearing Logan ask his mom why his *Zietta's* present was going to take so long, Cynthia decided to cut in. "Priscilla, open the envelope next to you."

Priscilla turned to find a mint green envelope with her name written in Cynthia's beautiful handwriting. Opening it up, she found what appeared to be a sonogram picture, with a tiny little bean-shaped blurb inside. "The little one on that sonogram says 'Hi' to their *Zias* Priscilla and Britt! You guys are going to be aunties in February!"

"Oh my god!" Priscilla exclaimed, vaulting off of the couch to envelop her sister in her arms, happy tears streaming down her face. "You're pregnant?!"

"I am!" Cynthia laughed as well while happy tears pooled in her eyes.

"I'm in tears!" Britt sobbed happily through the phone.

"Congrats, guys! I'm so stoked to have a niece or nephew!" They could hear the grin in Cade's voice. "Blue, let me get you a tissue," he chuckled.

"*Zio?*" Nine-year-old Logan's soft voice came from the line.

"*Sí, nipote?*"

"*Zia* Cynthia is going to have a baby, right? Would they be my cousin?"

"Yes, Logie!" Cynthia exclaimed.

"Would it be ok... if I called them my brother or sister?"

"Of course, you can, Logan! We have all taught you as you've grown that family is far more than blood, which I think you know well. It is a great joy and honor to our hearts that you look at our baby as your sibling. You will be the best big brother to them, I just know it," Antonio replied proudly.

Although part of her heart ached at the news that her brother and sister-in-law would be having a baby, while she should have had one of her own years ago, the rest of it soared, and Priscilla could not wait to hold the precious baby in her arms and spoil them to death. She hoped that someday in the future, she would be able to give her loved ones the same news, though she was afraid to even try. Shaking off the storm that was trying to ravage her mind and steal her joy, she hugged Cynthia and Antonio again, finding comfort in their warmth and contagious happiness.

Knockin' on Heaven's Door

February 6, 1994

"*Figlio di puttana!*" Cynthia roared as she pushed with every last ounce of strength she had left.

She had gone into active labor only four short hours ago, but was exhausted, and so over the pain of childbirth. While several people had tried to convince her to give birth in the hospital with an epidural to take away the pain, she had decided she wanted to have her first baby all natural at a birthing center. Big fucking mistake, she thought an hour into it. Her midwife was shocked about how quickly she was progressing, especially since this was her first baby. It seemed the child was in a hurry to get out.

Antonio hated seeing his wife in so much pain, but he didn't dare complain one bit when she crushed his hand during an intense contraction or yelled mean expletives his way. He was in awe of her, and he so desperately wanted to tell her so, yet he knew that now was not the time for that.

A rowdy cry broke through the tense atmosphere as their baby entered the world. "It's a boy!" The midwife, Andrea, beamed, handing the 8 lb 13 oz baby to his mother.

All thoughts of pain and exhaustion quickly left Cynthia's mind as she gazed in the face of her perfect, baby boy. He had quite the mop of cayenne-red hair, just like hers. But the angles of his cheekbones, the shape of his nose, and the warm brown eyes she could barely see a peek of were all his father.

"*Lui è perfetto*,"[110] Antonio whispered hoarsely, tears streaming down his face as bent down to give his son a tender kiss on the top of his soft head. "You did great, *amore mio*. I love you so much."

"He really is, isn't he? I love you too," Cynthia breathed, holding her son tightly to her chest as she nuzzled him.

"I'm proud of you," Alexandra Springer murmured as she brushed a couple of curls out of her daughter's face and wiped the sweat off of her brow with a cool rag. "He sure was in a hurry to meet his mom and dad!"

"His *nonna*, too!" Antonio chuckled, giving his mother-in-law's hand a loving squeeze.

"Let's get you cleaned up my dear," Andrea smiled as she walked back into the room, Britt in tow.

"So, boy or girl?" Britt asked excitedly.

"You have a *nipote*!" Cynthia laughed as she handed the baby to Antonio so Andrea could help her deliver the placenta and finish cleaning her up and preparing her for recovery.

"Oh, *Björn*, Cynthia! He is so precious!" Britt cried as Antonio brought the baby over to her. "I'm in love!"

"Am I late?!" Priscilla's panicked voice filled the room as she burst through the door. "Dammit, I missed the birth!" She sighed as she caught sight of her brother holding the baby.

"Only by like eight minutes," Antonio grinned as he beckoned his sister over. "Meet your *nipote*!"

"Look at that hair!" Priscilla grinned as she took the baby in her arms. "He's beautiful. Hi, sweet boy. I'm your *Zia* Priscilla, and this beautiful lady right here is your *Zia* Britt!

---

[110] He's perfect

248

You are so loved," she choked, tears filling her eyes.

"Alright you two, what's his name?" Britt laughed.

"His name is **Drake Luther Moretti**," Antonio stated proudly, loving the names his wife had chosen.

45 minutes later, the birthing room was clean and peaceful, and Cynthia reclined in her bed, holding her son to her shoulder as she burped him. He had been ravenously hungry, and it made her laugh how similar he already was to his father. Antonio sat beside her, his arm around both of them. Hating the feeling of being useless, he rubbed his wife's back and shoulders as their son had nursed, and he'd marveled at the way the baby gripped his finger so strongly with his tiny little hand.

He knew his life would never be the same, and he was so in love with his newborn son already. Holding them both in his arms, he thanked God for this wonderful blessing. "You're beautiful and awe-inspiring," Antonio murmured as he kissed the top of Cynthia's head.

She smiled up at him and kissed him in reply. They were entering a new season of life together, and Cynthia was so grateful that she had him beside her always.

April 1994

Priscilla paced up and down the hallway of her and Jack's house, trying desperately not to throw up from the immense anxiety she felt. They'd been careful, extremely careful. She'd been on birth control religiously for years, and she almost always made Jack wear a condom. It shouldn't have been possible for her to get pregnant, but here she was, and she was terrified.

It'll be alright, won't it? I'm graduating in a few weeks, we've been together for years, so surely he won't be mad. Right? Oh shit, what am I going to do?

The sound of the front door opening interrupted her thoughts, and she sighed as she looked at the watch on her wrist: 3:42 A.M. Hearing stumbling as Jack took off his shoes confirmed that he had once again stayed out all night drinking. It was nearly a nightly thing. She hoped that the buzz was strong enough that he wouldn't be mad when she told him the news. Taking a deep breath and swallowing the bile that threatened to leave her body, she strode to the entryway.

"Jack, you're home!"

"Mhm," he grunted. "Why you up sssooo late?"

"I wanted to tell you the happy news," she said, biting her lip.

"Whass that?" Jack slurred.

"I'm pregnant, Jack."

The heaviness left her boyfriend's eyes, and in its place was the terrifying rage she hoped to never see again. She couldn't do anything; she was frozen in fear, even as her mind screamed at her to run. The last thing she remembered was Jack's fist flying towards her face before everything went black.

Her body ached, and the dim light in the room was too bright for her eyes when she tried to open them. From the feeling of the clothes on her body and the blanket on the bed, she knew she was in a hospital room. Hearing someone shift beside her, she slowly turned her head and opened her eyes once more. She found Edward's red-brown eyes staring back at her.

"Priscilla…" he choked out, grabbing her hand gingerly in his. "He did it again. He hurt you!"

She swallowed, but didn't say anything; she didn't have to. He knew everything he needed to know. "I'm glad you're here," she finally whispered, knowing that the choice of keeping him as her emergency contact would always be something she would never regret.

"I'll always be here. But you can't just expect me to sit around and do nothing after he laid hands on you again!"

"Edward, you can't." Tears streamed down her face as she closed her eyes, unable to look at him.

"No, he can't keep hurting you like this," his voice broke. "You deserve so much better than that piece of horse shit."

"I can't explain it, but I love him. It was my fault for getting pregnant again—the baby! Is the baby alright?"

The heartbreaking look on her friend's face told her everything she needed to know: Jack had forced a second miscarriage. Sobs wracked her body, and Edward scrambled out of his chair to wrap his arms around her. She was grateful for his embrace, fearing that if he wasn't holding her, she would completely fall apart. "What am I going to do?"

"You are going to leave him and come home with me, back to your *famiglia* who love you and will take care of you. And then your brother and I are going to cut that *bastardo* into millions of pieces and scatter him across the state."

"No! You can't tell Antonio! Edward, you mustn't!" She panicked. "And you can't hurt him!"

"Priscilla, I didn't tell him the first time, but how can I keep this from him any longer? How can you expect me not to retaliate? How can you expect me to just let you go back to him?"

"Because you're my friend, Edward. I love him so much, I can't live without him!"

Knowing that he wasn't going to get anywhere with her, Edward took a deep breath and doused the fire raging inside of him. "I'll drop the subject for now. You need to rest and heal, uno dolce. I'm not leaving your side. You're safe. Go back to sleep."

No sooner had Priscilla fallen asleep than her hospital door banged open. "Priscilla! Oh my god, baby! I'm so sorry!" Jack exclaimed as he rushed into the room, a large bouquet of salmon-colored roses, sunflowers, pink carnations, lavender alstroemeria, and hypericum berries in his hands.

Edward was out of his seat faster than should be humanly possible, his hand around Jack's throat as he shoved him up against the wall. "What the fuck are you doing here?"

"I c-came to s-see my g-girlfriend," he wheezed.

"I think the fuck not! Not after what you did to her! Get out!" Edward roared as he used every ounce of self control he had not to snap the man's neck.

"Edward! Let him go!"

Seeing the panicked look on her face, Edward sighed and did as he was told, but he smirked when Jack fell and crumpled on the ground with a satisfying thunk. "You do *anything* that I find even minimally threatening, and I will kill you," he said through gritted teeth.

Nodding, Jack quickly scrambled up, grabbing the flowers as he did so, and rushed to Priscilla's bedside. "Forgive me, baby! I was a drunk, I didn't know what I was doing! You have to believe me! I love you more than anything. Priscilla, will you marry me?" Jack rambled, fumbling as he dropped to one knee and pulled out a ring box.

Edward's jaw dropped as he watched the scene unfold. He felt as though he was watching someone else's life as Priscilla nodded her head, her wild curls flying in all directions as she pulled her abuser into her arms and kissed him. Jack triumphantly slid the ring onto her finger, and as Priscilla adjusted it, Edward's heart dropped into the bottom of his stomach. It was all he could do not to rip the man off of the sister of his heart and throw him through the window and watch him drop the eight stories to the ground below.

Swallowing the bile that was coming up his throat, Edward quickly stalked out of the room and made a beeline for the exit. He didn't stop until he reached the streetlight next to his parked car. Pulling his arm back, he punched the pole as hard as he could and let out a frustrated yell. He was so angry and full of adrenaline that he didn't even feel that his right hand had shattered. Ripping the driver's side door open he jumped inside then slammed it before he peeled off and sped towards the airport. Edward wanted to be nowhere near the two of them; he just wanted to go home. *Uno dolce, you are making a huge mistake.*

July 23, 1994

Priscilla gazed at her reflection in the mirror as she smoothed her wedding gown. She and Jack decided to have a very quick engagement, and here they were, merely three months after they became engaged, about to get married. Her stomach was a jumble of nerves, but she was excited as well.

While everyone had guessed she would choose to have some sort of mint in her wedding dress, she had gone for a different look than everyone had pegged her for. No dress had caught her eye while she, Emily, and Cynthia had gone dress shopping, so she'd had a custom gown ordered. What had arrived was breathtaking. The white gown had an off-the-shoulder neckline with delicate floral lace straps hanging below her shoulders. Its natural waistline suited her perfectly, and her figure was accented with floral lace appliqués. The trumpet silhouette fell to a floor-length hemline and a brush train.

She had chosen not to wear any jewelry, save for her mother's wedding band on her right hand and small diamond studs in her ears. To complete the look, she wore white, one-inch heels, with the heel itself being mint green. And even in the simplicity, she saw her mother's elegance and grace reflected back at her.

A knock at the door stirred her from her thoughts. It didn't sound like Antonio's usual knock, and as she glanced at the wall clock, she realized it was far too early for Antonio to come get her. She had requested an hour of solitude to grieve the absence of her parents and prepare herself for becoming a married woman. Taking a deep breath and readying herself to scold her brother for interrupting her moment of solitude, she opened the door, an insult on her tongue.

The frustration died in a second as she found that it was not her brother that had been at the door, but Edward. "Edward? What are you doing here?"

Without answering, Edward pushed past her into the bridal chamber and shut and locked the door behind him. He took a moment to gather his thoughts before meeting her eyes. "*Uno dolce*, you look simply radiant in your gown... but I beg you, please reconsider this marriage!"

"Reconsider?" Priscilla gasped. "Why would you ever ask me to do such a thing?"

"Because you shouldn't marry him!" Edward yelled. "Priscilla, you deserve so much better than Jack. Someone who will love you unconditionally and who would never, under any circumstances, lay a hand on you. You are a brilliant, beautiful woman worthy of so much more. Please don't marry that man!"

His words tugged at her heartstrings, but she smiled sadly as she shook her head. "I know you mean well, Edward, but I love him. I can't imagine life without him. He loves—"

"And I can't imagine life without you! Can't you see? One of these days he's going to snap, and you won't wake up when that happens."

"He won't kill me. I know he loves me, I just have to make sure I don't do anything to upset him. That's all. And besides, who would love me so much more? You?" She laughed sarcastically.

"I've said it before and I'll say it again, you are my sister, just as much as Emily is. I can't just stand by and let you marry him without trying to convince you otherwise. You still have 20 minutes... *Uno dolce*, please leave with me. My car is right out front. We can get out of here and I can keep you safe until things die down. Please!"

With a sigh, Priscilla closed the distance between her and the brother of her heart. She gently placed her hands on either side of his face and smiled softly at him, though tears threatened to fall. It felt like she had been punched in the stomach when Edward opened his eyes to meet hers, tears falling freely down his face. "I know you mean well, *Fratello*, and I love you for trying. But I'm going to marry Jack. I love him. Please support me. I... I can't get married without you here."

Edward shuddered as she leaned in and placed a whisper of a kiss on his lips. It was at that moment that he knew he would never be able to convince her to leave Jack, but he made a silent vow to always be there when she needed him. With a heavy sigh and shoulders slumped, he took a step back and did his best to stop the tears. "Alright, Pris. I'll be here."

And with that, he quickly exited the bridal suite. Pausing in the men's room, he took a flask out of the inner pocket of his suit coat and downed the contents. He figured he'd be able to get through the wedding if his mind was numbed somewhat. Rinsing his face, he took a deep breath, and made his way to his seat, just in time to watch the sister of his heart walk down the aisle to her doom.

Nothing Else Matters

March 18, 1996

Antonio decided the day his son was born that there was no sound as beautiful as the first cry a baby made. That sentiment was further cemented on a beautiful March afternoon when their tiny little girl with a mop of black hair was born. Cynthia held the beautiful baby to her chest, and Antonio fell in love with her all over again. Looking at his wife, son, and baby daughter snuggled on the hospital bed, he knew their family was complete, and he felt a sense of warm contentment in his heart.

Just looking at her face, Antonio knew his daughter was going to be trouble, and he couldn't wait to see what she'd do. She'd been early, so Britt and Priscilla hadn't been able to make it in time, and Cynthia's parents were on an anniversary cruise, but it was nice just having it be the two of them in the room for the last baby. A soft knock followed by the quiet platter of feet caught Antonio's attention, and he grinned as he looked over to find his two sisters coming towards them.

"Priscilla, Britt, meet your niece. **Launa Carmella Moretti.**"

March 30, 1996

* * *

Priscilla grinned as she surveyed the dinner table that she had decorated beautifully and had laid out a feast fit for a king on. Jack would be coming home that evening from a recruiting trip, and she wanted to make the evening extra special. After spending time with her baby niece, she couldn't help but be hopeful and excited about the news she was going to share with her husband: she was pregnant with a baby girl.

She had decided when she found out she was pregnant to wait to tell Jack until she was far enough along to learn the sex. She hoped that if he knew the baby's sex, they would seem more real to him, and he wouldn't want to hurt her and cause another miscarriage. Priscilla had always wanted a baby girl, and she smiled as she daydreamed about a little, curly haired toddler with bows in her wild mane running around their home, giggling with glee.

The front door opened and she glided to the entryway, throwing her arms around her husband. Things had been good with them, though Jack seemed to be drinking more and more these days. She could smell the alcohol on his breath, and her smile faltered, but she plastered it back on her face as she led him to the dining room.

"Oh? What's all this?" Jack asked as he took his seat.

"Dinner for my husband, of course!" Priscilla grinned, sitting next to him.

They made pleasant conversation while they ate their meal, and Priscilla was delighted to discover that Jack had been given a substantial raise. Seeing her chance, she decided that now was the perfect opportunity to tell him her secret. "The raise will definitely come in handy now that we will have a daughter to raise."

"I beg your pardon?" Jack coughed, setting his wine glass down. "What daughter?"

"Our daughter. We're having a little girl. I'm 21 weeks along, and she is growing beautifully. You've been gone a lot lately, so you haven't really noticed. Look at my bump!"

Priscilla stood and lifted her silky cream shirt to reveal her pregnant belly. Jack stared at her with wide eyes, and for a moment, it seemed like he would smile back at her. He didn't.

Jumping out of his seat, he had her pinned against the dining room wall by her throat in seconds. "You're worthless!" He screamed in her face. "If you're going to give me a damn child, then it better fucking be a boy! What makes you think I want a pathetic little girl?"

"B-but... you seemed to be alright with the idea of expanding our family. Jack, please, let's just talk about this."

"Shut the fuck up!" Jack slapped her so hard across the face that she fell from his grasp. "Since I know you won't get rid of it, then I will."

"Don't touch me!" Priscilla roared, standing up as she moved toward the table to grab her steak knife. "She's a person! Look!" She shoved the sonogram she'd had in her pocket towards him. "She's our daughter! Please don't..."

But Jack didn't care. He ripped the sonogram in half and grabbed the knife out of her fist, not even caring that it sliced his hand open as he threw it to the ground. And then he began his all-too-familiar violent tirade as Priscilla did her best to wrap herself around her stomach.

She wasn't even surprised when she came to in the hospital once more, nor by the scent of Edward's distinctive cologne. Though it hurt, she breathed in the familiar scents of the cardamom and orris of the Clive Christian Original collection. She never had to use her eyes to know that the brother of her heart was there. "I know what you're going to say. Please, just don't," Priscilla sighed heavily without opening her eyes.

"*Uno dolce...*" Edward began. He wanted to berate her for

staying with that cruel, inhuman man she called her husband; but he couldn't. The pain she was in was evident on her face and the small swell of her belly that he could barely make out stilled the fire inside of him for a moment. All he wanted to do was protect her. Instead, the only thing he could ask was, "How far along are you?"

"21 weeks. It's a girl," she whispered, opening her warm brown eyes to meet his barely held-back tear-filled reddish ones.

"H-have you felt her move yet?"

"Yes! It is the most amazing feeling in the world. She typically moves around a lot when I'm laying down. It's odd... I don't feel her now..."

Before she could express her concern, her doctor came in, a cheery smile on her face. "Priscilla, my dear! Are you going to tell me what happened?"

"I... had an accident," she lied.

The woman scrunched her brows, not believing her patient for even a second. Sighing, she sat beside the bed and prepared to do an ultrasound. "Well, we need to make sure baby girl is alright after this 'accident.'"

Priscilla repositioned herself on the bed, pulling the hospital gown up to reveal her abdomen. Edward leaned forward in curiosity as the doctor moved the wand around her stomach and a picture came up on the screen. He was in awe that a tiny baby was so clearly visible, and he squeezed Priscilla's hand encouragingly. However, any hope that all was well quickly faded as the doctor began mumbling about not being able to find the heartbeat.

After searching for several minutes, the doctor turned the screen off and turned to her patient sadly. "Priscilla, I am so sorry... I can't find her heartbeat. She's gone. We need to induce you right away, and you will have to deliver her. Is there anyone else we can call to be here with you?"

She shook her head rapidly as sobs wracked her body and tears streamed down her face. "Just Edward."

The delivery room was quiet and somber as Priscilla labored in her bed, Edward holding her hand and her knee as she pushed. No one dared make a sound, except to encourage the young woman to keep pushing. The sweet relief of delivery never washed over the young mother as the tiny infant was born and quickly swaddled up. Where there would normally be melodic sounds of a baby's first cries resonating throughout the room, only deafening silence followed. Several doctors and nurses worked on her, trying to breathe life back into her tiny body, but to no avail. She was truly gone.

"Can I hold her?" Priscilla whispered.

"Of course you can. We will leave you to have some time alone and to grieve. Press your button when you're ready." Her doctor replied, placing the tiny bundle in her arms before ushering everyone out the door.

Taking a deep breath, Priscilla moved the blanket aside so that she could gaze upon her daughter's face. "She's perfect," she gasped. While the baby had only been 21 weeks gestation, she was developing perfectly. Her tiny little nose looked just like her mother's, and she had pretty lips. There was already quite a bit of dark hair on her tiny head, too.

"She is absolutely beautiful, *uno dolce*, she looks just like you," Edward murmured, touching the baby's cheek softly. "What is her name?"

"What?" Priscilla sobbed. "You think I should name her?"

"Of course. She may no longer be living on this earth, but you are her mother and she is your daughter, and she deserves to have the name I know you've chosen for her."

With a sad smile, Priscilla lifted the baby closer and kissed her downy head softly. "My precious daughter, your name is Ilaria Hope Taylors, and you will forever be loved and missed."

Two weeks later, Priscilla walked into her childhood home with a bag on her shoulder and a tiny urn in her hands. All she had told Antonio and Cynthia was that she had been pregnant but had had a stillbirth, and she just needed to be with them. She'd said that Jack was so distraught in his grief that he threw himself into the only part of his life he had control of, his job. They didn't need to know what had really happened. Hearing his sister come inside, Antonio ran like his life depended on it down the hall and caught his beloved little sister in his arms as she collapsed to the ground, sobbing.

"It's alright, *uno dolce*, I'm here. I've got you. I love you, so much..." it broke his heart seeing his sister like this, and knowing how broken her own heart was, but he was determined to help her pick up the pieces of this unimaginable loss in any way he could. Carrying her like he'd done when they were little, he made his way upstairs and to her old bedroom. He laid down in the bed and held her close, rubbing her back as she sobbed violently, and silent tears fell from his eyes.

Ilaria Hope Taylors, the niece he had only just found out about, was gone before he could even be excited about her existence, whom he loved so deeply even though he would never know her. He didn't understand how life could be so cruel to his sister, but he prayed that she would one day experience the joy of motherhood.

January 26, 1997

Antonio stared out the window of his office as he watched the rain fall. Something was coming, though he couldn't quite put his finger on what. Aside from his sister's marriage and heartbreak, the past couple of years had been relatively quiet and peaceful. He *loved* being a father, and though he was still head of both Moretti Industries and the Black Death Mafia, he made being present in his children's lives a priority, just as his father had done.

Each new thing his children experienced amazed him. He'd cried when both Drake and Launa had taken their first steps and said their first words. It hadn't surprised him in the least that Drake's had been "mama," but when Launa had uttered "dada" as her first word in her sweet little voice, it had brought him to his knees. Those two were his entire world, and he could not get enough of them.

And above all of that, what he had loved the most since becoming a father, was watching Cynthia become a mother. While he had no expectations of what roles women should be in, there were two things his wife was *born* to do: one was owning and running her own business and the other was being a mom; it came to her almost effortlessly. Before motherhood, Cynthia had little to no experience with babies, but when Drake came along, it was as if she had trained her whole life to care for him. It didn't seem to matter that their son was not a good sleeper and demanded to be fed every two hours and that she was exhausted, she never complained a bit.

When Launa was born, she transitioned into being a mother of two so seamlessly, that it constantly left Antonio in a permanent state of awe. And he never missed an opportunity to tell her so. He was perpetually falling in love with his wife over and over again and never wanted that to stop. Craning his head to the side, he sighed at the stillness of his home. The usual sounds of Drake's little feet running around the house and his and Launa's giggles that echoed throughout were missing today, and it saddened his heart.

Cynthia had taken them to Oregon to visit with Britt and Logan for a few days. While Antonio always gave her the space she needed away from their babies without hesitation, and he had offered to keep him in Los Angeles with him while he wrapped up some business, his wife had insisted on taking them. "They need to see their *Zia* and she needs to see them," she shrugged.

Britt and Cade were wrapping up their divorce, and the family of four had planned to go be with Britt as she dealt with the aftermath. However, Antonio had to meet with Alejandro Torres, so he would be following them the following day. It saddened his heart that his sister was going through a divorce, and he liked Cade, but he also knew that it was a long time coming. They'd done the best they could for years, and while it was a sad time, it was also a time of hope and happiness for the futures they would have apart. He also knew that they would always love and care for each other, and never let their separation get in the way of their love and devotion for Logan.

A knock at his office door startled him out of thoughts and he turned to find Everett standing in the doorway, hair and clothes soaking wet. His bright blue eyes were wide as he stared at his young boss. "I came as fast as I could!" He panted. "And I'm surprised you didn't hear me running down the hallway."

"I was lost in thought," Antonio chuckled. "What's going on?"

"One of my contacts spotted Casimir Syzmanski at the Port! He's returned to L.A.," Everett stated grimly.

Hearing the name of the enemy that had eluded him for nearly 14 years made time seem to stand still as Antonio gaped at his mentor. The man that had convinced one of the mafia's most loyal men to betray them; the man that ordered his parents' assassination; the man whose blood Antonio had been craving. They'd been searching for him for the last 13 years, 8 months, and 68 days, all without seeing him once, as he seemed to always be one step ahead of the Black Death Mafia's maneuvers since he'd gone to ground.

Narrowing his eyes, Antonio stared evenly at Everett, "Casimir's head is mine. Call the men. It's time to end this."

Everett nodded then made his way to the phone situated on Antonio's desk. He'd already told his son to meet them at the Moretti Mansion with his gear, and as Everett connected with Grant first, he could see Edward's car speeding up the driveway, water spraying everywhere.

While Antonio had been looking forward to this day for over a decade, he was not expecting the cool calm he felt washing over his body. He quietly walked upstairs to his bedroom, barely hearing Edward's exclamations from the office below. Without even really seeing what he was doing, Antonio changed out of his business suit from his earlier meeting with Alejandro and into his mafia gear. Once he was dressed, he took a deep breath and called his sister.

"*Ciao, Fratello!*" Priscilla's bubbly voice answered.

"It's finally happening," Antonio breathed, not quite trusting himself to speak.

"What's happening?"

"Casimir has been spotted at the Port. I'm getting ready to head down there and take his head as my prize."

"Holy fucking shit!" Priscilla screamed into the phone. "I wish didn't live so fucking away! I should be there to put a bullet in his head."

"I know, *Sorella*, you deserve that. But I'm afraid we can't wait. We have to move before he goes back underground. I'll call you when it's done. I love you."

"I love you, too. Antonio, make him *pay*."

Everett drove the armored car and discussed what the plan was while Antonio and Edward rode in the back. In the quiet, rainy night, several other armored cars fell into line, each one driven by one of the original guard members and a couple of other mafia members. Antonio couldn't help but grin as he silently named them: Grant, Tahir, Roy, Jeremiah, Zachary, and Michael. They would drive down the Port of Los Angeles, then spread out as they silently made their way toward the main dock where, according to the contact, Casimir was still conducting business.

As they pulled up to the Port, Antonio fingered his father's plague doctor mask, before donning it to finish off the last man responsible for his death. The group of 20 men silently spread out, keeping to the shadows, which they blended in well with. They silently crept alongside and on top of cargo and trailers, making their way painstakingly slowly toward their target. Antonio led them, and coming to the final hiding place, stuck his fist in the air, stopping everyone in their tracks. With a quick, small nod at his best friend and brother, Edward unleashed three razor sharp knives from his wrists, killing each of the three men surrounding Casimir Szymanski in complete and utter silence.

Before the leader of the Silver Serpents knew what was happening, he was surrounded and disarmed by the most powerful men of the Black Death Mafia, with nowhere to run. He had made a fatal risk coming out of hiding this evening, and he knew it. Casimir watched Antonio walk up to him and stared at him with resignation, but he kept his chin up.

Antonio was surprised by how much the man had aged. Casimir's once dark brown hair was now completely silver, fitting for the mafia he was the head of. "You have seen your last day, Casimir," Antonio growled. "Any last words?"

"*Pierdol się*[111]!" Casimir grinned, spitting at Antonio's feet.

With a grin of his own, Antonio snapped his fingers and Roy swiftly broke the older man's knees, Casimir yelling in agony as he went down on his broken kneecaps. Tahir

---

[111] Fuck you

crushed Casimir's fingers with his steel-toed boots before allowing Jeremiah, Michael, and Grant to break other bones of their choosing. When his enemy's body had been sufficiently broken, Antonio stepped forward and grabbed Casimir by his silver hair, forcing him to look into his eyes. "This is for my mother," he whispered menacingly as he produced a knife and gutted the man.

"And this is for my father," he finished, slitting Casimir's throat and watching the life drain from his eyes. Taking out a special card he'd made years ago for this very moment out of his pocket, he placed it over Casimir's lifeless face. The card was the traditional plague doctor calling card of the mafia, with the only difference being the giant, silver foiled script read: *Death to the Serpent*.

Satisfied with the bloody mess he was leaving behind for some poor fool to find, Antonio stalked back towards the parking lot, his men on his heels. He took off his mask and breathed in deeply. *I've finally avenged your deaths, Mamma and Padre, I hope you can Rest In Peace.* As the men made their way to the warehouse for a celebration, someone stepped out of the shadows at the Port.

The figure, wrapped in a dark jacket, wiped away silent tears as she stood over the broken body of the man that had been her world. Placing a hand on her swollen belly, she vowed to make Antonio Moretti pay, one way, one day. It did not matter how long it would take: she would have her revenge.

Crazy Crazy Nights

March 2000

Antonio watched Cynthia as she read a book to their kids, the four of them sitting in the family room. He had insisted on carrying on his parents' tradition of spending time together every evening, and he loved the expressions on Drake and Launa's faces each time he took their mother in his arms and danced around the room with her. It was crazy to him that they were already six and four, and both in school. Drake was already very tall, and Antonio knew that someday his son would surpass him in height. And Launa, though she looked dainty, was a strong-willed little girl who he knew was going to rule the world.

Their front door opened, and Edward walked in, his shoulders slumped. He looked like he hadn't slept in days. "*Zio* Edward!" Drake and Launa exclaimed, jumping up from the couch and rushing to their uncle, arms outstretched.

Edward, to his credit, plastered the easy-going smile he only reserved for the kids on his face, lifting them both in his arms, chuckling as they wrapped their arms around his neck. "How are my favorite kiddos doing today?"

"I puncheded a boy in the face today for puwing my hair and calling me a swimp!" Launa squealed excitedly as she threw her uncle a smirk and flexed her arm. "I have an in-school suspension tomorrow but I don't care."

He threw back his head and laughed heartily. Antonio grinned and Cynthia did her best to hide the proud smile that was spreading across her face.

"Never let anyone put you down, princess," Edward said as he kissed her forehead and set her down. "And what about you, Drake?"

The young boy ran a hand through his cayenne hair, mussing it up, and shrugged. "School was alright. But I got to call Logan today, and he and the boys played me their brand new song! They are all so cool... I want to be cool like them."

"They're pretty talented, huh? Drake, you are the coolest kid I know, and someday, you'll be the coolest man."

"Thanks, *Zio*. They said they're coming to visit in June and that they will take me to a live show!"

Noticing the tired, pleading look in their friend's eyes, Cynthia rose and strode over to her children. "Alright you two, off to bed. Your *Zio* needs to talk with your father."

"Actually, I could use you both," Edward said nervously.

Cynthia raised a brow but nodded. "Give me five minutes to lay these little terrors down. Drake, Launa, say goodnight."

The two rushed toward their father and into his open arms. Antonio hugged them both, kissing their foreheads, reminding them how much he loved them and how proud he was of them, and bidding them goodnight. He waited until they were upstairs before he turned to his best friend, his brother, and grinned. "You look like shit. What crawled up your ass and died?"

Edward rolled his eyes but tiredly plopped down in a chair, running a hand through his hair. "I'm in big trouble brother."

"What happened?" Antonio asked, his voice laced with concern.

But Edward just shook his head. "I'll explain when Cynthia comes back down."

Cynthia hurriedly tucked her kids in, her mind a worried jumble as she tried to focus on making sure they were settled. She had never seen Edward look like that in all of the years she'd known him. The 30-year-old, who always appeared youthful, looked as though he'd aged about 10 years overnight. Rushing back downstairs, she quickly took her seat next to her husband but leaned over to the chair Edward was sitting in and took his hand in hers, squeezing it encouragingly. She gasped as she felt him shake.

"Edward, what's wrong?" Her voice rose slightly as she tried not to panic as she watched him shake harder, tears spilling down his face.

He sobbed quietly for a few moments, and Antonio didn't quite know what to say. "I've messed up," a whisper escaped his lips.

"Whatever it is, we will get through it together," Cynthia stated firmly.

"*Fratello*," Antonio began, maintaining a calm and even tone that commanded his friend to meet his eyes directly. Edward's red-tinged, dark brown eyes met his light ones. "What happened?"

Grabbing a handkerchief from his pocket, Edward wiped his face and blew his nose. Taking a deep breath, he simply stated, "I'm going to be a dad."

"What?" Cynthia and Antonio stated in unison.

"I, uh, had a one-night stand with my favorite stripper from Misty's..." he groaned, his face flushing from embarrassment. "Her name is Regina Cromwell. Gorgeous woman, with full lips... but a nasty attitude."

"And you're sure she's pregnant?" Cynthia asked. "And not just trying to latch onto California's most eligible bachelor?"

"I'm sure, I went to the sonogram appointment today. She's definitely pregnant."

"But the baby might not be yours," Antonio started but stopped when his best friend held up a hand.

"The timing lines up exactly with our tryst. The baby is mine, I feel it in my bones, and I'll know for sure when he or she is born."

"Well, having a baby isn't a terrible thing," Cynthia said softly. "You could get full custody, you know."

"Well… I think I'm going to ask Regina to marry me."

Antonio, who had just taken a sip of bourbon, choked as he tried to swallow. "I'm sorry, I don't think I heard you correctly. Did you just say you're going to ask her to marry you?"

"I did. Can I have some of that?" Edward sighed, motioning with his head to the bourbon.

"Ice?" Cynthia asked as she rose and walked over to the liquor cabinet.

"Please."

She poured him a sizable glass and handed it to him as she sat back down. "Edward, do you love this woman?"

"No. But I… I think maybe in time I could learn to. For the baby."

"You don't have to marry her just because she's having your baby. Especially since she has a nasty attitude. She's probably a gold digger," Antonio shook his head.

"I have to try, though. It's the right thing to do. I have to accept the consequences of my philandering ways. It's amazing I made it past 30 without it happening sooner," he chuckled wryly.

Cynthia reached over and grabbed his hand, waiting until he swallowed the large gulp of bourbon he'd taken. "Don't marry her, Edward. You can do the right thing and raise your child with all the love in your heart without being married to their mother. It's not worth the heartache or a strained relationship. And she's a stripper… Not saying that strippers are inherently bad, but is she going to stop?"

"She said she would," Edward shrugged before finishing the last of the bourbon in his glass. "I've made up my mind. I just… I need your support to get through this. I have no idea what I'm doing when it comes to babies."

"We will be with you every step of the way. And what do you mean you have no idea what you're doing?" Cynthia grinned.

"I'm pretty sure you've changed your fair share of diapers and have plenty of experience with feeding small children since you helped us out so much after Drake and Launa were born. You're going to be a great dad, Edward," Antonio added encouragingly. "As much as we don't want you to rush into a marriage with her, it is your choice, and we will be by your side when you marry her."

Relief visibly settled over the man as he placed a head over his heart. "Thank you."

May 2000

Hope. Excitement. Joy. Priscilla felt all of them as the words her doctor had just told her, the words that were echoing in her mind: "It's a boy!"

Jack and Priscilla had sold their home in Stanford the year before and moved to Los Angeles, buying a house on a quiet street. The action was part of the apology and promise he had made to her after the loss of their daughter, the loss he had caused. Things had been better the last few years, though, and he had murmured in her ear one night as he made love to her that he was ready for a family now. She knew he still wouldn't be happy with a girl, so Priscilla had prayed and prayed that God would bless her with a son this time. And

He had.

She couldn't wipe the smile off of her face as she drove home, the sunshine beaming down on her. Jack still traveled to recruit for Stanford, but he was no longer required to keep strict office hours, which had allowed him to move away from the city. He was home today, and for the first time, she felt no sense of anxiety at the news she was going to share with her husband. Pulling into the driveway, she parked her cherry red Mustang and sprinted inside.

Priscilla found Jack sitting on the couch, reading the newspaper, and drinking... water. The clear liquid in his glass surprised her, and it boosted her spirits knowing he wasn't intoxicated this morning. "Jack!" Priscilla squealed, rushing to her husband and plucking the paper out of his hands.

"Good morning, babe," Jack chuckled, his eyes darkening with desire as Priscilla sat on his lap, straddling him. "What is making your face shine so exquisitely?"

"I have a gift for you, something you've always wanted," Priscilla breathed as her lips brushed his.

"Oh? What is it?" He asked huskily as her lips brushed his neck in the spot that always got him going.

She leaned back, her eyes sparkling as she ground her hips on him, making sure she had his full attention. When his eyes met hers, she lifted her mint-green shirt off of her body, flinging it behind her onto the living room floor, revealing her small, swollen belly. "A son," she whispered.

"A son?" He repeated, his eyes flashing from her face to her stomach and back again.

"Yes!" Priscilla exclaimed, pulling the sonogram picture from the back pocket of her jeans, where an arrow pointed to the anatomy that clearly indicated that she was indeed carrying a baby boy in her womb.

Jack's eyes filled his love, admiration, and... tears. "The greatest gift you could give me," he said in a voice so soft and loving, a tone she had rarely heard.

His warm hands encompassed her abdomen, feeling the swell of her stomach. She shuddered under his touch; he had never been so tender with her. "Are you happy?"

"Happy? I am over the moon!" He exclaimed, standing up with her in her arms as he carried her to their bedroom, admiring her swelling breasts. He laid her on their bed, flinging his own shirt aside. "And I am going to thank you properly."

He worshiped her body that morning, in a way he never had before, and Priscilla finally felt secure in their marriage. She was having a son, and as her husband made love to her, she vowed silently to the baby inside of her that she would protect him with her life, and love him always.

June 2, 2000

Drake and Launa, up since 6:00 A.M., stared expectantly out the bay window of the living room. They had been waiting as patiently as children that age could for their big brother to arrive. It had been nearly three hours, and Antonio and Cynthia marveled at their children, chuckling as they watched them buzz excitedly. As the clock struck 9:00, a sapphire blue car sped up the driveway toward the mansion, and both children screamed in delight.

Cynthia laughed as she watched her children race to the front door, ready to pounce on their brother the moment he stepped out of his Mitsubishi Eclipse. "Logie! Yous hewe!" Launa cheered, her braided pigtails bouncing with every jump as she flew down the stairs from the porch.

"Move it, *pipsqueak!*" Drake yelled as he grabbed his sister by one of her braids, pulling her out of the way.

Antonio laughed, watching his children, not bothering to intervene, his baby girl could handle her own. "Shut up *quacky*! I is not pipsqueak! I is gonna kick you butts!" Launa screamed as she connected her tiny fist with Drake's left eye as if to prove her father's point.

He and Cynthia both chuckled as they watched the four teenage boys watch their children pummel each other, their expressions a mixture of dumbfoundedness and amusement. "Man, Logan, I never knew you were so popular," they heard Pablo explain as he turned to their nephew.

Logan laughed, remarking, "Yeah, this is honestly nothing new. What can I say, they love me!"

Deciding that he'd let his children beat up on each other long enough, Antonio descended the front porch stairs, sighing heavily as he pulled them apart. "*Che diavolo? Non di nuovo*[112]." Turning to the boys, he greeted them with a grin. "I trust you four had a safe trip."

"Hey, *Zio*! We did. So, I take it these *piccoli mostri*[113] have gotten worse since my birthday," Logan quipped through giggles.

"Ugh... I don't even know what to do with them. I am exhausted and I handle criminals for a fucking living."

"Drake Luther Moretti and Launa Carmella Moretti! What have I told you two about fighting!" Cynthia belted in a stern, yet harmonious voice, deciding she should probably do what a good mother would and scold her children.

Hearing the tone of their mother's voice, both children instantly hung their heads with tears brimming in their eyes. "Sorry, Mama. We shouldn't fight because we are family, and family sticks together," Drake swiftly spoke up.

"We's sowwies, Mama. We's just happy to see Logie," answered Launa in a pitiful tone.

"That may be, but this is not how we behave. You two are

---

[112] What the hell? Not again.
[113] Little monsters

to go to your rooms and let the boys settle in. Once they awaken you may talk to them, but not before." Seeing her children about to protest, Cynthia quickly remarked, "And do not even think of protesting. If you do, no ice cream tonight when we all go out."

She watched as Drake took his sister by the hand and solemnly made their way inside. Shaking her head and chuckling, Cynthia turned to the boys. "I'm sorry you had to see that ridiculous display. Logan, if you can't tell, they have missed you very much."

Embracing the woman before him, Logan looked down and smiled, "It's ok, *Zia*! I love their antics. He hugged her for several moments, and Cynthia marveled at just how grown her nephew was, and her heart felt full at the fact that he still showered her with love in front of his friends. She was beyond proud of him. She smiled up at him, willing the tears in her eyes to disperse, and he gave her a crooked grin in return as if he knew what she was thinking.

Logan turned to his best friends and introduced his aunt. Cynthia gave them all her infamous *mom look*, all four of them shuddering in fear. "Boys, it is so nice to finally meet you all. I trust there has been no more trouble with cars or your mothers, right?"

"Yes, ma'am. Thanks so much for hosting us," Pierre responded, feeling genuinely grateful that the couple had opened up their magnificent home to the four of them.

"Alright, *amore mio*, stop scaring the shit out of them, and let's show the boys to their rooms." With that, Antonio beckoned them all inside, showing them to the three guest bedrooms next to and across from Logan's permanent bedroom for when he visited the house. Although he had told Cynthia not to overwhelm the boys, she had insisted on decorating them all to their liking and had chatted with Logan and Britt to discover their favorite things. They were in awe as they took in their rooms.

Antonio followed Logan to his room and leaned against the doorframe as he watched his nephew unpack. "Hey *Zio*, where is *Zietta*? Do you think I will get to see her? Mom said something about her being pretty sad."

Exhaling deeply at the painful memories of his sister's heartaches over the last few years, Antonio strode over and clasped Logan's shoulder affectionately as he responded, "Don't worry *nipote*, she's doing okay now. You will see her later tonight when we all go to dinner; she has a big surprise for you."

After making sure the boys were settled in, Antonio headed to his office in order to give Britt a call to let her know the boys made it safely. He dialed her number as he sat in his chair, putting his feet up on his desk, his wife slipped into the room as the phone rang. "Hello?" Britt said as she answered the phone.

"*Cerva*! I just wanted to let you know the boys made it here," he greeted the sister of his heart warmly.

"Oh, thank you, Jesus! *Bjorn*, I was so worried."

"I think the boys drove all night because they were a haggard-looking bunch when they drove up."

"Teenage boys," Britt laughed.

"There was a bit of a ruckus with Drake and Launa, but nothing is new there."

"Those *piccoli mostri!*" Britt laughed once more at the thought of her rowdy niece and nephew. Pausing for a moment, Britt asked, "Hey, *Bjorn*, is Cynthia there? I need to talk to her for a minute.

Feigning offense, Antonio retorted with fake tears, "I see how it is! Now that you got what you want from me, you're just gonna throw me out."

He could practically hear her shaking her head through the

phone. "Oh, hush you *patata sciocca*[114], and put your wife on the damn phone. Love you, brother!"

Chuckling, Antonio returned his affections to Britt before handing the phone over to his loving wife. As Cynthia took the phone, Antonio couldn't help but fall in love with her all over again. Her lovely cayenne red waves flowed down her shoulders and her bright green eyes sparkled with joy as she laughed on the phone with Britt. The cream-colored blouse and peach lace skirt Cynthia wore only enhanced her light rose skin, giving her a heavenly glow. Walking down the hall and upstairs to talk to his children, Antonio thanked God for sending him an angel to light his darkness.

---

[114] Silly potato

After the boys finally awoke and readied themselves for dinner, they met Antonio and Cynthia in the hallway. Antonio had requested they wear blazers with their ripped jeans since his wife's restaurant was at minimum semi-formal. "You know, *nipote*," he mused as he took them in, "I never will understand these ripped jeans, How can you not want to feel the power that a well-fitting suit gives you?"

"Well, *amore mio*, not every teenage boy is taking over a mafia dynasty," Cynthia chimed in with a wink. "I think you boys look ruggedly handsome." All four boys blushed at the compliment, sheepishly expressing their gratitude. With a smile, Cynthia went to fetch Drake and Luana while Antonio requested that the boys join him in his study for a quick conversation before getting in the limo that would transport all eight of them to *Bel Fiore*.

"Boys, the reason I have called you in here is that I wanted to let you know that my best friend, and right-hand man, Edward will be joining us for dinner with *quella dannata donna diavolo* he chose to marry! *Stupida cagna*."

Logan laughed before translating for his friends. "So, *Zio* called Edward's wife *'that damn devil woman'* and a *'stupid bitch.'*"

Antonio grinned as the other three boys burst into laughter. "Damn, sir! Why don't you tell us how you really feel?" Shaw jested.

"Oh trust me, boys, if she wasn't pregnant with Edward's child, I would shoot her in her fucking face and not blink twice, but since she is carrying innocence within her womb, I can't."

The shock on Pablo, Pierre, and Shaw's faces was something Antonio had long since grown accustomed to, and he now found it quite comical. Logan, however, had doubled over in laughter, tears dripping from his eyes, as it was the first time the boys had really heard this kind of talk.

With a wink toward Pierre, whom Antonio had picked up on a silent darkness within when they'd met back in February, he said, "*Figlio,*[115] if you want to work in this world, you have to develop thicker skin."

Motioning with his head toward the door, Antonio strode off down the hall, the boys on his heels as they made their way to the limo where Cynthia, Drake, and Launa were waiting. The drive to the restaurant was full of lively conversation, and Antonio beamed at the way the four boys treated his children. Drake looked at them in awe, as if they truly were the coolest people on the planet, and they answered every question he had patiently.

Launa couldn't seem to tear her eyes away from Pablo, though. She peeked up at him through her lashes and beamed every time he smiled down at her. "Looks like someone is developing a crush," Antonio murmured to Logan.

The two chuckled, but as Logan turned to tease Launa, the limo pulled up and parked in front of *Bel Fiore*. They all climbed out and headed inside Cynthia's restaurant to find everyone waiting for them. Priscilla, Jack, Edward, and Regina greeted them all as they walked towards the table. Spotting Priscilla, Logan quickly made his way to her and embraced her lovingly, not even giving her enough time to stand up.

"*Ciao Zietta!*[116] *Zio* said you have a surprise for me."

Laughing, Priscilla remarked, "Oh, *mio bel nipote*[117]! You have grown so much! You are so tall now, and your friends are so handsome as well!" She laughed once more, noticing that the young men blushed at her compliment. Continuing,

---

[115] son
[116] Hi Auntie
[117] My handsome nephew

Priscilla said as she stood, pulling her mint green dress flush against her waist, "Yes, I do have a surprise for you!"

As soon as Logan's eyes met Priscilla's tiny six-month pregnant belly, tears welled up in his eyes. "*Zietta*! You're pregnant?"

With tears of joy in her own eyes, Priscilla embraced Logan deeply once more, exclaiming, "Yes! We also found out we are having a little boy." It warmed her heart to finally share this news with her precious nephew, and she was so excited that she was finally allowed to have a child. Though, she would never admit that truth out loud.

"Another brother? Oh, *Zietta*, I am so happy. Mom didn't even say anything to me."

Laughing through her tears, Priscilla stated, "That's because I told her not to. I wanted to see your reaction for myself." Grabbing a napkin that Jack was holding up lovingly for her, she wiped her eyes before continuing, "So, is everyone ready to hear what we are naming this little boy?"

A cheer resounded throughout the table, causing Priscilla to burst out in laughter once more, especially seeing that her brother could hardly contain himself. Antonio had been begging her to tell him for months. "I will take this as a solid yes! We are naming our little boy Mikah Lee Taylors."

After the excitement had settled, dinner arrived and everyone settled into casual conversation. Antonio had requested the chef make Dianne's famous *Lussekatter* for dessert, and while it was very close, no one made it as good as his *Tant*. Much to Edward's dismay, Regina began pouting during the meal, as she had a very difficult time with not being the center of attention. She wanted to be happy for Priscilla, who she knew was like a sister to her husband, but Regina couldn't help but feel jealous and overshadowed.

Not wanting to feel left out any longer, Regina sharply remarked, "You know Priscilla, Edward and I will be finding out what *our* baby is next week. I mean, can you believe that I get the honor of carrying the *very first* Sommerset grandchild? Anything else really is second rate."

At the sound of his wife's comment in regards to his sister, who was not present to defend herself, Edward tightly squeezed her hand while giving her a look that said it was best to leave well enough alone. "Regina, love, I think everyone at this table will agree that *all* babies are a blessing, no matter when they come."

As much as Priscilla wanted to throat chop the hag the brother of her heart had married, she restrained herself. "While it is exciting that you are having the first Sommerset grandchild, Emily's baby will be just as special and important. It doesn't matter that the baby will be born three months after yours."

Rolling her eyes in response, Regina retorted, "Ah yes, it may be so that all babies are special blessings, but in my family at least, the first grandchild is always *the* most special."

Logan was completely flabbergasted as he looked at Antonio and asked, "*Zio*, is this bitch for real! What the fuck was Edward thinking?"

Laughing and shaking his head, Antonio simply replied, "Sadly, yes. This is Regina. She can't even blame her bitchy attitude on pregnancy hormones.

Noting the looks of disgust Antonio was giving her as he grabbed a saffron bun and placed it upon his plate, Regina curtly remarked, "Easy there *potato*, you don't want those sweets to go to your waistline now do you, I mean, you aren't eating for two as far as I'm aware!"

The look on everyone's faces was that of pure and utter shock. Swiftly removing her earrings and handing them to Priscilla, Cynthia was about to embrace the ghetto hoe residing in her spirit, which she was able to easily keep in check. "Edward, you best take this bitch out of here before I bash her fucking face in! And don't worry, her ugly ass face ain't pregnant!"

Antonio had never been turned on more by his wife than he was at that moment. If he were being honest, he would have enjoyed her embracing this side a little more, however, he would not change his sweet angel for anything. He loved that she wouldn't allow anyone but family to call him by his nickname, which was his rule anyway.

Pinching the bridge of his nose in frustration and embarrassment, Edward huffed out trying not to make a decision he would later regret. "Are you shitting me, Regina? One night. One fucking night for you not to be a crazy bitch. Is that too much to ask? Grab your shit and move it to the car now. If you hesitate, I will throw you over my shoulder, dump you on the sidewalk, and leave your ass here." Turning to Logan and his friends, he apologized for his wife's actions and hoped that he could talk with the boys personally at a later date, *without* his wife.

Once the "happy couple" left the restaurant, Pierre, Pablo, and Shaw released the breaths they had held in. "Damn, I thought my family had drama!" Shaw stated with nervous laughter.

Embarrassed by her outburst, Cynthia apologized to the boys for not remaining calm and collected. It wasn't like her to lose her temper. Drake and Launa stared up at her with awe, and she giggled as her son winked at her. *So much like his father*, she thought.

"Don't apologize, ma'am. I hope we will all be lucky enough to have women who will stand up for our names to stupid bitches," Pablo expressed wholeheartedly. Usually a gentle, poetic boy, Pablo's response took his friends by surprise, and they couldn't help but agree with his sentiment. Once the ruckus died down, everyone who remained enjoyed friendly conversation before returning to their homes and calling it a night.

As Antonio lay down that evening, the overwhelming joy he felt, between the visit from Logan and his friends and the upcoming births of three new babies into the family, made it impossible for him to fall asleep. Even though Emily and John didn't hang out with the family very often, they still knew how loved their baby would be by the Morettis'. He was sad that they hadn't been able to join them for dinner, but it was probably best they missed the occasion because even though Emily was firmly about justice, he knew she would have pummeled Regina for her words.

As sleep began to overtake him, Antonio held his wife close and thanked God for all of the blessings he had been given, knowing he deserved none of them.

Priscilla and Jack welcomed their son, Mikah Lee Taylors, on September 5, 2000. He was 8lbs 4oz and 20in long. Looking at her son, her precious rainbow baby, Priscilla couldn't help but love him. The only thing Mikah received from Jack was his pale complexion, the rest of him, however, was full Moretti–from a full head of black curls, like her own, to the warm brown eyes. With determination in her heart. Priscilla vowed to protect her miracle with everything she had, even if it meant her life.

Edward and Regina welcomed their baby, a little girl, three weeks and four days later on September 30. She was a tiny little thing, barely weighing 6 lbs when they left the hospital. They had made a deal that if they had a boy, Regina would name him, and if they had a girl, Edward would choose her name. As he held his daughter for the first time, he marveled at her tiny, perfect face. She had his complexion, his unique eye coloring, and his mother's nose. The only thing Regina had passed on to their daughter was her full lips. Pressing a kiss to her downy head, he whispered, "Eleanora Rose Sommerset, my little rose, I will love and protect you until my last breath."

A month and a half later, on November 18, Emily and John welcomed their own little girl, Freya Renee Blankenship. Freya was every bit the stereotypical Scandinavian princess (genetics pulsed through the bloodlines of both families). She had the fairest complexion and brightest blue eyes, and blonde hair was so pale it could be easily mistaken for white. Edward and Emily were thrilled that the cousins would get to grow up so near each other, even though the latter lived an hour away from L.A.; they were also happy that they would grow up alongside Mikah, too.

Approximately 15 months after Emily and John welcomed their daughter, Antonio, Cynthia, Priscilla, and the three children between them, traveled to Oregon to be with Britt as she and her boyfriend, Dean, welcomed their first daughter, Eloise Elise Anderson, into the world. Antonio beamed with pride as he watched Drake and Launa treasure their newest "little sister," and he couldn't help but tear up a bit when Logan gently cradled Eloise in his arms; the scene reminded him of when he first held Logan.

Daylight Dammit

June 2004

It was a beautiful, warm, early summer day in Los Angeles, made even sweeter by Logan's visit. He had come down to California to stay with his *Zio* and *Zia*, bringing along his professional camera to add the scenery of the state to his ever-growing portfolio. Antonio was proud of his *nipote* and had several of Logan's works framed and hung at the Moretti Mansion, Moretti Industries, and even at the Black Death Mafia's warehouse. Not only were his works as a photographer taking off, but the band he and his friends had created, *Beyond Oregon*, had become a sensation in the punk world. He was recognized everywhere, and Antonio was grateful that he was recognized for the good he was bringing to the world, not the destruction that he, himself was known for.

Hearing that her beloved nephew was in town, Priscilla loaded Mikah, the big four-year-old, into her Mustang and drove the mansion. She found Antonio, Cynthia, Logan, Drake, and Launa spending time outside at the playground that her brother had built for his children in a section of their yard. Mikah squealed when he spotted his cousins, and as soon as Priscilla unbuckled him, he sped off to hug his family before quickly calling dibs on his favorite swing.

"*Ciao, Zietta!*" Logan called, grinning broadly at her, his camera around his neck.

"*Hallå*, Logie!" Priscilla exclaimed, throwing her arms around him. She still couldn't believe how tall he'd gotten, and it blew her mind that he was already 20 years old. "I'm so happy you're here!"

Hearing some childish laughter, Priscilla turned to find her brother, a 34-year-old man, acting like a child. Antonio had his eyes scrunched up and his tongue sticking out as he pushed Mikah on the swing by his feet, her four-year-old squealing with utter delight. Priscilla, in a moment of true, genuine joy, threw her head back and laughed deeply. Logan, having noticed the absence of such laughter in his beloved aunt for several years, quickly brought his camera up to his face and took the perfect picture. It was one he knew he would treasure for life. He had never seen her look so beautiful. *This will make the perfect Christmas gift for Zietta*, he thought to himself as he lowered his camera once more.

Two weeks later, Priscilla dropped Mikah off at Edward's house for a playdate with Eleanora before heading to her doctor's appointment. She and Jack had decided it was finally time to give Mikah a sibling, and she had just hit her 20th week of pregnancy, though she had not told a single soul. Although Jack's drinking had gotten better after Mikah's birth, it started to slide when he turned two. He promised her that he would not hurt her, and that he would love this baby, no matter if it was a boy or a girl. So, with her heart full of hope, she walked into the hospital for her ultrasound.

A girl. She was carrying another baby girl in her womb. Priscilla could hardly believe it as she drove home to tell her husband the wonderful news. She would finally have the daughter she always wanted. But one step into her dark home told her that Jack would not keep his promise to her.

"We're having a girl, Jack," She started timidly. That was all he needed to fly into a rage.

Priscilla was surprised she woke up at all, given the look of absolute murder in her husband's eyes and the way his knee had slammed into her abdomen, and every impact afterward. "Why did I ever think it would work out? What did I do to deserve this, Edward?" She asked quietly, not even bothering to look over to where she knew the brother of her heart was sitting.

Edward sighed heavily and reached over to grab her hand softly. "You did nothing, *uno dolce...*" He trailed off, not knowing what else to say, and knowing he could *never* comment on the fact that she'd married an evil man.

"She's gone, isn't she?" She asked numbly, already knowing the answer, her womb feeling the loss.

Before Edward could confirm what she already knew, her doctor walked through the door. "Priscilla, I'm so sorry..." The doctor began, but Priscilla held up her hand and cut her off.

"Tie my tubes."

"I beg your pardon?" Her doctor gasped.

"I said, tie my tubes."

"Priscilla, you need to heal before I can do that. But I will schedule an appointment in four to six weeks..."

Seeing red, Priscilla reached over, shoved her hand down Edward's jeans, and pulled out his 9mm, aiming it at her OBGYN. "I said: tie my *fucking* tubes!" She roared.

With fear in her eyes, the doctor nodded and hastily left the room to prepare everything for her patient's request. "Priscilla," Edward said softly, laying a hand on her arm, still outstretched with the gun pointed toward the door. "Please give Jane back to me."

Sighing and slumping back against her bed, she let the handgun fall into Edward's palms. "I still hate that you named that beautiful weapon *Jane*."

"What can I say, it's a classic, timeless name!" He shrugged, holstering it once more. "Was that really necessary, *uno dolce*? You could have just threatened her with the mafia, you didn't have to aim a gun, *my* gun, at her."

Priscilla rubbed her face, tears streaming from her eyes. "I'll apologize. I'm just desperate. I love Jack, and I don't plan on leaving... but I just *can't* get pregnant again. I can't go through this again. Four times, Edward. It's too much."

Wishing he could just shoot the bastard and be done with him, Edward kept his mouth shut and held her hand. He would be there for her through this, just like every time before. After her tubes had been tied and she'd rested for a few hours, Priscilla was ready to get out of the hospital. Rousing Edward from his nap, she quickly dressed and checked herself out, much to her doctor's dismay. Giving him directions, they drove in silence until they came to a tattoo parlor. Edward raised a brow and smirked at her before following her inside.

Greeting the shop owner, who had tattooed every member of the Black Death Mafia with a tattoo, she told him she wanted two tattoos and would pay him extra to stay past closing to get them done. Late into the night, she left with four small black hearts in a column on her right wrist and forearm, one for each of her angel babies. And over her heart was a watercolor cloud raining down to create a rainbow, for Mikah, her one and only rainbow baby.

The following March, Priscilla could not bring herself to join Antonio, Cynthia, Drake, and Launa as they traveled to Oregon for the birth of Britt's third baby. She sent gifts and a card with them and called to congratulate her sister on her beautiful baby girl whom Britt named Rosalie Cerise. It was just too hard. It hurt her heart too much, because her baby girl, Farrah Marie, would have been five months old, and the loss was still too fresh in her heart and spirit. Someday, she promised herself she would go and meet the sweet baby, but not yet.

Fall 2008

For as long as Antonio lived, he would never, ever, be able to rid himself of the sound of Eleanora's scream. It was the sound he had made on the inside but never dared to voice out loud on the day his parents died. Walking over to the petite young girl, he wrapped his arms around her while she sobbed. He had made it to the scene of the accident just as the police informed Regina, whom Edward had thankfully divorced two years prior, and little Eleanora that Edward had been killed.

Someone had planted a bomb in his car, and when he hit the preset speed, it blew him and his car to smithereens. There was nothing left of him, save for his wallet, which somehow survived the explosion. At least, that is what he and Edward had planned to tell everyone. Looking over toward the trees he knew his best friend was hiding behind, he shook his head once, knowing the brother of his heart had heard his daughter's heartrending scream of agony, and would say "fuck the mission" to remedy her pain.

Antonio hated doing this to Eleanora, but he kept reminding himself that it was only temporary, and it was to keep her safe. No one, save for Cynthia and Margaret knew the truth, that they had faked his death. Everett had sadly passed away the previous year after a long battle with colon cancer, and he knew he could not cause Margaret, the woman that had stepped up to raise him, with anymore anguish. He willed tears to fall from his eyes as he swallowed his guilt and rubbed Eleanora's back. "It will be alright, Ella Rose. I promise," he murmured.

Six months ago, Edward went undercover to infiltrate a sex trafficking ring that Antonio had caught wind of. While the Black Death Mafia did and tolerated a lot of very bad things, sex trafficking was something Antonio would not allow in his city if he could help it. They had made a deal with both the LAPD and the FBI to do the sting, and it had been going very well. But about a month ago, Edward's identity was somehow leaked, but instead of coming after him, they started making very real threats against his 7-year-old daughter. Pictures of her playing outside, at school, and shopping, appeared at Edward's door.

They left messages saying they would leave Eleanora alone in exchange for Edward's life. With no other alternative, seeing as how they had not weeded out the leader yet, they decided the best course of action was to fake Edward's death until they could take down the operation. To begin their plan, they hid Edward's car in a sealed room in the warehouse and bought an identical car. Then they discreetly bought a pig carcass, minus the head, to put in the driver seat. Antonio's bomb-maker, a man whose tongue had been cut out in his home country, wired the bomb into the car, swearing secrecy.

They picked today, a foggy, wet, gloomy day for the occasion. Edward had made the most of the time he had left with his daughter and had sobbed in Antonio's arms about the pain she would feel and the fact that she would have to live with her hateful bitch of a mother, who didn't want anything to do with their little girl, no matter how temporary. To ease his best friend's mind, he vowed to always have a detail posted outside the house, out of sight, to make sure she was in fact safe.

Walking over to Regina, he placed Eleanora in her arms, then stood up at his full height. He was a very imposing man, and he glared at her with all of the ferocity the leader of the Black Death Mafia was known for. "You *will* take care of this little girl, or you will meet *your* end. Do I make myself clear?" He growled, pure death in his eyes.

Regina, to her credit, swallowed hard and nodded quickly. Turning on his heel, Antonio went to talk to the police and fire chiefs. Edward, taking one last look at his daughter, turned and ran through the forest to where a truck was waiting for him. He smiled sadly at the woman in the driver's seat, his bodyguard for the foreseeable future. She gripped his hand and squeezed it reassuringly before throwing the truck in drive and heading out of California.

December 31, 2008

Christmas and New Year's was Antonio's favorite time of year. Partially because he got Dianne's sweets, but also because he got to see his beloved Oregon family. This year Britt, her husband, Dean, Logan, Eloise, and Rosalie had all come to stay with the Moretti's at their mansion in L.A. He couldn't contain his excitement and joy about the fact that he got to spoil those precious little girls in the same way he had spoiled Logan at that age, so many years ago. To say there had been a lot of presents under the Christmas tree for all of the kids was an understatement.

Drake, at 14, had finally gotten the street bike he'd been asking for for the last four years. Launa had pouted for a few minutes until Antonio and Drake had promised to teach her how to ride it. Then she'd perked up and hadn't said anything else about it, which had seemed somewhat strange to both Antonio and Cynthia. Now, on New Year's Eve, Antonio, Cynthia, Britt, Logan, and Dean sat in the family room sipping spiked hot cocoa, with Drake drinking a soda. All of the kids had just been laid down, save for Launa who had excused herself early, claiming that she wasn't feeling well.

The six of them were laughing and playing a rowdy game of MAD GAB when sirens blared up the driveway. Four police cars pulled in a slammed to a halt. Antonio tilted his head in confusion but stood up and took a deep breath, getting his easy-going smile and charm ready. Cynthia folded her hands in her lap and tried to remain calm, as the police, in all of the years that they had been together, had never come to their home. Britt, on the other hand, folded her arms and raised a brow at her brother. Antonio just shrugged and headed toward the door as a loud knock sounded on it.

"Good evening, officer, how can I help you?" Antonio greeted the men on his porch, charm lacing his voice. "Wait, Chief Walker?"

"Antonio, I came as quickly as I could. Launa has been in an accident and has been rushed to the emergency room. All I know is that she was hit by a drunk driver and she appears to be in critical condition."

An animalistic sound burst out of Antonio's throat as he hit his knees. "My baby girl?"

Cynthia sprinted into the foyer, eyes wide at the words, tears welling up in her eyes. "Not Launa? She's supposed to be in bed!"

The police chief wrung his hands together as he took them in. "It's Launa. I'm so sorry. The reason there's four of us is to escort you to the hospital as quickly as possible."

Antonio stood in shaking legs in time to catch his wife who was desperately trying not to have a panic attack. "Dad!" Drake yelled, peering out into the driveway. "My bike's gone!" Panic rose in his voice at the realization.

Logan ran into the foyer, Antonio's keys in his hand. "I'll drive, Zio. Let's go!"

Britt, tears in her eyes, turned to Dean who hugged her tightly. "Go. I'll stay here with the girls. I love you, Blue."

The five of them ran to Antonio's car, Logan sliding into

the driver's seat and Antonio taking the passenger side. Britt held Cynthia in the back, both women praying with all their hearts that Launa would pull through. "She's only 12," Cynthia cried softly. Drake sat next to his mother, sobbing silently, his shaking hands balled into fists.

True to their word, the police escorted them as fast as they could to the hospital, two cars in front and two behind the Moretti's car. Throwing the car in park, Logan barely managed to take the keys out of the ignition before his legs carried him to the emergency room doors as everyone sprinted inside. "Launa Moretti, where is she?" Antonio panted when he reached the front desk.

"Mr. and Mrs. Moretti, over here!" A doctor called out, waving them over before the person at the desk could even answer. "I'm Dr. Davis, and I've got your daughter in the OR right now with the other attending surgeons on call this evening."

"Please, Dr. Davis, tell us what's happened!" Cynthia cried.

"Launa was riding a street bike with all of her gear and appeared to be following all rules of the road from what first responders were able to determine. A drunk driver swerved into the opposite lane where she was riding and smashed right into her. One of the handlebars pierced clean through her abdomen. Luckily another driver saw the accident and called first responders immediately. She is hemorrhaging badly, and we are still trying to assess the overall damage to her internal organs. I'm going to have a nurse show you to a private waiting area, but I want you to be prepared to be here for several hours, as she is in critical condition. We will do everything we can to save her life, but..."

"Don't finish that sentence," Antonio growled.

Dr. Davis' face paled, but he only nodded in response. "I'll send someone to update you when we have more news."

The next eight hours crawled by with only a brief update

every two hours or so. Antonio barely sat, pacing the room until his legs could no longer hold him up. His little girl was hurt beyond measure, and there was nothing could do. A knock at the door to the private waiting room roused everyone from their thoughts, and they all looked up to find Chief Walker stepping into the room. "How is she?" He asked.

"Still alive, that's all we really know," Cynthia sighed sadly.

"My prayers are with her," Chief Walker replied. "I came to update you on the status of the driver."

At this, Antonio perked up, and it did not escape Britt or Cynthia's notice that he had a fire burning in his eyes. "Is that fucking bastard in this hospital?"

Chief Walker ran a hand through his sandy hair and chuckled nervously. "No. He's in the morgue. He was killed on impact after he ran off the road and drove headlong into the bank."

Antonio clamped his jaws hard, the monster inside of him seething with rage. "Thank you for coming to tell us," Cynthia said with a small, tired smile.

"Of course," the chief nodded. "If you guys need anything, please don't hesitate to reach out. I will come by once the doctor lets me know she is up and ready to give a statement."

Britt walked him to the door, thanking him once more. Drake's hands were shaking once more, rage building inside of him at the fact that he couldn't take his anger out on the man that had hurt his beloved little sister. "Goddammit!" Antonio roared, standing up and slamming his left fist into the wall. "It's *my* job as Launa's father to... to make sure that fucking piece of shit paid for what he did! And now, I can't even give that to her."

Cynthia walked over to her husband and placed her hands on either side of his face, his eyes immediately meeting hers.

"Revenge doesn't matter this time, *amore mio*. Our daughter and her recovery are what matters the most."

"The best thing you can do for Launa, *Björn*, is to be there for her and let her know how much you love her. She's going to need her daddy," Britt added. Turning to Drake she continued, "And she's going to need her big brother, too."

"But if I hadn't been asking for a street bike, this never would have happened!" Drake exclaimed, tears streaming down his face once more.

"Oh, sweetheart!" Cynthia rushed over and pulled her son into her arms, and she was surprised once more at his height, already almost as tall as his father at only 14. "This is not your fault. No one blames you. Your sister chose to sneak out and ride your bike without permission or help, and that man decided to drive impaired. Do not blame yourself for this."

Drake nodded and hugged his mom closer. Antonio walked over and wrapped both of them in his arms, holding them tightly. Logan, not knowing how to express his own rage and sadness, simply wiped tears off of his face and joined his family. Britt snapped a picture of the moment on her cellphone, and as she took a step to join the group hug, the door opened once more.

"I'm pleased to tell you that Launa is finally stable and is in the ICU recovering," Dr. Davis grinned. "She won't be conscious for some time yet, but we put her in a private room that you guys can join her in. I had the nurses bring in a couple more chairs and an extra bed so you can try to get some rest."

"Oh praise God!" Cynthia burst out in tears.

"And what was the extent of the damage?" Antonio asked wearily.

Dr. Davis sighed heavily, his shoulders slumping. "She lost a lot of blood, and we had to give her over 100 bags during the surgery."

298

Britt gasped in shock, and everyone in the room paled. "That's not the worst of it, is it?" She asked.

The doctor shook his head. "No, it isn't. There was some damage to some of her internal organs but most of it was miraculously minimal. However, the handle mainly went through her uterus. Her ovaries burst, and we could not save any of it. We had to perform a full hysterectomy on her. I am so sorry, but Launa will never be able to have children. But, her spine wasn't damaged, and she should make a full recovery."

"Oh... oh my god," Cynthia breathed, collapsing into her husband's arms. "My poor baby."

"It will be alright, *Bel Fiore*, she's *alive*," Antonio murmured against her head.

Several hours later, after Launa had awoken and was informed of what had happened, Britt took Logan, Cynthia, and Drake home to get some rest, leaving Antonio and Launa alone, at Launa's request. Father and daughter sat in silence for nearly half an hour before Launa's hand squeezed Antonio's. "Daddy?" She whispered.

"*Sí, pertardo*[118]?" He asked softly, noting the fear in her voice.

"What if no one wants to marry me because I can't have babies?" Launa's voice and chin quivered, a tear rolling down her right cheek.

Her spoken fear felt like someone had punched him in the gut. Here his 12-year-old little girl was, worried about whether someone would want to be with her given her fertility status when all she should be worrying about is what she wants to wear to school. "Oh baby girl," he murmured,

---

[118] firecracker

sliding onto the bed next to her and pulling her gingerly into his arms. "You listen and listen well. Any man that doesn't want to be with you simply because you can't have babies isn't worthy to even breathe the same air as you."

She smiled up at him, and he smiled back as he brushed a stray curl behind her ear. "Someday, you are going to meet a man who worships the very ground you walk on. He will love you, every single part of you. He won't care that you can't have kids, hell, he might even be glad you can't. That man will be worthy of your love, and ours. Know your worth, *mio piccolo amore*[119], and *never* settle for less. But don't worry about all of that right now. Focus on healing and growing up first."

"Thank you, Daddy. I love you!" Launa exclaimed, putting her arms around his neck.

Once Launa had fallen asleep once more, Antonio pulled out his phone and decided to give one of his best friends a call for some advice. "Hey, Antonio, what's up?" The voice on the other end answered.

"Hey, Cade..." Antonio began before telling Cade everything that had happened. Even though Britt and Cade had been divorced for nearly 12 years, the two of them had remained friends and Antonio always paid him a visit whenever he was in Oregon. "I just don't know how to help her through this. I mean, everything I told her was true, and it will hopefully help her, but I know that it can't be enough since none of us have any experience with infertility. Do you think that Cate might be willing to have a chat with her about it once Launa has recovered and I can bring her up for a visit?"

"Of course, *Fratello*! Now how much do you want Cate to talk about?" Cade replied enthusiastically.

---

[119] My little love

300

Feeling a bit of the weight lift from his shoulders, Antonio relaxed into his chair as he chatted with his friend and watched over his daughter sleeping peacefully.

Heavydirtysoul

April 10, 2015, was a beautiful, sunny spring day. Antonio was enjoying a quiet afternoon gardening in his backyard, loving the feeling of the warm soil in his hands and the chirping of the birds. It was peaceful. Cynthia was at *Bel Fiore* celebrating her favorite hostess' engagement, and this year he had decided to give his son more responsibility in both Moretti Industries and the Black Death Mafia. Drake was 21 now and had grown to be several inches taller than Antonio. He had a good head for business and was nearly as fierce as his father when it came to dealing with the scum the mafia dealt with.

Launa, at 19, had grown into a stunning young woman, who was just as feisty as she'd always been. She was certainly his firecracker. She was just as involved in the family businesses as Drake, and had begged her father for more responsibilities as well. Knowing it was time, Antonio had happily obliged, and he loved the extra time he got to himself, just him and his garden. As he was tending to the tiger lilies, his phone rang.

Antonio always thought that nothing could possibly be worse than losing both of his parents on the same day, by murder no less. *He was wrong.*

Wiping his hands off on his pants, he grabbed his cell

phone and smiled when he saw his nephew's name. "Hi, Mikah," he said as he answered the call.

"*Zio!* My mom..." Mikah sobbed. "My mom is dead. He fucking killed her!"

All sound faded as the words rang in Antonio's ears. "What?" He whispered, hoping he'd heard wrong.

"M-my d-dad k-killed m-my mom!" The strangled, choking sounds of crying followed Mikah's reply.

And in that moment, Antonio's world shattered in a way he never thought possible. His precious, beautiful, full-of-life little sister, was gone. He wanted to scream and shout and pound his fists into the earth, and it was pure willpower that allowed him to swallow the urge to do so. Mikah needed him right now, he could break down later. "I'm coming, Mikah. I love you."

Running faster than he thought he could, he jumped into his car and flew down the road. His vision blurred with tears, but he forced his pain and emotions down deep. He *had* to be the strong, unaffected leader of the Black Death Mafia in order to handle this. Later. He could *feel* later. Pulling out his phone, he called Drake. "Son, I need you. Jack killed Priscilla. Mikah needs us. Please call your sister and mother and tell them." He hung up before his son could respond.

It took him far less time to reach Priscilla's house than it should have since he drove like a madman through the city. Jumping out of his car, he ran over to his nephew, who was standing on the front porch sobbing, and pulled him into his arms. Mikah couldn't speak, and Antonio didn't try to say anything, either. A few minutes later, Drake and a couple of their men pulled up. Drake's eyes were red from crying, and he searched his dad's face for answers. "Come here, *piccolo cugino*,[120]" he said quietly, pulling Mikah into his arms.

---

[120] Little cousin

"Where is she?" Antonio asked, willing his voice to stay even.

"Their bedroom. And so is he," Mikah choked out.

Taking a deep breath, Antonio stepped inside his sister's house and headed toward the stairs. He took them slowly, one by one, and did his best to prepare himself before stepping through the master bedroom door. And there she was. Priscilla was sprawled out on the hardwood floor, her wild black curls splayed around her head like a halo. She was still in her nightgown, indicating that she had been killed that morning, and she was laying in a pool of coagulated blood. Tears burned his eyes as he knelt to brush his fingers against her face, and he tried not to recoil at how cold her skin was. Her chest was peppered with holes, obviously from a shotgun at close range.

"*Uno dolce, mia Sorella,*" Antonio choked. Once more, he swallowed the grief and stood. Turning to the bed, he found his sorry excuse of a brother-in-law lying dead on top of it. Striding over to see what the coward had done, he found the shotgun lying beside Jack's body, half of his skill missing. There was brain matter and blood sprayed all over the bed, wall, and ceiling from shooting himself in the head.

"You fucking *coward!*" He gritted out through clenched teeth. "Fitting that your first name is Judas, you backstabbing betrayer."

"Shit!" Drake yelled from behind him. Antonio whirled around to see his son, anger raging across his face, which had gone pale at the sight of his aunt. "*Zia...*"

"Come, Drake. We need to get Mikah out of here," he motioned to the door. They walked together down the stairs, where they found Mikah sitting on the couch, Travis and Bryce standing next to him.

"Travis!" Antonio barked, grabbing the man's attention.

"Yes, boss?" Travis replied.

"I want you and Bryce to clean up the mess and take the bodies to the funeral home. Keep it on the down-low."

Travis and Bryce nodded before grabbing their supplies and heading upstairs to get to work. "*Zio?*" Mikah asked hesitantly.

"What's on your mind, kid?" He replied gently.

"I don't want people to know that my dad killed my mom... then killed himself..."

"Hmmm, yes, I can see how that could be compromising. I'll have it covered up."

"Thank you."

"You're welcome," Turning to the police officer that had just walked through the door, Antonio said, "Joe, I want the police and medical examiner's report to rule the cause of death as carbon monoxide poisoning."

Joe, the Moretti's most trusted man on the police force, replied, "You go it, boss," as he took out his paperwork and signed off on it.

"Drake, take Mikah home."

Antonio escorted the bodies to the funeral home to give them instructions. Judas, as Antonio would forever refer to him now, was to be cremated. Priscilla was to be embalmed for the funeral they would hold. Leaning over his sister as the body bag was unzipped, he kissed her forehead and allowed a single tear to fall from his eyes. When he got home, he found Launa and Drake holding Mikah between them on the bed in a spare room, his 14-year-old nephew sound asleep.

Making his way upstairs, he walked into his bedroom to find Cynthia sitting on their bed, her knees pulled up to her chest, with silent tears running down her swollen face. "Oh, Antonio!" She sobbed, opening her arms to him.

Antonio, however, could no longer stand and dropped to his knees in the middle of their bedroom. He couldn't hold back the tears, and they came with a vengeance as sobs wracked his body. His world felt like it was ending, and he couldn't breathe. Cynthia flew off the bed and collapsed onto the floor next to him, wrapping her arms around him as they cried together. They stayed like that for nearly two hours.

"So, what happens now?" She asked quietly.

He sighed heavily, his soul heavy. "Now, I step back even further from Moretti Industries and the Black Death Mafia. Mikah needs us, so we will raise him together and shower him with love."

"Of course. Should we move into that townhouse we've been eyeballing?"

"I think that would be for the best. It's closer to his school, and I guess now is as good a time as any to relinquish this home to our kids."

"With rules, of course," Cynthia giggled, albeit sadly.

"I need to go tell Britt," Antonio breathed. "Will you be alright for a few hours if I fly to Oregon?"

"I'll be fine. Go!" She replied, squeezing him tightly and kissing him passionately.

Taking nothing with him, Antonio drove silently in his car to the airstrip. The pilot nodded at him sadly but said nothing. The flight, though fairly short, was miserable. Tears came and went, and it was like that on the drive from the airstrip to Britt's house. It was 10:00 P.M. by the time he pulled into her driveway. Dragging himself up the steps and to her door, he knocked three times.

A sleepy-eyed Britt answered the door, but before she could open her mouth to ask what he was doing there, Antonio started shaking as the tears began once more. "Priscilla's gone," he choked out, falling to his knees.

In utter shock, Britt collapsed to the floor beside him, her heart utterly broken, and sobbed in a way she never had before. They didn't care that it was late or if they woke anyone up. The chosen siblings grieved together on the porch, wondering how they would ever truly heal from the loss of the sister they loved so dearly.

The End

Song List

1. Simple Man (1973)
    2. Dream On by Aerosmith (1973)
    3. He Stopped Loving Her Today by George Jones (1980)
    4. Hells Bells by AC/DC (1980)
    5. Let it Be by The Beatles (1970)
    6. War Machine by Kiss (1982)
    7. Hello Darlin' by Conway Twitty (1970)
    8. Mama He's Crazy by The Judds (1984)
    9. Girls Got Rhythm by AC/DC (1979)
    10. Growing Up by Sammy Hagar (1982)
    11. We Are Family by Sister Sledge (1979)
    12. Welcome to the Jungle by Guns N' Roses (1987)
    13. Head Games by Foreigner (1979)
    14. Night Moves by Bob Seger (1976)
    15. Waiting for a Girl Like You by Foreigner (1981)
    16. Bad Reputation by Joan Jett (1980)
    17. Working for the Weekend by Loverboy (1981)
    18. Carry on Wayward Son by Kansas (1984)
    19. Before the Next Teardrop Falls by Freddy Fender (1974)
    20. Shameless by Garth Brooks (1991)
    21. Knockin' on Heaven's Door by Guns N' Roses
    22. Nothing Else Matters by Metallica (1991)
    23. Crazy Crazy Nights by Kiss (1987)

24. Daylight by David Kushner (2023) AND Dammit by Blink-182 (1997)

25. Heavydirtysoul by Twentyone Pilots (2015)

Acknowledgment

This book has been a long time coming, and one I have been utterly excited to write. Antonio took on a mind of his own, and it was fun seeing how his character developed, even though I originally wrote him first in book three. While Antonio's story took much longer to write than I anticipated, it was a labor of love full of laughter and tears.

As always, I am so thankful to God for the creativity He has given me. It is through Him and His son that I am saved and have hope, no matter how dark things may seem.

To my husband, Dean: thank you for supporting me in this book writing endeavor. For listening to me as I was working through some issues, and helping me finish this book. Thank you for staying up late and looking up your favorite rock songs to help find ones that fit for chapter names and making sure the lyrics had aspects that I needed. I love you so much, and am so thankful God chose you to be the person by my side.

To my best friend Leslie, whom this book is dedicated, thank you. You were the one who first planted the seed of giving Antonio his own story. It is because of you that I wrote this book, that it exists at all. Thank you for helping me bring him to life, and for sharing your book world with mine. You are the sister of my heart, and I thank God that he brought you into my life. I love you.

To Kathryn and Brianna, two of my best friends, thank you for always supporting me in my writing endeavors. For sharing your thoughts and encouragement, and always being there when I need you. I love you both so much!

Meghana and Skye, thank you for being such heartfelt supporters of my writing, and being willing to beta read this book, even with all of the dreadful mistakes before I could edit it.

To my students, whether you ever read this book or not, this book was also for you. Thank you for being invested in my writing and my life. I always thought being a teacher meant that I would be invested in yours, and not that it would go both ways. You helped write this book, by giving me names and ideas, and I thank you so much for that.

And you, my dear readers, I thank you for giving Moretti: The Making of a Mobster a chance. I know it is not your traditional mafia book, but that was the whole point. I didn't want to write a stereotypical mafia book where the man hates women and relationships and treats them like garbage. No, I wanted the opposite. I hope you loved it anyway. Thank you for coming along on my writing career, and I hope you stick around, as this is only the beginning of the Black Death Mafia. Until we meet again, my dear readers.

Britt Richards grew up in a close-knit family in a small Oregon town. From the beginning, her parents instilled the importance and strength of family bonds. Eventually, Britt's family moved to Alaska. Here she met, and married, the love of her life, and gave birth to her pride and joy; her adorably sassy daughter. As a young mother, Britt obtained a Bachelor's degree in History with a minor in Anthropology from the University of Alaska Anchorage; which she followed up by a Master's degree in Education from the University of Alaska Fairbanks. After obtaining her degrees, Britt and her family relocated to the pristine shores of the beautiful Lake Erie in Northern Ohio, where she currently resides.

Britt is a self-proclaimed bibliophile who gained a love and panache for writing in high school. Writing would become a minor hobby as she entered college and pursued her true passion, history, and all things King Richard III of England. With the pressures of motherhood and college, Britt once again decided to pursue her beloved hobby of writing with her debut novel, _Pushing Through_. When Britt isn't writing or teaching, you can find her spending time with her family, whether that be a game night or something outdoors, or curled up with a good book and cup of coffee.

Currently in the works for Britt is _Unsuitably Bad_, the second book in her Black Death Mafia Series. She loves hearing from her readers! You can contact her through her Instagram: @brittrichardsofficial or by email: brittrichardsofficial@gmail.com

You can find all things Britt Richards Publishing and more on her website, www.plague-poppy-books.square.site

Other Books by Britt Richards

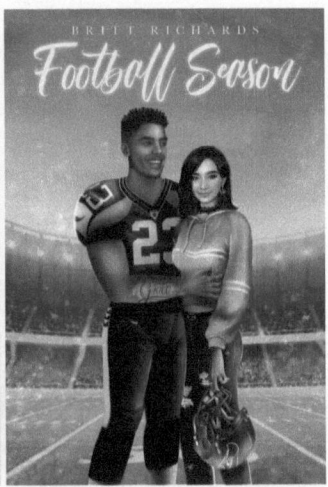